—THE—
GALE
—AGE—

ETHAN DANIEL

Cover and interior layout by Blue Pen

Published by Gloomwagon Press

ISBN: 979-8-9929130-2-6 (hardcover)
ISBN: 979-8-9929130-1-9 (paperback)
ISBN: 979-8-9929130-0-2 (ebook)

CONTENTS

THE NINE GALES

Gods of the Gale Age

The Yellow Watcher

She favors: the observant, the inquisitive, the inventive, the optimistic, the defensive

Her clouds: provide daylight, consistent shapes and speeds, form few hazardous combinations

The Red Rider

He favors: the bold, the passionate, the acrobatic, the competitive, the primal

His clouds: provide heat, often form thick fronts, form some hazardous combinations

The Blue Lady

She favors: the spontaneous, the industrious, the seafaring, the musical, the creative

Her clouds: send rain, often flat, form some hazardous combinations

The Orange Arbiter

She favors: children, the playful, the just, the diplomatic, the nurturing, the generous, the agrarian

Her clouds: provide nutrients, linger less often before rising, form few hazardous combinations

The Green Grinner

He favors: the poor, the unfortunate, the divergent, the charismatic, the humorous, the resilient

His clouds: spread fog, erratic shapes and speeds, form many hazardous combinations

The Pink Pilgrim

She favors: the adventurous, the dreamer, the refugee, the family, winged creatures, lofty places

Her clouds: bring wind, very fast, rarely thicken, form many hazardous combinations

The Purple Prince

He favors: ghosts, the otherworldly, the elusive, the lonely, subterranean creatures

His clouds: cause lightning, emit a faint glow, often spiral, form many hazardous combinations

The Teal Stranger

She favors: the loyal, the philosophical, the infirm, the quiet, the caring, the steadfast

Her clouds: bring cold, often branch into multiple currents, form some hazardous combinations

The Brown Hood

He favors: the outcast, the earth, the nomadic, the humble, the resourceful, flightless creatures

His clouds: carry dust, slow, linger longer before rising, form few hazardous combinations

CHAPTER 1: MADI

Six porcelain puppets jostled inside of Madi's black bag as she hurried to the drop point. The order was specific: six toy soldiers with internal gears linked to eight pins and a dial. The toys were to be polished with a tampering brew. Three wore pink cloaks. Three wore green. Madi fingered the bag's clasp, worried her toy creations might be used in an illegal ciphering system, but it was a risk she was willing to overlook. The payment was too important: forged identity papers, documented and sealed by an oracle of the Pink Pilgrim, confirming her new name and occupation—*Madi Amriel. Toymaker.*

Rain seeped into the cracks of an untended boardwalk, and Madi tilted her head away from the wind, tightening her grip on her bag. Aerial fussed inside her pouch as water dripped from Madi's hat onto her daughter's tiny head. This was Aerial's first journey to Greenpond, and a four-hour wagon ride with a four-month-old was going to take some getting used to. One day, she'd be old enough to ask questions, but how would Madi answer? She'd already lied to her husband about these visits. Would she lie to her daughter, too?

The drop point was a locked gambling box, carved into the alley between a fishery and a gambling den. The alley was tight, suffocating beneath the smell of fish and furnace smoke. A few men stood at the wall, opening boxes. Smooth bits of glass jingled as they bet on the stars above—which would fall and which would shine. How could they gamble over life and death so carelessly? Madi pressed her lips together. The rain tasted as bitter as her regard for gamblers. She glanced skyward, catching sight of a star, breaking apart and falling toward the earth. Celestials were sent from the world above to fight and die so these greedy men could live, laugh, and eat their smelly fish.

Only two things could free a Celestial from the magic binding them to the stars: death or escape. Madi had come very close to both—close enough, it seemed, to free her from her life of service—but not close enough for complete comfort. The subtle strings of uncertainty tugged her back to this box twice a year. What would the Gales do if she didn't deliver? Did gods consider cheating death a crime? This chore was her insurance, just in case.

Before approaching her box, she waited until most of the men had trudged away, praying for luck beneath their droopy fishing hats. Her metal lock-box was cold, wet, and significantly more rusty than last year. The box squealed open, cutting Madi's breath short. Six toy soldiers, covered in crumbled leaves and cobwebs, stared at her from inside the hole in the wall. Their staunch eyes and grins glowed as lightning flashed. Why hadn't the client picked up the last delivery? Where was her payment? There was hardly enough daylight to see. After a quick search, she'd fished out little more than soggy leaves and the acrid aroma of rust and rainwater.

Golden dayclouds drifted high in the sky, dimmed now by the storm's dark, purple-lacquered shimmer. Blue and purple clouds collided overhead, causing a thunderous *boom*. Lightning sliced through the watery atmosphere, accompanied by heavier rain, which pattered Madi's befuddled face. Why was last year's delivery still here? Where was her payment?

A betting box slammed shut, sparking her first hint of panic. A drunkard stumbled by, cursing as he dropped his nets and hooks. Madi's skin grew rigid with chills, and she checked over her shoulder.

There, in the orange glow of the gambling den's largest window, a hooded silhouette watched, moving away when she looked. Hopefully, it was nothing more than coincidence, but the sharpness of her chills had her spooked. If the rumors were true, then sudden chills meant a god was watching.

She closed her lock-box and stuffed an old toy soldier into her bag alongside the new ones. Aerial chirped from her pouch and reached for the toy, but Madi pushed her daughter's arm away, distracted. An oracle had given her this last task on behalf of the Pink Pilgrim. Gods never let someone just walk away from their task. Did they? What if this meant the task was complete, and Madi was now free without question?

But if that's the case, why do I have so many questions?

Thunder clapped, pushing her pace. Sembetra, the oracle who'd signed her papers, lived at the end of the boardwalk somewhere. She would know what was going on. Madi couldn't remember the address, but she remembered a very colorful garden next door. After adjusting Aerial's pouch, she set out. Unfortunately, this colony had changed drastically since her last visit. Everything sagged beneath the storm—soggy buildings, soggy boardwalks, soggy people.

"I don't know you," a man grunted when she asked for directions. "There's an administrator in the town center. Ask him."

Madi didn't recognize anything, and most of the alleyways were barricaded with signs of *NO ENTRY*. Last year, this lake had been a healthy green, abuzz with insects and lilies and frogs. Small fishing boats had dotted the water while jovial fishermen joked atop the jetties. In the bright sun, they'd worn wicker hats and smoked long pipes that smelled somewhat decent. Not like this year.

Now, there were more abandoned buildings in Greenpond Colony than people. Mud and moss lined the boardwalk, muffling Madi's steps. A stench rose from the lake, which was black and bubbly, like a bowl of burned soup. The once colorful waters were fading to Gloom—along with everything in it. A fish, as pale as a ghost, eyed Madi from a patch of sickly gray reeds.

Along each pier, magic lanterns *clicked* and *fizzed*, confirming her suspicion. Greenpond's lanterns were running out of Gale. Without fuel, this colony would fade—and by the look of things, it was happening quickly. A foul wind blew in from the far side of the lake, where gloomy trees swayed in an unbreathable air. Aerial squirmed and whimpered.

"I don't want to stay here any longer than you, baby girl," Madi whispered and started walking again. "Sembetra will tell us what's going on, if we can find her."

A few golden dayclouds shined amid the rainstorm, weaving between the wet blue clouds and the sparking purples. Wooden boats lined the piers, and raindrops danced down a wall of clean nets, freshly organized. As Madi walked, laughter from the gambling den faded, and prayers from the Gales' temples began to echo.

She greeted a woman who was kneeling in the mud, pulling weeds from a dreary garden bed. This wasn't the colorful garden from last year, was it? The woman looked up, the creases around her eyes curling kindly.

"Is that the home of the Pilgrim's oracle over there?" Madi asked.

The woman stared at the crooked tower for a moment. The windows were boarded, and Madi lost hope in the question as soon as it'd left her lips.

"Nobody lives in that old tower anymore," the woman answered. She hunched back over her flowers and shook her head. "So many people are moving away. Our lanterns are very dim. Hardly any color left for my flowers."

Rain pattered Madi's hat. She didn't know whether to be terrified or excited. Sembetra had moved, and the client wasn't picking up deliveries anymore. Did this mean she was free? No more reading the sky? No more strings of starlight? Just her new life with Aerial and Dario.

Black bubbles simmered on the surface of the lake, smelling of rot and dousing her brief bit of hope. More likely, this meant something had happened. The task had changed, and she'd missed the sign. She'd been so content on Lamptree, it'd been years since she'd last used a telescope to read the sky.

Madi reached into her coat and unfurled her identity papers from her pocket, glancing at the date of expiration—ten days from now. Rain pattered the page, which began to sag. "Are there any other oracles here in town?" she asked the gardener. "Or a roaming astronomer?"

The woman filled her palms with dirt and dumped it at the base of a sickly white flower. "You know where to look, temples or the astrohall. Astrohall is down the road. Temples are back the way you came."

"Okay," Madi said, shifting Aerial's pouch to better see the garden. It was in a sad state, and she pitied the woman, who worked in the pouring rain to save it. "Sorry about your flowers."

The woman wiped her hands on her apron. The mud was unholy black, like soot. "It's not your fault," she said. "It's my colony's lanterns that are dimming. I'll be moving soon, too, I suppose."

"You should come to Lamptree Colony. Our lanterns are always full."

"I may," the woman mumbled. "Or I may wait . . . just a little longer. Maybe things will turn around."

Madi fanned a mosquito away from her face. She despised this smelly swamp-hole, but she understood the sentiment. This woman had planted her heart here. *Just like I've planted my heart on Lamptree.*

"Good luck to you, whatever you decide," Madi said. She regretted leaving the woman there, kneeling over her doomed garden. Any decent person would have offered her a wagon ride to Lamptree, but that would take time, and Madi was in a hurry for answers.

The astrohall was closest, far from the pond, in the heart of the colony, where every window and door seemed to be boarded up and barricaded. Two colonial militia in green cloaks patrolled the street. Each carried a spear, a torch, and a backpack with a lantern of Gale hanging from it. A faint haze rippled from the lanterns, surrounding the two guards in a vibrant sphere of color. As they walked, healthy shades of green, brown, and silver spread to nearby homes, and to the road beneath their feet.

One of them hammered a sign onto a wall: *If you fear you're fading, report to the health minister for help immediately! If you suspect anyone of hiding a fading condition, report them to the health minister. If you see a shadowman, RETREAT IMMEDIATELY and REPORT DIRECTLY to city watch!*

Stained glass windows decorated the dome of the astrohall, depicting black skies filled with glowing constellations. It was the only stone structure in the whole colony. The doors were open, and Madi found someone right away. A plump woman rushed back and forth, ferrying scrolls and books to a small wagon outside.

"Excuse me, are you an astronomer?" Madi asked.
The woman's face was flushed with exhaustion, though only a few books filled her cart. "No time!" she said, pushing past Madi with an armful of dusty pages.

"I can pay," Madi said, coughing.

The stargazer used her large chest as a ramp, sliding the pile of books into her cart. Afterward, she placed a monocle in her eye and inspected Madi. "You don't look rich enough to afford me, darling."

"I'm rich enough."

The woman glanced at Aerial, at Madi's bag, then at the sky. "I only accept shards of glass, no bits. I only study a constellation if it's close. I only provide you with the pattern potential, no interpretations or religious flummery."

"I just need information about a glyph," Madi said.

The woman leaned toward a lantern on her cart. Healthy color surrounded it, staining a pile of books in refreshing hues of blue, red, green, and brown. The astronomer drew a deep breath and then walked back inside.

"Name and constellation?" she asked as Madi followed.

"I'd rather not give a name, but it was in Constellation Maya."

"Maya?" The woman squinted thoughtfully and flapped her lips. "I thought Constellation Maya disappeared years ago."

"It did," Madi said. "But there should still be a star up there that belonged to it."

The astronomer rolled up her scroll, took a deep breath, and then frowned. "Darling, if you don't understand how constellations work, don't waste my time."

"I know how they work," Madi replied. "A constellation represents a celestial company. Each glyph in the constellation represents one of the celestial warriors who fights for that company."

"Then you know what happens to their glyph when a constellation falls?"

Madi sighed, letting her head sag. "The star falls from the sky," she answered. "And the Celestial who the star belonged to . . . dies."

But I DIDN'T . . . she wanted to add, if only to deflate this lady's astronomical ego.

The stargazer wiped the sweat from her monocle and let its string slide between her breasts. "I can't help you, darling," she said. "The glyph you're looking for fell, and the Celestial it belonged to is dead. I'm sorry."

She lifted a pile of books from a table and waddled outside. Madi's sigh echoed in the empty astrohall. Now, she was too confused to panic. Had the Gales forgotten about her? If so, it could be a dream come true. A flicker of excitement got her walking, almost skipping. She'd cheated death, but had she also escaped the starry strings tying her to the sky?

She found an alcove, bright with candlelight, and sat down. Meanwhile, Aerial cooed toward the warm light. Madi opened her bag and retrieved the old toy soldier, wiping a cobweb from its face. The soldier grinned bravely, and the candlelight revealed something she hadn't seen in the alley. On the toy's ear, the switch connecting the internal gears had been touched. Someone had coded a message!

Gears clicked as she wound up the toy. The soldier waved its sword in patterns. Madi opened a tiny panel hidden beneath the soldier's boot, and the tip of his sword sparked yellow, leaving a faint trail of light. The glowing symbols hovered in the air for a moment before fading. Madi shielded the toy's message with her body. It'd been years since she used logograms, and she was slow to translate:

> *They know how you survived, Nariah Maya. They know what*
> *Lamptree is. The Gales will destroy it. Destroy you. DO NOT*
> *GO BACK! Please. I studied your glyph. Saw your death.*
> *~Your friend Sembetra*

Madi clutched the toy to her chest, disturbed. She hadn't been called Nariah in over three years. Who was 'they?' And what did Sembetra mean: *They know what Lamptree is?* It was a colony, a giant tree, the only place she'd ever found peace. What else could it be? The message made no sense. But would Sembetra lie? Never.

Voices echoed at the entrance of the astrohall, where two cloaked men talked to the astronomer. When the astronomer pointed inside, Madi rose, along with her heartbeat. She waited for the men to near her alcove before creeping back outside, certain they'd seen her through gaps in the shelves. Sure enough, the two men were follow-ing, and there were no crowds large enough for Madi to hide in. *The men are probably just inspectors,* she thought. *I've committed no crime. My papers are valid for a few more days. I should stop.* But Sembetra's message wouldn't let her. *They're going to fight over Lamptree. Over you.* What did that mean?

The rain turned torrential, and chills gripped Madi's whole body, like invisible hands. Did Sembetra mean the Gales? Were gods watch-ing right now? It certainly felt like it. The thought made her run, stabling Aerial's head in her pouch. The Gales' magic weaved through the world like webs, and Madi was being very careful. Magic was sticky, and every contract had a cost.

The boardwalk was too exposed, so she turned into an alley and climbed a barricade despite its warning: *No Entry.* She splashed into a puddle and proceeded down a colorless street. This alley had faded to Gloom. Gray wood stained abandoned shopfronts. White mist lingered atop the shadowy street, which felt mushy as Madi walked. Aerial coughed, and Madi's own throat itched. She unchained her lantern from her belt and held it close to her daughter's face. Green-pond's lanterns must be dangerously low for a street to become this gloomy.

She halted when she saw someone sitting at the far end of the alley—a forlorn figure. She set her lantern on a barrel and reached into her bag for her knife. Galefuel swirled slowly inside her lantern—a sticky black substance, twinkling with every color imaginable. She'd carved this lantern herself, in the shape of a bird with its wings raised. The wooden capsule was small, but custom made, so that the nozzles automatically trimmed to adjust to the amount of Gloom nearby. The lantern's nozzles widened with a series of quick *clicks*, then color spread from it in a sphere, painting the barrel brown.

The figure looked up, and a flash of lightning revealed its face.

Madi's skin went cold. It'd been a long time since she'd seen a shadowman. Her fingers tightened around her short weapon as she recalled what Celestials called them—Ashen. There were no features on its face, not even the glimmer of eyes. Rain spattered its grainy flesh, which was dappled like sand, and as dark as a shadow.

Aerial shuddered in her pouch, and Madi immediately withdrew, right into the arms of her two pursuers. "There's something wrong in your head, lady," one of them whispered, gripping her arm and pulling her back toward the barricade. "Running into a quarantine with your kid."

The other man showed Madi his inspector's pin—a red horse and rider. "We're inspectors from Mount Anchor, here on behalf of the Red Rider," he said, rain dripping from his thick mustache. "Would you mind dropping your knife? We have some questions for you."

Madi complied. Then, gripping her by the arms, the men led her back onto the boardwalk and gestured for her to sit beneath an awning. Rain pattered the canopy as the men looked through a small book. Aerial continued to whimper, and Madi cradled her as she waited for the men. The one with the mustache kept sniffing. He was either sick, or not used to being in a colony that was fading to Gloom.

"Why were you running from us?" he asked

"I saw two cloaked men following me in the rain and the dark," she answered. "I didn't know who you were."

"That's a fancy flier you're wearing. Can't say I've ever seen a colonist with a metal flier before. Only Celestials."

Madi's flier, *Flicker*, clattered as she turned in her seat. Usually, she kept it hidden beneath her cloak, but all the running must have loosened its harness. Both men eyed the elegant contraption on her back. Its ten, long, golden arms were in the closed position, furled against her back like a rib cage.

"No, it's made of wood," Madi lied. "I polish it to shimmer like metal."

Thunder rumbled as she eyed the turbulent sky. She could have flown, but she was unwilling to risk the storm's swirling currents while carrying Aerial.

The mustached man smirked. "Shame about the weather. It seems the gods are eager for our little chat to take place."

Madi disliked this man. Everything about him made her uncomfortable—his invasive posture, his dry smirks, his wet mustache. She much preferred the bald man, but he was by far the quieter of the two.

"Let's see who you are."

Madi handed him her identification, signed and sealed by Sembetra:

Madi Amriel – 24 years of age
Residence – Lamptree Colony, 84 Toucan's Branch
Occupation – Toymaker
Celestial Glyph – None
Curses – None

"What's in the bag?"

"Porcelain puppets and money," Madi answered. "I'm a toymaker working for a client here."

The men inspected one of the toys, clueless as to its inner workings. "And you deliver to a gambling den lock-box?"

"That's where the client wanted it delivered. I don't know why."

The man fingered his mustache. "Interesting. And how long have you lived on Lamptree?"

"Close to three years."

"Where did you live prior?"

"I moved around," Madi replied honestly. "None of the colonies lasted, or I just didn't feel at home."

"You feel at home on Lamptree?"

"Absolutely," she answered, watching the man take a seat across from her, sniffing all the while. "It's different. You can tell just by how the children smile. Living there, it's easier to forget what happens in the Gloom. I would have faded if I hadn't found Lamptree."

That last part was a lie, and Madi worried the man had seen right through it. He eyed Madi's skin, mostly covered by her coat. "Are you fading now? Is that why you ran?"

Celestials couldn't fade. Only colonists could. The Gales' starlight protected Celestials, or so it was said. Madi had no idea, but as long as these men thought she was a colonist, the most they could accuse her of was being in the wrong place at the wrong time.

"I *was* fading, I think," she lied again, employing their false assumption. "But Lamptree cured me. I couldn't imagine raising my daughter anywhere else."

There was something supernatural about it, Madi had to admit. Lamptree Colony was different. Magical. But not like most magic. It comforted instead of controlled. Lamptree wasn't a web, gripping her. It was a rope she'd grasped, reeling her in from the brink.

"Have you seen any activity on Lamptree that you would consider out of the ordinary?"

Madi was the only unordinary thing about Lamptree. "No," she replied.

"Do you know of any Celestials living on Lamptree?"

This question pushed like a bony knuckle against Madi's chest. "No," she answered evenly. "They visit. But they always go back to their wagons."

"You asked the astronomer here to interpret a glyph from Constellation Maya for you. Has a Celestial from Company Maya visited Lamptree?"

"I don't know."

"Then why did you ask about it?"

Madi didn't know what to say. She'd just wanted to see if the Gales had changed her task. She hadn't asked about her glyph in years, and now of all days, she made the mistake of asking. Forging papers was a cursable offense.

"Why did you ask about Constellation Maya?" the man repeated.

Madi shrugged while she invented another lie. "A Celestial paid me to ask. I don't know why. I'm just a toymaker."

"Who asked you? What did they look like?"

"I didn't see." Madi's voice quickened with her false tale. "He was wearing one of those magical cloaks they all wear."

The men exchanged a cryptic glance before looking at their book again. "The oracles of the Red Rider believe there is a person of interest hiding on Lamptree. Any information you provide will be rewarded."

Madi relaxed. She didn't have to lie anymore. "If someone is trying to harm my colony, I'd do anything to stop them, but I haven't seen anything out of the ordinary."

"But it sounds like you have," the mustached man said. "You said Lamptree changed your life. Extraordinarily, it thrives while other colonies struggle. Why is that, do you think?"

Madi glanced at her toy in the inspector's hand. "The people," she answered. "They overcome suffering with sacrifice. If enough people sacrifice, no one loses so much that their hope breaks."

"People don't make a tree grow supernaturally," he said, frowning. "Lamptree is a thousand times the size of a normal tree."

"Are you accusing me of making the tree grow?" Madi asked.

"No, I'm asking you if you've seen anyone suspicious." The man loomed.

"I haven't. I'm sorry." Madi stood, but the mustached man grabbed her arm.

"We're not done," he said.

"I have to go," she insisted. "My colony's wagon is waiting for me."

"She doesn't know anything," the bald man said. "She's just a colony girl."

The mustached man's grip tightened. His breath smelled like fried fish from the den. "Maybe, but her story stinks worse than this swamp-hole," he said. "She knows something. She can lie to us, but not the oracles. Come with us, *toymaker*."

They tugged Madi, but this time, she resisted. She was a small woman—even the short shaved man was a head taller than her, but together, the inspectors couldn't budge her. The men glanced at each other and then at Madi, eyes narrowing. They pulled harder, but two mere colonists could never overpower a Celestial—no matter how strong they were or how loud they grunted.

"She's a Celestial?" the bald man uttered, releasing his grip. "But her papers—"

"Were forged," the mustached man said. "By a pinker no less."

The men stepped back, cloaks flowing as they drew their swords. Beneath their outer garments, they wore crimson leather, bearing the emblem of the Red Rider. Their armor glistened wet, practically drooling in protective brews.

"In the name of the red oracles and our god, the Rider, you're under arrest. On your knees or be declared a Shade." The mustached man angled his sword. Its proximity to Aerial made Madi angry for the first time during this encounter.

"Stay back," she warned, shielding her daughter. "You would drag me onto a stage I fell from a long time ago. I'm just a toymaker now. A mother. Please, just leave us alone."

"The Gales decide when you're done dancing, not us!"

"Please, come quietly," the bald man added. "We don't want to hurt you or your daughter."

Madi lowered her chin and glared. "You won't."

Cradling Aerial's head, she bounded over her chair and ran down the boardwalk toward a growing crowd of people. Chills came again, and Madi felt like she was running away from the gods' invisible hands. As rain slid across her face, she imagined herself peeling their web of magic from her body. All she had to do was keep running.

Long lines of refugees snaked through the streets toward the sound of a loud *gong*. Where were all these people when she'd needed them earlier? Some carried bundles, bags, and packs while others pushed carts, full of furniture. The gardener wasn't exaggerating. Everyone was fleeing Greenpond.

The gong echoed again, and this time Madi saw where it was coming from. A large wagon rolled toward the gatehouse. A celestial company was here! They must have been tasked with escorting the refugees through the Trade Gap. As Madi weaved through the lines of people, she heard children pointing out each famous warrior by name.

Aloof and wary, a dozen celestial warriors watched over the gathering colonists. Two of them stood atop their battle wagon, rain pattering their shoulders. They carried long swords and wore their fabled celestial armor—thick cloaks, light as feathers, but stronger than iron and conjured from their own minds. Madi had almost forgotten how much the cloaks resembled a mixture of matted fur and greasy mist.

Colony girls smiled and giggled. Colony boys pushed out their chests and tried to walk taller. Everyone eyed the Celestials—their guardians from the sky. One Celestial faced the crowds. The other faced the quarantined alleys. Together, they scanned the city at the same careful pace.

Madi approached them. "Two men are chasing me," she said. "They came from the quarantine. I think they're fading."

The Celestials hopped from their wagon, twirled their swords, and walked—with a bit of bravado—toward the two inspectors. Madi remembered when she'd walked that way. The temptation was strong. Celestials were like gods to colonists, but every Celestial knew deep down: *We aren't gods. We're their puppets. Our strings are drawn in starlight, and the Gales hold them.*

Madi held up her identification paper for a guard to see, and she was shortly waved through the gate. Throngs of refugees fled the colony, and Madi hid among them. Greenpond was defenseless compared to Lamptree, though it did have one strength—a swamp—sticky and impassable, even for shadowmen. She wouldn't be free until she traversed a series of long wooden bridges, which first had to be lowered.

Once across, she looked back toward Greenpond's soggy walls. There, the two inspectors searched the crowd. Madi calmed her step as she neared the wagon corral, where friends from Lamptree were already prepping the wagon. She fixed her hat and tucked a loose strand of dark hair behind her ear. Her coat had enough pockets for a tinkerer's every tool, and she untangled a bit of bronze coil that had knotted.

She was a colony toymaker now, and she played the part very well.

Chapter 2: Dario

Dario's breath frosted the side of his telescope as he calibrated the dials. Above him, clouds glinted in starlight. Teal currents stretched across the sky like shards of ice, bringing snow. Energetic pinks billowed through the teals, howling with wind. The combination of clouds made Company Lire's hilltop perch a frigid landscape, but light-colored clouds always made for easy stargazing.

Hundreds of constellations filled the sky—a chandelier of lights and patterns, like a frozen lake glazed in frost. With each click of his instruments, Dario brought Constellation Lire into better focus. His glyph, and the glyphs of his friends, shimmered and changed. What did the changes and patterns mean? That was always the question.

"Two prongs. Slight top drift," Dario muttered, his fingers delicately tuning the cold bronze dial.

"Two prongs. Slight top drift," Wardan Lire repeated. He leaned over a large wooden table, etching the patterns onto a parchment. No torches or daylight brews were allowed on the hill. One flame could dilute the starlight, and the company might misinterpret a Gale's task.

So Company Lire worked in the cold, with only their tattered battle cloaks to keep them warm. Dario's cloak clung tightly to his skin. The magical garment was emaciated, shriveled, and barely shimmering with any mist. As snow piled upon his shoulders, an icy melt leaked down his back. He adjusted his lenses once more, sighing into the night. Constellation Lire was dimming by the day.

"Plus one dot, left wing," he muttered.

"Plus one dot, left wing," replied the interpreters.

Six other Lires stood next to Dario, aiming their telescopes at Constellation Lire. They also muttered patterns in the cold, and the interpreters scribbled those down too. He took this moment to magnify his scope toward his own glyph. It was near the middle of the constellation, his very own amorphous puddle of light.

Had it changed recently? He was curious. He couldn't stop thinking about Madi and Aerial, and he figured if his glyph hadn't changed, it meant they were safe. This was the month of the Brown Hood, so it was Madi's turn to lead Lamptree's trade wagon to Greenpond. Dario had asked her to find someone else to go, but she'd insisted she could do it. She had been uncharacteristically stubborn about it. Why risk traveling for a couple of crates of fish? Maybe obstinance was a permanent side effect of pregnancy? Dario smirked. He sure hoped not.

As he gazed, his body caught chills, and not because of the cold. The light of his glyph was moving! Patterns bent and flickered. Faint lines of starlight shifted. He gripped his telescope and squinted hard. This was the closest a person could feel to the Gales, watching them etch and alter the sky as though they'd dipped their pens in shining ink.

He desperately wanted to call out the change, but tonight wasn't for personal glyph reading. Wardan and the other interpreters would just scowl and ignore him. Tonight, Company Lire studied the shape of their constellation as a whole, in search of the Gales' next task. Dario hadn't much appetite for the gods' desires. People were beginning to whisper—these were the last days. If they were, he'd need a miracle to keep his family safe. The Gales refused to provide one, so he'd been busy conjuring his own.

"One prong, north, slow blink." Lire stargazers were still muttering patterns.

"Distance?" Wardan asked.

"Measuring."

Dials clicked in the cold. Dario gave his eyes a rest, and held his hands to his mouth, blowing. He missed Aerial's tiny body—the warmth of her little heart, beating rapidly against his chest.

"Five clicks," Koka answered.

The interpreters scribbled quickly, switching between pens, compasses, and calipers. "That's close," said Wardan. "Trouble in Brittlehorn Colony."

"It's a double prong now," Koka said with a shiver in her voice. "Big shimmer, could be a triple soon. It's the Rider! He wants us moving!"

A gust of wind swirled through the interpreters' tent, snatching some of their parchment. "Pack up!" Wardan announced. "Have bundles of food, water, and lantern fuel ready to offer refugees in need."

The bald hill, which had been silent, erupted with activity. Telescopes and tools were packed away, and sentries came out of hiding. Dario struggled to collapse his telescope's stand. This was a portable scope, not as sturdy or accurate as the giant lens on the observatory wagon. Frozen snow crunched beneath his boots and refused to release the instrument. When Dario kicked the stand, pain shot through his spine, all the way to his feet. The nerves in his back squeezed, and his muscles swelled, like there were fingers deep inside his skin, gripping his bones, trying to control him.

Dario reached out his hand and thought of an object he'd memorized long ago. Mist curled toward his palm, turning to matter. The magic sounded like a crackling fire, and sweat dripped down his brow, despite the cold. The mist solidified into the shape of a long crutch. Dario stabbed it into the frozen earth and pushed his body upright, feeling bone and tendon stretch along his spine—easing his discomfort.

He didn't need the crutch to walk, but it helped with the pain and the hunching. The crutch was as black as charred bone, with a pale blade set beneath the sharpened edge of the armrest. The heirloom was Dario's only inheritance from his family in the world above. It'd fallen with him into this world, and it was the first object he'd committed to Galecraft. He'd memorized its every property—the weight, the grainy texture, and even the bitter thoughts it conjured.

The second object he'd memorized was a large book, which he wrote in every day. After nearly two decades, he hardly had to think to conjure the object from his glyphlight. Most days, the book just lingered, dangling from a chain belt, forever on his mind. This made it an easy thing to commit to Galecraft, but a heavy magic to bear—so many stories, so many questions—page after page weighing down his mind, but he couldn't stop writing, especially when activity swirled around him.

> We've been ordered to march to Brittlehorn, so this will be a short entry. My starlight changed today. I don't know why. Maybe it has something to do with my condition? I experienced another episode just moments after the patterns in my glyph flickered, but I still don't know if there's a connection. If only I knew of another Celestial with my condition. I've interviewed colonists with similar sensations, but all of them were sick with shadow. They said it felt like something inside them was moving their muscles and they couldn't stop it. Many of them faded not long after. But I am a Celestial, and so I cannot fade. And yet, I have suffered from this condition since I was a small boy—since my parents hurled me into this world. Why?
> ~Dario Lire 3.14.2f

Company Lire descended the hill into a sparse forest, naked except for a thin garment of fresh snow. Dario balanced his scope over his shoulder, using his crutch to fight the sensation in his spine. Starlight streaked through the trees, and shadows danced all around. These days, color faded from the land and the sky almost as fast as hope seeped from people's hearts. A quiet countryside haunted the horizon—trees with white leaves, fields with black grass, and abandoned villages with no sign of life at all. Every dark home worried Dario, and he wondered how long it would be until Madi's home turned to Gloom too. Lamptree's lanterns wouldn't last forever.

At the base of the hill, Company Lire regrouped near their travel wagons, where a group of sentries stood guard. Illio Lire was among them, and when he saw Dario, he helped load the telescope into the wagon's storage compartment. He was shorter by a head, so it was easier for him to tuck the telescope into the carriage's crawlspace.

"Do we have a task?" he asked, his voice muffled by baggage.

"They're sending us to Brittlehorn," Dario answered.

Wardan Lire stepped between them and hurled his mapping tools into the compartment. "Are we crafting our wagons, sir?" Illio asked the commander.

"No wagons," Wardan answered. "We ride fast."

"Our lantern wagons won't be able to keep up," Illio warned.

"I know, but when the Gales send you a triple prong, you hustle. Everyone, carry a hand lantern," Wardan ordered. "We ride through the Gloom!"

Short and burly in his cloak, like a badger, Wardan was a grizzled veteran. Requests weren't in his vocabulary and he'd been around the longest, but the real reason he commanded Company Lire was because the sky decreed it. Somewhere on Wardan's glyph, the Gales had placed their favor.

"Why's he so pious?" Dario asked Illio while they fetched their horses. Rolly was a thoroughbred Dario had bought in the Umber Plains, while Grunt was a wild horse Illio had rescued from the Gloom.

"He's survived a long time, longer than most. Maybe he's just grateful."

"I should be grateful," Dario admitted, stepping into his stirrup. Before mounting, he waited for the pain in his legs to stop, but it didn't. It just kept pricking him, over and over, up and down, deep in his spine, pulling his tall frame into a hunch. "I wouldn't be alive without Company Lire, but I just can't bring myself to thank the Gales for this life."

Illio rolled his saddlebag around the hilt of his sword and exhaled a frosty breath skyward. They both knew where this conversation was going—the same direction it'd gone a dozen times.

"Dee, the Gales didn't hurl you into this world."

"No, my parents did."

"You don't know that either."

"My glyph says so."

Illio fastened his travel pack to Grunt's saddle, yanking the clasp. "Glyphs only reveal so much about our past, and they're never clear. I'm still not certain that astronomer was sober when you asked him. Maybe you weren't sent here to fight like the rest of us. Maybe it was unfair to you, but in the end, becoming a Celestial is a blessing. You serve the Gales now, and they're good."

Dario's throat knotted. The knots were getting bigger these days—tangled with frustration, fear, and uncertainty. "Are they?"

"Look out there, and you tell me." Illio pointed toward the bald hill where they'd just been stargazing. A gloomy atmosphere crept along the hillside, and everything that was once colorful there turned gray. Rocks blackened, and the sparkling snow lost its luster. Meanwhile, Illio's lantern jangled as he lifted it. Healthy air wafted from the glass, soothing Dario's lungs and turning the collar of his cloak a shade brighter.

Dario slouched in his saddle with a huff. Illio had a point. Gale protected life. There was no denying it, but that didn't mean the Gales were good. It just meant they were powerful. He'd written about it just a few days ago:

> *The word 'Gale' means 'breath of color'. The oracles say that clouds come from the gods' breath, which is why we can breathe in the Gale but not in the Gloom. They say there was a time when people lived without lanterns—when colonists spread Gale through joy and worship. But now, we all suffocate from this war. We dig for crystallized cloud deep underground, and use it for fuel in lanterns.*
>
> *A refugee asked me, "What did we do to deserve this? Why can't the Gales end this war?" I couldn't answer him. I've asked myself the same questions, and I began documenting this war in hopes of answering them.*
>
> *~Dario Lire 3.14.2f*

Company Lire thundered into the gloomy countryside. Out here, the earth groaned, and strange echoes filled the air. No travelers had used this road in days, maybe months, else there would have been at least some hint of color in the grass. Instead, the horses galloped atop dull and colorless fields. Even the clouds here were indistinguishable shades of white, black, and gray. Snow fell like ash, and a suffocating breeze burned Dario's lungs. He held his lantern close to his face, taking long, deep breaths. He wished he could have been with the sentries on the lantern wagon, or even better, with Madi on her tree-house balcony, or even more better, with Madi in a warm bed.

The air tasted hopeless. With each breath of toxic sky, a sad sensation settled inside Dario's stomach. Abandoned homesteads dotted the fields, separated by a long black fence. The remains of an evacuation lined the road—carts, clothes, children's toys. To make matters worse, Dario hadn't seen dayclouds for many, many hours. There was a wisp of light here and there, but no yellow clouds crested the horizon yet, so Company Lire found the gates of Brittlehorn stained in torchlight and blood.

A company battle wagon blocked the road, and a Celestial manned the ballista. "Company Lire! We read you were coming!" she shouted. "Welcome to the creep!"

Wardan signaled the company to a halt. "Shadowmen giving this place the haunt, eh?" he asked.

"Everything they got!" the Celestial replied.

"Who are you with?" Wardan asked.

"Company Veeren. We arrived a few hours ago and pushed the Ashen back to the trees. They're out there, watching us, and they'll be back," the Celestial said. "Got a lot of people here wanting to leave. Got some wanting to stay. We're not sure what to do. Our astronomers are reading the sky now. They're near the town center. Look for our telescopes."

Wardan spurred his horse forward as the gate opened. Once they'd dismounted, he split the company into pairs. While he talked strategy with the Veeren commander, everyone swept the town for shadowmen and provided supplies and medical aid to the people. Dario and Illio patrolled together, as always. Splintered homes vomited glass and furniture into the streets, sometimes a bloodied body. The air tingled, like a thick blanket had been thrown upon the town and every breath and whisper was trapped here, lingering, turning stale, and spoiling to shadow.

"The Gloom is so active here," Illio said.

Dario warily lifted his lantern toward the wall, which was quickly turning gray. "Because the colonists' minds are active," he answered. His lantern clicked and sputtered. Color spilled from it, but the wall kept fading. There was a much stronger magic at work here. The woodwork was wet, and a foul mist lifted from it. As Dario crept through the haze, his chest tightened and trembled. Celestial magic was grim, to be sure, but colony magic—it unnerved him. His was a physical magic. Theirs: psychic.

"Someone's still in here," he warned as Illio took the lead.

His friend's torch revealed a smoldering schoolhouse. Floorboards creaked, and dust floated amidst the rubble. Illio waved his hand, culling bits of fallen debris. Yes, Celestials could manipulate mist and matter with Galecraft. Yes, they possessed supernatural strength and vitality. But in Dario's opinion, Celestial magic paled in comparison to the power of colonist magic—the power to spread Gale—the source of all color and breath. With joy and bravery, Madi and all her Lamptree friends possessed this magic, but they also carried its curse. If they despair, they spread Gloom. If they lose sight of hope for too long, they fade to shadow.

"Please, Gales, protect them. Please, keep them hidden . . ."

A woman's voice rippled through the gloomy mist, and each sad syllable scraped color from the walls. Dario tracked the whisper to a toppled table, where he found the woman, cradling her head. With each prayer, color flickered from her body, like a lantern. But when the woman opened her eyes and saw the building burning around her, Gloom spread from her.

"Did they take them?"

"Take who?" Dario whispered, nearing.

"Stay away!"

"Look at me, mother," Illio said, addressing her respectfully. He knelt next to the woman. "We're Celestials. We can help you. The Ashen are gone." He held out his hand, and when the woman saw his healthy skin, she gripped him.

The woman covered her ears. "But I can still hear them. Whispers in the Gloom."

Glass and parchment scraped the floor as Illio took a seat, setting his lantern next to the woman. "Breathe, mother. You're safe now."

Dario retrieved his journal from his belt. He flipped to an empty page, passing hundreds of stories he'd recorded and pictures he'd drawn of desperate mothers and fathers and children. So many of them had died or faded, Dario couldn't let their stories fade too. He immediately began sketching this woman. She clutched her chest with one frail hand while gripping Illio's arm with her other. Her skin trickled with blood. "Celestials?" she asked in a gloomy accent. People who lived in towns with dim lanterns often developed a peculiarity of speech. Dario was sure it was a sickness in the lungs.

"Celestials, yes. We are," Illio replied, wagging a finger between his chest and Dario's.

"Did they take them?" she mumbled, tugging Illio toward a collapsed corner of the room. Glass crackled beneath her shoes.

"Take who?"

"The children."

"Was this your home?" Dario asked, scribbling notes.

"Yes. Orphanage."

"What happened here?"

"Shadowmen tunneled under the wall," the woman answered tearfully.

The woman held her key close to her chest, shuddering as she glanced around the ruin. She muttered prayers to the Gales, weeping and pleading. Her emotions wavered, as did the atmosphere within the dim room. The veins on her forehead bulged, and tiny shadows seemed to linger on her brow, like parasites. This woman's brain was bound to this world—like Dario's body was to the stars. As he recorded this event, he did not envy her.

The atmosphere around us reacts to her struggle. Color and shadow ripple through the wall, and I can hear her fears faintly in the mist. Her orphanage was destroyed, and I fear her fate depends on whether

*we can find her children or not. All I can think of as I watch her
search is how much I miss Aerial and Madi.*

~Dario Lire 3.14.2f

The woman gripped her long skirt and stomped on an earthen
hatch. It opened a moment later, and no fewer than a dozen young
children climbed out onto the cold ground, grabbing their bare
legs. When the woman saw them, she fell to her knees and wept
over them. Tears of joy stained their skin. They glistened
brighter than both Dario and Illio's lanterns combined, and soon,
color crept back into the courtyard.

There were children of all ages, one nearly as young as Aerial. Dario
quickly unwrapped a bundle of supplies. The contents rolled onto
the ground—dried fruit, canteens of water, and vials of lantern fuel.
The children scrambled all at once, not for the food or water, but for
the fuel. Hands shaking in the cold, they poured it into their empty
Gale-lantern. The black fuel sizzled and then sparkled, like a star-
filled night. The grass immediately turned a shade more green, and
the children fought to press their faces to the glass, breathing deeply.

"You must get them out of here," the woman pleaded. "Take them
with you."

"We can try," Illio said. "But I'm not the Celestial in my company
who evacuates children, but I'll take them to her. Does that make
sense?"

"Yes. Praise you."

"Eljay!" Illio called down the street. "I've got a dozen kids here! Is
our bunk wagon here yet?"

"It just got here!" she answered. "I'm coming!"

"You should go with them," Dario told the woman.

"No, I stay," she said, shuffling back inside the smoldering
orphanage.

"Why would you stay?"

The woman groaned as she bent over and picked up the bundles of food and water. "Celestials bring supplies to us, but then you go fight the shadowmen. Bad people come and steal what you give us. Someone has to make sure food and water go to people who need. So I stay."

Dario scribbled the woman's answer beneath her portrait, and not long after, Eljay Lire arrived. She always wore a wide smile for children—a smile second only to Madi's smile, though both could win a child's trust faster than a basket full of candies. Eljay waved her hand in a large circle, crafting a giant blanket.

"Magic!" the children shouted, gasping and giggling and shivering toward the blanket. Gale rippled from their laughter, and Dario wondered if the children knew they possessed a magic even more powerful than Eljay's Galecraft.

A large rock soared over the colony wall. Burning with black fire, it whizzed through the air and crashed into a tower near the town center. Splinters rained down. Shrieks and wails filled the night—not of pain, but of impatience. These people had seen this before, and they just wanted it to be over, but if Dario had learned anything from his journeys, he knew: this war was not ending any time soon.

"Why do you draw us?" someone asked him.

"People need to know your story," he answered, looking up.

It was a woman. Blood stained her face, and her clothes were smoldering. She tried to groom herself and burned her hand. A second rock hurtled overhead, and she cursed in the direction it'd come from.

"They do this to us all day," she whimpered. Her hand shook as she massaged her bleeding scalp. "Boom! Boom! All day. Shadowmen break our cloudcrawlers so we can't escape. They want to keep us here," she said with glossy eyes and a grin hinting of terror and broken nerves. "They want to break our minds. They want us to fade." The woman touched her forehead and began to cry. "I just want it to end."

Her tears sank into the cobblestone street, spreading Gloom. She looked into Dario's eyes, and he wanted to cry too. Magic had sapped her mind dry, and exhaustion drooled from her expression like a dying lantern.

"I do too," Dario said before asking her name.

The woman bit her bottom lip as it wavered, refusing to answer. "Who will read your book?" she asked afterward. "Colony archivists already record the war, but nothing changes."

Dario looked skyward. "If I can get back home, then I'll make sure the Gales read this book. And when they read your story, and all the others, they'll come down and end this war themselves."

The woman narrowed her eyes, grinning sourly and then walking away. She didn't believe him. Illio didn't either, it seemed. He grunted for Dario to follow and then sulked for the rest of the patrol.

"You okay?" Dario asked as they returned to camp.

"If the oracles find out what you're writing, they'll burn your book as blasphemy," he said.

"I write what I see."

"You blame the Gales for what you see. You write like there's no hope. You'd rather escape than fight. I told those orphans that you'd *DIE* for them, Dee. That you'd stand in the way of shadow so that they didn't have to. Was that a lie?"

"I have a family now, Illio. The only people I'd die for are Madi and Aerial . . . and maybe you, on a good day. We need to escape before it's too late," Dario replied. "Even if this war is somehow won, Company Lire won't survive to see the end of it. We are *dimming*! I feel my glyph dwindle every day. Why are we delivering bundles? Why aren't we chasing important tasks?"

"It's important to these people," Illio said, pausing in the street.

"Patrolling a ruin doesn't bring us any fame," Dario said. "Walking in circles won't make our constellation shine any brighter."

"It won't," Illio said. "But if we were off fighting legions of shadow-men, or hunting notorious companies of Shades, who would be here to make these people's lives just a little less miserable? We serve the sky, and our stars sent us here to save these people. You care about them, Dario, I know you do. That's why you write about them every day."

Dario glanced at his belt, where his journal dangled by a rope. "I do," he answered. "But that's what scares me. Colonists have Celestials to look out for them. But who looks out for us? Who races to our rescue when shadowmen tear through our cloaks?" Dario paused, letting silence fill the empty street. "No one! Constellation Lire is fading. If we don't finish a real task soon, something legendary, something people will talk about, we're both going to die. You know what I fear most? That I won't be there when Madi and Aerial need me. If Constellation Lire falls, who will protect them?"

"What do you want me to do, Dee? Challenge a Shade to a duel? Win fame by killing outlaws?"

"It wouldn't hurt."

"I can't." Illio touched his sword, shaking his head. "I can't go off on my own again. Not right now. Wardan needs me."

"It doesn't matter," Dario said. "I have a better idea."

When they returned to the town center, Wardan gave the order to craft wagons. The skies were unclear, and Company Lire would stay in Brittlehorn until the interpreters could decipher the Gales' will. Dario reached out his hand while also reaching deep into his mind. There was a special part of every Celestial's glyph dedicated to the memorization and recreation of matter: Galecraft.

Mist rose from the cobblestone street, and dust drifted from the beams of the nearby homes. The particles gathered toward Dario's palms. In front of him, a wagon took shape, a piece of his mind, like his cloak, in physical form. He wondered which looked wearier, him or his wagon. The wood was warped, the wheels were bent, and arrows littered the frame. A long brown tent covered his room. Narrow slits, cut into the cloth, let out a hint of candlelight. Inside the cabin, there was a cot, a desk, and a hook for his crutch. Everything else peeked out from beneath mounds of paper. Dario liked to think of his cabin as an unbound book, a history of past places and lost faces.

Illio followed, tramping mud onto the floorboards. Dario felt wet earth dribble onto his brain. He knew exactly which part of Illio's boot the mud had come from and the moment it'd fallen.

"What's this?" his friend asked.

A dozen parchments hung above Dario's cot, forming a series of intricate maps. Ink moved across the pages all by itself, as though a ghost were drawing it.

"Brewed inks," Dario revealed. "I bought them from an archivist in the Brink. I've been slipping the brew into our deliveries to the oracles' stronghold on Mount Anchor."

Illio shut the window flap and quickly touched a finger to his lips. He moved close to Dario and snatched one of the maps, whispering as he inspected it. "You're spying? On . . . an oracle?"

"Why not? They spy on us," Dario replied. "I told you I'm getting out of here. This is a mimicking brew. Cost me a fortune. When the oracles use my vials of ink, everything they write gets copied here."

Illio shook his head, thrusting the map toward Dario's chest. "This wasn't the plan," he whispered. "You told me you were going to get Madi and Aerial somewhere safe."

"The world above is safe."

"Yes, Dario, and you're a Celestial. If you return there without permission, it's treason." He raked a stool across the floor and sat down. Dario felt the chair rumble across his brain, and afterward, he sensed Illio's weight sink into it. His friend was angry—much angrier than expected. "You don't think the oracles are used to idiots trying to steal from them?" he asked.

"Which is why I had Madi build a trick lid." Dario's tone was calm and confident. It was a risk, but he'd taken the precautions—with Madi and with the oracles. "She thinks it's for a practical joke. Really, I brought the lid to a tinker in the Brink, who duplicated it for me. I've seen the oracles' servants test the vials. Remember? When we made our first delivery. They dip directly into the lid. They'll never know."

Illio inspected the maps as the ink danced across the page, un-hindered by any pen. A hundred miles away, some scribe was hidden away in some vault etching the location of every celestial company under the Gales' control, and it was all being copied here.

"There's magic in this ink," Illio warned, scratching his beard ner-vously. "Oracles know inks better than anyone, even you. They'll see residue. They'll track it to us."

Dario glared at the parchment, where the glossy emblems of a dozen companies glided across a map of the Carnation Region. "Or-acles don't know inks better than I do," he mumbled. "How could they? They're blind. They don't see anything but smoke and starlight."

"Then why would they have their servants draw magical maps?" Illio asked.

"Who's to say they know their servants are drawing them?" Dario answered. He settled into his hammock and stretched his stubborn spine.

Illio let out a long huff, his voice barely audible afterwards. "I can't, Dario."

"Can't what?"

"Can't go with you."

"Yes, you can," Dario pleaded. "I NEED you. I don't want to leave you behind in this world, and—"

"And you can't fight to the top of a city of escape without me."

"Yes, that too. Please. Our whole company needs to escape. That's why you have to talk to Wardan for me."

"No. We climb ONLY when the Gales grant us permission to climb. Which isn't happening any time soon because all of those cities are destroyed."

Dario stared at a remote coastline, far to the north of the Carnation Region. There, the inked symbol of a towering city disappeared behind black clouds. "Not all of them."

CHAPTER 3: MADI

Wagons splashed and spattered through Greenpond's swampy outskirts. Madi sat on the back of Lamptree's trade wagon, letting her feet dangle over the bulwark, cursing her complacency. One careless day threatened three years of careful living. She'd worked so hard to conjure a peaceful life for herself—and she'd done it without a stitch of magic. Now, she just needed to get home, to Lamptree's heights, where she could come up with a plan.

The caravan weaved through marshes until finally emerging on drier ground. Pink currents of cloud whisked the horizon, carrying a blustery wind and a coral-colored atmosphere. Madi's scarf fluttered at her neck. She sat exposed to the wind, behind the battened cargo, with Aerial tucked beneath her shirt while she nursed.

Lamptree towered on the horizon, and Sembetra's warning lingered. *Don't go back.* But where could she go? She couldn't hide anywhere else. She'd prepared caches, secret rooms, and escape routes. Sembetra didn't understand. It was too soon to give up Lamptree without a fight—too soon to become a refugee again, like so many in this caravan.

There were too many wagons to count—hundreds of rickety shapes with wheels—filled with refugees. Their belongings burst from each cart, and children clung to their clothes and blankets to keep them from blowing away. Madi pitied their muddied faces and blank expressions. They just wanted a home—a real home—a place to play and dream, a place to forget the nightmares. Guilt dragged her gaze downward. For three years, she'd hidden from her tasks, hidden from this war. But what could a lone Celestial do without a constellation? Nothing. She was better off bringing children joy by crafting them toys.

I'm supposed to be dead. This is the most I can do.

Madi touched her hip, where her identity papers lay—expiring—in her coat pocket. No matter how many toys or colony friends she surrounded herself with, one mystery still haunted her: *Celestials die when their constellation falls. How am I still alive?*

Sembetra had warned that the Red Rider's oracles knew the answer, but after what had just happened, Madi doubted they had her best interest in mind. *Inspectors investigate dark magics, not happy endings.* What's more, Sembetra would never leave without saying something. She was either arrested, forced into hiding, or worse, killed. The Red Rider was rumored to be brave, but also brutal. Madi cupped her eyes with her hand, wishing she'd had more time to investigate.

She glanced to the caravan's rear, expecting to see those two inspectors galloping after her. She couldn't rid herself of the sensation that she was being watched. It rode with the wind—an unnatural chill, causing her skin to tingle as though she'd been brushed in the dark by an unwelcome breath.

The caravan traveled at an irksome pace, rumbling along a road formed by two grassy ruts. This beaten path wandered for miles through a shallow valley—from Greenpond's swamps, through Lamptree's forests, all the way to the foothills of Mount Anchor, where the Red Rider's oracles were rumored to keep magical maps within pitch-black vaults.

Lamptree's trade wagon rolled in the middle of the pack, where the clatter of carts and chatter of refugees were loudest. Larger celestial wagons guarded the perimeter, gliding weightlessly compared to the colony carts. Sharpened ammunition glinted from their ballista nests, where Celestials stood guard, eyeing the treeline. Madi didn't envy their task. They looked tired. They were trying to hide it, but she could tell. It wasn't in the eyes; it was in the posture. Subtle twitches, and yawns. The celestial companies were vastly outnumbered, and large caravans like this were prime targets.

Here, though, in the heart of the Trade Gap, there was little trace of Gloom. Red and yellow flowers speckled a harlequin hillside. Pines shivered on the ridges, and above them, pink clouds mixed with shades of green, orange, and yellow. More dangerous flying weather. As the colored currents combined, the atmosphere turned green, and soon, a comet storm hissed overhead. Balls of green cloud wailed as they shriveled and burst.

Madi eyed the rear of the caravan again, clutching herself with a shiver. With each flash of green, she thought she saw the shape of someone watching her in the distance. It could have been a shadow-man, looming on the ridge, but if it was, why weren't the Celestials chasing it away? They didn't even seem to notice.

She tried to shake the feeling away, but her chills followed, even as the caravan changed directions. A hill shielded the wind, but Madi's skin was still bristly beneath her coat. The wagons rumbled and turned off the beaten path, forcing her to grip one of Greenpond's slimy cargo crates. She remembered this detour, and quickly curled her body onto the wagon. Her legs became hollow, and tingles skittered along her fingers, turning her palms sweaty.

In the middle of the valley, a giant pit billowed cloud, like a mouth silently exhaling color. All clouds rose from pits like this, or from crevasses and cracks in the earth. These currents were mostly pink, with some greens and golds mixed throughout. Grass turned to gravel as the wagons rounded the gaping abyss. By the look of things, shadowmen had long since abandoned this entrance to the underworld. Crude scaffolds and staircases lay in ruin.

Nevertheless, two Celestials stood atop a wagon, guarding the underworld passage. Colonists from Greenpond worked nearby. They wore the same floppy hats as the fishermen. They'd constructed long chutes, which snaked down the hillside toward the gaping abyss. Dirt flowed down the chutes and poured into the hole. Did they really think they could fill it in? The project was pointless. Madi had seen many entrances to the underworld, and the shadowmen were digging more every day. Only Celestials could keep underworld passages safe—not buckets of dirt.

Madi didn't believe in an underworld until Company Maya was tasked to purge a pit much like this one. Her company never reached the bottom, but she saw enough evidence of a world below—subterranean rivers, forests, and caverns as vast as this valley, full of clouds. She'd seen the ground give way to empty air. She'd seen tides of shadowmen emerge upon dark staircases of stone. She'd seen company towers tumble amid bursts of crumbling dirt and rock . . .

She'd survived the deep, but she returned with a terrible fear: the ground wasn't trustworthy. It could open up without warning. If there was an underworld, what kept this world from crumbling into it? Lamptree was the only place she trusted now, with its long curling roots holding fast to the earth. The wagon jostled, and Madi closed her eyes with a gasp. She clutched Aerial and leaned close to the cargo. Drawing a deep breath, she tried to imagine herself high on Lamptree's branches, safe above its colossal roots, where the earth couldn't betray her.

Clouds billowed from the pit. Whispers, too. They trickled with the wind, and it was impossible to tell exactly what it was. Deranged laughter? Weeping? Hollow cries for help? Madi looked around the caravan, wondering if anyone else heard the foul sounds. She couldn't tell. Colonists often said the Gloom spoke to them, and they'd even given the sensation a name, Madi recalled with a shiver—the White Whisperer.

Cloud belched from the abyss, and the ground shook. Madi took a deep breath and curbed her thoughts. She pushed everything out. Everything except Lamptree, Dario, and her daughter. She touched her nose to Aerial's beautiful face. Her eyes were two tiny pits of joy, two imprisoning pupils into which she'd gladly fall for the rest of her days. Pulling Aerial's cheek close, she made a silent promise.

We're never leaving Lamptree again.

Lamptree Colony was the size of a thousand trees. It was leafy green and full of thorns near the top, viny and budded with lavender in the middle, and dashed with honeysuckle near the bottom. Rising above a gloomy forest, the colossal keyhole-shaped tree rose like a candle in the dark. Four longroads surrounded the colony, reaching outward like the spokes of a wheel for refugees to follow.

The caravan arrived at the colony just as the last dayclouds disappeared behind Mount Anchor. The mountain erupted in the distance, spewing plumes of teal cloud, ice, and snow into the sky. There, Anchor Colony glowed like a gemstone beneath snow-capped peaks. Madi imagined the Red Rider's oracles searching for her from those heights, but they were too late.

Her nerves settled as her colony's colossal gate of dark brown bark came into view. Lamptree grew from a pine forest, which was odd, considering the giant tree was nothing close to coniferous. It was shaped like a cedar, she supposed, with massive branches all the way up and down, glistening with civilization.

A blanket of brown needles muffled the arrival of refugees and merchants. The scent of pine filled the air, kicked up by excited footsteps. Children leapt up and down. They pointed and stared. Their jaws unhinged. All the while, Madi beamed with pride.

Voices filled the forest, echoing beneath the colony's bright glow. Administrators organized the refugees into lines, while Madi and other citizens were waved through the Trunk Gate. New arrivals were everywhere, surrounding the Shivering Sapling, an inn built into the cleft of Lamptree's trunk. Flutes, drums, and guitars battled the chaos with a musical beat. Refugees bartered for housing, and merchants barked orders. Workers unloaded cargo. Giant cranes churned, carrying crates upward, while mechanical lifts carried people. One of those lifts required a cog Madi had recently repaired. She smirked with satisfaction as it spun with a gentle *clatter*.

Already, the amount of commotion put Madi at ease. In this vertical colony, the constellations were only visible on the highest branches. Down here, in this honeycomb of gatehouses and corrals, she was certain even the Gales would have to look twice to spot her. Merch masters sorted Lamptree's trade wagons into warehouses. Madi, and the others from her wagon, unloaded quickly. The sooner they finished, the sooner they could begin the long climb to their cottages on Lamptree's upper districts.

Once the wagon was unloaded, Madi's companions said their goodnights and made for the nearest lift. She followed, but then paused when she heard her name. Not her new name—her old one.

"Nariah Maya?"

The warehouse was empty, home now to a lonely chill. Madi's spine straightened, and her coat provided no warmth. Wagons lined the corrals, and the smell of timber and lubricating brews filled the air. Music and commotion echoed outside, but otherwise, it was completely quiet—until a frost crackled across the wagon window. In the glass, Madi spied the reflection of two people standing behind her—a man in a black hat and a woman in a long crimson coat. There was a hole in the woman's jacket, just above her heart. Stranger still, her coat fluttered in a wind, but there was no wind at all in the warehouse.

"Madi Amriel?" the man asked. His voice was familiar and friendly, albeit a bit arrogant. "A pleasant name, I think. Did you make it up yourself? Or did Sembetra?"

Madi turned, her heart shaken by the mention of the oracle's name. But she recognized the man immediately, relaxing some. His black coat, wide-brimmed hat, and tall frame made it easy. This was Bandico, the Celestial Sembetra had tasked with forging Madi's documents. Madi's friend had only signed them.

Bandico stood as rigid as an icicle, with his hat tipped so that Madi could see little more than his lower lip. His oversized coat draped his body, making him look shorter and younger than he was. The woman in the crimson coat was nowhere to be seen, but Madi spied a puddle of dark water beginning to form where she'd been standing. The water rippled as dark as night, and it evaporated quickly.

"Bandico!" Madi turned. "Please tell me you know where Sembetra is."

The Celestial cocked his head. His hat's long shadow shrouded his face. "Haven't seen her since she paid me," he answered in a tone not nearly as grim as his garb.

Madi pressed a finger to her temple, and her stomach turned sour. Maybe it was just the smell of old merch wagons, but somehow, Bandico's presence felt like more bad news. He showed up out of nowhere, today of all days, him of all people.

Bandico stepped closer, shedding the shadows like a cloak. "You're clearly busy, so I'll cut straight to the gut." He unfurled a parchment and set it on the wagon's step-board. "I'm on a task for the Green Grinner, and I could use some trustworthy local knowledge. Have you seen this symbol anywhere inside Lamptree?"

Black chalk smeared the parchment, forming the shape of an arrow pointing upward toward a circle. Madi squinted and tilted her head as Aerial squirmed. At the right angle, the symbol looked ominously like a shadowman—if the circle was its head, and the top of the arrow its arms.

"No, I'd remember this ugly thing," she answered. "What is it?"

"A way-mark for a group of very dangerous people," Bandico replied. He stuffed the parchment back into his pocket and retrieved a second paper. This one was folded and smeared with blood. "I have a manifest here that shows a shipment was sent by barge from Oakenhole to Lamptree. There's no river in Lamptree Forest. How would the crates get here? Who is W.L.?"

Madi eyed the page, worried by the flakes of dried blood drifting across it. She saw the initials *W. L* on the manifest. It wasn't a person. It was a place. The Waterlog was a subterranean river. It flowed through a canal carved from wood in Lamptree's lowest district—the Roots. But, wary of the bloody page, she remained silent.

Bandico gave little reason for anyone to trust him, but he didn't seem to care. He wore all black. His hands and fingers were mostly covered by his oversized sleeves, and two sharp hatchets peeked from his belt. He turned his attention toward a crowd outside, and when he saw a group of Celestials questioning them, he retreated from the door and tucked into the shadows.

"Are they looking for you?" Madi asked.

"Maybe. I didn't ask who you were running from when I helped you," Bandico replied. "I knew you were scared and needed help, so I helped. Look, I don't know what Sembetra told you, but I'm not a bad person. I'm caught on the bad side of some magic, just like you. You're trying to hide from yours. I need to outrun mine. Okay?"

His plea sounded genuine, but it would have helped if he'd at least made eye contact. Madi had never seen his face. What if he was fading? What if he was a Shade—a cursed Celestial, marked as an outlaw and wanted by the oracles.

Then again, I'm wanted by the oracles now, she realized. *What if I've been marked as a Shade for hiding from my tasks? Maybe he can help.*

Bandico wore a dark coat, long and black, with several belts and buckles. Strands of mist weaved across it, a protective entanglement of vines. Madi hated how a celestial's battle-cloak devoured their clothing, robbing its purpose, turning it into an armor. Dario always said: *a glimpse at a celestial's cloak reveals exactly how powerful they are.* It wasn't always true, but it gave a good idea. Bandico's cloak was thick and strong, hinting of green, with generous amounts of mist curling across his collar. But his jacket bore something a strong Celestial ought never have—holes and tatters, like a moth chewed through the fabric, even now, as he wore it.

The commotion outside grew, and several of the Celestials began searching the neighboring warehouse. Bandico retreated further into the dark, where Madi could barely see him. "Look, are you going to help or not?" he asked. "If I don't complete this task, I'm going to die."

"Because of your ghost?" Madi asked.

Bandico didn't answer immediately. His feet scraped glass on the floor as he searched for another escape. How could he see anything in that darkness?

"So you did talk about me."

"Sembetra told me you were haunted," Madi answered. "But I thought ghosts could only haunt places."

Bandico quietly stepped back into the light, rubbing his chest. A bandage covered his palm, and Madi spotted a second bandage peeking through a small hole in his sleeve. Mist from his coat hissed as it repaired the hole. His skin wasn't fading. It was rotting.

Something really is killing him.

"Here's the ten-second answer. A longer one costs your cooperation," he said quickly. "My ghost chose me as her haunt, meaning she survives by feeding off my glyph. When I complete a task, she takes a share of the reward. When I eat, she feels full. When I sleep, she feels rested. I'm what keeps her anchored to the land of the living, until I wither away to nothing and we both die."

Madi scanned the warehouse for any hint of his ghost. The air was prickly with an unseen presence. The window of the trade wagon was still frosted cold. Dark water dripped from the driver's box now, as though the ghost was sitting there, drenched in rain. Madi believed him, but what was his task? She didn't want him hurting anyone, and he'd been vague for a reason.

But so had Sembetra.

Madi didn't know who was using her ciphers or why. *The purpose didn't matter, just the payment.* So how could she judge Bandico? She couldn't. He reminded her of the haunted mansion in Lamptree Forest—encased in vines, slowly collapsing. Now, as he studied his two crumpled parchments, she pitied him. *What would I do in his position? Give in to the ghost leeching my life away, or fight to stay with my family?*

A pair of Celestials neared the warehouse door, which *squealed* as they opened it to its fullest, shooting rays of light into the large storage area. Bandico hid behind a box, tugged the brim of his black hat downward, and checked the time. Sand sifted through a small clock on his belt, clicking a timing bead.

"We need to find a way out of here," he whispered toward the wagon.

Was he talking to his ghost? Madi shivered and tightened Aerial's pouch. "I know a way," she told him.

The hall was unlit, and Madi walked with her hands outstretched, following a crease of light coming from the far door. A stack of wooden crates clattered as she bumped them, and the Celestials shouted something from the far room. Bandico took the lead, snatching Madi's hand and leading her to the door. His bandage was coarse and damp with sweat—or blood. He walked quickly, but he guided her gently through the pitch-black hall. Beneath his hat, his eyes gave off a faint white glow.

The alley led back into the clamor of Lamptree's Trunk District. Bandico quickly adjusted his hat. Here, torch-lit fortifications mingled with the influx of refugees—inns, markets, and hastily constructed tenements. Lamptree's main avenue, the Mossroad, was nearby. Madi eyed it briefly, but that road curled upward, around and around, toward the top of the tree. Bandico's task was below, in the Roots district.

"Follow me," she told him. "I know where you need to go."

She pressed through the crowds and took a shortcut through a shrine to the Pink Pilgrim. Wooden archways separated a courtyard from the bustle of the street. Prayers echoed, and pink incense spilled from bowls at the base of a statue. An argument broke out, stirring the pious blanket of mist. Some refugees had led a lamb into the courtyard, and they carried a knife with a purple sash.

"You can't do that here!" a man shouted.

Sacrifices were illegal on Lamptree. The Pilgrim favored explorers and those who journeyed to sacred places—not blood.

"The Pilgrim isn't the only Gale," someone answered. "We worship the Purple Prince. Our home is gone. What do you expect us to do?"

Tempers flared. A censer clattered to the ground, and colored incense clashed—purple and pink. The argument drew attention from the street, and several Lamptree rangers rushed to the scene, cutting through the mist in their dark cloaks.

Madi kept moving, and Bandico followed close behind, muttering, "The Gales' alliance will never last."

"It needs to," she replied. "Or the shadowmen will win this war."

By the look of it, they were winning already. Refugees poured in from the countryside, and Madi had never seen the Roots district so cramped. Health ministers patrolled the streets, offering fresh clothes and warm handshakes. Each of them carried a glass goblet and a belt of daylight brews. Their hospitality was genuine, Madi believed, but their duty was obvious: they were checking people's skin to see if they were fading.

Two ministers spoke gently to a gaunt woman, sitting on the steps of a tenement. Her hand trembled, shaking what little flesh clung to her emaciated arm. The minister raised his glass cup, into which he poured a drop of daylight brew. As soon as the yellow brew touched the water, the goblet glowed bright. Bandico shielded his eyes, but Madi slowed down to watch. It'd been a long time since she'd seen someone fading within the walls of Lamptree. Was it so hopeless out there in the wild that the mere sight of this colony hadn't cured this woman?

Shadows shimmered deep beneath the woman's flesh, like distant water, rising. Even now, it spread up her neck. Most of her flesh was dark gray and sickly, with a texture like sand. Bits of mist peeled from her arms and legs, like dust. Her pupils were dark, dilated, and traumatized. Madi shuddered, sensing the Gloom eyeing her from inside.

"Don't give up," a minister told the woman. "You haven't lost everything. You're a colonist. You have the power to spread Gale. Not even the most powerful Celestials can do that, and the shadowmen can never snatch that power from you."

"Breathe in, now out," said the second minister. He lifted a small lantern to the woman's face.

The woman lifted her chin, grimacing in the lantern's colorful glow. Her hair dangled, black and greasy, down her shoulders. Her cap, which appeared to have once been red, was turning white. Bits of mist frayed from her clothes, which were dark and tattered. The last bit of colorful flesh she had left was on her arm—the one that was shaking. It was as though all the life in her body had fled there, and the rest, the Gloom had seized. When the woman saw Madi—and Aerial sleeping in her pouch—a tear slid down her cheek, smearing her flaxen flesh. She blinked sadly, and then her eyes turned dark gray and melted away.

Madi's heart hollowed at the gaze. She'd just faded . . . right in front of everyone! The woman's arms dropped hopelessly to her side, revealing an empty pouch on her chest, frayed and graying. It was a pouch just like Aerial's—only empty. Seeing the empty pouch paralyzed Madi, and her heart groaned for the woman. She clutched her daughter, realizing what the woman had lost, realizing why she'd given up hope.

"Move along. Everyone, move along!" the minister shouted. He turned to his partner and lowered his voice. "We need a ranger here now."

The crowd started moving again, carrying Madi like a current. She couldn't get the fading woman out of her head. She couldn't stop squeezing Aerial, keeping her as close to her chest as possible. Today just needed to end. She needed a drink and a long night's sleep. Tomorrow, she'd visit the governor and come up with a plan. She tried looking back toward the faded woman, but the road angled downward, taking her deeper into the district, where Lamptree's roots meandered into an underground cavern.

Madi took a deep breath as the cave widened. If not for Lamptree's thick curling roots all around, she would have been too terrified to continue the descent. The Waterlog glistened blue, slicing through the Roots within a canal carved from the wood of the tree.

"A subterranean river," Bandico muttered. "So this is how they smuggle them." He'd been muttering throughout their walk, and Madi still wasn't quite sure if he was talking to her or his ghost.

The Roots looked more depressing than the last time she was here, a few months ago. The houses at the bottom of the cave seemed so distant and hopeless—covered in dust from the crissle mines, where the sound of picks echoed in search of Galefuel. The houses higher up were teased by light from the surface. Clothes dried on lines, adding a bit of color to the dim chamber. Some trees and gardens grew, and wisps of orange cloud rose through the underground chamber, providing nutrients.

Bandico walked toward a few children playing with a ball on one of the rooftops. When a stray ball rolled toward his feet, he picked it up and threw it back to them. They thanked him and returned to the game without a thought, but he stood there, watching them play. Their legs were so skinny, Madi wondered how they had the strength to kick the ball.

"Are you hungry?" Bandico asked them.

"Yes, sir!" they replied.

Bandico strayed from the road to the nearest vendor. A vat of soup steamed behind him. "Why don't you give them food?"

The man swallowed and shied away. "I-I did sir, up to their ration. They-they don't have money."

Bandico's tongue pushed against his lower lip, and he flung a glass shard into the man's chest. "Now they have money. Give them all they can eat . . . and let them warm themselves in your treehouse some . . . and get them a better ball."

The vendor fumbled for his ladle. "Yes, sir," he said.

The children cheered and rushed to thank Bandico, but he passed through them without a word, parting them with his hands. Madi followed, pinching her lower lip. If Bandico was a good person, and it certainly seemed he was, why did he seem so sad? The way he moved was like the people of Greenpond, slow and soggy beneath his oversized hat and coat.

He walked to a pier, where a crane lifted cargo onto a boardwalk. Water lapped the edges of the canal, where he stood and studied the scene. "What can you see?" he asked.

"Nothing out of the ordinary," Madi replied, scanning the slums.

"Sorry, not you. I was talking to Raven."

Madi tread carefully across the slippery boards. "You speak to her? I thought she's killing you."

"She is, but we've come to a sort of understanding. You see, if I die, so does she. We spent a long time working against each other, but that had to change for us to survive."

As he spoke, he took one of his hatchets and cut away at some signage, revealing a way-mark, identical to the one on his page. Frost crackled along the windows of the nearest warehouse, and Madi caught the reflection of a long red jacket in the chilled glass.

"Raven says it's this way," Bandico told Madi.

A narrow scaffold led to a lone structure built high above the canal. Madi cradled Aerial's pouch as they crossed. Here, she spotted another way-mark, etched faintly into the boardwalk. Who were these dangerous people?

"Should I report this group to the governor?" she asked.

He crept closer to the building and its glowing windows. "Won't need to once I'm done," he whispered.

"Why? What are you going to do?" Madi asked, eyeing the man's hatchets.

"What my task requires."

He paused at a large door and brushed his fingers along the height of the entrance. Iron bars blocked the door, but Bandico reached out and formed a fist, culling the iron. A fond scent filled Madi's nose—the smell of mist and matter mingling. Celestials could craft or cull any material they'd memorized and committed to their glyph. The Gales had bestowed this magic on Celestials, but Madi refused to use it anymore. Galecraft required a magical connection to the world around you, and if she was done being a puppet, she couldn't afford to have any strings attached.

The iron bars turned to mist and floated away, leaving a bare wooden door. Bandico placed his hand on the door, and tried to cull it, forming a fist. Nothing happened.

"It's not culling. Why not? Do you know what kind of wood this is?" he asked.

Madi waited before answering. "You talking to me, or . . ."

"Yes, you."

"It's Lamptree wood."

"Is that like oak? I've studied oak. Why won't this cull?"

"Because it hasn't been cut from the tree yet," Madi revealed, eyes raised toward the cavern's heights. Lamptree's roots curled from the surface, gleaming with streets and scaffolds. "Every building here is carved from Lamptree. The wood is still alive, and living things can't be crafted or culled."

Bandico turned back to the door. "No, but they can be haunted. Raven, we need to get through here."

He paused, and then spoke again.

"Inside? How many?"

He paused again. Madi turned her ear, but she couldn't hear anything, not even a faint whisper in the air.

"Okay, try to find out what brews they're using. Dry them if you can." Bandico paused again, hiding beneath a window. "Right. I'll wait."

Madi waited and listened, but noticed no sign of movement from the ghost. Water trickled through the canal below, and children laughed on the rooftops above, but here amid the warehouses, it was quiet.

She tapped Bandico on the shoulder, hoping he'd look her in the eyes. He didn't. "So, uh, recently, I've felt like someone's watching me, following me, like your ghost follows you," she admitted. "Do you think I could be haunted?"

"Maybe. Do you have many enemies?"

Madi shrugged. Her only enemies escaped when her company left her behind. "Not anymore," she replied.

"Then probably not," Bandico replied. "Ghosts know that they feed off of their haunt, so it's rare they pick a person they love. Still, happens though. Love can be prickly poison."

"So, Raven wasn't your friend then?" Madi asked.

Bandico chuckled. "No, she hated me. Correction: she hates me. But we both need to climb out of this world before I wither away, and we're stuck with each other until we do."

The door began to hiss. It was happening! Raven was . . . doing something—moving between worlds. Vines on the wall shriveled and died. The entrance shook amid a series of rumbles and a loud *crunch*. Cracks formed on the wood, tearing through the door's handle. Aerial cried out, and Madi leaned away. Splinters rained into the air alongside a ghostly wail. Bandico readied his hatchets, and as soon as the door crumbled, he charged inside.

A ballista bolt shot out from the door, narrowly missing Madi as she ducked. The defenders had been ready, but against a Celestial, they stood little chance. Shouts echoed, turning bloody. Bodies tumbled to the floor, and Madi retreated across the scaffold, away from the violence. Through the windows, she tracked Bandico's silhouette through the flickering light. The whole structure turned dark, but Bandico's assault continued. When he emerged, it was quiet.

Blood dripped from his hatchets as he crossed the bridge. His hat hid all but a callous grin. "I'll show myself out. I don't want any of this getting tracked to you."

"You killed those people."

"I'm a Shade. You knew that."

"I wasn't sure, but it's no excuse!" Madi said, stroking Aerial.

Bandico adjusted his hat, revealing a reserved smile. "It keeps my curses away. You'd do the same if you were in my position."

Madi caressed her daughter's forehead and eyed the extinguished hideout. The fading woman was still fresh in her memory—the empty pouch, her hopeless posture. She gathered her lip between her fingers, worried she'd have done Bandico's task and more to keep from losing Aerial.

"See? You already know. Forged papers won't save you, Madi," he continued. His tone hardened, cold and resolute. "You're going to have to do more to survive. . . like I do."

As he walked away, he stepped through a puddle. It splashed. Then, it splashed again, and Madi glimpsed the reflection of Raven in her crimson coat, trailing Bandico step for step.

CHAPTER 4: DARIO

Night echoed with the sound of shifting starlight—lofty wails and airy rumbles. Dario sat at the door of his wagon and watched Constellation Lire shimmer while stretching his legs. He'd been too nervous to sleep. Illio had made it sound like the Gales were omniscient. *But if they were, they'd have cursed me a long time ago.* No, the sky was a checkerboard of tasks, and the Gales were too busy pushing important pieces to notice one little pawn sneaking away.

Daylight peeked over Brittlehorn's wall when news came from the observatory wagon: A new task from above. Company Lire was to escort a caravan of refugees through the Trade Gap—first to Greenpond, then to Lamptree, Oakenhole, and finally Mount Anchor.

"Cull cabins!" Wardan commanded. "Clear out your food and your friends for the night."

Dario limped up the ladder into his cabin and closed the flap behind him. Hidden from the stars, he took the mimicked maps and sorted them onto his desk. Dozens of pilfered pages flickered in the candlelight. The ink was still moving as he sewed the pages into a fresh binding. His heart pounded, but it was too late to turn back now. His family's only escape was upward.

He buckled the stolen maps to his belt and joined the others outside. Company Lire wagons bordered the narrow avenue, where the smell of a savory breakfast added some sweetness to the smoldering ruins. Apples dipped in bacon grease were a Lire tradition after long periods without dayclouds. Colonists milled about the street, weary-eyed and restless. Meanwhile, Dario wrote.

> *In the daylight, we can see the extent of the devastation. This was more than a few shadowmen sneaking into a settlement to ambush someone in their bedroom. This was a well organized raid. Many were taken. We've yet to be tasked with going after them, which likely means they've already suffocated in the Gloom and faded.*
>
> *Raids like this are why I'm convinced the oracles are lying. These people on the frontier know it too. We're not winning this war.*
>
> *~Dario Lire 4.14.2f*

Three girls watched Dario from the doorstep of a cramped row-home. He guessed they were sisters, based on their assorted heights and matching dresses. After ensuring each girl received a candied apple, he reached out his hand and culled his magical wagon. Really, there was no wagon—no wood, no rivets, no spokes. The sisters, like most colonists, didn't understand. The wagon was Dario. It was an extension of his mind, just like his arm extended from his body. All along the avenue, celestial wagons shriveled to a mist and disappeared.

"Where did it go?" the youngest asked Dario, wearing the same awestruck expression as her sisters.

Dario grinned and pointed toward Constellation Lire, which glistened—even during the day. The sisters squinted, as if to see a tiny wagon dangling from a star. But that was another thing they didn't understand. Celestial glyphs held more than just light. It contained every material Dario had ever committed to Galecraft—as well as every fiber that made him, *him*—from his memories, to his dreams, to his very soul. Galecraft didn't come cheap either. This magic belonged to the Gales, and the cost was servitude.

The small girl chased a strand of Dario's dissolving wagon into the street, but he stopped her. Like all magics, Galecraft had its dangers. Further down the street, someone had forgotten about an apple inside their wagon. It hissed, shriveled, and popped as the wagon faded. Bits of apple flesh spewed into the air. Chuckles skittered across the street. Organic matter couldn't be crafted or culled using Galecraft, but an exploded apple was better than an exploded bed-friend.

> *I can only think of my daughter as I watch these young girls. I bore a child into this war, and I feel responsible for getting her out of it. But when I look around—at the smoke, at the rubble and the blood—I fear I'm taking too long. I think I speak for all the parents here. I see it on their faces.*
>
> *~Dario Lire 4.14.2f*

"Signal departure," Wardan ordered. "First stop, Greenpond."

A bell sounded, and refugees filled the streets, burdened with belongings.

"Chess, Gable, up boys!" Eljay coaxed Company Lire's two adopted strays onto the bunk wagon. The dogs barked and clambered inside the cabin, where Company Lire stored food, passengers, or anything else that couldn't be stored or recalled with Galecraft. Dario usually stayed away from the bunk wagon. Every cot and curtain was riddled with dog hair.

Celestials from Company Veeren watched the departure from their battle wagons. "Good luck, Lires," they said.

"Good luck, Veerens," the Lires answered.

"I worry for them," Dario whispered to Illio. He looked back at the smoldering settlement. Veerens patrolled the palisade, watching the forest, and the shadows shifting within. "This frontier is too dangerous to hold."

"I worry for them, too. Celestials bear a bond no one else could ever understand. We're the Gales' warriors. We fell from the sky. We sleep in wagons. None of us know what home really means, and yet we fight to protect it for others. It's a noble calling."

"That's not what I mean," Dario said. "I worry that the Gales' tasks don't have our best interest at heart—not ours or the colonists of Brittlehorn."

Illio scowled. "The Gales aren't evil. People are. Evil happens when we misread the sky. That's why you have a book full of sad stories."

Dario sped to a gallop, frustrated. He'd fought side-by-side with Illio for years, experiencing the same war, but they'd reached two opposite conclusions. *He trusts what he doesn't see, but I trust what I've seen.*

A large sphere of color surrounded Company Lire's lantern wagon. Here, the air was fresh, and the grass green. Large flocks of birds circled the giant lantern, bickering for a spot in the healthy atmosphere. Hundreds of them perched atop the iron cage guarding the lantern, and atop the nearby observatory wagon's bronze telescope.

Company Lire formed a perimeter around the caravan, which grew longer with every passing hour. Travelers poured in from the countryside, where rumors of a celestial escort had no doubt spread. Every hour, Dario uttered a battle hymn with the rest of his company, which was more of a melodic chant than a song. Tradition said that the hymns were meant to ward off shadowmen and alert nearby refugees to safety. Dario thought it was just a clever way to see who was awake or not.

Rolly flicked her ears as Dario patrolled the edge of a forest. She'd heard an animal, or something else. Dario leaned back on the reins, sat still, and listened. Leaves crackled in the forest, but then the sound stopped. He scanned the dreary woodline. There was some color this far from the lantern wagons, but not much. He relaxed his grip on the reins and squeezed his calves against Rolly's side, signaling her forward. Pain coursed through his lower body. Usually, he gave verbal commands, but now he wanted to keep quiet.

Rolly churned through a blanket of dead leaves for about a minute. When she stopped, churning continued elsewhere, echoing deeper in the forest. Nervousness knotted Dario's stomach. If sudden chills meant a god was watching, then a sudden weight in the gut meant shadowmen were watching. Dario narrowed his eyes toward a hint of movement. A dark figure peeked out from behind a tree, revealing just its head and hands.

Slender creep.

Oracles called them Ashen, but most people just said shadowmen, because that's what they were. Bodies like a human, skin like shadow. Their faces were as featureless as a cloud and as ominous as a growing storm—not even eyes glowed from their empty visage.

"You good?" Illio asked, riding to Dario's side.

The shadowman's fingers curled around the tree, turning the bark black.

"They're all around us," Dario muttered.

"I know." Illio faced the opposite direction, scanning the hillside. "This caravan has grown fat and slow. I haven't had time to talk to Wardan yet." He peeked toward Dario's belt, eyeing the stolen maps. He pressed his lips together pensively, like he was fighting hard to resist some mortal temptation. Had he finally started to consider escape?

"But you've had time to think about it?" Dario asked, smiling.

Illio tapped the hilt of his sword. His fingers jutted from his torn gloves. There was a time when Illio's cloak was the thickest and strongest of all Lires. He'd go off on his own, and Dario remembered watching his glyph grow brighter and brighter, but then they became friends, and Illio stopped chasing after renowned tasks. Instead, he started looking after Dario. Ever since then, he'd slowly been withering—along with all of Company Lire.

"I have, and you're right about one thing. Something has to change," he said. "Maybe it's time I start competing for tasks again."

"It's too late for that," Dario countered. "And too dangerous."

"You think treason is less dangerous?" Illio whispered. "I said I'd talk to Wardan for you, so I will. Just don't do anything stupid until I do, and don't be surprised when he has us both flogged."

He rode off, leaving Dario alone with his journal.

Today, I asked people what they thought about the cities of escape. Most think they're a myth. The rest think they're all destroyed. They ask me, "If the cities are real, why aren't we going there?" I'm afraid to show them the maps I've stolen. I don't want to cause them any more reason to despair, but they need to know.

I carry proof: Cities of escape are real, and the oracles are hiding them. I don't know what to do. The refugees probably wouldn't even believe me. My best friend doesn't. I wonder if my wife will.

~Dario Lire 4.14.2f

Hundreds of small colony wagons formed a disheveled line. Wagons covered by canvases, wagons shaped like wooden boxes, wagons that barely moved—they all rolled down a hill, splashed across a shallow riverbed, and rumbled up another small hill. Company Lire was stretched thin, without enough eyes to track all this activity.

Many more wagons passed Dario's position on the embankment. In one cart, a young mother carried an infant in a sash, just like Madi carried Aerial. Their wagon rumbled violently over the ford. Amid a string of vicious coughs, the mother reached down to fill her canteen. The wagon bumped, and the canteen slipped from her hand into the water, but she didn't stop to retrieve it.

Dario clicked his tongue, and Rolly descended the hill. He retrieved the floating canteen, filled it, and held it next to his lantern until the gloomy water turned a sparkling blue, cool and refreshing. When he spotted the mother's wagon again, he rode to it.

He overheard the mother muttering a prayer. "Please, Stranger, if this sickness is a sign, I don't know what it means."

Another cough cut her prayer to the Teal Stranger short, and she covered her arms with a shawl.

"Sudden chills?" Dario asked her.

The woman nodded, eyes red with exhaustion. She took a rag to her nose and blew. "Sir, I've heard chills can mean a god is watching. Is that true?"

"Sometimes. Sometimes it's just your body telling you to rest."

He offered her the canteen back.

"Thank you, sir," she said after drinking. "I have papers, here, somewhere."

She fumbled at her pockets, but Dario gestured gently. "Stop. Why would I need your papers?"

"I saw you watching me," she admitted. "I was afraid I'd done something wrong."

"No, nothing wrong. I have a daughter the same age as yours."

The grime of travel smudged her skin, yet the way she cradled her child cut through Dario's charade of toughness. He was a Celestial. People watched him from every wagon, waiting to see him slice a shadowman in half with his crutch. But this mother exposed what Dario truly felt like: a frightened father.

"What happened to your home?" he asked.

"Shadowmen found it. One night, my husband and I saw one peering through the window at our daughter. She's barely lived," the mother said, cradling her daughter. "I don't care what happens to me. I just want to find a place where they can't reach *her*."

The baby yawned, and Dario thought instantly of Aerial. It'd been six weeks since he'd seen her—since he'd touched her soft skin, listened to her tiny breaths, and gazed into her innocent eyes. Uncertainty filled the air, and as Dario drew a long breath, nervousness poured into his lungs, squeezing them tight. Lamptree wasn't safe, not nearly as safe as Madi promised it was.

He cleared his throat and tried to sound confident. "Your husband, where is he?"

"Driving our cattle. He's a few days behind, but he'll catch up."

"I'm certain he will," Dario said, turning his attention to commotion near the woodline. He had more questions he'd have liked to ask, but a shout sparked his adrenaline, and he spurred Rolly toward the hillside, where a group of young men had gathered too close to the valley's edge. Here, the colorful field met a gloomy forest—branches dangling like limp fingers.

"Come out, come out shadowman!" the boys taunted.

A lone shadowman emerged from behind a tree, arms dead at its sides. The boys cursed at it and threw rocks. The Ashen stood com-pletely still as rocks whizzed by its body. Meanwhile, the boys inched closer to get better throws.

"Get away from there!" Dario shouted, guiding Rolly between them and the shadowman. "It's luring you in."

"Sir, it's just one," they said. "Drag it here! Let us kill it!"

"There's never only one," Dario warned. He spurred Rolly into the tall grass, sweeping his crutch. Immediately, five more shadowmen hopped up from hiding places and scampered back toward the woodline. The young colonists' eyes swelled. As Dario shepherded them back to safety, a rock struck him in the back. Now, a dozen Ashen stood at the woodline, holding rocks, taunting *him*.

"Back to your wagons," he told the colonists.

A second rock hissed from the forest, striking Dario in the shoulder. Thirteen shadowmen gathered now. Fourteen. Fifteen. The sharp weight in his stomach returned.

"Should we call for help?" the boys asked.

"No," Dario said. He set his crutch across his lap. "They'll need more than this to get past me."

The boys retreated, and Dario let the Ashen see the bladed edge of his crutch. The shadowmen peeked out from a dozen different hiding places. He expected they would test the strength of his cloak soon.

Sure enough, an arrow hissed from the forest, directly toward Dario's face, but as it struck, the mist from his battlecloak swirled into a white mask, shattering the arrow. He'd seen his mask form in a mirror once: it bore his exact face, pearly white, but far braver than he felt. The shadowmen fled as it flashed, only to return a short time later, in greater numbers.

Dario remained at his post, enduring more rocks, until the deafening sound of a sky-quake scattered the shadowmen. Like a long trumpet blast echoing high in the air, sky-quakes occurred when a constellation shifted more quickly than usual. He grimaced, the hairs on his neck rising. While common, such a sound in the sky often signaled death.

If this is what a Gale sounds like, he thought. *How can Illio say they're good?*

The sound smeared the clouds, first like a low horn, then like a series of shrill echoes, as though the stars were about to shatter. Dario scanned the caravan for the sick mother and her daughter, but he couldn't spot them in all the activity. Children ran to their carts, dogs barked, and the observatory wagon was abuzz.

Dario fingered his new map book beneath his cloak. The stolen tome was heavy on his belt, and as the sky quaked, he felt as though the Gales were calling for it. Were the gods omniscient like Illio thought? No, probably not. If they were, this war would be over.

Nearby, Wardan walked quickly across the deck of the observatory wagon. He bit down hard on a pipe in his mouth while drawing back a bow. He fired several arrows into the sky, which exploded into smoke, forming a series of logograms.

Abandon posts. Form battle line. North. All wagons into formation. North. Shadowmen. Many.

The message withered to smoke and lingered alongside the unease in the air. Dario found Illio near the front of the caravan, carrying a frightened cat back to a colonist. "What happened?" he asked.

Illio returned the cat to its owner, ignoring Dario until they were alone. "That quake, it was for us. Constellation Lire is shifting fast," he said. "I overheard Adacus and the interpreters. Fast updrift. Twelve doubledots. Four prongs."

Clouds moved quickly through the sky, disturbed by the quake. A purple current mixed with a blue. The combination of cloud erupted with sparks and flashes of lightning.

"Twelve doubledots!" Dario had to have misheard. Such a change, at such a pace? It could only mean one thing. "That's a tide."

Illio retrieved a bundle of bandages from his saddlebag. "Yep. Over a thousand shadowmen just climbed from a nearby pit, and the Gales want us to head them off."

"Can we stop that many?"

"The Gales told us to," Illio said, spurring his horse along the caravan. "Whether or not we can is irrelevant."

Piety and naivety, they sounded so similar to Dario sometimes. He frowned toward a gloomy gust of wind, spitting the distaste from his tongue. "One company, against an entire tide of shadowmen?" he asked. "That merits questioning."

"Companies have withstood multiple tides."

"Strong companies have," Dario said, shaking. He'd heard the tales—companies tasked to a fool's mission, never to be seen again. Was Company Lire to become just another fable, whispered to children beneath a sky full of celestial glyphs. "We're not strong enough to do this. You know it. Are any other companies close? Are the Veerens coming?" He imagined lines of shadows clashing with lines of flesh. White and red blood would soon mingle upon these fields. Unless the Veerens reinforced, there was no chance.

Illio didn't even bother glancing at the sky. "I don't know."

Company Lire's wagons turned against the flow of the caravan. Celestials left their posts and weaved through the convoy toward the rear. The colonists appeared both confused and concerned. Where were their protectors going? Were they coming back?

Dario wished he knew. He trembled. Two very different forces were pulling him in opposite directions. Love pulled him toward Lamptree. The will of the Gales pulled him toward the gloomy hillside.

"If we obey this task, we're going to die," Dario said.

"We'll die if we don't," Illio replied. Finally, he met Dario's gaze, a challenge in his eyes. "This is the kind of task you've always wanted, right? These people need us. We can't leave. We're connected. Can't you feel it?" he asked, looking toward the refugees.

The colonists cheered. They waved as Company Lire formed a battle line. They shouted and prayed. They filled the air with hope, and Dario felt their magic coursing through his muscles. It was called Co-alescence—Madi's favorite kind of magic, the only magic she seemed to care about. When enough colonists gathered together, sharing joy or hope or bravery or any powerful emotion, they could spread an abundance of colorful mist, Gale which seemed to rise all the way to the stars above—strengthening nearby celestial glyphs.

Dario took a long, refreshing breath. It was as though his lungs had doubled in size. All soreness left his body, and amid the colonists' encouragement, a lively tingle crept over his body, readying him for war. He *did* feel it. The Gales' magic. And it made him sick. Even if they won here, it would just lead to another task . . . and another . . .

and another. He wanted to flee—back to Madi's warm embrace and the coo of their firstborn. But he couldn't. Constellation Lire flashed overhead, and the sky quaked again. If Company Lire fell, so would he, even if he fled. So, he marched.

Twenty-six Celestials, ten battle wagons, the whole of Company Lire, turned toward the Gloom. Meanwhile, the caravan continued to safety. Refugees waved white fabric and colorful flowers as the Celestials departed. They cheered, and the air glowed with Gale.

"Sir, what's your name? So that I may pray for you in battle," a woman called. It was the sick mother and her daughter. She offered Dario a teal scarf, which she tied to his crutch.

"Illio Lire," Dario said, turning Rolly toward the hills.

The woman nodded and waved. Eventually, she disappeared within the stream of refugees.

"Why'd you give her my name?" Illio asked as they rode up the hill.

Dario untied the teal scarf and gave it to his friend. "Why bother the Almighties with a name they'd just ignore?"

"But they haven't, Dario. This is the answer to your prayers! You were right. Constellation Lire is dimming, and we need tasks to make it shine. We're going to make it through this, and when we do, the Gales will reward us. You'll be able to ask the oracles for anything you want!"

The proposal sank like a rock in Dario's gut. False hope. Pious words for an impossible prayer. He shook his head, skeptical.

Company Lire gathered on the ridge. Here, the Ashen had pried a giant lantern from its post. The capsule of glass and wood lay shattered against the rocks. Galefuel leaked from it. The liquid was black, but also full of light, like a starry night—dark, swirling, and colorful all at the same time. The fuel floated from the lantern, leaking skyward. As its glimmer died, shadows stretched from the opposing ridge. Long black shadows. They inched toward the wagons like sharp teeth.

The Ashen marched, spears and black banners jutting upward. Dario had never seen so many. His stomach grew heavy, so much so, he vomited his candied apple. Other Lires did too. A distant sky-quake echoed in the Gloom, and clouds gave way to starlight, like a torn curtain. Dario was certain this time—the Gales were watching.

Wardan raised his lance. "Company Lire, forward," he said, never one for speeches.

"My life for the company!" two dozen Lires shouted back.

Dario lacked the will to shout. Instead, he thought, *My life for my family.*

War wagons released a barrage of bolts and rocks. White blood sprayed into the air. No cries, no calls, the shadowmen stepped over their dead and marched closer. The host of shadowy bodies kept coming, and Dario wished they would just wither into the air like ghosts, but they weren't ghosts. Their marching grew louder. Their feet bent the grass and the flowers. Their black swords made a loud *crack* as Dario thrust his crutch. They looked like shadows, but those bodies were very real.

Company Lire's battle wagons crashed through the Ashen ranks. Starlight glittered against their armored hulls, scythed wheels, and caged driver's boxes. The wagons smashed through the shadowman formation, cutting apart like their sandy flesh. Puffs of white blood sprayed into the air as two more war wagons followed, Lires shouting atop them. Seeing his friends charge into those shadowy ranks, watching each wagon carve into that dark sea of shadows, Dario sucked in a quick breath: This was a fight to the death. If he ever wanted to see Madi or Aerial again, Company Lire had to win.

For what felt like hours, Lire wagons weaved back and forth, preventing the Ashen from reaching the hill in large numbers. Sweat poured down Dario's face as he passed ammunition to Illio and refilled the lanterns. They fought atop a battle wagon now, which rumbled violently. Dario's spine seized, nearly throwing him from the deck. He grit his teeth and held fast. Wind and clouds whipped around him, gray and suffocating.

Thunder cracked, and the shadowmen shifted course, silently running up onto the ridge. They tried to spill into the valley, but Wardan ordered half of the company to dismount. Led by Illio, the detachment met the Ashen with swords, lances, and shards of Galecraft. Dario fought directly behind his friend, using his crutch as a spear—a tactic they'd practiced. No other Lire would have risked fighting alongside Dario. No one but Illio. As the battle progressed, Dario's seizures became more and more severe. More than once, his bones seemed intent on throwing him into the shadowmen's grip.

Illio pushed him behind a war wagon. "Rest!" he shouted amid the crack of ballista fire.

"But I'm not tired!" Dario answered. "Our constellation is shining! We have a chance!"

Illio dipped his hands into a bucket, washing away slick white blood. His gloves and battle-cloak were no longer tattered, and the mist's healthy shimmer reminded Dario of the Illio of old. People all over the Gloom were watching, praying, betting on this battle. Dario gazed upward, his chest swelling with hope.

"Fight, Lires!" Wardan shouted from the top of the observatory wagon. He thrust his hand forward, crafting a bronze pin identical to the pins holding the telescopes together. Wardan's Galecrafted spike flew forward, striking a shadowman in the chest.

Hundreds of shadowmen died climbing the ridge, but hundreds more came after them, pushing Company Lire into the lowlands. The soggy ground forced the wagons onto drier ground while the infantry struggled to keep the Ashen lines from crossing the bog. Several wagons became stuck in the mud, far behind Ashen lines. Not long after, starlight drizzled downward. Sadness welled inside him. He didn't know whose glyphs were falling, but it meant Lires were dying.

"Fight, Lires!" Wardan's voice echoed from somewhere in the fog, this cry more desperate than the first.

Glyphlight trickled to the ground in long golden lines. The battlefield glowed in the light, revealing an endless tide of shadowmen. The urge to run once more flooded through him.

He gasped, knees begging for rest, realizing he was trapped in a broken body. Trapped in a fading world. Trapped in a web of magic his parents had hurled him into.

A loud shriek pierced the night, not far from them. Shadowmen had cut through Eljay's battle-cloak, metal through mist and mind. She cried out as they overwhelmed her, tugging her in different directions like wolves fighting for a piece of meat. There were just too many. In complete silence, their boots sloshed through the blood-stained soil, slipping and sliding through the bog water. Eljay, meanwhile, groaned. Her body grew stiff in their arms, and the pain in her voice slowly began to numb.

So many children owed Eljay their lives, but by the time they reached her, she was already dead. A roar fought its way up through Dario's chest. Mere steps away, he gazed upon Eljay's lifeless form and tasted the suffering that he wrote about in his book, every day. Eljay's starlight fell as innocently as her spirit had lived—drifting downward like pure flakes of snow and settling upon her body, shim-mering no more. Dario called for Chess and Gable, but the two dogs refused to leave. Loyal until the end. Loyal in a way he wished he could understand.

"Fight, Lires!" Wardan shouted once more. Shadowmen surrounded the observatory wagon. The telescopes were still. No one looked to the sky. Everyone fought for their life. Flashes of Galecraft were the last signs of their commander in the fog.

More glyphs fell from Constellation Lire. As Lires died, Dario's strength waned and bits of his cloak frayed, withering too greatly to defend him from an attack. Arrows cracked against the trees and splashed into the bog. He took cover behind the lantern wagon, where Lires fought desperately to keep the shadowmen from breaking it. Illio fought near the front, his cloak littered with arrows, no longer beaming with power. His movements slowed, and his fingers jerked around his sword's hilt, as though fighting to keep a grip. If only Dario could pull him to shelter and give him a moment to breathe. By the time he reached him, his friend's cloak was little more than a frail bit of cloth. Blood smeared Dario's hands. Red blood.

Illio gargled as he fought to breathe. Panic crawled into Dario's throat, strangling the sob that fought to escape. His friend strained for air, blood speckling his lips. Even as he stumbled into Dario's arms, he killed another shadowman, gasping. Pangs shot through Dario's legs as his friend's weight fell onto him, and they both slumped to the ground. He loosened Illio's collar, feeling a cold sweat on his neck.

Glyphlight fell freely now, drizzling from Constellation Lire, which appeared disfigured—a gaping wound of light. Illio's eyes drifted toward the stars, and his body shook, as if trying to rise. Dario opened his mouth, but no words came out. What could he say? Illio was always the one with the words of encouragement. This was their battle! This was the moment, the gift from the Gales that would see them escape this war! Dario leaned forward, aching to hear his friend whisper those words. To see the stilted rise and fall of Illio's chest. *Nothing. Just another unanswered prayer.*

A sluggish breath passed out from Illio's lips, but no more. The sky shook, sending down a torrent of glyphlight. His glyph was breaking apart! Illio's body went limp, pushing heavy against the denial in Dario's heart.

No. Not yet.

He squeezed his friend, as if that would somehow stop Illio's glyph from falling. The sky groaned, and starlight gushed about, like a capsizing ship. The sounds echoed through the swamp, filling Dario's heart with loneliness. No last words. No apologies. No shared memories. Just a short farewell glance, after so many years together. Illio didn't deserve this. He deserved to be famous. He deserved statues and stories and songs.

He could have been anything he wanted, but he chose to look after me.

Anger and guilt shook Dario's mind and heart. Paralyzed, he knelt over his friend, ignoring all other Lires' cries for help. Illio's glyph descended upon the bog like golden ribbons. Dario extended his hand, catching a strand of light. It was weightless, wet, and warm, and he wondered if he was holding his friend's soul.

The glyphlight slipped through his fingers and settled atop Illio's body. He tried to cling to it, but with every grasp, the warm wisps of light slipped through his fingers. He pressed his palm against Illio's chest, and through the tattered cloak, he felt no heartbeat.

A voice called to him, shouting from the deepest recesses of his mind. A voice that sounded eerily like Illio. *Run to your family. Find the city of escape before it's too late. Run!*

It wasn't Illio speaking, Dario knew. It was fear. But he listened anyway. Turning his back on his company, he stole the nearest horse and fled toward Greenpond, sparing only a final glance back at Illio's body. It was selfish, cowardly, and wrong, but if it meant seeing Madi and Aerial one last time before he died, it was worth it.

As he fled, shadowmen shattered the lantern wagon. Glass cracked and Galefuel exploded into the sky. Color filled the bog for a moment, turning even the tiniest frog green, and then everything went gray.

Chapter 5: Madi

"Don't worry, Ms. Amriel. They have no jurisdiction here." Governor Kipps stood and brushed the crease of her pink blouse. "If red inspectors harassed you in Greenpond, I'll take it up with the Rider's oracles personally."

Madi paced the governor's office, dissatisfied. Her boots clapped the floorboards. She'd worn her best outfit for this visit—a white trench coat with black buttons and laced sleeves. The office was polished and clean, brightly illuminated by a circular window behind the governor's desk. Lorani Kipps had a penchant for perfection, especially before a Lamptree festival, which meant nipping troubling news in the bud.

Pausing at the window, Madi scanned the horizon, where a gloomy mountain loomed beyond gray forests. "It takes a week for a flying bottle to reach Mount Anchor," she said. "I'm worried the men will follow me here."

"No need for a bottle," Governor Kipps replied. "A delegation of red oracles is coming here."

"Here?" Madi asked, spinning around. "They can't!"

Governor Kipps chuckled. "Oh, but they can. I will inform the gatehouse to deny any red inspectors, but I can't possibly deny oracles. They may worship another Gale, but they are still our allies in this war, and my authorities."

"What about the Pilgrim's oracles here?" Madi asked. "Can't they do anything?"

"Ms. Amriel, the event you described to me sounded like two men fabricating reasons to put their hands on a young woman. They will be dealt with, harshly, but I wouldn't dare involve our oracles unless there was truth to the inspectors' claims, which you've assured me there's not. It would only escalate the problem, and the last thing we need during our festival is bickering oracles. There are enough rumors going around as it is."

The governor rose and walked to a platter, which jingled as she poured out two glasses of Lamptree cider. Madi drank, and the liquid settled hot in her gut. She would need more alcohol than this to soothe her nerves.

"Rumors?"

The governor sipped before answering. Madi's cup was already empty. "Yes. Everyone knows the Red Rider and the Pink Pilgrim have warred in the past. We don't have a garrisoned company of celestials here like they do on Mount Anchor. Imaginations ran wild when I announced the oracles' visit."

"Why are they visiting, if I may ask?"

"They've asked for our cooperation locating a thief," Governor Kipps answered, taking Madi's glass and setting it onto the platter. "That's all I'm obliged to say, though I do hope this all passes quickly."

"So do I," Madi admitted, turning to gather her coat and hat. "Thank you for your time, governor."

"Of course," she said, flashing a smile. "Your daughter will be with Annea in the Glass Hall, second door on your right. Which reminds me. My sons are already talking about the surprise toys you give out at every festival. Their excitement is contagious. I've never seen their bedroom so vibrant. It's an important role you play here, bringing joy to the children. They are the purest of us all." The governor returned to her desk. "Times are dark," she said, glancing out the window.

"Hope must continue to grow on the branches of Lamptree if we are to continue spreading Gale, which is why this festival must be perfect."

"I'll do my part," Madi said, waiting to be ushered from the room.

The mansion guards were slow to open the office's double doors. When they finally opened, the hall was full of administrators and clerks. They gathered at the windows, pointing in the direction of Greenpond. Glyphlight glittered on the horizon. The sky echoed and boomed in the distance. A constellation was falling, its starlight sliding down the sky like golden tears. Before panicking, Madi tried to remember. Where was Company Lire? Dario had sent her a flying bottle not long ago. He was east of Brittlehorn, deep in the wilderness. It was far enough from Greenpond for her to breathe easily, but close enough for her to wonder.

The governor's voice echoed in the other room. "Celeste, what is going on?"

"A constellation is falling, my lady," her secretary answered.

"Oh dear." The governor's boots clapped toward the window. "I want our rangers patrolling the long-road. Travelers will be coming to the festival, and I want the roads safe. Do we know which company it is?"

"Not yet. I've put in a request to the observatory ."

Madi found Aerial in the Glass Hall, sleeping in the caretaker's arms. Other guests stared out the windows, dressed in their fancy clothes, like a new painting had just been added to an exhibit. They didn't understand. Yes, they were solemn. They knew Celestials were dying, but they just didn't realize the horror they were watching. At this very moment, lives were being ripped apart. Celestials would likely survive this battle, but with their constellation shattered, they would die slowly, painfully, and alone, without any of their lifelong friends.

Madi received many concerned glances as she exited the mansion.

It was no secret Dario Lire was Aerial's father. Outside, the Mossroad bustled with activity. With the Lamptree festival just two days away, final preparations were being made. Carts, filled with decorations, rolled silently along the trimmed roads of green moss, which curled up and down the tree like garland.

Colony rangers, in their dark cloaks, descended the tree. Madi's good friend, Elduko, was with them, dousing his clothes with a protective brew. The bitter liquid dripped down his sleeves and filled the air with a metallic taste. "We're headed out," he said. "I'll check on you and Aerial when I get back, okay? Don't worry about Dario. I got a good look at the falling stars, and they didn't look like Constellation Lire to me."

Madi nodded. There was a time she'd thought Elduko was trying to impose on Dario's absence, but then she'd learned it was the ranger's habit to check on all the mothers and fathers left alone on Lamptree. Still, his reassurance failed to stem the surge of uncertainty souring her thoughts. The sight of that sinking constellation had thrown her heart off balance, slowing her step and spilling a nervous sweat down the insides of her sleeves. Aerial's pouch became hot and unbearably heavy, and it wouldn't stop until she knew exactly whose stars had fallen—until she was certain her daughter's father lived.

The Pilgrim's oracles would know, but a colony toymaker would have to wait months to inquire of them. The astronomers in the astrohall could look, for an unrighteous fee. They read the more subtle aspects of the sky, leaving the Gales' will out of their interpretations. This made them popular with merchants and explorers, but also smugglers, pirates, and Shades—anyone looking for answers in the grayer regions of the sky. Madi considered the price, until Aerial woke up, squirming and squawking in her pouch. She wanted to nurse, and the astrohall was far away, on the Owl's Branch.

"News from Greenpond! News from Mount Anchor!" a young crier flew over the Mossroad. "News for a bit of glass!"

In the center of Lamptree, there was a circular hole in the bark called the Whole Story—an archivist headquarters. All day long, orphans flew in and out of the hole, like bees in a hive. Adult archivists traveled with celestial companies to document the war, but young criers spread the news around the countryside. They wore fliers on their backs—glossy, bone-like contraptions with ten spindly arms that shot outward and mimicked the motion a glove the child wore. Madi had constructed many of those fliers herself. She'd even taught some of the orphans to fly.

Madi flagged the crier. "News from Greenpond?" she asked, giving the girl one glass bit.

The girl leaned close and whispered in Madi's ear. "Outbreak of faded in the streets. Red inspectors asking questions about Lamptree. People leaving in drones."

"In droves, I think you mean."

"Oh. People leaving in *droves*. Want to hear more?" the young crier asked, holding out an empty palm.

Madi gave the girl a second bit. "What about the constellation that's falling? Whose is it?"

"Everyone's asking about that," the girl answered. "I'm carrying the morning news, so I don't know yet. Once I get back to the Whole Story, I'll gather all the spooky details for you, like I have about the vault explosion in Mount Anchor. Want to hear more?"

The girl's empty palm was back, and Madi gave her five more bits. "No, thank you."

"Hey thanks, miss," the crier said, dropping the extra glass into a purse. As she wiggled her fingers into her flying gloves, her flier sprang to life. Ten spindly arms curled from the contraption's spine, just as Madi had designed them to do. Reaching upward, the girl pulled herself into the air and flew off. "News for a bit! Paper for twenty-five!"

Madi wandered toward her cottage, still unsettled. Row houses nestled against Lamptree's core, with tiny garden plots next to each house. *Trees growing on a tree?* Dario had remarked the first time he walked this path.

Please, Pilgrim, Madi prayed. *Please keep him safe.*

Boots and carts rumbled along a rickety pier where a giant cloud-crawler slowly moored, its oars glinting. Madi remembered the days when a dozen of those flying ships came and went with the currents, soaring atop the clouds with goods from distant colonies. But now the tide was rising, and colonies were disappearing from maps faster than the ink could dry.

Shouts echoed from the Raptor's Claw—another brawl by the sound of it. Lamptree's gambling den overlooked the port from a high crotch of branches. Madi rarely ventured onto Petrel's Branch, but when she saw the crooked telescope glinting from the den's rooftop, she thought she could try asking around the den.

"It's my glass!" Mr. Ardenoy shouted.

A skinny man backed away from the baker with his hand clutched to his chest. "Not yet, it's not. The den's telescope ain't official. It don't have details."

Mr. Ardenoy reached for the man's palm. "It don't need details," the baker said. "We bet on the result, and the Lires lost. Hand it over."

The argument stopped as soon as Mr. Ardenoy saw Madi. A long staircase led to the den, where men and women spent their off-hours, perched like birds, exchanging gossip and glass. They shied away as Madi moved closer, her expression quickly falling numb. The Lires lost? Was that what they'd said?

"What company fell?" she asked Mr. Ardenoy, hoping she'd heard wrong.

The baker ran a finger through his graying beard. "We're not sure. You know the den's lenses," he said, shrugging. "They're no good."

"What company?" Madi repeated, her eyes warming with tears.

Mr. Ardenoy averted his eyes and spoke softly. "Company Lire. We think. We—We're pretty sure."

Madi's throat tightened. It squeezed until she couldn't breathe. Finally, she gasped for air, tasting a tide of emotions—disbelief, sadness, loneliness, and then anger. Bits of glass glinted from people's hands. She cursed everyone on that pier and then she slapped the skinny man's palm, scattering his money.

"Bet on your own lives!" she shouted, looking skyward. Hot tears streamed onto her cheeks, one for every memory of Dario—starting with the day they'd met in Lamptree Forest. Madi had volunteered to be a ranger. She preferred patrolling the wilds over moping around the colony, looking for a reason to keep breathing. She'd been tracking a girl who'd been snatched by shadowmen, but all she'd found was the girl's doll. It seemed her miserable life had wandered into another dead end.

But then Dario rode into the glade, wearing that precious expression—a cute combination of concern and curiosity. He wanted to hear her story, and so she made something up. None of it was true except the emotions behind it, and Dario sensed them through the lie. He waited for just the right moment to turn his horse and reveal the missing child, clinging to his waist. That was the same day he convinced Madi to leave the rangers and build toys for children.

Dario Lire was not like any other Celestial Madi had ever met. He didn't care about the legend of his own glyph. He cared about the story of a weeping colonist in the woods. She adored him because of that, and ever since *that* day, she'd feared *this* day. Fond memories sparkled through her tears, and for a moment, she felt weightless, timeless, like she'd always dreamed of being. She wasn't even sure if she was standing anymore.

"Madi, please. Let me help you home," Mr. Ardenoy said.

She let out a tearful moan when a hand touched her arm. Her eyes swelled, hot and blurry with tears. By now, Aerial was shrieking, too. Mother and daughter, mourning together as Dario's glyph slid down the horizon. A crowd gathered. They said they would take Madi home, and all she could do was put one leg in front of the other.

Dario dead? She'd feared this day would come, but not this soon. Not yet. Not before Aerial grew up and learned what a brave father she had.

The walk upward felt like an eternity, and Madi clung to the hope that the gambling den's crooked lenses could be wrong. After stumbling to the upper branches, Madi no longer heard Mr. Ardenoy, nor could she smell his beer-stained clothes. Instead, she heard her friends and neighbors gathered around her.

Madi's small cottage was tucked into a notch of the Toucan's Branch, near the top of Lamptree. There, she was surrounded by colorful clouds and her favorite sounds—a lofty wind, the gentle squeak of pulleys, and the distant murmur of townsfolk. But now, the sound of mourning drowned the chattering leaves and distant birdsong.

Madi's two closest friends, Tatina and Vishi, remained with her for the rest of that day, cooking her meals, comforting her, and holding Aerial. But even amid their kindness, it hardly seemed like they were there at all. A numbness paralyzed Madi, a numbness only Dario could cure—like he'd cured on the day they'd met. She sat in her kitchen, staring into a bowl of soup, imagining it was the sky and Constellation Lire was still glistening in it. Her stomach was too full of doubt to eat. For much of that afternoon, all she could do was swirl her spoon and hope the gambling den lenses and the drunkards who tuned them were wrong.

Clouds of daylight drifted toward the horizon, and night crept through Madi's curtains. Vishi and Tatina put Aerial to bed and eventually returned home, but Madi lingered on her balcony, staring at a black slice of sky where Constellation Lire used to be. What was she supposed to do now? Just keep living without him? She groaned as she thought of their last conversation together. It hadn't been a romantic one.

He didn't want me going to Greenpond, but I had to. He didn't understand, because he doesn't know I'm a Celestial.

Madi walked into her workshop, which was hot and stuffy in the clutches of a dusty brown cloud. Mud caked the windows, obscuring the constellations. She didn't want to see them anyway. Tugging a canvas, she uncovered a project on her table she'd been working on for almost a year—a flier for Dario. With its black glossy skeleton and long spindly arms, the contraption looked like a dead spider. Madi kicked the table with all her might. It slid across the room into the wall, knocking tools to the ground with a cascading clatter. Every joyful thought became bitter, and Madi understood why so many people were fading these days.

A doorbell rang in the night, startling her. She was slow to walk across the balcony into her cottage. The bell continued ringing, and Aerial awoke in her little bed, tilting her head toward the sound. Madi put on a coat, wiped her eyes, and approached the repeated knock at her front door.

Peeling back the curtain, the flickering torchlight revealed Elduko, Governor Kipps, and Dario. Madi nearly ripped the door from its hinges and ran outside. Dario shivered in a wool blanket. He looked up, hunched and covered in blood—both white and red—which stuck to Madi's skin as she hugged him. His battlecloak was emaciated, clinging to his body by a mere stitch. She hugged him tighter, but he lost his balance, and they both teetered.

"Easy," Elduko said, catching them. "We found him on the long-road. His horse was barely breathing. He must have rode from Greenpond without stopping, through this dust storm too."

Dario nodded. Mud caked his face and hair, and he coughed violently. Madi pressed her brow against his forehead, wishing she could stop time. It was HIM—and she wanted to keep him. But as sweat slid between their flesh, she already felt like she was losing him again. When she looked into his eyes, she knew he was thinking the same thing. Their grip around one another tightened.

"He told us to bring him straight to you," Governor Kipps said. "Should I send for Doctor Nariel?"

"No," Dario whispered. "There's nothing a doctor can do. I'd like to speak with Madi alone, please."

"Yes, sir," Elduko said, guiding him into the cabin. Filth from Dario's boots smeared the floor.

The governor watched Dario with wary eyes, and she wrung her hands together. "As you wish," she said. "Let my office know if you need anything."

"I need to get back out there," Elduko said. "We found shadowman tracks in the woods. We think they're gathering nearby. A lot of them. Where's Vishi?"

Madi softened her eyes toward her friend, and spoke as appreciatively as she could. "Home. She was helping me earlier. I'll be alright now that Dario is here. Thank you, Elduko. Thank you so much."

The ranger collected his bow and closed Madi's door. When she turned, a weak smile crossed Dario's face. Sweat slid from his shaved black hair and settled into the sallow creases next to his eyes. Barbs, black from Ashen arrows, clung to his tattered cloak, which revealed oozing wounds and swollen skin.

"Save your strength," Madi said, stooping beneath Dario's arm. A barb pinched her neck. "Lean on me."

Aerial cried in the bedroom, and Dario hobbled toward the sound. "Wait, I want to see her."

He paused in the doorway, and Aerial looked at him, wide-eyed, from her bed. Dario picked her up and touched her gently to his blood-stained cheek.

"Careful of the barbs," Madi warned, tugging Dario's shirt away from their daughter's skin.

He gazed deep and long into Aerial's eyes, like he was never going to see her again. His expression wavered between joy and despair. All the while, Madi begged the Gales: *spare him like you spared me. Please!* She put Aerial back in bed and helped Dario onto the balcony, where there was an extra cot with enough room to wash him and bandage his wounds. The dust storm swirled amid the branches, making the task more difficult.

Above the cot, a small windmill powered Madi's workshop. She'd come to enjoy the clatter of toys passing along the conveyor, but tonight, the windmill squealed anxiously amid the storm. Lamptree was a vertical colony reliant on pulleys, elevators, and cranes. They always needed new cogs and pivots. Most days, Madi had more adults lining up outside her workshop than children.

Madi brought Dario a light blue brew. Frost licked the top of the glass as she held it to his lips. "Drink this one first," she said.

"It's freezing," Dario said, shivering. "I'm already freezing."

"It'll bring your fever down," she answered, handing him a second vial, which was dark brown. "This one will help you sleep."

"Brews aren't going to help me, Madi," Dario replied. "Sleep isn't either."

"Yes they will."

"Madi." He took her hands and pulled them to his cheeks. The mud on his face was dry now, and it crumbled down Madi's fingers, tickling her wrists with each of his erratic breaths. "You need to understand, I'm dying. Medicine can't stop this. My constellation is gone."

Madi refused to answer. She nodded, but inside she was still praying for a way. *Pilgrim, please. There has to be a way. I'm alive, somehow, without my company. I'll do anything. Anything, if you spare him.* She gazed skyward, but the stars were veiled behind a canopy of chattering leaves and the brown swirl of the dust storm.

"We should move inside," she whispered.

Once he was settled in her bed, she kissed him. His lips were drier than sandpaper, and she could taste the frosty brew on his breath. They laid together there for a few minutes, until she saw that Dario's eyes were still open.

"What are you doing?" she asked him.

"Planning."

"Planning isn't resting."

"There's no time," he said, revealing a book she'd never seen before. Its binding was torn and covered in mud. Dario opened the pages, and Madi's eyes swelled when she saw the magic. Ink snaked across the page like it was alive.

"Brewed inks?" she asked.

Dario groaned as he sat up. The look in his eyes was frightening— wide and delirious, frantic even.

"Yes," he replied. "They're attuned to the constellations, and they're recording the companies' movements. You can see the date changing here."

Inked emblems crossed the page—celestial symbols Madi hadn't seen in years. Outside, the dust storm scraped at the shutters. Mud balls beat at the bark of her treehouse, like someone was out there, trying to get in—trying to get something back.

"Dario, where did you get this?" she asked.

"Watch the ink!" he said, in a hushed voice. His eyes were wide, like a child marveling over a new toy. "They're tracking us. They're looking for something. They're looking for the same thing I've been looking for. And I think they found it."

Dario spoke with a nervous energy, frantic, almost possessed. He'd been working on something and he hadn't told her. "What were you looking for?" she asked. "Who's tracking you? The oracles?"

"No. They don't need maps like this," he whispered, unable to keep the page from shaking. "I don't think they know about these maps."

Madi thought of her toy ciphers—the porcelain soldiers she delivered to Greenpond every few months. This map made her fingertips tingle the same way those toys did.

"If it's illegal, why do you have it?" she asked.

Dario was too fixated on the map to answer. "Watch what happens. There!" He tapped the page as the ink moved, thrilled at his discovery. "Every company that travels this far into the wild redirects course, straight toward these mountains. Every time. You know what that means? It means they saw something *over* the hills. Something tall. Towering. They found a city of escape." He adjusted the page for Madi to see. Ink shimmered as the dates changed. Dario pointed to a symbol, which abruptly shifted course and then disappeared. "Gone! They're gone! These companies either escaped, or they were killed before they could."

Madi seized the book. "STOP! You're scaring me. Why don't you answer? How did you get these maps?"

"I stole them."

The answer struck like a stone, squeezing through her ears and settling hard inside her throat. "So, it's you?" she uttered.

"What do you mean, me?"

Madi let the map book fall to the floor, her hands frozen with fright. "Dario, the oracles are coming here. They say they're looking for a thief."

Dario scowled toward the fireplace. His face flickered between confidence and confusion. "Okay, but I didn't draw these maps. I-I'm not the thief. I mean I'm not the thief they're looking for. I stole from their servants. These aren't even the original maps. They're copies. They don't know I have them."

Wind howled outside. Leaves and dust chattered across the balcony, piling up against the back door. Madi paced the room while biting her nails. "So, that's your plan to escape?" she asked. "Fight through tides of shadowmen with your daughter in your arms?"

"I was thinking you'd carry her," Dario replied with a grin. Afterward, his expression and posture sagged. Fresh blood flowed from a gash on his scalp. Without magic from his constellation, his body refused to heal. His eyes looked like hollow glass, and he wheezed with each breath. "Company Lire was starved for tasks. Our stars were anemic. It was only a matter of time before we fell, and it's only a matter of time before this colony falls too."

Madi turned away with a frown, pacing the cold corners of her living space. She rubbed the shivers from her arms. Although she disagreed, she hadn't forgotten what had happened in Greenpond. Dario wasn't the only Celestial the oracles were looking for. She peered from her balcony toward Lamptree's lower districts. People moved up and down the Mossroad like ants, and she wondered if Bandico had made it safely out of the colony. He'd said he was trying to climb a city of escape, too. What if he could help?

"Say we leave together. How do we get there?" she asked. "You can barely walk."

"I'm not sure yet," Dario said, moving to Madi's side. He eyed the piers and the flying vessels moored there, their long oars obscured by the dust storm. "There are cloudcrawlers over there. How many people would we need to pilot one of those things? We could hire a crew."

This was a ridiculous conversation. Dario was delirious and desperate, but Madi was beginning to share his desperation. Red oracles were coming. She could lie to inspectors. She could outrun them too. But she couldn't lie to the oracles, and no one could outrun their curses. Were they really here to look for a thief?

Or are they hunting me?

Sembetra had warned her not to return. Madi balled her hands in front of her lips, smelling the soap she'd washed Dario with on her fingers. Maybe running was the only option.

"It depends on the size of the crawler," she answered. "A dozen crew, minimum, I'd think. And we'd need a captain who could chart us a course across currents of cloud. I can navigate with a flier, but crawlers are a much larger breed of bird."

Dario hobbled back to his cot. "Do you know anyone up to the task?"

Madi thought of a few decent Lamptree captains. "Maybe."

For the first time in a long time, she was tempted to tell him the truth—that she'd climbed those streets already, where fliers cease to fly, and the sky starts to shimmer like a dark sea. Dario was dying, and she wanted him to know she was taking this seriously, but a whisper deep within warned her to keep quiet. Nariah Maya was dead. *And if I want to keep my family safe, it's better she stay dead.*

Suddenly, the thought of saying goodbye to Lamptree weighed heavily upon her heart. Supernaturally so. Dario would say it was just a tree, but could "just a tree" grow this tall? Could "just a tree" grow hope like fruit? Would Sembetra have fled, risked her life, maybe even died, to warn Madi about "just a tree?"

What if Lamptree is the answer, not the problem.

She didn't know what to do, and judging by Dario's trembling chest, neither did he. Together, they watched a cloudcrawler depart Lamptree's port, rowing across a current of brown cloud, like a caterpillar. Its long oars sliced through the spattering mud storm, and soon, its silver hull disappeared into the dusty brown atmosphere. Madi was certain Dario was thinking the same thing as her. A cloudcrawler could work. One fast enough to outrun the shadowmen's phantom ships. A Tern-class smuggler would do. Dario would need to learn how to operate a flier, for safety.

But if I teach him, she worried, *we'll fly right back onto the stage Nariah Maya died on.*

CHAPTER 6: MADI

Madi woke up with a pounding headache. She'd dreamed of asking Bandico for help finding the city of escape. In the dream, Bandico was still here, in the colony. He gave her newly forged documents, but the page was charred black and covered in curses. The ink glowed red: *Nariah Maya. City of Escape.* That's when Madi woke up, unsure of what to make of it.

She groaned, sweating beneath her bedsheets. The whole room was stuffy. This always happened when she slept with the shutters closed, and a headache always followed. Dust from the storm lingered atop her loft, floating delicately between shelves of books and the creaking beams supporting them. Aerial's crib was empty, and frost crept from the mouth of the fireplace, where a teal flame cooled the room. Dario must have doused the logs with a chilling brew before taking Aerial onto the balcony. Their muffled voices brought some comfort, as did the cold fire, which crackled like ice as it released a refreshing froth throughout the cottage.

Madi closed her eyes and listened to her colony wake up—the distant clamor from the piers, the schoolhouse bell, birds in the gardens. She loved these sounds, but none of them came close to the joy of hearing Dario and Aerial together.

This is it, she prayed to the Pilgrim. *This is all I want, my lady. To grow old here with that man and our children. Please, heal him. Please, let me keep this.*

She opened the windows, one by one, and the smell of cinnamon and apples swept into her home. The brewery was on the branch below, and it was never too early for Lamptree cider. For a moment, it felt like yesterday had never happened, but her headache and the dried blood on the floor reminded her that it had.

She wrapped a blanket around her body and opened the door to the balcony—into the heat of an oppressive red atmosphere. Daylight sliced through Lamptree's green canopy, where globs of mud crumbled as they dried. Hot red clouds mingled with the brown, filling the air with an earthy scent only slightly more tolerable to Madi than the smell of manure. She massaged the side of her head while brushing dust from the doorframe.

She'd designed this balcony herself, ensuring the architect obeyed every detail. Her favorite feature was a circular dip in the wood, meant to be a play area for her children. That's where Dario and Aerial were now, bathed in giant red leaves. Aerial chirped as Dario scooped her up inside a leaf twice her size. This sight filled Madi with hope, making her feel as light as a feather. This was a glimpse of the future she'd dreamed for her family. But then Dario winced in pain, and prongs of uncertainty pierced her pleasant expectations, forcing her back to reality.

Without a miracle, he will die.

Madi's balcony connected her cottage to her workshop, which was caked in dust from its recessed doorstep to the tip of its windmill. The tower scarcely made a squeak, and dried mud dribbled from it. Only the rain-catcher had been safe from the storm, hidden in a shady nook and concealed by a wooden lid. Madi scraped the bottom, scooping up what water was left in the heat. Flower boxes lined the edges of the balcony, filled with fruit-bearing plants. She plucked a handful of berries and munched on them, taking a sip of water to wash down the mouthful.

"Have you eaten?" she asked, offering Dario some. She'd hoped he'd improve by morning, but now he looked worse. Beneath stale bandages, his skin seemed to wrinkle in the daylight.

"Not hungry," he answered while fanning Aerial's face with the giant leaf. Aerial smiled, fluttered her eyelashes, and tried to grab it.

"What hurts?"

"Everything. You might have to fill me with cogs and wind me up to keep me going." His tone was humorous, but his posture exhausted. Had he slept at all?

"I was hoping Lamptree would heal you," Madi admitted. "I overheard two inspectors say a Celestial was healed here once. There's still a chance a Gale will grant us a miracle."

Dario sighed loudly, sinking into the bed of leaves. He didn't believe in miracles. He'd made it clear many times, but Madi had to believe. A miracle was keeping her alive. She just wished she knew more about it. What kind of magic was it? Was it really the Pilgrim's, as Sembetra promised? And why was it granted to her while other Celestials were left to die alone.

Dario leaned toward a small telescope on the edge of the balcony. It was a weak lens—a toy for Aerial and her siblings when they were older. Madi imagined they might spy on shadowmen in the bog or watch the long-road for their father's return.

"I've been trying to calculate exactly how long I have left," he admitted. The tiny telescope creaked as he tilted it and spoke in hushed desperation. "If you look carefully, you can still see it. My glyph. It's there. Barely clinging to that black curtain."

The softness of his voice soured the grapes in Madi's mouth. She stopped chewing, and pressed her tongue against her teeth, angry and frightened. *My Lady, if you were merciful enough to preserve me, why can't you save him? Why don't you tell me what to do?* While praying, Madi secured her hair with a pink bandana..

"Dario, I'm sorry if I haven't seemed urgent," she said, dampening her tone to match his. "I was just so happy to see you alive. It made me wonder if there was any way we could stay here."

"I know," Dario groaned, letting his head sag. "It's alright."

"No, it was silly, and I've wasted your time," she whispered. "We can leave as soon as you'd like. We'll stow away if we have to."

"Slow down," Dario said, catching Madi's hand as she tied her bandana tight. His arm was heavy, and coated with crumbled leaves. "We need a plan. We only have one go at this, and our daughter's future depends on it. If we stowaway and get caught, I'll die in a dungeon before an oracle even sentences me for treason."

Madi's breakfast circled inside her stomach, and she regretted eating. Dario's hand shook as she took it. Desperation trembled from his bones into hers, making her shake alongside him. "Do you know how long your glyph will keep shining?" she asked.

"Days. Maybe a week. But I intend to prolong that time by completing tasks if I can." He cradled Aerial and then pulled Madi close, touching his head to hers. "I'm going to hold on, Madi. Deep down, I just *know* my light can keep shining until we escape. Someone out there is praying for me. I feel it. The colonists my company sacrificed themselves for are looking up at my glyph, wondering what my fate will be."

His earnest expression and voice were like a river running dry. The combination brought Madi to tears. "We're leaving this world together," she replied. "As soon as possible. Give me one day. I'll have a cloudcrawler and a crew ready."

Dario touched his belt. "I have no money."

Madi took Aerial and tugged Dario toward the workshop. "I have enough," she said.

"Enough to hire a captain on such short notice?"

Madi could afford a small fleet. She'd been left behind with Company Maya's fortune. She'd tucked most of it away beneath the floorboards of this very workshop. The door was stubborn at first, blocked by globs of mud. She pushed her way inside, disturbing the coffin of tools and tracks. Completed toys stood atop every table and chair. Even the conveyor was hidden beneath a legion of stuffed animals and flying puppets—thousands of toys—a year's worth of work—all to be given away during the Lamptree Festival. This entire week, she'd been sorting and counting—a far less enjoyable task than building.

Dario peeked into the workroom. His eyes widened, and he smiled. "That's a lot of toys. No wonder you're rich."

"Actually, I don't make any profit off my toys. I make money repairing the colony lifts, and on occasion, I sell fliers. You're going to need to know how to use one if we're traveling by cloud."

Madi weaved through the workshop maze and opened the store room door, where six fliers hung on the wall. Daylight glistened against the contraptions' long glossy spines. Each flier had ten spindly arms, five per side. For now, they remained tucked, rigid against the spine. Dario shuffled closer, wide-eyed.

"Pick one," she told him.

"I'm broke. Which one's cheapest?"

"Shut up and pick."

Dario hummed, gently brushing his hand across each flier, inspecting their colorful shimmer. Each wooden contraption bore a faint glow—a color, which would trail behind the flier as it flew. This was common knowledge, and buyers often selected fliers in the color of their favored Gale. Dario didn't seem interested in any of these.

"What about that one?" he asked, pointing to a discarded flier in the corner.

It lay on the floor, curled, and covered in dust and broken tools. Madi had completely forgotten about it. She frowned as Dario lifted its dark and colorless spine. Memories rushed into her mind—nightmares belonging to Nariah Maya.

"Oh . . ." she stuttered, lost in thought, faking a smile. "That was my old flier. It broke . . . one day."

"It looks okay," Dario said, brushing it off. The bone-root spine jangled. The sound gave Madi the chills.

"I fixed it," she admitted. "But when the spine cracked, it lost its pink hue. I was never able to get it back, and every brew I tried just turned it more black. It's hideous."

Dario smirked. "I kind of like it."

"Then try it on," she suggested with a shrug.

"Will it bother you? It looks like it's bothering you."

"It just annoys me that I couldn't fix it," she lied. Really, she wished she'd thrown it into a pit instead of hiding it in that corner. "If that flier makes you happy, Dario, then I'm happy. Try it on . . . outside, please, or you'll probably break everything in here."

He did it right the first time, placing the flier on his back and sliding his hands into the wiry gloves. In its closed position, the bony device looked like a skeleton's ribcage. Madi restrained a frown. That flier was light, but Dario still hunched, and it looked like a bug had hopped onto his back. Was he already too weak to operate it?

She pinched her chin. "Try opening it."

Dario spread his fingers. Ten long appendages whistled out like a spider's legs. When he raised his hands, the flier mimicked the motion. Mist gathered around each appendage, and seconds later, he rose a foot into the air. That was more like it! His legs and spine stretched, weightless, and his turbulent expression settled into absolute wonder. Confidence gushed into his expression, and he looked like a king.

"I've always wanted one of these," he admitted. "Every real archivist has one."

"Most of their fliers are made of polished flex-wood," Madi explained. "That one is made from bone-root, just like the one I wear now."

"What does that mean?"

"It means it won't break as easy."

"You expecting me to fall a lot?" he asked, inspecting himself.

Bone-root wasn't good for falling. It was good for fighting. Company Maya had used their fliers as weapons, but naturally, Madi kept her mouth shut. She lifted Aerial and wrapped her tightly in a chest pouch. After it was secured, she gathered her hunting pack and a small bag of bolts. Then, she unhooked her flier, *Flicker*, from the wall. Its spine was pearly white, with streaks of pink and a sheath for her crossbow.

"Lesson one," she said, facing Dario. "Flying is like swimming, but your buoyancy comes from your flier, not you. You'll fall like a rock."

"Rocks don't splatter."

"You'll fall like a grape, then."

Dario gave a juvenile nod of approval. Madi rolled her eyes, but she was happy to see him so excited. "To protect your grape-self, you need to learn to time each stroke correctly. Practice grabbing and pulling a few times, but not too high. Just get used to the motion."

He grunted and bobbed up and down. "This is harder than it looks," he said, wobbling.

Madi stabilized him. "Don't fall to death in front of our daughter, please."

Dario turned sideways. He lost balance and slipped into the pile of leaves on the balcony. Aerial erupted in laughter. Madi wished she could laugh, but she couldn't. Dario was in no condition to fly. His body bruised immediately, and he already looked exhausted, but he tried again—over and over—ignoring her calls for rest. After an hour of thrashing and falling, he began to understand: delicate pulls for balance, long pulls for speed.

"Use your fingers as much as your arms," Madi told him. "Grab. Pull. Float. Grab. Pull. Better! Really, that's pretty good. Most people don't pick it up this quickly."

"Necessity, I guess," Dario replied. "I don't have weeks to lear—hearn." He wobbled, then righted himself. "Okay. What's next?"

"Fliers don't need much mist to work," she explained. "Big cloud-crawlers like the ones on the pier have to stay atop a current, but we can go just about anywhere, so long as there is a current nearby. Now listen, the closest visible current dictates how your flier will respond. The first thing you'll need to pay attention to is the shape of a cloud. Puffs, flats, streams, bubbles, vents—your flier's buoyancy depends on each cloud's shape."

"I've heard fliers can get stuck in dense clouds. True?"

"Yes. Certain combinations of shape and color can be very dangerous, which is why the second thing you'll be paying attention to is color—not just the color of the atmosphere, but the shade of each cloud. Color affects weather, speed, and slickness in the sky. Some currents we use, some we watch out for. Okay? Follow me. Slow."

Madi secured Aerial in her pouch before jumping. She spread her arms and pulled through the air. She soared over a small patch of gold and dashed through rings of red, white, and pink. The wind lifted her chin and filled her nose with the healthy atmosphere of Gale. All the while, Aerial babbled to the clouds.

The heart of Lamptree buzzed beneath them. Rows of skinny homes bordered each branch, tied together by lines of laundry. Smoke drifted from chimneys, carrying the smells of breakfast. Children ran through a maze of alleyways toward the schoolhouse bell. Their voices echoed upward. The Lamptree festival hadn't officially commenced, but the tree was ready and excitement filled the air.

Some of Lamptree's branches were hollow, revealing an inner scaffold, where mechanical lifts carried goods up and down the tree. The costume parade was tonight. By lunch, music would fill the streets, accompanying a long line of colorful garments. Kites and balloons floated above the branches, and criers darted between them on fliers.

From the air, Madi saw some children skip school and run straight to a moss field with a tossball in their hands. Every home on Lamptree glittered with light. It was a tradition to cut leaves from the tree, dip them in daylight brews, and hang them from doors and windows.

Together, Madi and Dario weaved through chimney smoke and flew above a crowd wearing colorful costumes. This was one of the happiest moments of her life, but she didn't know if this was the beginning of a wonderful dream, or the end of one.

Dario wasn't half bad. He pulled faster and more confidently now. She gave him some instruction and then showed off by somersaulting. Dario copied her. Madi could hardly tell this was his first time flying. He may have limped on the ground, but in the air his movements were smooth. A life with a wobbly spine had taught him balance, which was key to masterful flying.

Rolling onto her back, Madi stroked across the weightless blanket in the sky. "I've always wanted to fly with you," she admitted, leading him away from Lamptree into open air. "It's been a secret desire of mine since we met."

"Why secret?" Dario asked.

"Because I'm afraid if I say my dreams out loud, they might not happen."

"All you had to do was ask."

"I could have, but then something would come up," Madi revealed. "Look, sometimes I just don't want any divine being out there to know my dreams, so they can't influence them."

"I understand," Dario replied. "I do. Completely. But did you ever think to whisper it to me . . . or maybe just slip me a note."

Madi smiled, but then there was silence for a time, as if they were both thinking the same thing.

The Gales discern whispers. They see through sealed letters.

Sky passed softly between them. Dario's eyes narrowed, but not because of the wind. It was the look he always had when thinking—or talking—about his parents, the world above, or the war. His breath came quickly, and he began to falter.

"You alright?" she asked. "Is it a spasm?"

"No," he replied. "Just frustrated."

"Stay focused," she warned. "Keep your arms tucked close when you bind, and try to lengthen your stroke, else you'll tire quickly. And never fly near Gloomclouds without a lantern. Remember, the color and type of cloud will change how your flier behaves. Thin currents are fast. Thick ones are slow, but they don't fade as quickly. They're more predictable. Blue clouds are slippery. Browns are easier to climb. You need to memorize every color and every combination. What two clouds create lightning when they mix? What combinations are poisonous? You need to know how every cloud will react when it flows through another. One wrong move can kill you," she warned.

Madi closed her eyes, dove through a puddle of daylight, and led Dario to a hill not far from Lamptree. Capped by a lone lantern, it was covered in white and yellow flowers and stood out from the Gloom like a lily on a gray pond. But beyond the lantern's reach, fields of black grass withered into a white-willowed swamp.

Madi landed and brushed her fingertips across the tall green grass. Dario descended hesitantly. He dropped his arms too early. His flier mimicked the motion and threw him off balance. He tumbled through the grass, grunting.

Madi couldn't keep from laughing. He looked like a splattered bug. "Landing is hard," she told him.

"The ground is hard," Dario replied, wincing.

She chuckled again, tasting both joy and sadness. This was why she hated magic, because it destroyed how beautiful life could be. The Gales were good, and their companies were fighting the rising tide, but sometimes, she wondered how perfect life could be if she and Dario had been born colonists.

"Thought of a name yet?" she asked.

"A name?"

"For your flier. Every flier gets a name. It's kind of a rule."

Dario squinted toward the clouds—threads of red, orange, and yellow. "I'm no good at naming things."

"I'm aware. You wanted to name our daughter Fairy."

"You said, 'think of things that fly.' I named something that flies," he said, waving his arms flamboyantly. His flier mimicked the action, throwing him into the ground again. "Gah! How do I stop this thing?"

"Take off your gloves."

Dario's flier collapsed onto his back once his gloves were off. "How about Nightfly?" he asked from the ground.

"Sounds fine to me. As long as it's not our daughter," Madi replied. "Flicker and Nightfly. I like it."

She scanned the Gloom for movement. This was her favorite hunting spot. Animals were often drawn to the Gale on the hill. Usually she only found snakes, frogs, and lizards, but sometimes, a faded boar or deer wandered in from the bleak lowlands and climbed toward the lantern.

"What are you doing?" Dario asked. "We need to plan."

Madi detached her crossbow from the spine of her flier. "The Rider's oracles will want meat during the feast. Governor Kipps asked me to help hunt. Don't worry. It won't take long. Besides, it will give me a reason to go about town. Call in some favors. Let's try not to act too suspicious, yes?"

"I suppose so," Dario said, stretching his legs. As he groaned, the clasp of his journal opened all by itself, and the hilltop wind rif-fled through its pages, allowing Madi glimpses at the sketched faces within—pain and desperation, expressions just like the one she felt herself making now.

Madi only ever read brief portions of Dario's magic book. Every time, the pages pulled her back into her past and she had to stop. While everyone else blamed the Ashen for the war, Dario blamed the Gales. That was why he used Galecraft to write his book instead of pen and paper. That way, he could hide it with a wave of the hand from those seeking to silence him. All of this worried her now, and she gripped her quiver tightly, fearing for her man sitting so humbly here on this hill.

"I hoped if I used Galecraft to create this book, people in the world above might be able to look down and read it in my starlight. Maybe they could transcribe the pages somehow," he told her, setting the book on his lap. "Because if I die, these pages will fade, and all the stories I swore to share will be lost. Their stories . . . Company Lire's story . . . Illio's story," he added, pursing his lips hard, holding back a deluge of emotion.

Madi's heart ached as he released a painful exhale, wobbly with sorrow. She curled her arms around Dario's neck and kissed the side of his head. Right now, she thought a silent touch had to be more comforting than anything she could think of to say.

With a slow wave of his hand, Dario crafted a fresh page. A milk white mist rose from the grass, moving sluggishly toward his palm. The page that formed was pale, tattered, and too frail to hold ink. Dario groaned and gave up before his Galecraft was complete.

"Go on your hunt. I'm going to rest here. I'm—I'm pretty tired," he said, staring stoically at the pages. The wind caught them once more, and this time Madi saw the most recent face Dario had sketched: Illio Lire.

Heartbroken, she descended the hill, looking over her shoulder more than once. Dario's pitiful form made her weep. She wished for his sake, and for Aerial, that cities of escape were easy to climb, but they weren't. They were riddled with webs of magic, just like everything else. When Company Maya climbed, they'd had the Gales' blessing, but it'd still ended in tragedy. Now, Madi and Dario were planning a climb with no blessing at all.

The large lantern chimed atop the hill, spreading a healthy atmosphere, breathing fresh air and color. Each wave spilled down the hill into the borderland of Gale and Gloom. Animals came here often to graze upon the green grasses before venturing back into the gray. She angled her crossbow toward a deer. She readied a shot, but then a cloudcrawler passed overhead, billowing red smoke and the Red Rider's banners. Sky shanties spilled from the decks, startling all the animals. The deer bolted, and Madi released a quick shot, unsure if it'd hit. She tracked the creature toward the Gloom, where the chirp of insects turned harsh and otherworldly.

On the banks of the colorless swamp, the air lost its warmth, and a bloated mass of gray clouds blocked the currents of daylight. Lamptree seemed to shrink in the distance, and soon, the only sound was the gargle coming from the bog. Aerial began to cough, and Madi shook her hand-lantern. Everything in the Gloom's colorless haze was boring and blurry, but she swore something moved. The deer?

No. It was a shadowman. Not far from the base of the hill, the dark figure swayed slightly, just enough for Madi to see it was alive. The deer was dead at its feet, muddied in half-faded flesh. Shadowmen didn't need to eat, but they often stole food from those who did.

Slowly, the shadowman brought a finger to its face—to where his lips should have been—for Madi to remain silent. She raised her crossbow, but the shadowman retreated into the rushes, dragging the dead deer away.

Chapter 7: Dario

That night, a sharp fever split Dario's thoughts in two, keeping him awake. Memories of battling Ashen merged with memories of flying with Madi. Anguish and bliss fluttered inside his head, uncertain of where to settle. Aerial squirmed in her little bed and began to squawk, so he lifted her from her crib and carried her toward the balcony. Meanwhile, Madi rolled from one shoulder to the other, anxiously wrestling the bed sheets.

Outside, Lamptree was quiet, its colorful leaves rustling. Celestial constellations peeked through the treetop. Each light was a life, a web of stories—a book, but not like his. They belonged to the Gales, glittering from horizon to horizon, full of secrets and deception. He let out a long breath, which flowed through his lungs like wind through a tattered sail.

"I wish Illio could have met you," he whispered to Aerial. Her innocent eyes glinted in the night. Every time Dario looked at her, the weight of responsibility crashed down on him—sliding down the slick sadness in his throat, squeezing between his lungs and rib cage, pressing his heart hard against his stomach until he felt nothing but panic. "Maybe then he would have understood how the sky makes me feel—small, helpless, caught up in someone else's arms."

Aerial yawned. With a stretch, she closed her eyes and settled her cheek into his arm. A nearby lift rattled, drawing Dario's attention downward, toward the curling alleys below, and nighttime glow of the denser districts. Torchlight and smoke blurred, making Dario dizzy. He stepped back, squeezing Aerial tight, as though she were the one holding on to him.

"I'm scared, Aerial," he whispered. "Not because I'm afraid to die, but because I'm afraid of failing you . . . like my parents." The thought caused a sourness to boil. What began as a spiteful simmer suddenly stirred up such a sadness—deep tears, old tears, painful tears. He peeked toward Lamptree's lower districts again, whispering, "They threw me down, into a war I don't want you to experience. Into a magic that has flowed from my blood to yours, binding you to a life I don't want you to live."

Dario grit his teeth and tensed his stomach. Something wormed inside of him, disturbing him. At first, he thought it was his fever, chilling his bones and causing every movement to ache. But now, it felt like a cold syrup creeping down the inside of his skin, leaking from his brain. He was thirsty, but he knew no amount of water could quench this thirst. It was the Gales' magic, his glyphlight in the sky, drying up.

Death clung to his thoughts, turning them acerbic. He rested on the balcony until late morning, wondering how many days he had left, and what tasks he could complete to prolong them. Aerial napped on his chest, and Madi worked in the kitchen. She'd hunted two large turkeys in the Gloom and hung them next to a lantern to cure. Faded animals had to be cured before becoming edible. Large game needed to bask next to a lantern for hours, sometimes days, before the flesh regained its color.

Dario eyed the countryside from his perch. Far below the branches, Lamptree rangers patrolled a gloomy swamp. Shadowmen lingered in the Gloom, peeking from behind trees and rocks. Company Lire had tried to cure an Ashen, once. It didn't work. Wardan locked it in a wagon with a lantern, but the lantern ran dry, and the wagon slowly lost color. All the while, the shadowman stood at the window of its prison, staring.

"Shadowmen can't be cured," a minister had told Dario during an interview. *"They are an illusion of life, an antithesis, a gray shell possessed by something or someone we do not yet understand."*

"What happens to a colonist when they fade?" Dario had asked.

"They relinquish control of their bodies to the Gloom, and become prisoner to their very worst fears," the minister had answered.

"Can they ever come back?"

The minister's answer was short and without explanation. *"No."*

Touching his chest, Dario felt his heartbeat flutter. Fear pressed like a glacier, cold and weighty upon his soul. Some people believed death was the end, a peaceful rest until the world ended, but others said there was more—a world below this one, far more dangerous than the Gloom. Dario didn't know which was true, but he couldn't imagine a fate worse than waking up on the shores of an afterlife, separated from his family.

The door to the balcony squealed open. Madi curled an arm around Dario, kissed him, and took Aerial. She'd bathed and smelled radiant. Her dark hair glistened wet against her skin, which hinted of rose. Dario leaned away, fearing his stink might spread to her. But she hugged him tighter, and her cool skin soothed his burning flesh. It was the little things, like this, that made Madi different. She knew the power of silence, and the hope that an honest hug could bring.

"I don't know how much more of this sitting around I can take," he told her.

Madi placed a cup of water in his hands. "I know," she said. "But Captain Tibet had one condition. She wants to spend the first day of the festival with her family."

"How's our crew looking?" Dario asked before drinking.

"Ragged," she admitted. "I found six, and the captain has ten. She says we can make it to The Brink with that, but we'll need to hire more hands when we get there."

Dario had only taken a sip of his drink when nausea gripped his jaw and a cold sweat dripped down his face. His stomach convulsed and he spat up the liquid. Afterward, all he could do was retch. A searing red atmosphere surrounded Lamptree, sizzling as yellow dayclouds sliced through it. Leaves fell to the ground, dried by the heat—withering like Dario's body.

"It's too hot," he said.

"The red currents will rise soon, and it will cool off," Madi said toward a silky combination of clouds. Shades of green and purple mist rose from the bubbling swamp. "A twilight is coming. Until then, you can move back onto my bed if you'd prefer."

"I'd prefer to go to the festival with you."

Madi grimaced. "Too risky."

"I'll say I'm dressed as a ghoul."

"Better that you rest," she replied, pecking him with a kiss. "I have to get dressed and go. I'm in some of the dances, and if I'm late, people will come here looking."

"Can I watch Aerial for you?" Dario asked, feeling useless.

"No, you hide here. It wouldn't look right, me showing up to the festival without her. I'm locking the door. I have a key. Don't answer for anyone."

Clouds churned, shifting in shape and shade as they combined. Dario wished he could stop time and sit here with Madi forever, on the edge of the oncoming twilight. Exhausted, he closed his eyes. By the time he realized he'd dozed off, Madi and Aerial were already gone from the house. Lamptree children followed Madi along the branch toward the festival, squealing with delight. She carried two large bags of toys over the laced shoulder of her costume, a black and pink jacket with a deep hood. Dario's heart palpitated. She was so beautiful—so innocent—and the thought of losing her made his love for her surge more than his breaking body could bear.

The air cooled, just as Madi had predicted. Twilight currents of purple and green pushed the red atmosphere past the horizon. Day-clouds lingered, glistening against a dazzling emerald atmosphere. Happiness filled the air—laughter, music, and applause—but Dario felt so detached from it, as though he'd already died and stood alone on an empty tree. The smell of savory soups, sizzling vegetables, and steaming loaves of bread made his nauseous stomach squirm. He imagined dancing with Madi, holding a kite with Aerial, and getting drunk on Lamptree cider. It was a glimpse of life without this war.

Fireworks crackled, lighting the swamp—revealing a mass of shadowmen amid the reeds. Dario blinked the blurriness from his eyes and retrieved a small telescope from his belt. When he looked again, he couldn't be sure what he saw—swaying reeds? Or swaying bodies, hiding amidst them? Scanning the hillside, he spied a lone Ashen, standing on the high-ground, where Madi had gone hunting. The dark silhouette stretched its arms, and then it pointed, signaling something—to someone. Dario's grip on his scope tightened. He'd never seen a shadowman act like this.

Tuning the telescope, he tried to track the gestures. If only his eyes would stop burning. His vision blurred as he peered through smoke, reeds, and dying trees. Lamptree rangers patrolled the long-road, which was empty at this hour, and Dario couldn't tell who the shadowmen were signaling.

He stumbled to his cot and retrieved the wooden crutch Madi had fashioned for him. It was smooth and delicately fashioned, but there was no magic in it. His spine tensed as he walked, and his tendons stubbornly gripped his bones. He paused with his hand on the back door of Madi's cottage, unsure of what to do. Could Lamptree's gates withstand an Ashen attack? Probably. But there was something strange going on out there, and the colony commandant had to know.

A bell rang, startling him. The bell was tied to a string, which he assumed led to the front door. He hid in the workshop and peeked across the balcony. After a second ring, there was a loud *crack,* and torchlight flooded Madi's house. Dario searched for a weapon.

Why are all of your tools so small, Madi? he thought, opening a drawer full of tweezers and glass eyeballs. *Don't you own a hammer?*

Another CRACK. Torchlight spilled across the balcony, and footsteps pounded the deck. The cot toppled over. Dario grabbed a large sewing needle and hid it behind his back. He opened the door of the workshop, faking confidence, though his heart was hammering. Four men, wearing the Red Rider's crimson leather had invaded Madi's deck, accompanied by a cloaked woman.

"Dario Lire?" a man with a thick mustache asked, flashing an inspector's medallion.

"No, you have the wrong house. Get out!"

The inspector turned to the woman. "Is that him, governor?"

The folds of Ms. Kipps' cloak rippled as she nodded. "It's him."

The men advanced. Dario struck first, but the mustached man caught him by the wrist, wrenching the needle away. He punched Dario in the gut, knocking the air from his lungs, and forcing him into a painful hunch. The inspectors checked his belt, and after they'd retrieved the oracles' maps, they dragged him across the balcony.

Dario fought and flailed through every inch of Madi's house. Dishes fell from the table. The kitchen lantern clattered to the ground, knocking over her drying rack. Somewhere in the sky, Dario's lonely glyph sparked as he mustered every last ounce of strength and tried to craft his bladed crutch. Mist lifted from the floor and walls, and even from the bubbles in the sink.

An inspector noticed. "Galecraft! Grab his hands! His hands!" he shouted. "Get him shackled!"

Dario roared as they tackled him. They rolled through the door and onto Madi's steps. A week ago, he could have overpowered all four of these men. Now, he feared his own arms might rip from their sockets. His Galecraft failed, and the mist fell back to the ground. Shackles jangled, and the men pinned Dario. He cursed as their fingers dug into his flesh, prodding his anger.

"You did this!" he shouted toward the stars, imagining his parents watching. "You let go of me!"

He was too sick to think and too exhausted to fight. His muscles burned as he tried to get free. Ripping his right hand away, he managed to wiggle it into his flying glove.

"His flier!" An inspector panicked. "Grab his wings!"

Dario leapt into the air with a smile, but his body lurched as they caught Nightfly's arms and whipped him back onto the boardwalk. The fall broke him, body and spirit. Splintered floorboards scratched his cheek, and he laid there, gasping.

"Why did you let go of me?" he whispered toward the stars, sapped of all his strength.

The horizon glowed with constellations, twinkling like a tapestry, a sea of shimmering stories. Illio had always called the sky a scroll, where the lives of heroes and villains would unfold. But for Dario, the sky and its tasks were nothing more than a net, tying him down. He often wondered if the people in the world above were watching and laughing at his attempts to escape.

A bony grip pushed him forward, but he refused to walk, so they dragged him. Large crowds filled Lamptree's moss road, but the inspectors kept to the alleys and catwalks on the sides of the giant branches. Gulls scampered into the air as they crossed a rickety bridge and led Dario toward Lamptree's dungeons, which were little more than a maze of gnarled notches, surrounded by thick bark and sharp thorns.

A ranger stepped in front of the inspectors, barring their path even after they flashed their crimson medallions. "Hold where you are! Weapons down, now!" he shouted, drawing his blade when the inspectors protested. "You've been barred from Lamptree!"

"I've suspended the order, ranger. Stand down," Governor Kipps announced, revealing herself. The soldier drew back as the governor's hood fell to her shoulders. "Their task is of great importance to the Pilgrim. Let them pass."

Gears churned and crows cackled as the prison's thorny gate rattled open. *Illio warned me I'd end up here,* Dario thought as his knees slid across a dirty floor, slick with hay.

"Put him here," Governor Kipps said, pointing to a wooden chair.

Two heavy hands forced Dario into the seat. Pain shot through his spine, and his legs seized. He stretched them to ease the pain. Governor Kipps lifted the length of her dress as she stepped over Dario's feet and crossed the floor.

"We have the documents," she said, offering the stolen map book to a Celestial. He hunched over a table holding a caliper to the edges of a sketched constellation. His thick battle-cloak shimmered with orange and brown mist. Illio once said that after enough successful tasks, a celestial's cloak would shine in the colors of the Gales they'd served. Some people still spoke of powerful Celestials with radiant cloaks of every color.

"Dim your light, woman," the man replied. "You'll dilute the stars."

The governor quickly spilled her glass goblet of brew onto the floor, where the golden liquid fizzed and went dark. "I've done everything you've asked. Now, let me go," she begged.

The Celestial drew a symbol on his paper and let out a long contemplative breath. Behind him, three more Celestials peered into telescopes and muttered patterns as they angled their scopes toward a wide window. The thorns there had been cut away for a clearer view. The stuffy cell echoed with the click of dials and the whir of bronze instruments.

"Where is my family?" Governor Kipps demanded. She paced the length of the cell, wringing her hands together. Dario relaxed his eyes, realizing he'd been scowling at her for no reason. She'd had no choice.

"Safer than you or I at the moment," the Celestial replied, etching another symbol. "The sooner we finish here, the sooner we'll both see our families again."

The Celestial dropped his pen, dragged a chair in front of Dario, and sat down. The chair creaked beneath the weight of his large forearms. "This is *him*?" he asked, studying Dario's emaciated form. "What company you with, son?"

The Celestial leaned into the light as he spoke. Gray hair speckled his chin, but his head was bald and scarred. Mist hummed gently as it weaved through his armor in organized lines and protective pools, revealing the strength of his glyph. He was an old badger in his cloak, just like Wardan had been.

"Company Lire," Dario answered.

The Celestial Commander looked skyward. His scowl relented for a moment, as if to briefly honor the dead, but then he turned back to Dario, scowling again. "I'm sorry, but you dug the grave you're sitting in." He placed his palm upon the stolen map book, then clapped the back of his hand against Dario's face. "DO YOU HAVE ANY IDEA WHAT YOU'VE DONE?" he bellowed, saliva spattering the book's binding. "The traitor in Mount Anchor was supposed to be discovered, but not by you!"

"Relax, I'm not the thief you're looking for," Dario replied, matching the man's glare. "You have bigger problems than me right now. A tide of shadowmen is gathering outside the gates."

The Celestial shook his head, eyes irate. "We already know. And you *are* who we're looking for. A tide of shadowmen is nothing compared to the mess you've made. Listen, boy! We've known for months that there was a mole inside the oracles' vaults. We left her there. She was the bait."

"For me?"

The Celestial chuckled, running a finger across the withered mist of Dario's battle cloak. "Do you know who we are?"

"No," Dario replied.

"We are Company Minoan," the man said, standing upright, drowning Dario in a broad shadow. "We hunt Shades. The sky has tasked us to kill Vetricus Perth."

Company Perth? The outlaws? Was that who the Ashen were signaling? Dario doubted it. Shades were cursed celestials, but they fought shadowmen like anyone else. Company Perth had done what he'd been too afraid to ask Wardan to do—openly defy the Gales. Vetricus and his Celestials had been declared Shades, and now they did what all outlaw companies did—they killed to keep their constellation bright.

Dario glanced at the Celestials in the room. The Minoan's cloaks were thick, and their faces grim. Despite their powerful postures, he noted hints of apprehension—glances, restless movements, faint prayers. Constellation Perth—despite being cursed—was the brightest in the sky. This made hunting Vetricus and his outlaws the most dangerous task Dario could think of. Some Celestials said Vetricus and his Shades couldn't be killed.

The Minoan commander paced around Dario's chair. "We spent a year, carefully leaking information so that his company knew exactly where the vault was and how to get inside. We spent months reconstructing doors and corridors, so neither they nor the mole, could escape. Do you know what happens when light touches a wall doused in black-light brew, son?"

"It explodes," Dario mumbled.

"IT EXPLODES!" the Celestial shouted, striking Dario across the chin. A painful *pop* echoed inside his skull. Blood splattered the frills of Governor Kipp's white costume. "Vetricus sent his thief to Mount Anchor! They were nibbling our bait, and then you came along and yanked the line! Not long after you planted those mimicking brews, the mole fled."

He cursed and stood, hurling his chair across the room. Wood splintered, and Governor Kipps gasped. "We were going to *kill* him, Lire!" the Celestial screamed, coming within inches. His breath reeked of cider and stung at the fresh wound on Dario's lip. He snatched Dario by the chin, breathing intensely. Blood leaked through the man's fingers, and a frenzy glazed his eyes. With every mention of the name Vetricus, Dario heard an obsession in the man's tone. Sweat slid from the old celestial's forehead toward his beard, glistening across his scars. "He's dangerous. SO DANGEROUS. Do you know what the Perths will do if they get their hands on this map?"

Dario didn't answer. Instead he focused on recalling all he could about the Shades. Perths were loyal once, supposedly. Now, they ravaged the Gloom, pillaging colonies, but nobody knew why. The trove in their company tower was said to be so large, you could see gold glittering through the gatehouse. When Perths fought, their constellation burned so bright, it out-shined dayclouds. Their glyphs bore so many curses, that each shade in the company had to kill every single day, just to keep their starlight from fading.

"THEY'LL FIND A CITY OF ESCAPE!" The commander screamed so loud, Dario's ears throbbed.

"I wasn't aware Vetricus was looking for one," Dario mumbled, itching his earlobe. The celestial's punch was still sending tremors through his body, but he'd rather act dumb than intimidated. "I'm just trying to keep my family safe."

"WHAT ABOUT *MY* FAMILY?" The Celestial kicked Dario to the ground, cursing him again. "He'll breach the world above, Lire! He'll open the horizon gate, and tides of Ashen will surge toward it. No number of companies will be able to hold them back. If Vetricus succeeds, there won't be a safe place for your family to flee! Nor mine."

The man loomed, clutching a necklace. Five small teeth rattled from it. He curled them around his fingers. Bones were sacred to the Orange Arbiter, and her followers often kept their children's first lost tooth. *He has five children,* Dario realized while massaging his chin.

"I thought Celestials devoted to the Arbiter were supposed to solve tasks *WITHOUT breaking bones*," he mumbled through his smashed jaw.

The commander scowled and raised his hand to strike, but a voice stopped him. The cell door opened, and a crimson mist spilled across the floor, bathing the dim room in a bloody haze. "Peace, Maz Minoan," boomed a deep and delicate voice.

Dials stopped clicking, telescopes stopped tuning, and everyone stopped and bowed. The voice came from nowhere, and everywhere, as though it wasn't a voice, but a thousand whispers hidden within the red mist. The smoke was warm and prickly to the touch. The floorboards creaked, and a dark red cloak brushed Dario's foot.

"Master Guldarion," Maz said, backing away. "I'm sorry. I just don't understand. If celestials like *him* would just complete their tasks and stop interfering with others, this war would be over."

Guldarion's boots paused in front of Dario. "There are many misguided minds in this world," the oracle answered. "Governors, celestials, even other oracles, we can all misread the sky, but the Gales' story shines true, above all else. We just need the eyes to see it. Stand up, Dario Lire."

Dario's skin chilled as the voice vibrated through his shoulders and down his spine. An oracle was here, which meant a god was surely watching—the Red Rider. Dario grit his teeth and tried to stand. He didn't want to appear weak, but the oracle's voice loomed like a thick fog. The room turned hot in a crimson haze, and Dario felt every particle latching on to him, pricking his skin, his skull, and his spine. Mist coiled around him. His legs buckled and seized, and a pain shot up his spine as if the oracle's voice had climbed into his brain.

When Dario breathed, the air tasted hot, and he heard the oracle's voice. "I see anger billowing from you. Why?"

Dario's brain burned, and he couldn't help but think of his past. Tears filled his eyes as a child's voice filled his mind: *His* voice—crying out as he fell—plummeting into this world, alone. The wail ripped not one tear from his heart, but a stream of them. Dario had been close to crying these last few days, but he'd resisted, as not to frighten Madi. But that sensation—that sorrowful sound that no child should ever make—Dario couldn't fight it. It was *his* voice, the sound he'd made while falling from the world above, and he hated that it was his.

"I see," the oracle said softly. "Help him stand."

Dario pushed their hands away. "Get off me!"

Snarling, he rose on his own. When he opened his eyes, he faced the oracle. The man was completely shrouded by a thick cloak with long sleeves. All Dario could see inside the hood was utter darkness—and two fiery red eyes, which disappeared as the oracle let out a puff of smoke. He held a pipe in his hand, which was connected to a tube and a device on his back. Something gurgled inside the tube, and as the oracle exhaled, a stream of red mist spilled from his hood.

"There is a boldness about you, Lire. Fickle and unfounded, but favorable to the Red Rider," Guldarion said, his deep voice billowing. Mist crawled across Dario's scalp, stinging, like a thousand termites were tunneling into his mind to retrieve his thoughts. "You've seen great suffering, and so you do not believe we can win this war. But I tell you, those people who suffer, the people whose stories you document, they suffer because they do not commit fully to the cause. Perhaps that is why *you* suffer?"

Dario eyed his journal. It dangled from its chain, laden with arguments that might suggest otherwise. "I'd like for you to read their stories."

"Sadly, I am unable," Guldarion said, sipping from his pipe. His hood filled with red mist, and two crimson eyes peered outward. For a moment, Dario saw the man's face, which was like rot. His nose was missing, and the sockets of his eyes were empty. Red smoke spilled from both, glowing. When he exhaled, the depths of his hood turned dark. "It is the price I pay to commune with those above."

"I could read them to you," Dario said unkindly. The man's visage was proof enough. The Gales were untrustworthy.

"No need. I can read the mist well enough," Guldarion replied while looking left and right. "Coalescence is strong here. Gale spreads from these people amid their celebration. This is how we win this war, Dario Lire. When people obey. It is my duty to ensure the sky is obeyed, and the sky is telling us to keep fighting, so we cannot flee. Not yet."

The oracle's tone was even, and yet, his words slithered like a snake. Nothing could make Dario trust the world above—or anyone who 'communed' with them. He'd seen enough suffering, and it had nothing to do with obedience. The sky was a messy checkerboard of wills—gods playing with their pieces instead of saving them.

"If you're going to curse me, just do it."

"I could," Guldarion replied. "Or I could redirect your rage. I offer you a task of redemption. In exchange for your service, the Rider will protect your family."

Dario's head grew heavy, and his spine sank into a deeper slump the longer this conversation lasted. His heart fluttered erratically, and his mind ached. Tasks of redemption were the stuff of myth—a cruel prolonging of the Gales' games of glory and graves. Even healthy outlaws struggled to complete them.

Dario narrowed his eyes, glancing around this dungeon. Thick vines, sharp with thorns, coiled around the walls and weaved through every window, strangling any thought of escape. This task of redemption wasn't generosity. It was the Rider's attempt to squeeze some usefulness from a withering pawn. But what choice was there?

"The Rider can save them?" he asked.

"Of course."

"Can he save me?" Dario asked, holding his gut.

The oracle stood silent for a moment, stooping beneath the weight of a device on his back. Steam hissed inside the device, which was black and adorned with red symbols. Judging by the oracle's posture, it was heavier than it looked.

"That depends on the outcome of your task, which is this: Rebuild Company Lire, at least twelve strong, and devote yourselves to the Red Rider."

"Impossible."

"Then die," Guldarion replied, turning away. Company Minoan bowed as the oracle moved toward the cell door. "Begin your task by helping the Minoans kill Vetricus Perth. His death will bring your glyph glory, perhaps even enough to survive a journey with your family. But you will NOT journey to a city of escape. Your task will continue at the Carmine Keep, where I will be waiting. Ensure your wife and child arrive there, and your constellation will shine again." The oracle's deep voice reverberated through the room.

Dario's head spun, and he fought to stay focused. Hands shaking, he unsheathed his pen and scribbled in his book. "C-Carmine Castle?—I mean Keep, where's that?" Dario followed the oracle, but then fell to a knee, losing grip of his book. "How long do I have until my glyph falls?" he asked, tasting bile. "How long do I have to fix this?"

Guldarion was already gone from the room. The dungeon door closed with a loud *boom*. Only a wisp of crimson mist lingered. From it, a deep whisper replied.

"Not long."

CHAPTER 8: MADI

Aerial snuggled deep inside her pouch. This was her first Lamptree Festival, and Madi wasn't sure how she would react. So far, she'd peered hesitantly from her hiding place, like a little turtle inspecting a new pond. Every so often, she shuddered at some new sound she'd never heard before. But she didn't cry. To Madi's surprise, her daughter grew more and more curious, as if to realize these were the sounds of celebration.

At times, Madi covered Aerial's ears. The noise was deafening. Drums echoed. Fireworks crackled across the sky. Thousands of voices rose from a vertical maze of branches. Shouts, chants, and whistles mixed with music, explosions, and applause, creating a cacophony of celebration. Purple and green clouds swaddled Lamptree, which seemed to sway under the weight of so much celebration.

The air was cooler now. People had taken to the streets, which glittered beneath a sea of constellations. Across every branch, crowds cheered as fliers raced through the twilight sky. Winged competitors rounded the tree, smearing wisps of color as they vied for position. Like spindly spiders, they skittered across the clouds. The Orphan Cup was over. The youngest racers had received their purses of glass, and now the fastest fliers from nearby colonies competed for the Lamptree Crown.

At the heart of Lamptree Colony stood the Ringed Hall, an enormous circular room carved from the core of the tree. The chamber's function changed as needed. Today, it was being used for the dances, which would continue for the next few days. A polished stage shimmered with brown and beige rings of sapwood and hardwood. Long tables surrounded the floor, rising upward like an arena three stories high. Madi had finished two performances already and was eager to complete her final performance so she could return to Dario. Giant archways lined Ringed hall, and Madi sat beneath one of them, on the promenade overlooking Lamptree's Core District.

Another firecracker shrieked through the air. After a loud *bang*, light twinkled through Lamptree's colorful canopy. Smoke from the fireworks descended, and smells from the street rose—hot food, sizzling and steaming. Fresh drink flowed, filling the streets with smiles and bibulous laughter. Governor Kipps and the ministry ought to be pleased. Coalescence filled the air—colonist magic—spreading Gale from Lamptree Colony like one colossal lantern.

In Madi's opinion, coalescence was the most beautiful sight in the whole festival. Even now, with her chin on her arms, she watched healthy color creep from Lamptree, through the twilight atmosphere toward the gloomy hills beyond the swamp. Fireworks lit the countryside, and with each glowing explosion, she saw more vibrant color spread—to the tops of the pines, to the flowers on the hillside, to the clouds in the air. Meanwhile, shadowmen watched. There were many now, standing at the edge of the swamp—staring at a celebration they were certainly not invited to.

Vishi paced the promenade behind Madi, holding Aerial and bouncing her to the tune of the music. She'd brought a plate of food and some glasses of Lamptree cider, but Madi wasn't feeling so festive anymore. She'd spotted the Red Rider's oracles—three of them. They paraded through the street below, slowly making their way into the Ringed Hall. People gathered on a bridge above and rained pink petals upon the procession, a warm welcome for old rivals. Madi scanned the crowd, where rangers escorted two men away. It appeared they were the source of some conflict, and she was glad that others were not pleased to see the Red Rider's representatives on Lamptree.

The Rider's oracles walked amid a host of servants, who swayed golden censers. Crimson incense spewed from the ornate vessels, spilling over the road, and rippling outward as the oracles walked. Dark red cloaks with deep hoods obscured their faces, and long sleeves draped over their arms. They each wore a device on their back, an ornate waterpipe—with elegant shafts, tubes, and pipes for smoking. Rumor had it that oracles had no eyes. Nothing but mist flowed through their empty sockets. Yet, somehow, they walked into the Ringed Hall, unaided.

Incense burned, and the air filled with the scent of amber and rose. Madi leaned away from the haze, her hands tingling. Supposedly, oracles saw through the smoke, and she feared if it touched her, they could peer into her soul. Lines of carved pumpkins adorned the Mossroad, and decorations dangled from every doorframe, but the oracles ignored everything. They moved with their heads slightly cocked, as if walking through a completely different world—one of only mist and starlight.

Vishi kept pacing. Just a little bit ago, she'd brought bad news about the escape plan. Captain Tibet's manifest had been rejected, and Madi was certain the oracles had something to do with it. "Why else would the governor's office reject our manifest?" she asked Vishi. "We're set to leave soon."

Colonists milled about the promenade, carrying plates, sipping cider, and watching the festivities. Once they were alone, her friend answered quietly. "I told you I don't know. I couldn't find any paperwork about it." A beaked mask hid much of her face, but it couldn't hide the angst in her voice. "The document I gave you will let you depart. Just don't expect other colonies to let you moor without question."

Madi inspected the folded papers. The wax seal was still warm. "What is this?"

"A governor's writ of transport," Vishi replied. She worked in the Bottle Catcher—a tower where all the flying bottles sent to Lamptree floated—so she knew her way around official documents. "It doesn't need a manifest."

"How'd you get this?" Madi asked.

"The window was open," her friend answered with an overt innocence. "There was a sudden gust. The paper must have blown into my bag . . . freshly sealed . . . and signed." Her voice became serious. "Just don't lose it, okay?"

"Thank you, Veesh," Madi said tenderly. She looked over the sealed document, fingering its fresh corners. The last thing she'd wanted was putting her friends in danger. "I didn't want you getting involved in this."

"Involved? I didn't even know you were leaving until yesterday." Vishi's tone soured with each word, and her lips pursed beneath the cut of her mask. "As your friend, I'd *love* to be involved, but you're not telling us anything. I hope you'll at least throw us a bottle when you get to wherever it is you're going?"

Madi grabbed the beak of Vishi's mask and tugged it until they were eye to eye. Rich brown hair blew across Vishi's face, and behind her mask, her eyelashes glistened. "I don't want to leave," Madi told her softly. Sadness choked her, and she fought not to cry. It'd been easy to plan an escape with Dario writhing on his bed, but here with her best friend amid her favorite time of year, the words seemed impossible to say. "This is my home. You're practically family. I would never leave unless I had no other choice."

Her stomach hollowed, and every sound caused it to flutter—drums, explosions, cheers. The last time she remembered being this nervous was the day she was grafted into Company Maya. Her parents were Celestials in Company Brazen, but their constellation wasn't bright enough to graft another Celestial into the company—least of all a child. So, they hid Madi for a time, but glyphs cannot be hidden, and Celestials can't survive without a constellation. It was a dark blue day, torrential with rain, when Company Maya came looking for a young Celestial to graft. Madi was only eight years old when they took her. She never saw her parents again after that, and today, she feared she would never see Lamptree again either.

"Toymaker's dance, up next," the master-of-ceremonies called, peeking onto the balcony.

Madi waved to him and rose, wiping her eyes and sweeping her hands along the cape of her costume. Tools jingled from her belt, and the festival noises deafened some as she curled her collar upward and placed a mask over her eyes—silver spectacles with many magnification loupes. The lenses clicked as Madi groomed her hair across her shoulder.

Meanwhile, Vishi whimpered. "It's because of Dario, isn't it," she said, gripping Madi's sleeve. Aerial cooed as she was squeezed between the two women. She squawked and yanked a strand of Madi's hair. "I can't stop worrying about what might happen if you go," Vishi admitted. "Celestials frighten me. They fight until their glyph falls. We're colonists. It's not safe for us out there. Stay. Please! Dario will come back when he solves whatever task he needs to solve. You can trust him. He's always come back to you."

Dario did always come back, but this time would be different unless she helped him. Madi turned toward the Ringed Hall, toward the sound of applause.

"Promise me you'll think about it," Vishi called.

"I am," Madi replied honestly.

She couldn't *stop* thinking about it, but each time, she concluded that finding a city of escape was the only solution. Madi wasn't just hiding herself. She was hiding Aerial, keeping her far from the celestial stage—intent on doing what her own parents couldn't—sparing her daughter from a life of tragedy. Aerial's glyph would brighten every year, until she was seven or eight. Then, a company would come looking—and they would take her away. Sembetra had promised to help find a solution, but now the oracle was missing. If Madi couldn't somehow sever the strings of magic binding Aerial to the sky, then the city of escape was her daughter's only hope.

Forged papers won't save you, Bandico had warned, and after what happened at Greenpond, Madi believed him.

A wooden catwalk creaked as Madi entered through the basement of the Ringed Hall. Footsteps thundered overhead as dancers leapt across the stage, depicting stories of far off colonies and famous Celestials. Applause echoed. Wheels squeaked as stagehands lowered a curtain and raised props for Madi's scene. She moved into position on a marked lift, where dust danced in a pale ray of light from the stage. The specks fled her lips as she sighed. Magic had a high price, but some people had miraculously managed to overcome the cost.

As a child, she'd watched the dance of Elio and Aegis—two Celestial lovers who overcame all odds and found a realm beyond this world's edge, in a place outside of time and trouble. These days, everyone dismissed it as myth—even Dario—but Madi coveted it as a dream.

The lift rumbled upward. Stuffy basement air gave way to the smell of a feast. In each large window, bowls of water glowed with drops of daylight brew. Hundreds of people sat at dozens of long tables, obscured by heaps of food. Madi stood in her starting pose, but she was so distracted in thought, she missed her cue. The music started, and she hurried to catch up.

Madi wasn't a dancer, and sometimes she wondered why she'd

ever agreed to perform. But when she saw the children gathered around the stage—their little bodies jittering with excitement—she remembered. It was for them.

Fortunately, the toymaker's dance was rather mechanical, with most of the props moving for Madi, stealing the spotlight. The audience murmured with delight as a blossoming dogwood tree rose from below stage—its branches adorned with toys.

Mysterious music welcomed Madi's enigmatic character. There was a story to every dance, and the toymaker's dance was no different. Every toy had a home—every flying puppet, every porcelain soldier, every mechanical doll belonged to one specific child, like dreams. To the children, toys were just toys. But to Madi, these toys were Celestials, and each child was the peaceful home every celestial puppet longed to find.

Violins accompanied Madi as she used *Flicker* to fly around the dogwood, retrieving toys and presenting them to approaching children. She glided around the tree, cutting strings and lowering boxes into the children's waiting arms. Wooden props slid across the stage, and Madi weaved between them, *Flicker's* long arms gleaming. The audience clapped as she demonstrated how some of the toys worked.

She threw her personal favorite into the air—a gliding squirrel. The puppet soared in a wide circle, casting off falling blossoms as it rounded the dogwood and glided over the children's heads, landing in the palm of a small girl. Delicate music accompanied the demonstration, which caught the attention of more than just children.

Standing upon the frame of each giant window, Celestials stood guard. As Madi performed, she noticed more and more of them turning toward the stage, watching. What company was this? Did they understand the secret meaning behind the dance? It seemed they did, and the thought made her skin turn cold. They longed for homes as much as she did—no more wandering in wagons, no more battling shadow, no more serving the stars.

Madi moved to the edge of the stage for her finale. The Ringed Hall was not nearly large enough for all the people of Lamptree, especially with the surge of refugees. Hundreds of people, with their children, watched from other branches. Madi waved at them—parents with children on their shoulders, peering from a distance. *A toy for every child—a home for every Celestial.*

After a burst of blossoms and a flare of music, Madi released a lever. Balloons and flying toys floated from the Ringed Hall. Crowds all across the tree watched and pointed as the wave of glowing balloons flew toward them. Slowly, they soared across the gap, toward those too poor to merit an invitation to the Ringed Hall. But Madi had made toys for these children also.

The crowd raised its voice, uncertain if all the toys and balloons would survive the journey, but Madi was certain they would. The music reached a crescendo. She raised her arms, and the balloons released boxes of toys—an entire year's worth of work. Children reached up, hands open, to snatch one of the gifts. Applause erupted across all of Lamptree, and color spread into the air, turning the twilight ablaze.

On cue, dozens of young dancers burst onto the stage for the next dance, puppets in hand. The dogwood was lowered on a lift, and new props took its place. Madi perched atop the dogwood as it descended, taking one last look at the room. Children showed off their toys to their parents, and cheer filled the hall. Outside, vibrant color spread from the colony in all directions. Madi took a deep breath and smiled. If this really was her last day on Lamptree, this was as perfect an ending as she could imagine.

The lift descended into the dim basement, where Vishi was waiting. As soon as Madi removed her mask, Aerial squealed with joy.

"That was beautiful. You were beautiful," Vishi said.

Madi sobbed, snorted, and wiped her nose. "I'm a mess."

Her eyes watered, and the more she wiped them, the more she smeared fragrance across her face. Some got into her eyes, causing a blinding sting. She gasped, trying to balance Aerial while blinking the irritation away. The pain in her eyes was exactly like the pain in her heart—a mixture of joy, sadness, and a burning blindness.

Ever since Dario's return, her heart stung like this, making it impossible to think. She could only react to the sensation—to Dario's situation, to Aerial's, to her own. But she had no idea if she was doing the right thing or going the right direction.

"I need a cloth," Madi said, reaching toward Vishi. "There's one in Aerial's bag."

Madi opened her palm, wiggling her fingers until she felt the cloth. It was warmer than she remembered, a little damp, and as soft as snow. She stooped and wiped her eyes until the burning stopped.

"Are you Madi Amriel?" an unfamiliar voice asked.

Madi blinked her eyes and looked up, surprised to see a young Celestial standing in front of her. The girl was tall, with blonde hair braided across one shoulder. She wore an amused smirk as Madi had just wiped her face with the edge of her battle cloak. The red and gray fabric glistened with wisps of mist, which curled around Madi's fingers, buzzing slightly. Vishi blushed and stared at the Celestial like an enamored little girl. No matter how beautiful a costume, there was no matching the grim glory of a celestial cloak.

Madi felt her own face flush. "I apologize, milady," she said, retreating and bowing.

Reverence rippled through her core as she stooped into the celestial's shadow. It'd been a long time since she'd stood this close to one of them. Dario didn't count. He was different—humble on account of his past. Bandico didn't count either. He was a Shade, an outlaw, walking heavy beneath his curses. But this girl stood upright, gleaming, proud of the magic connecting her to the sky.

Vishi clenched her hands together, visibly shaking in the Celestial's presence. Madi had lived on Lamptree long enough that Celestials were no longer her comrades in arms—they were foreigners. She trembled some too, wondering: what was this Celestial's task?

The Celestial cocked her head, and her blue eyes twinkled like stars—innocent and dangerous all in the same gaze. "They said your company escaped," she said, pausing skeptically. "So how are you still here?"

Madi swallowed as she thought of what to say. *She knows who I am? How?* A nervous knot squeezed down her throat and settled firmly inside her gut. She gripped Aerial and exchanged a quick glance with Vishi, whose jaw still hung open.

"I-I'm afraid I don't understand, milady," Madi stuttered, struggling to keep her act convincing. "You must have the wrong person. I have papers here, somewhere."

She rummaged through her pockets, trying to buy time. She was very close to dropping the act now. Her heart drummed against her chest. Run or don't run? She eyed the celestial's frame, wide and rugged on account of her cloak. Madi could outrun inspectors, rangers, and even shadowmen, but she doubted she could outrun this Celestial. She looked powerful—her skin and cloak were healthy. Mist flowed freely through the fabric of her armor, glistening with tiny specks of color, mostly shades of red, brown, and orange. A second Celestial blocked Madi's retreat, sealing her decision.

"This way, please. We don't need to see your papers," she said, angling an open palm toward a curling staircase. Mist lingered at her fingertips, and Madi knew—these Celestials could craft their weapons in an instant. "Madi Amriel. Toymaker. Twenty-four years of age. No curses. Lamptree Colony. The oracles have summoned you. It's our task to deliver."

"Yes, milady," Madi replied, lowering her chin. Feeling utterly exposed, she dropped her leather-bound booklet. The documents Bandico had forged for her, year after year, tumbled onto the boardwalk.

Madi followed slowly, taking the time to look back at Vishi, who stood with her hands clasped against her chest, utterly confused. Madi's cheeks burned with embarrassment. It'd been a risk to go about the festival, but would hiding at home have been any wiser? She shook her head, tucking her hand around her daughter's body. As she ascended, she felt a noose being tightened around both their necks.

Two Celestials escorted Madi through the upper corridors of the Ringed Hall, where garlands of orange and yellow leaves adorned wooden columns. The scent of cinnamon and pine filled the hall—familiar scents from hundreds of walks through these passages. Either way this meeting went, Madi was certain this would be the last time she walked through this place. Music echoed from the stage, growing louder as the Celestials opened the doors to the oracles' booth.

Red and pink mist flowed through the double-doors as they opened. Five oracles were seated in the booth—three red, two pink. Before they even turned, Madi felt their gaze cling to her. Deep hoods, oozing mist, obscured the oracles' faces. The air was thick—not only with the smell of red and pink incense—but with something else, a magic that seemed to slither through Madi's nose, reaching for her mind. She held her breath and shielded Aerial's face with her hand. Her arms trembled, and chills rolled across her body. If Celestials were the Gales' swords, then the oracles were their eyes. A black void filled their hoods, and as mist frothed from their faces, she felt an otherworldly eye upon her.

Lamptree's two oracles, Tenti Ordecon and Valemon Ordecon,

sat at the end of the table, nearest Madi. They wore pale pink cloaks, nearly white, with dark pink veins shimmering across the fabric like a wind. Incense surrounded them, which smelled of lemon and pine. Madi took some comfort. The Ordecon siblings were rumored to be wise and fair.

Mist lingered around every object in the booth, forming a warm haze that filled the air with a sense of lethargy. Even the music from the stage seemed to dim. Madi couldn't hold her breath much longer, so she breathed in slowly, sensing a tingle inside her skull. Meanwhile, Aerial whimpered.

A gentle laugh rippled out from Tenti Ordecon's deep hood, alongside an exhale of mist. "Don't worry," she said. "The smoke has no lasting effect on your eyes, only ours." Her hood tilted slightly, but the kindness in her tone failed to match the black abyss where her voice originated. "Please, come closer," she said, extending an arm. The long sleeve of her cloak covered her hand and fingers.

Madi received the gesture. The oracle's arm felt brittle within her cloak, as though there was nothing beneath but bone. Slowly, she guided Madi toward the nearest chair. None of the oracles looked directly at Madi. Instead, they angled their hoods in her general direction. She tried to peek at their faces, but saw little more than a hint of flesh.

"We apologize for the brevity of introductions, but time and trouble often dictate terseness," Tenti said. She gripped a slender pipe within her sleeve, which she brought to the mouth of her hood. A moment later, mist exhaled, and her voice seemed to slide across it. "I am Tenti Ordecon. My brother Valemon and I make pilgrimage here several times a year to serve our god. Today, we are accompanied by servants of the Red Rider, who have brought to our attention some troubling notions. They've requested an audience with you, which we've granted. Since there are no oracles of the Orange Arbiter nearby, my brother and I are here to act as arbiters for you in their stead." She brought her pipe into her hood again, and a dark pink mist billowed afterward.

Madi sat rigid in her chair, every word from the oracle's hood tightening around her stomach like a vise. "I would prefer to leave," she declared, glaring at the crimson hoods across the table. "As I don't serve the Rider."

"You serve the Pink Pilgrim, and she too wishes to *see* if there is any truth to these claims," Tenti replied. Two coral colored orbs blazed beneath her hood like eyes. "I see your mistrust, but by our divine obligation to safeguard the Gales' realms, we must insist on your cooperation. Guldarion has assured me this won't take long."

"It won't," the Rider's oracle replied. His voice was deep, almost too deep for Madi to understand. It rumbled with a wave of smoke, vibrating against Madi's chest. "Collecting Nariah Maya isn't the only task we're here to complete. We've more than one Shade to eradicate."

"Nariah has not yet been declared a Shade," said Tenti. "You are still devoted to the Pilgrim, are you not?" she asked, turning to Madi. Her sleeve dangled over a full cup of cider, which Madi quickly took and drank.

"Yes. I never intended to hide from my tasks. I consulted an oracle."

"Who?"

"Sembetra," Madi replied.

Guldarion grunted with satisfaction. He felt the table for his fork, and after studying his steaming plate, he selected a bit of carved turkey. The fork disappeared momentarily into his hood before emerging empty. "You heard her," he said, munching. Red mist escaped his hood with each munch. "She consulted . . . Sembetra."

There was an obvious distaste to the name. He sipped his pipe and exhaled a plume of red smoke across the table before snatching a palmful of nuts from a bowl. As dancers bowed, he clapped with the rest of the hall, his palms muffled by his long cloak. Salt sprinkled from his sleeves onto the golden tablecloth. Clearly, he was pleased with how this conversation was going.

"How did you survive your fall from the city of escape?" one of the other red oracles asked, her voice feathery and frail.

"I was wearing a flier. I managed to lock the wings before I fell unconscious."

"Can you still practice Galecraft?"

"I can," Madi answered. "Though I've forgotten many materials."

"Interesting. Have you experienced any sudden illnesses? When you travel, perhaps?"

"Just homesickness."

"When was the last time you gazed at your glyph?" The questions came quickly now, from each oracle, in turn.

"I can't remember. Years ago."

"Was Sembetra gazing for you?"

"Yes."

"What did she tell you?"

"I can't remember."

Guldarion dipped bread into honey, bit into it with a *crunch*, and then washed it down with a sip of Lamptree cider. Madi saw a hint of a ragged white beard on his chin. "You're lying. I can't see you, Nariah, but I can see the color of your words, and there are white whispers among them."

Aerial grew heavy in Madi's arms, and beads of sweat dripped down her face. The haze in the booth was warm, buzzing, and prickly. She felt it crawling across her cheeks, searching for a way into her mind.

"When I consulted Sembetra, she couldn't figure out how I survived, but she was intrigued and decided to help me," Madi revealed truthfully. "She began studying my glyph to determine if I was free from its magic. She studied my daughter's glyph also. In return, I created ciphers and delivered them to a gambling den in Greenpond."

Guldarion's eyes flared from a calm crimson to a bright and bloody red. "Was this before or after she told you to move to Lamptree?" he asked, mist hissing from his hood.

"After," Madi said, hesitating. She felt like she'd just incriminated herself, but she still didn't know what she was being charged with. "She said I might find peace here, and I did. It's one of her sanctuaries."

"You were misled," Guldarion said. "Your friend Sembetra is a heretic, and I'll prove it to you." He placed his hand on the table. Pale fingernails peeked from his sleeve. Gray bone, and hardly any skin at all. Madi froze to her seat as he revealed a small porcelain soldier, broken, weathered, and smeared in blood. "This place, Lamptree, is *not* favored by the Pilgrim, despite your friend's reassurance. And this cipher, which your friend requested, was taken from the corpse of a Shade."

The toy soldier stood crooked upon the table, its wooden body shattered, its inner workings revealed. Blood stained its face, and Madi reached slowly to touch it—to ensure it was hers. It was. But if Sembetra wasn't serving the Pilgrim, who was she serving? Madi's whole body tingled, as though she'd been dipped in a bath of black magic. Sembetra wouldn't lie. Would she?

Madi turned to the Pilgrim's two oracles. Pink mist flowed over their hoods like a veil, moving faster and more erratic than the red incense fuming from Guldarion's hood. "Is this true?" she asked.

The Ordecon siblings nodded simultaneously. "It is," Tenti replied. "Which is why my brother and I are here. The power preventing your glyph from fading is *NOT* that of our goddess, nor is Lamptree one of her holy places. Contrary to what many believe, we do not come here to commune. We come here to study. There is a foreign magic at work here, and you may be our key to solving it."

Madi tightened her grip on Aerial. "So you've come to *collect* me?"

"Master Guldarion spoke out of turn."

"I did not." The red oracle crossed his arms. He puffed at his pipe and exhaled a crimson cloud. "Our god is bold and so are we. It is our task to ensure the celestial companies obey their tasks, and I am here to ensure that THIS Celestial obeys hers. It is our task to investigate dark magic and any other threat to the Gales and their realms, so I will solve the mystery you have failed to unravel."

Dark magic? Good magic? Was there a difference? The cost was too high either way. Still, this notion eased her somewhat. If this was some foreign magic she'd stumbled into, then the Gales could still favor her. They could save Dario! If she had something they needed, then maybe a deal could be struck.

"What would the Pilgrim have me do?" she asked. "If Lamptree isn't hers, whose is it?"

"We would need to study it—and you—more thoroughly to say," Tenti replied.

"You've had your chance," Guldarion interrupted. "This issue has been tasked to those cloaked in crimson now. The Rider's task for you, Nariah Maya, is to journey to the Carmine Keep, our stronghold west of the Carnation Region. There, we will study the manner of this magic."

Applause rippled through the hall as a dance ended. Curtains fell, and props emerged from below the stage. Meanwhile, Madi squirmed in her seat. Sembetra wouldn't lie, but in her warning, she'd said the oracles knew how Madi had survived. She'd said they knew what Lamptree was. She said they'd destroy it, but none of those things seemed true now. Something wasn't adding up, and she couldn't bring herself to condemn Sembetra.

"Don't the Gales know whose magic this is?" she asked, hoping to coax more information.

Incense curled across the table as the oracles angled their hoods toward the question. They sat, rigid, in their seats, slowly lowering their pipes. Had the question offended them? Perhaps it had come across as irreverent, but Madi didn't really care at this point. Dario questioned the Gales all the time, and maybe he was right to do so.

"They have their suspicions. As do we," Guldarion eventually replied. "Our enemy is cunning, and the White Whisperer has been known to impersonate our gods and sow dissension among celestial ranks."

"Wait, what?" Madi sat upright, needles pricking her skin. She drew a quick breath and curled Aerial close to her heart, which began to beat faster and faster. Her chair seemed to grow beneath her, making her feel smaller and smaller—a bug in an ever-growing web. "The Whisperer? She's real?"

"It is beginning to seem so," Guldarion replied, breathing more mist into the booth. Madi didn't mind so much now. His voice seemed warmer now, as though the thought of a god in the Gloom had suddenly made them allies.

The White Whisperer was said to rule the Gloom along with her brothers, the Black Knight and the Gray Ghost, but they were made up. Their names were an invention—villains in dances to frighten disobedient children. The only comforting thing about the Gloom was that nobody ruled it. It was like a storm that came and went, snatching people away with it for no reason. But if this was true, it meant someone ruled the Gloom—someone with their own magic, their own intentions.

A chorus of boos rippled across the Ringed Hall as an actor in dark gray rags leapt onto the stage, portraying a shadowman. He carried a black flag and twirled it to a twisted tune. The song stung at the shock shaking Madi's core, and she wished it would stop. She started to shake, and the oracles turned their hoods toward her—no doubt sensing the spark of fear.

"Don't be afraid, Madi," Tenti said softly. "I don't sense the Whisperer in this place." She paced the far side of the booth. Gray hair slipped from her hood as she lifted her gaze. "Nor do I see any sign of the Knight or the Ghost. There is no Gloom here. This magic is foreign. Perhaps even originating beyond the borders of this world."

"The Whisperer only needs a shred of Gloom to deceive, Lady Ordecon. It's her for certain," Guldarion countered. "My inspectors have yet to search every gnarled nook of this colony, and once they do, I'm confident they will find a trace of our adversary. Meanwhile, I will escort Nariah personally on her task to Carmine Keep."

"I serve the Pilgrim," Madi said. "I've no reason to trust the Rider."

Guldarion stood, incense fuming from the folds of his cloak. "And he has no intention of giving you one. Reasons to trust are not nearly as powerful as reasons to obey."

He slowly set his pipe on the table. His pale fingers were little more than bone. Crimson smoke spilled from his hood, heating the cup in Madi's hand. The oracle leaned close, and when she saw his face, she gasped and covered Aerial's eyes. There was barely anything left of this man! Flesh gave way to bone. Crimson mist coiled around his skull as though it'd devoured all the organs inside. The smoke snaked through Guldarion's two empty eye sockets, like worms. His nose and ears looked as though they'd rotted. Mist spewed from his pipe, and as it sizzled against his flesh, Madi wondered if anything besides magic was holding this man together.

Sembetra had said that she'd sacrificed her eyes so that the Gales might peer into this world, and that she might peer into theirs. But she looked nothing like this. She was young, though—only a few years older than Madi. Would her body one day rot from the inside out like this man's? Why would anyone agree to this magic?

Guldarion sipped from his pipe, and this time, Madi saw the fumes pass through his skull. The mist swirled, forming two crimson eyes—bright and foreign, like a distant and unfamiliar star. Madi froze in her seat, clutching Aerial.

"Let me reawaken your dulled sense of reality, Nariah Maya." Guldarion's voice slithered through the smoke. "You are a Celestial. You will obey your task, or you will be cursed. But since I can see what you fear, we will not curse you. If you fail this task, we will curse your daughter."

Madi recoiled, shielding Aerial's body. She wished the oracles would stop staring at her. Their gaze burned now, like a steady thrust of a spear.

Tenti pressed a hand to Madi's arm. Pink mist spilled from her hood, curling around Madi's body. It felt as slick as a lie. "Madi, we can see that—"

"That I'm upset?" Madi interrupted, freeing her hand from the oracle's bony fingers. Her heart throbbed—shaking her entire body—blurring her ability to think. Her chest rose and fell with such force, Aerial began to fuss. "How can you let him do this?"

"It's only temporary." Tenti Ordecon returned to her seat beside her brother, smoothing her robe with her hands. "After what we've heard here today, the sky is clear. The Pilgrim and the Rider are in accord. You will travel to Carmine Keep to aid in this research. As a precaution, your daughter will be marked as a Shade. If you stray from your task, the curse will burn. Once you arrive at Carmine, we will lift the curse."

Madi dropped to the floor. Aerial a Shade? What was happening? What had she done? She crawled to the door of the booth, rising slowly. Her knees trembled, and the air seemed to boil. When she tried to leave, two Celestials blocked her path.

"Let her go," Guldarion said. "She will obey."

His confident voice slithered coolly amid a crimson mist, which coiled around Madi's body like chains. She ripped herself free from the Celestials' grip and glared at the oracle, hating him, hating the sound of his voice, hating the way he was using Aerial. He dipped his hood slightly, and Madi knew he could see her hatred.

She fled the Ringed Hall as fast as she could, eager to get home —to Dario and their plan. She'd never felt more united with him. But what would he say? How would they escape without losing their daughter? She raced along the Mossroad as fireworks flashed above, spilling smoke across the rooftops. The street was empty this far from the festival, and the air grew colder. She sped her pace, kicking up strewn bits of garbage. She'd never gripped her daughter so tightly. The desperate trill of music followed from the Ringed Hall as she ran, and chills clung to her arms all the way. But when she arrived at her steps, gasping for breath, she found the front door broken open.

CHAPTER 9: DARIO

Dario stood at the window of Company Minoan's hideout. Constellations shimmered and changed shape, quaking high above. Airy trills and distant rumbles signaled the Gales' pens were moving. Tasks filled the twilight air—and Dario's stomach—with a sense of dread. Company Minoan must have felt it, too. They sat in solemn silence while their astronomers tuned their telescopes toward Constellation Perth.

"Two crests, mirrored. Light fracturing, quickly now," a Minoan astronomer announced. "They're traveling in pairs. I think Vetricus may already be inside the colony."

"Everybody up!" Maz ordered. "Tell the governor to announce the dance."

Company Minoan rose, forming two lines on either side of the dungeon hallway. Instead of their battle cloaks, they wore costumes. Their plan was an ambush—like the one Dario had inadvertently foiled. Only this time, there wasn't an exploding vault involved—just an exploding book.

"Ready, Lire?" Maz asked. "You look as pale-eyed as a puffer."

"I'm the one holding the bomb," Dario mumbled. His head sagged toward the two books on his belt: his journal and the stolen maps. They bumped against one another as he shifted his weight, and he worried the map-book might explode at any moment.

Let Vetricus steal the map from you, but make it look convincing,"

Maz replied. "You're the bait, but his ego will be his downfall. This only works if he believes you're being sentenced during this dance. We kill him, you get a share of the glory."

"I get it," Dario replied.

He'd watched Company Minoan soak the stolen pages with black-light brew—a thick, gooey slop. If given enough time to dry in complete darkness, the brew would explode at the slightest touch of daylight. Nobody was going to discover any secrets from these maps. By now, the brew was probably dry, meaning as soon as Vetricus cracked the binding open, he'd find a face-full of inferno. But would it kill him?

Dario limped to his place in the center of a large lift, wondering if they were the ones walking into a trap. On either side of him, Celestials prepared themselves for the ambush. They wore festival masks and dance costumes, but beneath them, they readied their weapons. Hooks and shackles rattled. Arrows fizzed as they were polished with brown 'muddy material' brews. Dario tilted his nose away. The foul glaze would make it more difficult for Vetricus to cull the arrows. Other colorful vials clinked as the Celestials added them to their belts—red combat brews, green poisons, purple spark pots.

Dario's only weapon was his pen, so he did what he always did—he wrote:

I ask the Minoans about their thoughts on the war, but they refuse to answer. They consider me a Shade, and they blame Celestials like me—and Vetricus—for the length of the war. But why are Shades to blame? They oppose the Gales' tasks, but the Gales themselves have opposed each other. In the past, they've tasked celestial companies against one another, and I intend to prove they still do. They prolong this war, not us.

~Dario Lire 6.14.2f

The lift lurched and rose, churning Dario's nerves. He tucked his pen away, refusing to accept that this might be his last entry. Governor Kipps' voice echoed down the shaft. *"Citizens and esteemed guests, friends of Lamptree, you may be wondering why our custodians are pouring sand onto the stage. As you know, tonight's festivities are in honor of our allies from Anchor Colony. Lord Guldarion has expressed to me his deepest gratitude for your hospitality, and he wishes to give us something in return. Tonight, our friends from Mount Anchor will be sharing a dance of their culture, in the bold tradition of the Red Rider."*

As the lift ascended, it passed open archways, blocked by iron bars. Dario peered at the activity on each floor. Cooks stirred steaming pots in kitchens. Stagehands loaded props onto lifts. Dancers rushed into their dressing rooms.

But on one floor, inspectors used tools to shave bits of bark from Lamptree's wall. The room looked evacuated, and Dario tilted his head, squinting as an inspector cut a leaf from the tree and placed it into a pouch. He knelt over a device—a box with a small telescope. Wood shavings had been cut from the floor next to him.

"What are they doing?" Dario asked Maz.

"Collecting samples," he replied. "They've been poking around ever since we got here."

"What are they looking for?"

"No idea. Focus on your own task, Lire. Not others."

But other tasks matter, Dario thought. The sky may have told a story, but it certainly wasn't as clear as Maz or Guldarion made it out to be. Dario's journal was full of discrepancies he'd witnessed. Sometimes, colonies were protected. Sometimes, they were ignored. Sometimes, Celestials worked together on a task. Sometimes, they worked against each other. Guldarion said the sky was full of good. So had Illio, but Dario couldn't see it. If there was anything the sky was full of—it was schemes.

He wondered which of the Gales had sent Company Minoan here. What kind of scheme had summoned such powerful Celestials to the stage? Whatever it was, company blood was about to be spilled—and Maz and his Minoans seemed well aware. A pensiveness pervaded their proud postures, and some whispered prayers to the Orange Arbiter. Even if Vetricus and his Shades fell for this trap, not everyone in this lift was going to survive.

Dario trembled, wishing Illio were here to offer comfort. *This is the kind of task you wanted,* he'd have said. *Patrolling poor colonies won't bring you glory, remember? Killing Vetricus Perth will. Complete this task, and your glyph will shine long enough for you to escape with your family.*

Light applause rippled through the shaft, alongside some consternation—nervous shouts, which Governor Kipps quickly addressed. *"Yes, traditional red dances are known for bloodshed, but I assure you, this is merely a demonstration. The dancers will be using wooden weapons . . ."*

Maz and his Celestials grinned. They carried wooden weapons now, but as soon as Vetricus appeared, they'd craft all manner of sharpened blades. The lift paused momentarily, and a group of dancers squeezed onto the platform, completing the charade. These were *real* dancers and they'd be the ones doing all the acting. He'd been told to just *play along*, whatever that meant. Stagehands moved props into position, and as music boomed overhead, the lift ascended. Waves of applause echoed in the giant hall, and a circular curtain fell.

The stage was covered in a generous layer of white sand. It'd been decorated to look like one of the Red Rider's arenas—crimson wreaths, red petals, hot braziers and an auburn atmosphere. Curved tables surrounded the stage, piled high with food and gifts. Each row of tables was carved from the wood of the tree, rising upward and outward, like an amphitheater. Dario searched for Madi, but there were just too many people—hundreds at every table, hundreds on the balconies, hundreds on the promenade. His eyes ached, and his vision blurred.

The only thing he recognized was the hall's ornate architecture—curved windows, sweeping arches, giant columns.

Vetricus could be hiding anywhere.

Sand burned Dario's shins as two Minoans dragged him. He didn't have to act like a prisoner at all. He felt just like one. Dancers twirled around him, characters he recognized. A woman in a white headdress always represented the colony. She released fireflies, which represented cloudcrawlers. Dancers wore different colored clothes: dark gray rags were shadowmen. Colorful clothes were colonists. Glowing garments doused in glittering brews were Celestials. Dancers in twisted masks were Shades—the more distorted the mask, the more infamous the outlaw.

The dancer portraying Vetricus Perth kicked and thrashed across the stage, spitting sand into the air. He waved a wooden sword and wore a hideous costume—white like death, stained in hues of dormant gray. The thick cloak curled high over his shoulders, like a hunched vulture, covering all but a pale mask—the color of bone. The mask bore a scowling face which was stained in black scars. A loud *crack* echoed close to Dario's ear as two dancers sparred. One of them fell to the ground. The audience clapped hesitantly at first, then more loudly, as the moves became more elegant—and the mockery of Vetricus Perth more obvious.

Every dance had characters and a story. Dario was the thief, a villain at first, but then a victim, forgiven by the Red Rider. By the end of the dance, he was the hero, battling Vetricus. It was a tale of redemption, of the Rider's power against shadow. The dancer portraying Vetricus flopped to the ground as Dario's strength "grew" and their wooden weapons clapped.

Dario felt like a fool. This wasn't real combat. He'd stand no chance in a duel with a Perth, even if Constellation Lire was still shining. Even Illio would have struggled. Glyphlight mattered that much. It was the magical pool Celestials drew their power from, and Dario figured a Perth's pool was near limitless. Oracles watched from a booth high above, like puppeteers, tugging Celestials by the strings. The dance mocked Vetricus, surely, but Dario was beginning to think it mocked himself as well.

At least the crowd seemed to be on his side. They cheered as he parried a blow and struck the dancer on the arm. For a moment, he felt a spark of energy. As the applause surged, so did his heart. Company Lire was gone, but Dario was still a Celestial, and colony magic still affected him. Coalescence washed over him like wet clouds over parched land. There were thousands of colonists watching right now— cheering, shouting, chanting Dario's name. What if their Coalescence was enough to heal him? What if this really was the Rider's blessing?

Curious, Dario struck three quick blows. The dancer leapt and spun, flailing his arms. The crowd cheered, and energy surged—from them, to him. It was working! Dario felt colony magic feeding his mind and muscle. It was only temporary, but he only needed their magic long enough to survive Vetricus—that was, if he was even here.

The dancer recovered, and this time Dario kicked him. Strength stabled his legs and spine, and for once, the violent motion didn't cause a spasm. Chills crawled all across Dario's body, causing him to smile. He'd never had so many colonists cheer for him at once. He'd never felt this kind of strength.

If only it were real, he thought, letting his smile fade.

People laughed as the dancer tumbled through a pile of props, stored near the edge of the stage. But when he emerged, his movements slowed. He dropped his sword and looked at Dario as though he'd broken the rules of the dance. There were no rules to the dance, Dario had thought. They were wooden swords after all.

The dancer clutched his stomach, then collapsed to the ground. The crowd applauded, but Dario knew something was wrong. Blood stained the dancer's fingers, and soon, it spilled onto the white sand, turning it crimson. Dario backed away as the red stain spread. The dance stopped as some of the actors shrieked. The crowd gasped, and the victorious music faded. Dario quickly inspected the dull edge of his wooden staff. It was dry.

The audience gasped again as Vetricus Perth emerged from the edge of the stage. His battle cloak was identical to the dancer's in appearance, but incomparable in glory. The other dancers backed away quickly. The music stopped, and the hall fell so silent, Dario heard Vetricus' boots press into the sand.

The whole hall was stunned. Not even the nearest rangers moved. Maz Minoan and his Celestials waited. They knew what came next. Dario did, too. His hands sweat against the leather binding holding back the inferno. Meanwhile, the stage belonged to Vetricus. He moved slowly, smoothly, studying the scene with sharp brown eyes. He seemed to revel in all the whispers and shot a quick smirk toward the nearest tables. Dark blond hair fell evenly toward each ear. His chin was bare, but bolder than any of the Rider's best champions. Stepping slowly into the trap, he dragged a razor-sharp sword behind him, painting a bloody line across the sand.

He stopped next to the dancer who'd been portraying him—the dancer he'd just murdered—and angled his sword at the man's mask, removing it. Two eyes, glazed with death, peered upward. Blood leaked from the dancer's mouth.

"The next time you choose someone to dance as me, choose someone tall enough," he told those nearest.

The clarity of the Shade's voice surprised Dario. Calm and articulate, his words didn't stutter or scrape like other Shades, burdened by their curses. In fact, Vetricus moved with such a light step, it seemed he wasn't cursed at all.

Red mist rippled from the oracles' high table, and Guldarion's resounding voice came with it, deep and daunting. "Vetricus Perth . . . leave." The word *leave* echoed, over and over, fainter and fainter, deeper and deeper.

Vetricus wiped his sword clean with his cloak and spoke as if taunting a thug in an alley. "You speak of thieves and cowards. All the while, you serve one."

Guldarion's deep voice boomed again, like thunder. "You will find no means of escape here. Only doom, for you and your company."

Behind Vetricus, Maz Minoan and his Celestials moved into position. Mist gathered toward their fingertips as they poised their palms for Galecraft.

"My constellation already bears every curse the Gales can conjure," Vetricus replied, turning his back on the oracle. "Doom comes when I shed those curses atop their thrones."

The Shade stood so still, Dario could hardly see him breathe. He was more like an idea than a man—an anger, a rage, an uncontrollable force. Strands of mist sizzled through his hawkish garb, crackling like a calm fire. His flesh and hair were healthy, but his battle-cloak bore obvious signs of curses. The colors from his completed tasks had faded—or maybe they'd been revoked—and so his armor sparkled in dull shades of gray.

He was a grim figure, but lordly and unashamed beneath a thousand scowling faces. Dario tingled, head to foot. This was the kind of celestial he'd dreamed of becoming as a child—not evil, but powerful enough to defy the sky. He struggled to remind himself: *this man is a murderer. His company is evil.*

"The maps, please, Lire," Vetricus said with piercing attention. Even his eyes held a familiar rage. "I'd rather not kill you. This dance made a mockery of us both, and I think you know it."

He remained at a distance, resting his sword on his shoulder. All Dario had to do now was hand over the makeshift bomb, but he hesitated. The book's chain swayed as his mind churned. He couldn't stop thinking that he was about to betray someone very much like himself. The rumors about this man were violent, but who was to say they were true? Dario wondered if Constellation Perth had the power to heal him. Shades were covetous of their glyphlight, but if any company had the strength to graft a dying man, it was Company Perth. If only Dario had something useful to give in exchange, but the book of maps was useless now.

There was only one other option. Kill Vetricus and trust the Red Rider—the thought twisted miserably inside Dario's skull. After all his unanswered prayers, after all he'd written against them, why would the Gales rescue him now? But what was best for Madi? The last risk Dario took ended in disaster, an act he was desperate never to repeat. Madi trusted the Gales. Dario knew they'd never protect him, but if he completed this one task, maybe they'd protect her.

Dario separated the books dangling from his belt. The chain jangled as he hurled the stolen map-book toward Vetricus. The Shade sliced open the seal with his sword. As soon as he cracked the brewed binding open, a flash of light erupted. The force of the explosion threw Dario backward. Vetricus' cloak swirled amid the explosion, and his mask formed in a flash. The inferno enveloped the Shade's grim silhouette, and the last thing to disappear into the flames was that mask—a pale thing. To Dario's surprise, the mask wasn't dark and disfigured. Celestial masks were said to be a glimpse into their souls—because they only flashed when death tried to take them. Vetricus' mask was not cruel, nor was it calm. It wasn't frightening, or brave, or even defiant. No, the bone colored mask mirrored Dario's own heart, bearing expressions of sadness, uncertainty, and fear.

The cloud of smoke and flames engulfed him, and the whole hall fell quiet. Many people ran from their seats, but some stayed. They covered their mouths, waiting to see if the rumors were true. Could

Vetricus be killed? Would the brightest star slip from the sky? Warning bells echoed outside, but Maz Minoan and his Celestials ignored them, stepping closer to the explosion, weapons poised.

The smoke parted, and Vetricus emerged from the inferno, his cloak wreathed in flame. Company Minoan roared toward him, loosing arrows and brews. The arrows shattered against the shade's cloak, and the brews were licked up by the flames with a loud *hiss*.

For being the brightest celestial in the sky, the shade's fighting form was unimpressive. His footwork was athletic, but inexperienced, and Maz Minoan easily hooked his arm. Vetricus spun away, underestimating the length of Maz's spear. The blade caught him squarely in the chest, but nothing happened. His cloak was so strong, not even a shred of cloth came free. Meanwhile, Maz recoiled, holding his arm like he'd just struck a rock.

Lamptree rumbled violently, catapulting dishes onto the floor. Bowls of daylight brew fell from the windows, shattering and spilling glowing water. Outside, a fiery atmosphere engulfed the nearest branches. Smoke curled through the windows, and a chilling cry echoed—hundreds of people shouting, all at once.

Dark shapes rode atop the twilight clouds. One of the shapes flew straight toward the hall. Twigs and leaves rained downward, crackling against the object. Only as it careened across the promenade, could Dario see what it was—a faded cloudcrawler with dozens of Ashen clinging to its hull. Its oars shattered, spitting bits of the faded vessel across the stage—colorless wood and metal as bland as shadows.

The crashed vessel tore across the stage, splintering wooden beams and scattering sand. Maz dove one way, while Vetricus ran the other. A plume of debris billowed across the stage, and Dario lost sight of the Shade in the smoke.

Maz's voice thundered through the chaos. *"FIND HIM!"*

Shadowmen leapt from the craft and thundered across the stage, trampling discarded costumes and props. Two dozen Ashen, at least, climbed from the faded cloudcrawler. Without a word, they invaded the hall. Dishes crashed as they leapt over the tables, muddying the golden cloths with their gloomy boots. They caught a woman by the hair, yanking her across a table and dragging her toward the vessel. Her feet flailed, and bowls and plates flipped as she struggled, catapulting water and food into the air.

Maz barked orders, commanding half of his Celestials to protect the Ringed Hall, while he pursued Vetricus. He said nothing to Dario, who took it as a sign of freedom. He'd done his part for the Rider's task. Now it was time to find Madi. Colony magic tingled through his body—the effects of the dance—and he felt strong enough to run. He rushed for the nearest door, but Lamptree rumbled violently. His spine seized, as if a hand had reached deep inside him and tugged him away from the exit. He fell with a grunt.

His senses swirled. Colony magic was strong, but it wouldn't last forever, especially amid all this panic. Soon, the same magic that had spread color to this hall and strength to his body, would turn this place to Gloom. But for now, the pain in his body subsided, and his thoughts came more clearly. As he lay on his back, Dario thought of Illio. Whenever his spine seized in battle, Illio would be right there. He'd carve his way close. Then he'd grin and reach down—white blood spattering his gloves—and pull Dario to his feet.

But Illio wasn't here, and the only figure to come close was that of a tall shadowman. Its dark boot stomped against Dario's chest, pinning him to the ground. The creature loomed over him, reeking of Gloom. It was slender, slow, and calculated, staring silently. Its body was dark gray, without any features or flesh. But as the boot drove further into Dario's chest, the weight and smell were very real.

This was a person once, and all that remained of their clothes were bits of gloomy fabric, which brushed Dario's face. It was coarse and cold like ice, foul like rot. The shadowman reached down and grabbed him by the neck. A low hum vibrated from its face, along-side a tepid mist. As foreign as these creatures seemed, there was something disturbingly familiar about them. Dario imagined what this person's face once looked like. Now, it was gone—like a page blotted out by ink—forgotten, the same way he feared the stories in his journal might be.

The Ashen pushed a knife through Dario's decayed battle cloak. Dario resisted, and the black blade sawed against his mind, back and forth, until he couldn't resist it any longer. The dagger cut through his cloak and drew blood. He cried out for Illio, but he didn't answer. Someone else did!

Madi soared through the hall as quick as a hawk. The wings of her flier whistled as she landed and raked through the shadowman's arm with five of her long wings. A puff of white blood sprayed into the air. She kept one hand close to her body at all times, keeping *Flicker's* wings curled protectively around Aerial's pouch. The tightly closed sack clung close to Madi's body, and Dario could make out little more than the lumpy shape of his daughter.

Three Ashen studied Madi, tilting their heads toward her flier as if they recognized it. Circling silently for a moment, they decided the fight wasn't worth it and ran. Bits of debris rained from the top of the hall, and Madi dragged Dario beneath a table.

"Are you alright?" she asked.

"No, but I'm still breathing, thanks to you. Where were you?"

Madi removed her flying gloves and pressed her hands to Dario's cheeks. Her fingers were frigid with fright, and she'd been crying. Bits of ash stained her costume. Some of the embers still glowed, burning tiny holes into her sleeves. She wasn't wearing her flying bandana, so her dark hair hung wild over her face.

"I went home," she said. "I thought you were still there."

"Well, we're together now, and it's time we leave," he replied. "Are you ready?"

Madi nodded, but her uneasy expression seemed unconvinced. She applied pressure to Dario's wound, pushing against his exposed tendon. Dario groaned. His skin hissed. Bubbles formed at the wound, and blood frothed, but the strength of a lone glyph was not enough. He needed his constellation. He glanced toward the window, where twilight glowed through Lamptree's vast canopy. Stars sparkled above, but Constellation Lire was no longer there to help him.

CHAPTER 10: DARIO

Lamptree rumbled with a thousand panicked footsteps. Colonists fled the Ringed Hall in every direction, pouring out of holes in the tree like bees. Dario and Madi were among the last to emerge onto the promenade, where a large crowd moved at a sluggish pace, hampered by costumes and a thick air of confusion. Rangers bellowed commands, fighting to restore some semblance of order.

"Proceed directly to your homes! Barricade doors and windows! Do not come out unless the evacuation bell rings or we've signaled that your district is clear!"

A loud *CLANG* echoed over and over from one of Lamptree's highest towers. Moments ago, people were celebrating on this wooden promenade. Now, there was only coughing and crying and pushing. Dario squeezed Madi's hand tightly, preventing the crowd from sweeping either of them away. After just a few steps, however, he was too dizzy to continue. He stumbled toward one of the promenade's enormous columns and stabled himself. Madi helped him. Blood stained the wooden pillar where their hands touched—red fingers and palms.

Chaos spread upward, from the base of the tree, where the surrounding forest shivered with activity. Thousands of shadowmen and faded animals emerged from the swamp, funneling toward Lamptree's massive trunk—a maze of thorns, bridges, and gatehouses. But something wasn't right. Something stirred in Lamptree's lower districts, causing the circular streets to bubble with erratic movement, like a pot of simmering water. Dario peered downward into a furnace of activity. He saw glints of steel, flashes of Galecraft, puffs of mist. Shadowmen had already breached the walls, and Company Perth was helping them from the inside.

It was the only explanation. It would also explain who the shadowmen were signaling to in the swamp. Vetricus came to the Ringed Hall alone, which meant his company was likely sabotaging Lamptree's impregnable wall of barricades, towers, and catwalks. But why?

A loud *BOOM* echoed below. Flocks of birds scattered from Lamptree Forest, catching Aerial's attention. The birds flew upward, and a thousand wings clapped at the nervousness in the air. Aerial silently pointed. She'd already developed a love of flying things, a trait she'd no doubt inherited from her mother.

The surrounding countryside swayed behind a thin mist. Shapes emerged. Every gray hill and white road produced all manner of Ashen—faded humans and faded creatures. Black birds circled the hill overlooking the swamp, where Madi had gone hunting. The lone lantern there was broken, bleeding a faint trail of Gale into a vast sky of gray. A pack of wolves gathered right where Dario had rested. They looked as though they were howling, but no sound reached his ears. All Ashen were silent, it was rumored, because someone in the Gloom had stolen their voices—the White Whisperer.

Dario often wondered if she was real during treks through the Gloom. There were many tales of the Black Knight and the Gray Ghost—but was no hard evidence, nothing he felt comfortable recording as fact. Illio had believed the rumors anyway. He'd argued that dark gods were the cause of evil, not the Gales. But Dario saw no reason for such beings to exist. There was no life in the Gloom, but today, he had to admit there was intelligence.

Formations of shadowmen moved in perfect coordination, without a single word or whisper. Colorless clouds filled the sky beyond Lamptree's lanterns. Sounds echoed in from the Gloom—groans, gurgles, wails on a high wind. Dario tilted an ear, wondering if the grim echoes were just sounds or something more—someone trying to communicate.

A gust of wind swept over the promenade, snatching hats and costumes. The air thickened with unintelligible howls and hisses, causing many of the colonists to look around, eyes wide. Others covered their ears. A second *boom* echoed below, followed by a wave of chilling shouts—hundreds of colonists crying out at once. Gloom spread from their panicked voices. Dario saw it almost immediately, on the pillar where he'd been resting. With each fearful shout, the colorful promenade and all its decorations turned a shade more gray. The twilight atmosphere faded, giving way to white fog, black embankments, and gray hazes.

"Steel your minds!" a man shouted. "Our home only fades if our hopes do!"

Bridges and gates boomed below, and Lamptree's warning bell tolled like a panicked heartbeat. Dario took Madi's hand, fighting a limp as he led her back into the stream of people. The loud clomp of boots softened as they moved through the promenade gate—from the wooden walkway onto the Mossroad.

Here, crowds converged from every branch, forming a long stam-pede upward. Chaos clamored from every alley, churning through the Mossroad like water through rapids. Bodies tumbled, and the force of people drove Dario and Madi apart, knocking them both to the ground. Someone's knee collided with his chin, cracking against his broken jaw. Pain sliced through his skull, ear to ear. He gasped for air and fought to his feet, crawling over the bodies of several others who'd been trampled.

The stampede carried Dario upward. Hints of gray stained the grassy road, as though the colonists carried a disease with them. In fact, they DID carry a disease. It was the cost of their magic. Every shadowman attacking this place was a colonist once, and Dario suddenly feared for his wife. This shadowy contagion existed in her body as well, waiting for moments like this to seize her mind. Dario listened for Madi or Aerial's cries, but every sound churned in the chaos. Bells clanged. A thousand voices blended together in one panicked chorus, spreading from Lamptree's trunk all the way to its top. Madi was impossible to spot amid all the costumes and masks, and she would have been just a small body among hundreds.

The stream of colonists rushed like water, and with every passing second, Dario feared his wife had drowned somewhere beneath it all. Had she flown? Unlikely. Twigs and leaves rained down. Kites burned, ribbons fell from their lines, and balloons popped as shadowmen wearing fliers darted overhead. Some colonists with fliers had tried to fly away, but faded birds swarmed them, chasing them back to the streets. Rangers leapt across the rooftops, manning towers and firing shrapnel from turrets. White blood spattered the leaves, and an Ashen flier toppled into the crowded street, its black wings sprawled.

"Madi!" Dario called, but his voice was lost amid a thousand others.

An arm curled around his elbow, and Dario turned to see his wife stepping through the crowd. She shielded Aerial's pouch, grimacing and smeared with sweat. "I'm here!" she replied. There was a rawness in her tone—a fatigue behind her eyes—something more than exhaustion. Her face bore the same limp gaze that Illio's bore in battle just minutes before he died. It was a terrifying realization, and Dario immediately pulled her close.

A horse and wagon careened up the Mossroad, out of control. The crowd surged, severing his grip on Madi's hand. She shrieked and disappeared in the flood of people. Dario fought his way toward her, roaring as bodies bumped into him—battering his broken body. Madi was so small, he worried she'd been swept away, but somehow, she'd held her footing amid the tide of people. Men much larger than her tumbled around her as she tilted her body, protecting Aerial.

"This way!" she shouted, tugging Dario.

She led him into an alley, away from the core of the tree. The sound of the stampede slowly faded, and eventually, Dario heard his own boots clapping the boardwalk. Here, tenement balconies overlooked a quiet avenue, laden with a thin fog and the scent of smoldering wood. Embers rained down from the branch above, drifting softly overhead. A metal gate squealed as Madi unlocked it. Here, colonists crept quietly through the twilight, making for their homes. Doors clicked shut, curtains were drawn. Some entryways were already barricaded.

One of Lamptree's giant lanterns dangled from the branch above, spilling color onto the secluded avenue. It *clicked* and *sputtered*, fighting to keep the atmosphere colorful. Nevertheless, Gloom appeared on the walls, rising from deep within the woodwork—like water beneath ice. Festival pumpkins turned gray, distorting their decorated faces.

Aerial whimpered as the alley grew dark. Madi comforted her and scampered up a tenement staircase. Dario's exhausted breaths echoed in an unlit entryway, where Madi fumbled with some keys. After a series of jingles, the door to a small apartment opened. Dario stood in the dark entryway, panting, while Madi strode throughout the unlit house, stirring the stale air. She seemed to know her way around.

After a hiss and a crackle, a bright orange glow flickered in a fireplace, illuminating a small living area. The room was completely barren, and the windows were already boarded. A few brown travel sacks hung on the wall. Madi snatched one of them and slung it over her shoulder. It jingled with vials. Dario stepped out of her way as she walked quickly to the other side of the room and pried up one of the floorboards.

"This was my old apartment," she said as she lifted a crossbow from the hiding place, along with another small bag. She sheathed the weapon inside Flicker's spine with a perfect *click*.

Dario took a seat on the hearth, stretching his leg toward the fire. His spine curled his shoulders into a hunch, but he was too exhausted to fight it. He'd thought the fire would soothe his aching skin, but it only made it worse. The heat nipped at the nerves on one side of his body, while his other half was freezing.

"Do all toymakers keep a secret apartment with weapons and supplies?"

Firelight danced across Madi's body as she opened a hidden panel and pulled out a small lantern. "I was a ranger before I was a toymaker, remember?"

Dario nodded while she quickly gathered supplies. There was no hesitation. No thinking. It was like she'd practiced this a hundred times. There was always something new to learn about Madi, some hidden talent. That *was* something he loved about her, but today, he wasn't in the mood for any more surprises.

He peeked through one of the boarded windows. Outside, footsteps pounded the wooden boardwalk, and he discerned some people running through the unlit street. One of them screamed. The shapes scattered. Aerial flinched. More footsteps followed, and shadows darted across the boarded windows of the apartment. Dario backed away, uncertain of who the shadows belonged to.

"If we stay here too long, we're going to get trapped," he warned.

"I know," Madi replied. "If the core wall is breached, the bells will signal an evacuation."

"Not if the Ashen took control of your bell-tower," Dario glanced through the boarded window once more, toward the distant *clang* of bells. A green mist obscured the tower, but it should have changed signals a long time ago. "I think they've already breached the core."

Meanwhile, Madi muttered prayers. "Please, Pilgrim. Help our rangers. Please protect Elduko. Help Vishi. Watch after my friends. Help them retake the bell-tower."

Hearing his wife pray had always irked Dario, but today it infuriated him. The Pilgrim didn't care about what happened to these people. All the Gales were the same, and all they wanted right now was to keep their secrets safe.

"Time to go," he said, interrupting her.

Madi opened her eyes, but remained seated. She caressed Aerial, wiping dirt from her face and grooming her little coat. "What was the name of the man in your book—the kind ferryman you wrote about?"

A heaviness in her voice insisted he stay, and Dario heeded her tone. "Totep," he answered, sitting beside her. "I met him when the Bleakbend fell. He could have been the first to leave, but he stayed to help refugees cross. He'd wave his red cap and wish everyone who crossed a swift journey. Illio and I went back one day, but we found his ferry burned."

Dario thumbed for the page in his book, but the dim light made it difficult. Inked faces gazed back at him from every page—portraits of people he'd met during his travels. Their stoic expressions flickered in the firelight, haunting him a little. Most of them were dead now, and he feared he could be, too, very soon. The book weighed heavy on his lap, and with each turned page, he felt a growing responsibility. He carried the last account of these people's lives, and he couldn't look at their pained expressions anymore and do nothing. People had to know who was responsible for prolonging this war.

"Totep sounds like my friend Elduko," Madi whispered. "People like him don't leave anyone behind. He's down there right now, in the chaos, and he won't climb up here until he's ferried every man, woman, and child to a lift first."

"He'd have made a good celestial," Dario replied. "The companies need more men like him."

"They do," Madi agreed. "He looked after us—me and Vishi."

"Her husband is a Celestial too, isn't he?" Dario asked.

"Yes. In Company Marrow."

Dario snorted and shook his head. "Figures."

"What's that supposed to mean?" Madi asked.

"You ever think Elduko might just be an oracle's informant?"

"Why would you say that?"

"Does this Elduko fellow look after anyone who isn't somehow related to a Celestial?

Madi scowled. "Yes! He does. EVERYONE. He's just like that."

Dario threw up his hands. "Okay. Sorry. My paranoia was kicking in. Had it since I fell into this world. Big bump on the head."

A resounding *gong* echoed from the top of Lamptree. Then again. Over and over. A different pattern than before. The shrill tremor sent shivers up Dario's spine. The sound stoked the siege, and he heard a flurry of movement outside.

"Oh god! That's it! The evacuation bell." Madi rose and rushed to the pantry, muttering. "Pilgrim, please! Spare this place." After fastening Aerial's pouch, she touched one of the shelves, and the pantry wall gave way to a narrow passage. "In here," she said, taking a candle from the wall and lighting it. "This will take us to the old pier lift."

The tunnel was dank and empty, except for barrels of cider. It curled upward, through what Dario guessed was the tenement block. Madi's candle hissed in the stale air, and Dario was quickly feeling claustrophobic. The chiseled passage twisted and turned through wood of varying shades of brown. After a few minutes, it was silent again, except for a gentle hiss, like steam rising from a kettle.

"What's that sound?" Dario asked.

Madi angled her candle toward the passage wall. "Water and nutrients flowing up the tree."

Dario touched the beige bark. It was smooth, warm, and vibrating with life. Who could have carved a passage so perfectly? It seemed impossible for any tool. Only Galecraft was this precise.

When they reached the lift, they found it closed, and judging by the rust and vines, it hadn't been operational for a long time. Madi lay on her back, tinkering with a series of gears near the lift's base. Meanwhile, Dario paced the old room with Aerial in his arms. Old benches lined the walls, covered by moss. Cobwebs dangled from the sealed door, and spiders crawled across them. Madi brushed a bug from her sleeve and tried turning one of the cogs. Despite her grunt, the gears did not move.

Boots rumbled in the tenements surrounding them, followed by a series of shrieks. Dario stared at the wall. He could only imagine what was happening outside this hidden passage—shadowmen invading homes—people fighting for their lives, screaming, clawing at every piece of furniture to keep from being dragged away. A faint mist lifted from the wall with a *snap* and a *spark*. Dario had learned that this meant Gloom had become very active. He'd seen it before, like with the woman in Brittlehorn. He tasted a sourness in the air—the taste of a psychic magic he didn't fully understand. He continued to stare at the wall, which seemed to absorb each and every disturbing sound.

Boots rumbled up and down staircases. Bodies tumbled. There were groans and shrieks. Broken furniture. Slammed doors. Shattered windows. Dario couldn't peel his eyes from the wall. The awful noises echoed, sweeping back and forth like invisible paintbrushes. With each stroke, the wall turned a darker shade of gray. White wisps wriggled across the wood, and in its center, an amorphous black puddle formed.

I'm not the only one writing a book. The Gloom is writing its own. It uses our world for its canvas, smearing an illegible horror of stained ink. I'd hoped never to see the day my own wife's colony fell. As we make our escape, I feel like—

"DARIO!" Madi peered out from beneath the lift. "Stop writing! Can't you hear our daughter?"

Dario blinked his eyes and stepped away from the gloomy wall, only then realizing that Aerial was sobbing. Her warm tears trickled down his hand as he tried to comfort her. Meanwhile, Madi tapped a bent gear with the butt of her crossbow. It pinged and then sizzled when she poured a vial of blue and brown brew onto the contraption.

"Try the gate now," she said, rising.

Dario turned a cold bronze crank, and the door to the lift squealed open. Bats burst from the compartment, screeching and flapping their wings. They flew down the tunnel, and Dario stepped tentatively onto the platform. "This doesn't look safe."

Madi took Aerial and placed her back inside her pouch. "It's safer than running the Mossroad."

The lift wobbled as they stepped inside. The door rattled shut, and Madi pulled a lever. Nothing happened. But once she'd kicked it, cogs churned and gears ground against each other. Slowly, the platform rumbled upward, and the sounds of the siege grew louder and louder. The shaft shook, and dust trickled from the small compartment's ceiling.

"Madi, I'm sorry," Dario said. "Company Perth wouldn't have come here if not for me. I didn't know."

Guilt gnawed at every organ in his body. Ever since his theft went awry, his collapsed conscience was squeezing stress into every breath. Leading Vetricus here was an accident, but still, the cost kept multiplying. People were dying, but this time, it wasn't because of the Gales' schemes. It was because of his own.

"We all make mistakes," Madi said. She stared at a long crack in the wall, watching the destruction outside. She remained quiet afterward, as though saying a final farewell to her home.

The lift lurched to a stop, and something scratched and beat against the door. Madi reached into her bag and tossed Dario a long knife. As she opened the gate, a giant mosquito with long black legs squeezed through the crack. Guarding Aerial with one hand, she fired her crossbow with the other. A sharp bolt pierced the faded creature amid a puff of white. Madi backed away from its wriggling body, which kept *buzzing* until Dario stabbed it.

Together, they forced the doors of the lift open and stepped onto the piers. Gale was still vibrant here, thanks to four giant lanterns hanging from the branches above. Leaves fell from Lamptree's heights, many of them smoldering. Night shrouded the horizon now, which was nothing more than a black curtain, surrounding Lamptree—highlighting how alone each colony truly was.

Hundreds of people emerged from the Mossroad. The poor carried candles. The wealthy carried cups of daylight brew. Some carried clothing. Others carried pets and valuables. But as they stepped from Lamptree's pier onto a large cloudcrawler, they all became refugees. Out there in the wild, they'd soon learn that the only thing that mattered was the fuel in their lanterns.

A cloudcrawler disembarked. Its long oars glinted atop a thick current of green and purple cloud. This particular vessel had a mast and sails, meaning it could also navigate the sea as well as sky—so long as the clouds met the water. But most of Lamptree's fleet seemed to be without mast or sail. Dario didn't know much about sky travel, but most of these cloudcrawlers looked like merchant craft—with tall lookout towers for spotting pirates, and cranes for moving supplies. They each had several decks, and many cabins. He always underestimated a cloudcrawler's size until he was up close—they were floating fortresses. Everyone on the pier seemed to agree. He spied an eagerness in their step and heard a nervous mutter in the air. How many cloudcrawlers were there? And would there be room for everyone?

A second cloudcrawler departed. Its forward oars moved first, followed by the middle, and then the rear oars. Up and down, they gripped the cloud and pulled in a staggered timing, like the legs of a caterpillar. The crowd moved slowly, funneling onto the narrow piers. Dario counted fewer than a dozen ships now. When a third ship released its lines, some colonists mobbed the pier, clambering desperately onto the departing vessel. As the ship ascended, dozens of people dangled from its hull, holding on for their lives.

Madi pointed to a much smaller cloudcrawler, an elegant and speedy-looking vessel with a blue hull. "There," she said. "Captain Tibet's ship."

Despite its size, colonists had squeezed onto the deck, and many more peered from the cabin windows, watching the chaos unfold. Panic trickled onto the piers, stirred by the sound of siege rising below. Dario tried to find a shortcut. He stepped onto an outer catwalk, but quickly spotted a dozen shadowmen racing upward. The wooden scaffold thundered beneath their weight. Dario bristled with fear as their footsteps hammered louder and louder.

"Not that way," he warned those who'd followed.

Panic trickled onto the piers. Bells clamored. Whistles blew. Crewmen barked orders, but the people didn't listen. More and more piled onto each ship, wherever they could find space. Colonists swarmed branches above, trying to climb down onto the decks. Branches creaked and groaned, and one of the smaller limbs started to crack. Leaves rained onto Dario's head as he pushed through the crowd, spotting shadowmen on the pier.

Shouts turned to screams, and soon, the whole branch shook with terror. People scattered, but Madi quickly took Dario by the hand. "Get ready. We're going to fly across," she told him. "Ready? Now!"

She leapt into the air and pulled toward the cloudcrawler, reaching the deck in three quick strokes, but Dario hesitated. His fingers felt stiff inside his gloves, and he eyed a giant black bug—an enormous beetle of some kind, as large as a keg of ale. Its wings vibrated violently, and arrows simply bounced off of its bony carapace. Rangers manned the branch's defenses, firing a net from a ballista. Wood churned and gears rattled as they spun their turret. Only after they'd brought the beetle down in a net did Dario risk flying across the gap, which had grown far larger.

Smoke filled the sky. Flames licked the streets below, where Gale and Gloom blurred. Dario immediately regretted looking down. His whole body tingled, and he couldn't remember anything Madi had taught him. Instead, he stood paralyzed. The air felt freezing, like he was standing at the bitter edge of the world. He couldn't bring himself to jump—until Madi called to him.

She coached him across the gap, reminding him how to read the currents. "Keep your eyes on me," she told him. He obeyed, and it helped. The chaotic background blurred away, leaving only Madi and Aerial. He watched her every gesture and listened to every word until he was on the bulwark next to her, clinging to her.

"Good job," she said, smiling proudly.

"Did anything almost eat me?"

"No, you did great!" she answered, but her body hardly matched her optimistic tone. She limped along the edge of the bulwark, clutching her chest. People squeezed across the whole of the deck, and Dario struggled to follow her. "Axis!" Madi called to a crewman. "Where's the captain?"

"Ms. Amriel! You made it! Hope you don't mind a few extra

passengers. It will take us longer to row to The Brink, but I'm sure you understand."

"We're not going to The Brink," Madi replied. "Where's the captain?"

"Not going?" The crewman looked confused, and so was Dario. "We've already charted the course."

Madi ignored him, repeating the question. "Where is she?"

"Below. Problem with the cargo, I think. Some unmarked kegs. Captain thought she smelled black-light brew. They're dumping it just in—"

An explosion rocked the deck. Wood blasted from the side of the ship amid a flash of light and the unmistakable smell of black-light brews. Dario's ears rang, and every sound blended together. Only one thought came to mind, swirling a sea of splinters: this ship had been sabotaged.

The cloudcrawler listed, and everyone clambered for something to hold on to. The vessel had already been under way, and now it couldn't stop. It slid too far across a purple current. Cloud gave way to open air, and the crawler tipped, echoing with a hundred frightened shouts. The ship's oars sparkled and then slid sideways, rumbling as they ripped free of their portholes. Wind whistled against wood—a sound Dario had never imagined could be so terrifying. He leaned over Madi and Aerial, gripping the bulwark as tightly as he could.

Branches thwacked and crackled. Sweat stained his eyes, so as they fell, all he saw of Lamptree was a smear of Gale and Gloom, billowing smoke. The vessel tipped, but not so severely. Dario could just barely see the top of Lamptree's forest before they crashed. There was a jarring stop, a gush of splinters and cracking of limbs, and then the overwhelming scent of pine and sap.

Dario and Madi crawled from the wreckage together. The top deck was spared from the brunt of the crash, but the decks below were an entanglement of shattered wood and broken bones. At times, he felt like he was sliding down a ramp of corpses and tattered clothing. Colonists stumbled from the toppled cloudcrawler, coughing and gasping. Only a few people had lanterns, which clicked loudly amid the fading atmosphere.

Embers rained from Lamptree, illuminating the forest floor. Shadowmen crept from the trees, pouncing on survivors as they fled. A young boy called out as a shadowman dragged him by the arm. Blood stained his costume. The boy beat against his captor's slender body, but there was little he could do to free himself. His legs went limp with fear, and he clutched something against his chest—one of Madi's toys. He closed his eyes and took a deep breath as he was dragged deeper into the Gloom.

White fog enveloped the forest, curling through the trees and releasing a haunting howl. Faded wolves raced from the woodline, hackles high. Jaws snapped, and people fell to the ground, screaming as they were tugged away. The Ashen hunted relentlessly, not giving a moment's rest. Dario and Madi gasped, side by side, as they ran. The ground rumbled, catching Dario off-balance. Pain shot through his legs, and he tumbled. Madi stopped to help, but then she froze—horrified.

Lamptree shimmered and glowed. There was a subtle hiss, then a loud crackle, like something enormous had bit into the bark of the tree. Madi squeezed Dario's hand, tighter and tighter, but she did not lift him. Instead, she sank to her knees, mouth aghast, eyes wide. Branches groaned and creaked. Leaves rained down. Lamptree grew brighter and brighter, until it kindled like a white flame and exploded.

The forest and sky roared, turning Dario's courage cold. Orange and white light melted the twilight atmosphere, scattering the clouds. Debris crackled amid a plume of smoke, and Dario covered his head, peeking out from beneath his arm. First, he was curious.

Then, disturbed. Lamptree didn't topple or fall. It simply vanished. How? There wasn't enough black-light brew in the world to pulverize such a massive construction, not all at once.

Slowly, Dario sat up, wrapping his arms around Madi, who sobbed into his chest, moaning and gasping. Her small body shook against his weakened spine, and he fought very hard not to spasm. He had to be strong for her now, as bits of her home rained down. It was an unforgettable image—the smoky skeleton of a once colossal tree—and Dario felt more helpless than ever. Even the shadowmen stopped and stared in silent awe of the destruction. Who could do such a powerful thing? And why? What kind of magic could turn a tree to dust?

The force of the explosion rocked the forest, bending the pines. Wood and ash scattered in every direction. But much of the tree had turned to mist, as though someone had culled it. The mist swirled, gathered, and then suddenly changed direction. Madi gasped and covered Aerial's pouch. Dario stood up and shielded his family, arms outstretched, but the cloud ignored his Galecraft, passing around him. The gust of wind curled around Dario's clothes, scraping and scratching at the withering remnants of his battle cloak, but when the gust struck Madi, she grunted and slumped to the ground.

The forest grew very quiet after that, except for the wails of those who'd just watched their home disappear. Dario knelt over Madi's body, dizzy and gasping for breath. The stars seemed to swirl overhead, and the cries of nearby colonists echoed in his ears. He wiped her hair from her eyes and touched her lips to feel for a breath. Nothing.

Dario searched his wife for wounds, his fingers trembling. Fearful thoughts popped into his head, one after the other, like shears of lightning illuminating the Gloom. Would she die? How could he go on alone? If she lived, would she fade? She loved Lamptree with all her heart, and someone had just extinguished it. Was it Vetricus?

Was it the Gales? An avalanche of thoughts burned Dario's brain, but they all stopped as he inspected his wife's skin.

It was perfect. No wounds. No faded flesh. Nothing. Her tattered costume smoldered, but the only wound he found was a recent cut on Madi's neck, where a large splinter had lodged itself. He expected blood, but none came out—only a familiar sound, which pricked his ears.

Her flesh hissed faintly, and skin closed up around the wound, pushing the splinter out. Dario's face tightened as concern turned into confusion. His heart burned, heating his entire body, cooking him in a sensation he hadn't felt since the day he'd learned that his parents hurled him into this world. Madi had lied, and though this sensation felt like betrayal, Dario wasn't angry. He was embarrassed. She was a Celestial? How could he have missed this? Why wouldn't she have told him? Had she not trusted him? These were many of the same questions he'd asked himself about his parents, and yet, he could not blame her the way he blamed them . . . not yet at least.

Dario's pulse pounded, and sweat trickled down his tingling palms. This revelation settled like a boulder on his mind, and it kept growing, an idea too large for his head. Doubt gnawed at him, spreading from ear to ear—doubt in himself, in his wife. But after a deep breath and a brief look at Madi's unconscious form, the sensation diminished, and he realized:

We've come this far because of love. Because of trust. He knelt over her, touching her cold cheek, wishing her eyes would open, sparkling. *She has her weaknesses, but deceit is not one of them. She would have told me if I needed to know. And if she had,* he decided, *I would have loved her all the same.*

Aerial wriggled in her pouch, squawking. Dario leaned close, hush-ing her as he removed the pouch from Madi's chest. He moaned in pain, adjusting the straps as he placed it over his shoulders. The weight of his daughter settled heavily upon his heart. *My wife is a Celestial.* He looked skyward, as if he could pick her glyph out from a hundred glowing constellations. *Whatever she's running from, I'll protect her from it.*

He touched Madi's heart, and when he felt a pulse, he dragged her toward cover. Everything seemed intent on stopping him—the branches, the soggy ground, his own depleted muscles. His family was falling apart in his hands, and he lacked the strength to hold them together. All he could feel was his starlight, peeling from the sky.

Branches rustled as colonists fled blindly through the brush. The twilight atmosphere—Madi's favorite sky—turned gloomy and gray, filling the forest with a thick fog. Soon it was difficult to tell colonists and shadowmen apart. A wolf leapt toward Madi's body, but Dario cracked it across the skull with a rock, cursing the creature as it stumbled away. The Gloom released a resonating roar, which echoed amid each colorless cloud. The ground shook, and trees bent as some giant creature appeared.

It stood on two legs, veiled in a thin fog. Dario reeled back when the shadowy creature stepped into view—a faded bear, bigger than he'd ever seen before. He picked up a large branch and stood over Madi's body. The bear raised a dark paw, but as it lunged for Dario, another bearish shape lumbered through the fog, tackling the animal.

It was a celestial, in a thick cloak—burly like Wardan's cloak used to be. He stood head-to-head with the faded creature, grunting and grappling it. Whoever this stranger was, he was huge! He carried an iron club, which bit into the bear's skull with a loud *crack*. Pine needles whisked into the air as the celestial fought to keep his footing. He caught the bear by the arm and hurled it into a felled tree, impaling it. Faded blood sprayed into the air—a puff of white—spattering the man's cloak, which was black and green. He peered at Dario through a mess of long braided hair, as black as the bear's fur. He had a wild beard too, which covered every part of his face that his dangling braids didn't. As Dario studied him, he decided this celestial looked more like a bear than the actual bear had.

He knelt over Madi's body, covering her face with his enormous palm. "Bandico!" he called out in a voice far more gentle than Dario had imagined. "I found her!"

A second celestial rode through the trees on a black horse. He carried a bow and wore a very large hat. His eyes glowed beneath the hat's floppy brim as he angled his bow and released an arrow into a shadowman's neck. When he saw Madi, he dismounted and opened his hand. Mist curled across the forest floor, gathering into the shape of a large wagon. Glyphs chimed overhead as the Galecraft formed.

"Get inside," the archer said. He looked at Dario, beckoning him. The wagon's rear hatch fell to the ground with a dull *thud*. "Let's go, Lire. You'll be safe with us."

"How do you know me?"

"I know Madi," the celestial answered. "I helped her a while back. She helped me recently. Now, I'm helping her again." The archer's big hat hid all but a subtle grin. "I'll be expecting her to help me again, you know, so we can keep this fun little pattern going."

The confidence in the celestial's voice calmed Dario's nerves. With his family safe, his muscles relaxed, but his pain returned—and so did his thoughts. *Why didn't Madi tell me? Was she trying to keep me safe? Or maybe Aerial?* The archer beckoned, but his voice was little more than a muffled echo now. Dario limped toward the wagon, but it seemed to move away from him with every step.

He stumbled. His battle-cloak was so heavy now. There was hardly anything left to it, but it felt like a thick blanket soaked with water. The cloak hissed and peeled, fading to a mist as it fell to the forest floor. A panic crept into his heart—a sharp fear he'd never felt before.

Breaths came slowly now, and he had to rip them from the air. His body vibrated with every loud wheeze. His jaw slowly opened, and an intense nausea hit him, like he was about to throw up his soul. He groaned loudly and then gagged. Pain pierced his bowels, and he imagined his heart tumbling through his intestines. Was this it? Was it happening? Celestials die without a constellation, but he never thought it would actually happen to him. He'd complete his task of redemption or outsmart the sky somehow. He'd never lost hope in that—until now—and it caused a chilling fear.

Graft me, please! he tried to scream to his celestial rescuers, but nothing came from his lips but a muffled moan.

He fell to his knees, and a searing pain burned inside his body, shriveling every organ to dust. Crying out, he thrust his gaze toward the sky. Stars swirled overhead, and a gushing sound filled his mind—like the rush of wind, or the trill of a thousand trumpets. He sensed his glyph, sinking from its place in the sky. The pain was worse than he'd ever felt, stinging every nerve—as though someone peeled his spirit from his flesh. He grit his teeth and cried out again, desperately focusing on his glyphlight. It dangled above, and he felt himself dangling with it—dangling over death. Tears filled his eyes as he imagined the abyss. He wasn't ready to die.

He squeezed Aerial, as if his daughter's tiny hand could somehow keep him in this world. Starlight shattered, and death arrived like a needle, pricking Dario's skin and plucking his last bit of starlight from the sky. He clutched Aerial tight, begging it to stop. She was his most important task, and he was seconds away from failing it. He fought for as long as he could, but then there was nothing left—no strength, no energy, no life.

He stared dully at the stars. Blood trickled from his nose onto his lips. He released Aerial's pouch, letting his arms drop to his sides.

The sky turned dark. The trees and forest disappeared. Then, he fell. He fell and fell and fell through a black sky. Glyph-light surrounded him, sparking, sizzling, and hissing. He tried to touch it, catch it, and hold on to it somehow, but his arms refused to move.

The light flickered, his heart stopped beating, and everything went black.

CHAPTER 11: MADI

Madi dreamed of birds singing on Lamptree's branches. She kept her eyes closed, expecting to wake up at any moment, but she didn't. Lamptree's Mossroad warmed her cheek, filling her nose with a fresh forest fragrance. Her fingers snaked through the street's soft texture as she sat up and looked around. Birds chirped and trilled, cooing gently as they gathered amidst the leaves, eyeing her. A squirrel scampered across the bark and paused, sniffing toward Madi.

The atmosphere was dark and quiet, so very, very quiet. Wood creaked, leaves rustled, creatures scampered across the branches—these were sounds she'd rarely heard amid all the bustle. Was this really a dream? Or was this death? Madi took a deep breath, deciding the air was too tranquil to be death. But if this was a dream, she'd never experienced one like this before. Her senses were too keen. Every sight, scent, and sound told her she was somewhere back on Lamptree, but that couldn't be. Lamptree had vanished in a flash of fire and cloud.

She curled a hand through her hair, which was full of crumbled leaves. The last thing she remembered was Dario shielding her from the blast. She touched her chest, where the explosion had punched into her body. There was no wound, only an aching pain, like a piece of her heart had been uprooted. Was Dario hurt? Where was Aerial's pouch? Had he taken it? Fear stalked the borders of her brain, but she didn't panic. Something about this place prevented her from doing so.

Perhaps it was the peacefulness in the air. More likely, it was something stronger—a magic, muddling her mind.

"Hello?" Madi asked, rising.

Birds scattered as she walked to a nearby lift. The door was sealed, and gears groaned stubbornly when she tried pushing the lever. She returned to the Mossroad, calling out louder, "HELLO?"

Her voice echoed. The path was completely empty. Wandering to the edge of the branch, she peered downward. The streets below were dark, humming with insects and tree frogs. What part of Lamptree was this? She wasn't sure she'd ever climbed this high. Thousands of lightning bugs clung to the branches here, illuminating the Mossroad and the boardwalks weaving across it. She looked for a working lift, but each time she strayed from the Mossroad, the fireflies stopped shining. She'd no choice but to follow their light, and soon, she recognized where she was—at the steps of the Bottle Catcher!

Vishi worked in this tower. A wooden staircase weaved through the leaves, and Madi ascended, carefully stepping around candles lighting the path. Flames flickered, leaves rustled, and birdsong echoed in the tranquil atmosphere. The Bottle Catcher was one of Lamptree's highest structures—a domed tower, built between two curling branches. Green vines crawled up the walls, curling around a series of nets and chutes designed to catch flying bottles.

Madi tread carefully across the high boardwalk, studying the horizon. There was not a strand of yellow cloud anywhere. No daylight. No constellations either. Other than the fireflies she'd been following, the only other light came from falling stars, which glided slowly from one side of the sky to the other. She'd never seen stars move like this, and so she stared, mesmerized by the sad march of light. Everything here was so calm, but also so lonely. Lamptree was empty it seemed, and yet, chills squeezed her skin. Someone was watching.

The door to the Bottle Catcher was open, and she walked inside, into the thick scent of parchment and polished glass. Hundreds of shelves lined the dome, filled with scrolled up messages and empty bottles. Wooden chutes curled throughout the room, funneling toward several wooden desks, each equipped with a ladder that moved along the walls. One of these desks belonged to Vishi, and Madi guessed it was the one with the bowl of dried apricots on it. So, this was where all of the flying bottles thrown to Lamptree were collected. Sometimes, bottles got stuck on other parts of the tree, where children would throw sticks at them.

"Hello, is anyone here?" she asked, rubbing the chills from her arms.

A door creaked open, revealing an ornate office. Madi peeked inside. Plush cushions adorned leather chairs, which overlooked a wood-fire stove, much like the one in Governor Kipps' office. Stacked documents lined a giant polished desk with an extraordinarily large chair. Madi rolled her eyes when she saw that the office even had a dumbwaiter. Apparently, whoever worked at this desk was too important to fix their own lunch.

Madi brushed her fingers atop some loose sheets of parchment and sat down. The leather chair crunched as she studied a series of gears connected to a small lever. The lever was clearly meant for the dumbwaiter, but Madi knew contraptions like this, and the cogs beneath the desk made no sense. There were too many, and they were in the wrong order—unless this lever opened more than one door.

She experimented by pushing and pulling—letting the pressure rest against her palm. Sometimes, unlocking a hidden passage was like opening a safe, and she'd found many secret doors during her time exploring Lamptree. The lever clicked, and sure enough, a panel opened behind the desk. Madi stepped inside, holding her breath as she was struck by the overwhelming scent of burnt paper.

Scorch marks stained a small staircase. Chutes lined the walls, much like the other room, but these chutes were charred and led to a small furnace. Broken glass covered the floor, crunching beneath Madi's boots. The small chamber gave Madi a foul feeling, like something very wrong was being done here. Some of the bottles had fallen, and bits of parchment had survived the flames. She sorted through the debris, piecing together some fragmented reports:

—*Thousands of shadowmen crossed the Scars yesterday. Hundreds of thousands—*

—*Front line failing. The colonies in the west are falling faster than the companies can evacuate—*

—*Ms. Marshall, just writing to let you know I've been granted an exclusive interview with famed celestial, Harriet Cowl. Full story to follow—*

—*Companies are in full retreat. I'm afraid we are losing this war, Governor. I'm trying to find a way home. Full story inside – Nubi Oshen, Archivist, 65.35 Lamptree time.*

Ash stained Madi's hands as she sorted through the soot. From all across the Gloom, Lamptree archivists documented dire news concerning the war with the Ashen. Their pens bore traces of panic. Blood stained some of the pages, and a few bottles contained pictures of the destruction, just like Dario had drawn in his book.

Many of these messages were addressed to Miriam Marshall, curator of the Whole Story, which meant someone was intercepting these stories before they could be printed. News around town had been that the war was a stalemate, and the companies were even having success in some places. Ms. Marshall and Governor Kipps had a loud history of opposing opinions on what news should be announced to the colony. It didn't surprise Madi in the slightest that Lorani Kipps would destroy news like this in order to keep people from fading, but she couldn't judge the governor, not after all the secrets she'd kept from Dario.

He'd discovered many of them, of course, but she'd thrown in enough lies to keep even him from piecing her past together. A cold breeze passed through the Bottle Catcher, and a glint of light caught her attention. Something floated toward her. It bobbed through the night sky atop a strand of purple cloud—another flying bottle!

Nets swung into position, snatching the glass capsule and sending it clattering down the chute. Madi caught it, uncorked it, and unfurled a fresh piece of parchment:

Lorani Kipps is guilty of hiding from this war, but so are you, Madi Amriel. Stop hiding from your tasks and start searching for your home.

Fear pounced on Madi's heart for the first time in this dream. She glanced across the empty branch. Lamptree's silence, which had been so tranquil, now haunted her. The streets were empty, but now she was sure someone was watching her. Had they sent this bottle? And why was its message making her so angry?

"This WAS my home!" she shouted, hurling the bottle into the furnace.

Lamptree rumbled violently. Candles hissed. Fireflies scattered. The shelves began to shake, and hundreds of bottles fell, crashing onto the floor all around Madi. She covered her head and woke up from her dream with a shout.

Madi sat up straight, breathing heavily. Pale light peeked through the porthole of a small cabin. At first, she thought she was on a cloud-crawler, but when she felt an earthy rumble and heard wheels churning outside, she realized she was in one of her least favorite places in the world—the stuffy interior of a wagon.

She clutched her chest, searching for Aerial, but her daughter's pouch wasn't there, just a pool of sweat. Beneath her tangled and muddied blankets, a wooden bed creaked. Frost glazed the porthole, and a howling wind sliced through a thick fog outside. Light from the window illuminated a strange texture on the wagon's wall. Madi squinted at the wood, letting her fingers run across tiny lines. There were words, chiseled into the wood, and she grew cold when she read some of them: *Liar . . . Murderer . . . We trusted you.*

The cabin walls buzzed, warm against her fingertips. Wood cut from a forest would have been cool to the touch, meaning this material was a product of the mind—Galecraft. This was a Celestial's wagon, but certainly not Dario's.

Madi pulled herself to a seat, searching for her husband. She glanced toward each dark corner of the long cabin, which was sparsely furnished. Locked chests lined the far wall, and judging by the scarred floorboards, they'd been dragged there recently. The near wall contained a pair of bunks, partially concealed by a tattered gray curtain. At the front of the cabin, two alcoves had been carved into the bulwark. Each contained a porthole, which spilled starlight across even more locked chests. Whoever crafted this wagon had trust issues.

Madi found herself in the second alcove. Her bed, she'd realized, was actually a desk. She'd discovered this after her knee kept touching a wooden stand, containing a magnifying glass. Several other small instruments surrounded a metal device, which looked like a printing press. Locked boxes, bundles of parchment, the smell of brewed ink, the printing press—this was a forger's wagon. And if the cryptic curses scrawled across the walls were any indication, this thief was being haunted by a ghost. Madi stood up, smiling as she tasted a bit of luck for once. There was only one haunted forger she knew of!

"Bandico?" she whispered.

As soon as the name left her lips, a hiss slid across the walls—a whisper, a faint answer. Bits of mist drifted across the floor, sparking gently. Madi tiptoed around it, toward the top-hatch's ladder, feeling the air turn humid. Magic wagons were an extension of a Celestial's mind after all, and she'd feel much safer topside, in the open air.

Next to the ladder, three other survivors huddled around a lantern on the floor. The lantern hummed, releasing a steady stream of Gale into the cabin, refreshing the air somewhat. She squinted, unable to make out much more than three swaying bodies. But as she stepped toward the candlelight, she recognized one of them.

Panima was a dancer—one of the older girls who performed after the toymaker's act. Madi had never spoken to the girl, but she'd seen her during rehearsals. Earlier today, she'd caught Panima crying backstage before the first performance—probably because she didn't get the role she'd wanted. Tears slid down her face, even now, as she angled her shallow gaze toward the lantern's colorful glow.

Next to her, a young boy sat with Aerial in his lap, dangling a toy soldier above her outstretched arms. Candlelight danced against the boy's body, revealing bright blond hair and a toy sword tied to his belt. His clothes were foreign to Madi—an assorted collection of mismatching garbs. She didn't think this child was from Lamptree, but she did recognize the wooden soldier in his hands. It was one of the festival toys she'd built. Madi quickly gathered her daughter, thanking the boy, but Aerial squirmed and reached for the toy. Little clattering objects always captivated her attention.

"He can see us," the boy warned, glancing nervously toward the walls.

"He can hear us, too," Panima whispered without taking her eyes from the lantern. Dark brown hair curled around her shoulder, spilling into her hands as she spun several strands around her finger.

"There are two of them," mumbled the third survivor.

He was by far the eldest, a young man, she realized. His face was coated by a thick layer of dust and mud, and he glared at a piece of rock in his hands. All Madi could clearly see were his eyes—and they were angry. He wore a mining coat, which was too worn to be a costume. No, this boy hadn't been at the festival. He'd been in the Roots, digging for lantern fuel. The rock in his hand was a small piece of unrefined crissle—stone as black as coal, but as smooth as glass. Tiny white dots glimmered on the surface. Once brewed, that rock would fuel a lantern.

"Two Celestials?" Madi asked.

When the young man nodded, she practically leapt over him with joy. She scampered up the ladder toward the top-hatch, nearly bumping Aerial's head along the way. Bandico and Dario were topside together, and oh what a pair those two rebels would make. This plan might actually work! She opened the hatch, shielding her eyes from a gloomy fog, filled with white dayclouds. Then, she sighed. There wasn't a hint of color in the sky, nor in the pines, nor on the road ahead.

A pair of tall Celestials stood beside a lantern, muttering softly. Their grim silhouettes swayed in stark contrast to each other. Madi quickly recognized Bandico's droopy black hat. He slouched against the bulwark, spindly like a scarecrow. The other celestial was enormous. He wore a battle cloak, hairy with mist and thick, like a buffalo's hide. This stranger's presence unnerved her, not because of anything he did, but because he was supposed to be her husband.

"Where's Dario?" Madi asked, gripping Bandico's sleeves. She'd never been so happy to see his big hat and cryptic grin.

He touched his hat hesitantly. The change in posture turned Madi's whole body hot with trepidation. Her head throbbed, and it seemed to take an eternity for him to answer.

"He didn't survive the forest. His glyph fell."

Madi slumped to her knees, gasping when she saw a canvas covering a body near the rear of the deck. She couldn't breathe. Her mouth hung open, but all that her lungs could suck in was sadness.

She clung desperately to other possibilities: Bandico was mistaken, Dario had slipped away in the chaos, the body beneath the tarp was someone else's. But her breath hitched when Bandico finished with a quiet finality.

"There was nothing we could do. I'm sorry."

Wind howled through the pines, battering Madi's body as she crawled across the deck, eyes fixed to the covered body, refusing to believe it was him. A light rain pattered the canvas, which she couldn't bring herself to untie.

"Help her, Bear," Bandico told his friend.

Madi's throat was still so tight, she could barely breathe, let alone protest. The giant Celestial lumbered over, his braids swaying as he loomed. He untied the top of the canvas, which crinkled in the wind. Madi steeled her gaze, preparing to see Dario's face, praying to see someone else's. When she opened her eyes, she saw Dario's short black hair fluttering in the wind, his eyes closed beneath them. His pale skin glowed gold with fallen glyphlight, like tiny stars seeping into his flesh.

It's him, Madi had to remind herself. It wasn't some prop for a dance. Not another dream. It was Dario. Her love.

She nodded and groaned. She'd prepared to see him, but now that she had, reality was slow to catch up. She knelt, paralyzed. The bottom of her heart opened up, like a torn net. Years of joyful memories and emotions poured out, along with all her dreams of the future. She touched his cheek, feeling a dryness in her heart and a sickness in her stomach. His eyelashes fluttered, but she knew it was just the wind. Dario was dead. Their escape had failed.

She pressed her forehead to the cold canvas covering him and sobbed. What was the point in running anymore? The man she wanted to live with—out of trouble and time—was gone. Emptiness enveloped her heart, and it showed no sign of stopping. She was certain the hole would soon devour her very soul. For what felt like a very long time, she stared at Dario's face, watching his glyphlight slowly fade. It could have been seconds, minutes, or hours. She didn't know.

Madi's arms were now slick with mist. She clung to Dario, shivering, but his body provided no warmth. Aerial fussed in her pouch, her nose and feet freezing. Madi wiped her eyes and looked around for something warm. When Bandico's friend noticed, he tilted his palms upward, crafting a blanket of mist, which slowly hardened into a blanket of fur. The Galecraft vibrated against her skin and heat settled atop her shoulders, melting over her entire body like a hug.

"Thank you," she said softly.

"Bereket," the man replied, even softer still. His gentle voice and smile were warmer than the blanket. "But you can call me Bear. I'm Bandico's brother."

Hearing this comforted Madi more than she ever thought it could. She was glad that Bandico and his brother were here. They seemed accustomed to suffering, which made sense since they were Shades. This comforted her, too. Dario was a Shade at heart—always blaming the Gales in secret.

Bereket stood watch inside a ballista nest, arms crossed. He looked nothing like his brother. Bandico had trimmed hair, while Bereket had wild braids. Bandico kept his eyes hidden beneath his hat, while Bereket's eyes peeked out from his long black hair like a curious cub. They burned like a fire—contemplative and comforting—and the longer he looked back at Madi, the more she realized that these brothers knew what she was going through. They'd seen pain like this before.

Bandico's wagon was black, and its decks were as bleak as its cabin—matching Madi's mood. Barren garden plots clung to the bridge connecting the mid-deck and the driver's box. Beehives glistened gold against the rear bulwark, but she didn't see any bees. There was an empty hammock beneath a canopy, and the ropes there were laden with frost. A pool of black water dripped from the bed, and Madi wondered if she was staring at Bandico's ghost.

Bandico stood in his driver's box, looking at a distant hill through a telescope.

"Those look like Veeren banners," he said.

Bereket angled the ballista toward the sound of shrieking artillery. Madi's neck ached as she lifted it for the first time in a long time. On the far hill, celestial ordnance whistled through the fog. Battle wagons formed a defensive line as shadowmen ascended the hill. The sky lit with Galecraft. Catapults *clapped*, releasing a barrage of exploding rocks. Madi collapsed onto Dario's chest, releasing a long moan. This was the war she'd been hiding from—the war that Dario had been documenting. The war that took his life. The war they'd both wanted to spare Aerial from.

A sky-quake rumbled overhead, smearing starlight across the sky, where a thousand tasks sparkled like riddles. Bandico and Bereket both looked skyward, with similar expressions of concern.

"We need to double back," Bandico said.

"Should we leave the Lamptree kids with Company Veeren?" Bereket asked.

Bandico's face soured. "I don't know," he said, scratching his bare chin. He looked through his telescope again and studied the distant battle. "The Veerens are tending the tide. It's not like the kids will be any safer with them, and if they see us, they'll try to arrest us."

Bandico lifted the reins. The wagon changed directions, and Madi cradled Dario's head in her lap to keep it from bumping the deck. Trees gave way to an open field, where ash and bits of clothing were still drifting downward. How long ago had Lamptree exploded? Madi still couldn't believe it was gone. All that remained beneath the gloomy sky was a crater, surrounded by rubble and felled trees. Hundreds of

Ashen corpses scattered the devastation, thrown outward by the blast, impaled on the fractured treeline.

The sound of battle echoed in the distance—exploding rocks and hissing Galecraft. Veeren wagons moved along the distant ridge, but there was little movement here amidst the debris. Bandico's wagon rounded the large pit left behind by Lamptree, churning atop splintered wood and shattered glass. A few hours ago, Gale was spreading from this stronghold, amid music and applause. Now, it was nothing more than a gray graveyard. Debris filled the remains of the Roots district—pieces of treehouses, boardwalks, and palisades. The Waterlog's dam appeared to have broken, flooding the streets far below. Madi looked away from the deep chasm, hands tingling.

She'd been so certain that Dario was going to survive, that she would be the one to die. Had he sacrificed himself for her somehow? The thought made her stomach tighten into an even more gnarled knot. What if she'd told him who she really was? What if she'd told him that she'd climbed a city of escape just a year before they'd met?

He'd never have stolen that map, she decided, weeping again. *Constellation Lire would still be shining. Dario would still be alive.*

The *CRACK* of artillery echoed throughout the Trade Gap. Ashen cavalry darted across the tops of the ridges, matched by celestial lancers. Bereket eyed them from the ballista nest, and Bandico tucked his wagon closer to the shadows. They each scanned the horizon. Exiled Shades never lived long, but Madi met Bandico three years ago, meaning these brothers had survived some time like this. What was their trick? How was Bandico's glyph surviving both curses *and* a ghost? Or perhaps it wasn't, thus the squealing sound of starlight above.

It was a horrible sound, like creaking metal, or like a sick star, gasping for life—long sad gasps—air struggling through a shriveled lung. Madi couldn't stop looking skyward, searching for the source of the disturbing sound. What bothered her the most, however, was that it seemed to be following them.

Gale still colored the eastern Trade Gap, where the wind howled and large lanterns swayed atop tall posts. Madi spotted the tail end of a caravan fleeing the valley. Here, Bandico's wagon caught up to damaged colony wagons and those who'd paused to bury the dead before the green fields turned gray. Colonists stood, solemnly swaying in the wind as they lowered loved ones of all ages into the earth—children, adults, and the elderly. There were rumors: burying a body in healthy earth eased one's passage to the afterlife. But bury a loved one in the Gloom, and they'd rise a shadowman.

"Would you like to bury Dario here?" Bandico asked. "These might be the last colorful fields we see for a while."

Madi gripped the canvas covering her husband, unwilling to part with him. "I don't know," she whimpered.

"We have glass, so he can afford a ghost to carry him to the shores of the underworld. We also have food we can spare, so he won't be hungry."

Madi remembered when she considered celestial customs romantic, but now they made her heart ache. Grave goods were an important part of company tradition. Food, clothing, weapons—these things were said to ensure easy passage to the underworld, but now, Madi just wanted to be free from magic, and she hoped that death had finally freed Dario from it as well.

"I don't think any of that matters," she whispered, clutching Dario's journal. Its chain rattled, tugging against his belt as she pulled it. He'd dreamed of delivering these stories to the world above, and if he couldn't do it, then she would.

"It matters," Bandico replied, pointing to the journal. "That book is Galecraft. If you don't bury it with him, it will fade forever. Is that what you want?"

No, it wasn't. But the thought of Dario's absence made it seem inevitable. If only there was a way she could copy his work, but there wouldn't be time. The binding cooled in her hands and ink faded from the pages. Madi had watched many celestial burials, but never like this. Never for someone she would miss so much. The rituals, the lantern, the trinkets—it all felt meaningless, as if she were packing for a hard journey Dario might never take. A hard journey she didn't want him to take. A hard journey he didn't deserve to suffer through.

"We don't know where death leads," she said. "Sleep is like death. And I've heard that our dreams are glimpses into the world our death leads to. When we die, we wake up in the world above."

Bandico grinned. "That sounds like the start of an extremely lucrative con for people who don't want to accept what death is. I'm surprised I haven't heard of it."

"I'm NOT making it up," Madi replied. "It's a real theory. People are talking about it."

"Rich people."

"Scholars," Madi clarified.

"*Rich* scholars," Bandico said, mirroring her confidence.

She shrugged, too exhausted to defend herself. Her body slumped over Dario's, and as her back ached, all she could think of was Dario's poor spine. Maybe there was an underworld, but it wasn't where the dead were. If it was, wouldn't hundreds of thousands of people have climbed back by now? If the dead were down there, more than just rumors would have surfaced by now . . . unless . . . the Ashen were preventing them from surfacing.

Madi grimaced and shook her head until the terrible thought was gone. Dario was somewhere peaceful now—a safe place, out of time and trouble—walking through a land of perfect Gale. His spine wasn't damaged anymore, and he'd be there waiting when Madi and Aerial finally climbed out of this world.

Bandico snapped the reins and huffed. "Fine, take your chances. Don't bury him," he muttered while turning away.

Take my chances? What does he mean by that, Madi wondered. Did he really believe that Dario was going to magically wake up somewhere underground? If so, how was dumping his corpse into a hole going to help? She groaned. Stress squeezed at her stomach, and every thought to enter her mind flooded the folds of her brain like a bitter bog.

She curled her fingers through Dario's hair, which was cold and wet with mist. Storm clouds brewed overhead—combinations of blue, purple, and gold—spitting rain on his body. Thunder cracked and warbled. Lightning flashed, flickering in a colored atmosphere stained with Gloom. Dario looked so different with this much hair. He'd always worn it closely shaven. As Madi combed it, bits of fallen glyphlight stuck to her fingers—warm strands of starlight. She tried to cling to them, those tender pieces of her husband's soul, but the wind carried them away.

"Madi, I know this is hard, but my brother knows a thing or two more than most about the underworld," Bereket said. The ballista nest squeaked as he leaned against it. "I *really* think you should listen to him. He just wants to help."

Madi pressed her lips together, fists clenched. She hated this. Every part of it. But the logic was there, hanging in the cold air between them. What if she was wrong? What if Dario needed this? She exhaled shakily, staring down at his lifeless form. Glyphlight was beginning to fade from his body now, and it was said, without that light, a Celestial might never find their way to the afterlife. Bandico's warning spun inside her head: why risk it?

"Alright," she said, glancing up at the brothers. "Will you help me?"

They agreed, and Bandico guided the wagon to a flat patch of grass which she'd pointed out. The hill here was vibrant green with yellow and white flowers. A lantern fizzed nearby, coloring the surroundings, even amid a fast approaching storm. Thunder rolled overhead as the brothers tilted their palms, crafted shovels, and dug a hole. The Lamptree children watched through the porthole, flinching as sparks of lightning crawled across an entanglement of blue and purple cloud.

Tears welled in Madi's eyes, and she watched like a statue, feeling nothing but cold and rain and the weight of misery. She clutched Aerial, cupping her daughter's warm head, but nothing eased the pain. Shovels sliced through the earth, scraping and sloshing. Stab after stab, dirt scattered into the air. The sloppy sound was like a soul being churned to mush—her soul. As Dario's grave opened, all of her dreams and desires poured inside.

Bandico and Bereket lowered him into the hole. Dirt sprinkled across his skin, which still glowed. Rain licked his eyelashes as though he were trying to open them. Madi wept loudly, realizing he'd died alone. She wasn't even there to help him, and she couldn't even re-member the last words they'd spoken together. After what his parents had done to him, the last thing he'd deserved was to be alone again.

The brothers carefully curled Nightfly's arms around Dario's body, and ensured his book was fastened to his belt. They placed a smooth shard of glass in his palm to buy a weapon in the afterlife. Then, they filled a bag with provisions and tucked it against Dario's shoulder. This was all according to custom, but Madi didn't believe any of it mattered. As Bereket filled the hole, Bandico took a small lantern from his wagon and tied it around Dario's neck.

"What's that for?" Madi asked, shaking her head.

"So he can breathe in the underworld," the Shade replied.

"He won't need it."

Bandico tightened the knot and squinted up at her, grimacing as lightning flashed above. "Just in case," he said, climbing from the grave.

CHAPTER 12: MADI

Dario's grave shrank into the distance. A gloomy fog enveloped his final resting place, and a similarly rancid haze clouded Madi's heart. All of her motivation and excitement for escape lay at the bottom of a hole, six feet deep. She pressed a hand to her face, hiding from the stars. Every breath trembled as it rolled over her swollen throat, and a sense of submission washed over her. She didn't want to feel this way—to bow before the sky that'd stolen her husband—but she was too exhausted to fight it, and if she didn't submit, Aerial would be next.

Smoke rose from Lamptree Forest, signaling to the surrounding countryside that something terrible had just happened. Refugees emerged from fields and homesteads, a few at first, then many—long lines of people, laden with possessions. Madi had seen so many refugees in recent months, but she never imagined becoming one of them.

Bundled in coats and blankets, they carried all manner of packs and bags. Children walked behind their parents, eyes dazed. The littlest of them kept looking back at Lamptree Forest, wondering why the colony wasn't there anymore. For all of their short lives, Lamptree had towered bravely against the gloomy horizon, spreading Gale, but now the only thing keeping this valley colorful was a perimeter of large lanterns swaying atop rickety posts. Madi knew it was only a matter of time before shadowmen reached them.

Pink clouds whistled over the hillside, scattering brown leaves across the valley, but most of the clouds today were orange. The crisp

autumn atmosphere curled across rows of crops, feeding them nutrients. Farmers paused bitterly beside their fields, a short, shivering
farewell to a harvest they'd never reap.

The callous wind swept across soggy stretches of soil, seeped with
rain—just like the lonely sensation swirling around Madi's heart,
seeped with tears. This weather was good for the crops, but miserable for travel. Families squished through thick globs of mud. Carts
creaked, burdened with more than they could carry. Boots, hooves,
and wheels struggled through the soil, adding to the audible tension
to the air. Time was not on their side.

Artillery thundered in the distance as Company Veeren held off
the tide. One of their wagons perched on a high hill, launching rocks
from a catapult. Stones hissed through the air toward Lamptree Forest,
where they exploded. Some refugees prayed for the Celestials, but
most remained silent. They were busy with another battle—the one
raging in their own minds. Colorful scarves blustered in the wind, but
as the colonists lost hope, Gloom stained their clothes. With every
slip and stumble, the grass became more gray. With every shed tear,
the healthy atmosphere faded.

A colony wagon rumbled nearby, its inhabitants hunched and
hopeless. Gloom appeared on the bulwark, swirling within the wood,
white splotches and black smears. The patterns repeatedly formed
and faded, reminding Madi of clouds condensing inside a brewing
vat. Shades of white, black, and gray spilled across the wagon like ink
in water, spreading into disturbing shapes—some like blinking eyes,
others like open mouths. Colonists covered their ears. Others tore
off their clothes, which bore colorless patterns just like the wagon.
They gathered close to their lantern, eyes fixed to its colorful aura.

Madi scanned the valley, disturbed. Something swirled inside
these mists—something alive. Gods in the Gloom? They felt more
real than ever right now. Fog veiled the hillside, shimmering with

splotches of black and gray and swirls of white. They fizzled and faded, like bubbles in a mug of cider. Were they random shapes? Or was someone communicating? Chills crawled across Madi's skin as she imagined a woman watching her from beyond the lanterns' healthy atmospheres—the White Whisperer.

Was she tormenting these people? Tempting them to fade? Was her magic keeping Madi alive? Each question filled her with a feeling of frailty. Celestial powers paled in comparison to such malicious magic. Finally, Madi understood Dario's frustration—his fear. He'd said it all along, yet she hadn't believed it until now: not all gods were good.

This revelation made Madi feel like a bug who'd only just realized she'd been walking beneath the shadow of an enormous boot. Birds cackled. Explosions cracked. Every sound made her shrink, and she longed for Dario's arms around her, but he was gone. She groaned and loosened Aerial's pouch. It pressed against her stomach, which was nauseous and unsettled. The pain was so sharp, she was certain she'd broken a rib.

Aerial squirmed and coughed, reminding Madi of her most recent task, and the cost of failure. Beads of sweat dappled her daughter's face, despite the chill in the air. "You're burning up," Madi said, brushing her daughter's head. She cradled her and stood, quickly studying the valley. Which way were they traveling? Toward Carmine Keep, or away?

"Where are you taking us?" she asked Bandico.

"That way," he answered, nodding forward. His hat covered most of his face, and he slouched in his driver's seat. She would have thought he was asleep if not for his habit of tapping his fingertips together. "Why? You got somewhere in mind?"

"I've been tasked to reach the Carmine Keep," she replied.

Aerial shivered in her arms, her tiny fingers curled and quivering. This was too much. Lamptree. Dario. And now Aerial. Madi glanced skyward, praying to the Pilgrim for mercy. She felt her chest ripping open, like some toy. Madi Amriel was just a creation, after all—*I'm a puppet with three cogs: Dario, Lamptree, and Aerial.* All the gears and springs she'd stuffed into her chest to forge a free life were bending and breaking.

Bandico adjusted the brim of his black hat. "Let me guess. The people you're running from told you to go to Carmine, and they cursed your kid to ensure you do."

Madi fumbled with the straps of Aerial's pouch. Something was caught, but she was too furious to take the time to fix it. She just tugged, harder and harder, angrier and angrier. There'd been no time to think about her task or what it might mean for her or Aerial. Was it a trick, like Bandico's tone suggested? Would the oracles honor their promise to lift Aerial's curse? What if they'd died on Lamptree?

After another strong tug, the pouch ripped and slid out from Madi's grip. Bandico leaned from his driver's box as it happened, reaching out and catching Aerial, allowing Madi to see his eyes for the first time. Beneath his hat's wide shadow, Bandico's eyes glowed with a gentle white hue. Aerial stopped crying, clearly captivated by the two pearly pupils.

"Rough day, kid?" Bandico asked her, grinning. "I know how that can be."

As he studied Aerial, Madi got a second glimpse at his eyes. Black scars stretched across each cornea. His eyes sizzled as daylight struck them, but he held the gaze, squinting at Aerial for some time. What could he be thinking about? He looked as though he might cry, but no tears came, only a wisp of yellow mist, which curled across his eyelash and disappeared.

"I can help you," he said, pulling his hat over his eyes. "But first, tell me who's hunting you, and why."

"The oracles."

"Whose?"

"The Rider's . . . and the Pilgrim's. Maybe all of them. I don't know." Madi was too overwhelmed to think, and she was so sick of these kinds of questions. "I don't know what they want! I don't know what's happening to me! I don't—"

Madi froze when she saw a faint figure standing behind Bandico. A woman. She was there, but not there—a distant haze of color and flesh. The figure stood with her hands stuffed into the pockets of a long crimson coat. His ghost!

She stuttered as the ghost faded in and out of her sight. Slowly, she pulled Aerial out of Bandico's grip. His eyes, which had seemed so fanciful, now seemed so dark and foreign.

"I don't even know who you are," she said, stepping away. She'd only met this man three times in her life. She didn't even know his company name.

"Do you need to know?" he asked. "When I helped you, all I asked for was your name and the new name you wanted."

"She doesn't trust you," came a woman's voice. The shrill whisper slithered across the wagon, startling everyone. It was more like a wind than a voice, and it rose from the deck, pricking Madi's skin with fright. *"And she shouldn't."*

Bandico quickly fumbled for a vial from his belt. Gritting his teeth, he took a swig of purple brew, coughing afterward. As he drank, the whisper faded. He continued coughing and eventually leaned over the bulwark and vomited. Blood came with it.

"Easy, or you'll overdose again," his brother said, coming over and holding his shoulder.

Bandico wore two brews on his belt, a small orange vial and a larger purple one. Next to them, he wore a sand clock, which was connected to a string of timing beads. After a final sip of brew, he flipped the clock and the beads reset with a spin and a *clatter*. He shoved his brother away with a scowl, and then shot a guilt-stained glance toward Madi.

The hatch to the cabin opened, and two of the three Lamptree kids poked their heads topside. It was Panima and the younger boy. "Did you hear that?" the boy asked.

Bandico removed his hat and ran a hand over his neatly shaved hair. His eyes sizzled in the daylight until he put his hat back on and tugged it downward.

"Where are you taking these children?" Madi asked, standing in front of them. Goodwill was rarer than ghosts in the Gloom, and shadowmen weren't the only monsters trying to snatch people. These men were Shades after all. They killed to survive and they took dark tasks to keep their glyphs from falling.

Bandico burped, grimaced, and held his stomach. "Give me a second," he replied, bending over while holding his knees. "You know, it's rude to question a man while he's vomiting."

"Where are you taking them?"

"I don't know. Anywhere. As long as it's somewhere I feel like going." Bandico spat over the bulwark. After a few deep breaths, he sat down. "Relax, Madi, we didn't kidnap them. We saved their lives, except for Corlan here, who thought he could stow away on a Celestial's wagon."

The little blond boy gripped Madi's hand and peered toward the Shade. "I didn't know you could see through the walls. You scared me!"

"I scared you? You scared me!" Bandico said, mirroring the boy's fear, hiding behind his giant brother. "There I was sitting in my driver's box daydreaming, and all of a sudden a half-naked child crawls inside my head. You can have whatever you want, just never do that to me again."

The children smiled, even Panima. Healthy shades of Gale shimmered through her costume. Maybe they trusted the brothers, but Madi was still unsure. Bandico seemed to come along whenever she was desperate, and she was beginning to think it was no coincidence.

"Is your ghost dangerous?" she asked.

Bandico spat overboard, wiped his mouth, and muttered, "Not to you."

"Then why do you have those?" she asked, pointing forward.

"Horses? They pull the wagon."

"Not them. You know what I'm talking about."

A string of brews jingled from the horses' harnesses. A faint noise echoed from the vials, like a distant wail. The sound had her spine straight as a needle. The glass was filled with an orange liquid, and the pattern inside gave its purpose away—a sparkling double-helix, surrounded by a halo. Only someone trying to keep a ghost away carried such a rare and expensive defense.

Bandico stared at the glass brews for several seconds, his lips some-where between a smirk and a scowl. "They're warding brews. They help keep Raven away," he answered. "I hung them there for you and the kids. I don't want her appearing or speaking to you, but sometimes she slips through."

"Are you afraid she'll tell us something you don't want us to hear?" Madi asked.

"No, it's because she leeches my life faster when she manifests," Bandico revealed. He checked the sand clock on his belt before tucking it into the folds of his over-sized black coat. "Every breath I take, Raven steals half of it. Brews can only slow the process."

"Will she steal our breath?" Corlan asked. His blue eyes peered out from his blond hair, studying the haunted wagon. A black fence curled around the bulwark, and Madi thought the deck looked more like a coffin than a carriage. Dario always said, "A glimpse inside a celestial wagon was a glimpse into their mind."

"No, kid, just mine," Bandico replied. "It's why we're looking for a city of escape."

Madi crossed her arms. "And you think I know where one is."

"I *know* you know where one is," he answered. "I know exactly who you are. Look, we'll offer you a deal: you tell us where the city of escape is, and we'll take you wherever you want to go."

"I don't remember exactly, but I can tell you roughly where I think it is."

"Then I'll take you roughly to where I think the Carmine Keep is," Bandico replied sarcastically. "Look, you know where that city is. Just take us there, and I promise, we'll get you to the top safely."

Madi cradled Aerial as she cried. "That's a promise you can't keep. I won't risk my daughter. Not for you. Not for myself."

"And the oracles know that!" Bandico replied. "You really think the Red Rider will lift your daughter's curse? Bow to one curse and they add another until your lips touch their feet. If you go to Carmine, you're going to die there."

Madi imagined herself curling up next to Dario in his grave. She was already so tired, and somehow dying inside the Carmine Keep seemed better than dying in search of a city of escape.

"If it means my daughter lives, then so be it."

"But she won't live," Bandico answered. "She'll be grafted into a company. She'll serve the Red Rider. She'll fight in this war, and one day, she'll die."

Madi shook her head, unwilling to entertain the thought. Instead, she skipped straight to a happy ending. "Then she'll be with her parents."

"Death is not the peace you're looking for, Madi," Bandico said sternly. "I don't know where you're getting your idea of an afterlife from, but the underworld is real. The dead are down there, and you need to do everything you can to keep from falling."

"Ease off, Bee," Bereket grunted. "We just buried her man."

"And if she isn't careful, we'll bury her, too!" he replied. "Look, you were on the right track, Madi, when you thought of forging a new name. When I met you beneath Sembetra's tower, you had the eyes of someone who'd do anything to survive. You have to keep thinking that way, otherwise you won't escape this world, and neither will your kid. The underworld is real, and the tide is rising. The only way we survive is by climbing."

"How do you know?" Madi asked.

Bandico glanced across the valley, squinting toward the caravan of refugees. Dead leaves tumbled across his hat, and in the chilled autumn atmosphere, his pale eyes turned callous. "Our father died when I was six. Bereket was four," he said, catching one of the leaves and crumbling it in his glove. "I'll never forget seeing his glyphlight fall. I thought he was invincible. Two years went by. Then, on my eighth birthday, there was a knock at the door. I thought it was a Celestial, coming to take me into their company. It was my year to be grafted. But when we opened the door, it was our father. He'd returned from the dead."

The Lamptree kids looked to Madi as if to ask if it were really true. She didn't know. She'd heard of people who knew people, who'd been told by people, that someone who'd died was seen walking the streets of their old town. Dario had even interviewed a man who'd said he'd climbed back into this world using nothing but a rope and a shovel. He was mad, and even Dario had to admit it. Madi felt her expression slide skeptically, but Bandico quickly defended himself.

"My father DIED, Madi. I *saw* it happen. Then, a few years later, he walked into our kitchen and ate three loaves of bread."

"It's true," Bereket said, leaning his giant arms atop the ballista, where a sharp bolt glinted from its groove. "But he wasn't the same after."

"He said we weren't safe," Bandico said, nodding with conviction. "He told us the Ashen tide was rising, and the only way to survive was to climb. That very same day, a company came for me and Bear, but we ran. Our father said he'd found a city of escape. We were halfway there when the oracles cursed our mother. She got sick. Her constellation stopped healing her. She had to rest a lot, and when we reached the Long Dark, she could barely travel. That's when our father left."

"The Long Dark. I've heard about that place," Corlan said. He'd wandered closer and closer to the story. Now, he sat near the brothers' black boots. "Is it true dayclouds don't rise there very often?"

"They *never* rise," Bandico answered.

The wagon was quiet for a time, rumbling atop rough terrain. Pale trees passed by until Corlan asked softly, "What happened to your mom?"

"She died."

"Is she your ghost?"

Bandico slouched deeper into his driver's box. "No."

He was done talking, but Corlan's curiosity was clearly growing. He paced the deck silently for a time, staring at the Shade, enamored. "How did you get—"

"He's haunted because of me, Corlan," Bereket interrupted, collecting the boy and steering him away from his brother. "I got caught in the Long Dark, and he rescued me. He rescued a lot of people. Don't ever hitch a ride there. It's a very bad place. None of us would have escaped without him."

The man's arms were almost the same size as the boy's torso, and he whisked the boy away like a little bird.

"I've heard of it," Corlan said, smiling as he became weightless. "You needed help escaping? You're HUGE."

"He was still my big brother, just like I'll be yours. You're one of us now, right? Right. Now, go on. Get below."

Bereket corralled the kids, guiding them below. When they were alone again, Bandico said to Madi, "Look, all we're asking is for you to mark down for us where you found one of the cities of escape. In return, we'll ensure you reach the Carmine Keep safely so the oracles can dissect your organs."

Madi curled her arms against her chest, uncertain. Burn marks covered her clothes, and all of her tools had fallen from her costumes' pockets. "You really think that's what they'll do to me?"

"No idea. But do you honestly think they're going to bring you in, feed you, bathe you, lift your daughter's curse, and then apologize for wasting your time? They're after something, Madi, and your life is going to get worse until they get it."

The warning sent a shiver down Madi's legs, which she rubbed with her hands. It sounded like something Sembetra would say. *Don't go back!* She heard Dario's voice, too. *Climb! Save our daughter before it's too late.* But could Madi find the city of escape in time? She didn't know where it was, and she'd no idea how long it'd take for her to find it again. Furthermore, the last thing she felt like doing right now was searching for a way back into her past.

"I need time to think. I'm sorry," she answered.

"Understandable," Bandico said. He faced forward and propped his feet atop the bulwark. "Take all the time you need. I charge by the hour."

Madi moved to the rear of the wagon, to a secluded nook behind Bereket's ballista nest. The warm hull of the wagon buzzed, which meant Bandico could still sense her if he wanted to, but at least she felt more alone here.

Red and yellow leaves drifted from a thin birch grove. Compared to Lamptree Forest, these trees looked very lonely. All around, refugees trudged through the quiet wood, churning the blanket of dead leaves. Aerial slept lightly, twisting and turning and whimpering in her pouch. What was there to consider? There was no good outcome now that Dario was gone. *Wherever we go, he won't be with us.*

Birds fled Lamptree Forest. Its pines shrank into the distance, tipped in black, beneath a completely gloomy sky. Hundreds of geese flew in long formations. Their squawks echoed, like a warning for all to flee the impending shadow. Smaller birds squabbled in the nearby trees, and Madi picked out a familiar sound—a low wail, like the coo of a dove or a warbling owl.

She'd only ever heard the sound on Lamptree, but she didn't know what kind of bird made the call—no one did. It'd echo elusively throughout the colony, and every one just called it the Lamptree bird. The thought caused her skin to tingle, and she scanned the trees. Rays of daylight sliced through the leaves, and the only movement was the slow trudge of refugees. None of them seemed to notice the sound.

Something small floated through the air. At first, Madi thought it was a bird, but it moved too slowly. Daylight glinted against glass, and she realized the tiny shape was a flying bottle. Mist curled through the trees, and the bottle wobbled from current to current, following Madi. Curiosity straightened her spine, bringing her to her feet. Was this bottle thrown to her? If so, it bore her glyph, but how could that have been? Only two people knew about Madi's glyph—Bandico and . . . Sembetra.

Madi reached out, her hands trembling. The cold glass capsule settled into her palms, frothing gently with white mist. A scrolled note was inside. As she eyed it, she strangled the bottle's throat. If her old friend was sending another warning, it'd come too late. She uncorked the bottle and unfurled a small bit of parchment:

If you want your daughter to live, go with them.

Madi's brain shook, and a million thoughts squeezed through the sorrow-stained passages of her mind. Chills clawed at her skin. She glanced side to side, searching the forest for someone watching her.

Daylight danced between the trees, and birdsong echoed beyond the mists. The wooden deck vibrated, and Madi jumped when she heard someone moving behind her.

She spun around, catching Corlan peeking at her from behind the ballista nest. An embarrassed smile curled across his cheek. "What are you doing?" he asked, eyeing her hands.

"I thought you were below."

"I'm real quiet," he said, glancing toward the front of the wagon, where Bandico talked to himself—or maybe his ghost. "I don't think he can see through the walls when he's distracted."

"We can't," Madi answered.

"You're one, too?" Corlan asked, eyes widening.

Madi studied the parchment. This wasn't Sembetra's handwriting. In fact, it didn't even look like ink. It looked more like . . . starlight.

Corlan crept around Madi, studying her hands. "What are you looking at?"

"A message came for me in this bottle, but I don't know who it's from."

The boy tilted his head, and his brow furrowed more than it already was. "What bottle?"

She lifted the bottle for the boy to inspect, but his hand passed right through it.

"Where?" he asked, grinning. "There's nothing here."

The bottle and parchment burned hot against Madi's skin, buzzing and blistering. When she let go, they fell to the ground and shriveled to a pink mist. The Lamptree bird echoed in the forest, louder than before. She held the side of her head, suddenly feeling very dizzy.

"Uh. Are you okay?" Corlan asked as Madi fell toward him. He grunted, lacking the strength to hold her. "Bandico, help!"

The wagon rumbled as the brothers hurried to the rear. Mist hissed toward their fingers as they crafted their weapons—a bow for Bandico, an iron club for Bereket. Rays of daylight darted between them as Madi looked up, her eyes beginning to blur. As she slipped out of consciousness, she imagined this was what it felt like to be buried. This was the last thing Dario's soul might have seen. So, where was he now? If only she could have crawled into that grave with him to find out.

Chapter 13: Dario

Dario Lire opened his eyes. Cold water sloshed through his clothes as he lay in shallow waters. A small wave rolled over him, scattering sand and shells across his body. The water was as black as ink, both frigid and foul, burning his throat and lungs as he accidentally swallowed some. When he lifted his head and gasped for air, the smell of salt and decay filled his lungs.

Lethargy bound his bones. Even in the ankle-deep shallows, it was difficult for him to sit up. He tried again, but a sharp shell slit his finger. The wound stung with a strange sensation—a subtle tug, as though something reached inside of him and tugged out the strands of blood. He bled freely now, and the red stream turned as pale as milk. He clutched his hand to his chest—teeth chattering, clothes dripping, body shivering.

Was this a dream? Or had he just woken up from one? Muddy memories disoriented him, pieces of his past all out of place, like a jumbled puzzle. He focused hard to reorient himself. He remembered suffocating and then falling, but what had led him to this place? His empty stomach gurgled, and the only substance he felt inside his body was guilt. He'd made a horrible mistake, but he couldn't remember what it was. All his most recent sensations stung with regret.

Faded gulls circled an unfamiliar sky, pale and cavernous. Far above, stalactites dangled through the clouds, reaching downward like gnarled fingers. Clouds of daylight danced between them, shooting bright rays across the colorless beach. A vast ocean swayed against a gray horizon. Swells of dark water surged into the lagoon where he'd awoken. The surf crashed and receded slowly, like dying breaths, pushing him bit by bit, further into the shallows.

Debris floated nearby—clothing, wooden boards, and a child's doll. The soggy toy reminded him of Lamptree. Memories came rushing back, fitting into place at a frightening pace, filling in his past. Company Lire. Illio. The war. Madi. Aerial. The festival. Even his death.

Each thought was more vivid than a recent dream, and yet, they all seemed to have happened so long ago and so very far away. *Somewhere up there*, Dario thought as he looked skyward. There were no stars above, just the shimmering reflection of the water. The glow was very bright, forming patterns as ominous as starlight. Meanwhile, a single consuming sensation filled him—separation. He opened and closed his fingers, shrugged his shoulders, and bent his knees. All his limbs were intact, but something else had been severed during his fall—his heart.

There, on the shores of the underworld, he wept. Emptiness ached inside his chest, and he loitered in the shallows, holding his shivering rib cage and hollow heartbeat. He'd lost the two people he valued most, and now he faced his worst nightmare alone.

There wasn't a hint of color anywhere. Everything was white, black, or a pale in-between. Dario's clothes were colorful, however, which meant Gale was coming from somewhere. A gust of salty air brushed his chest, rattling a small lantern tied around his neck. *I don't remember putting this on*, he thought as he touched the soggy rope. There was a pouch there, too, filled with some seeds and nuts, which he devoured, ignoring the briny taste and mushy texture.

Dario searched his pockets and found some tools for survival, including flint, a small knife, and some rope. These were grave goods, meaning the rumors were true. There was magic in burial. *But who buried me?* Madi? Or maybe those two Celestials? Dario's brain throbbed as he focused, trying hard to remember. The Celestials in the forest—they'd said, *"We found her!"* Why were they looking for her? Were they members of Madi's company? What company did she even belong to, and why was she living under a different name?

Amriel wasn't a company name, which meant Madi was hiding from someone. The thought of her lying to him didn't make him angry or bitter. It made him afraid. She loved him. He knew it without question. *Whatever she was hiding, she kept secret to protect me or Aerial.* Dario's shoulders sagged beneath the weight of failure. She needed him now more than ever, and he wasn't there to help her.

His thoughts came keener now, except for his sense of time. How long ago had he died? It seemed like ages—in another world. He imagined Aerial all grown, and Madi old and frail. The thought sparked panic, and he quickly began searching for a way inland.

I HAVE TO GET BACK!

A distant moan echoed, like that of a singing whale. A faded fish surfaced, spouted black water, and cracked its massive tail atop the sea. The fish submerged, but the wailing continued. The lamenting calls were rhythmic, human almost. It wasn't the whale calling. It was something else. Dario squinted toward the waves, and there, he saw a tiny boat bobbing up and down. Two blurry figures sat inside, watching, wailing. They were little more than a haze, and the sight of them chilled him to his core.

The figures gestured, but he didn't understand. Why didn't they come closer? Could they help him? He limped toward the boat, clutching his bleeding hand to his chest. Even the wind seemed to grasp at his wound. Dario tensed as the frigid water reached his waist. In the boat, the gestures became more frantic, signaling for him to go back. A black wave roared toward him. His eyes swelled, and the rising waters made him fear for his life. Why? He was already dead.

He tried to run, but the wave caught him, lifted him up, and threw him back toward the shallows. He tumbled through seaweed and shells—and something else—human bones. As the waters receded, he lay there gasping, right where he'd started. Beside him, water trickled from the empty sockets of a human skull.

He checked his lantern, fearing it'd broken. It hadn't, and he found something he hadn't noticed before—a small piece of wood. Words were scratched onto it, as though by a nail. Dario wiped the sand away and read:

> *Run quickly to the cliffs. Do not fly. Help is near.*
> *Trust the Stranger in this strange place.*

He looked back toward the waves. The boat hadn't moved, and the people inside were still surrounded by a faint haze. Were they ghosts? Their wails were chilling and unintelligible, and they pointed inland, toward a sheer cliff.

Dario shivered. "That's t-too far." He was already short of breath, and his clothes were so heavy with water it hurt to move.

The figures in the boat wailed again and pointed somewhere else now, toward a formation of shadowmen walking across the shallows. That's when Dario realized he wasn't alone on the beach. A wave crashed, leaving behind a few bodies. Another wave came, leaving more bodies behind. Then another. More and more bodies. Slowly, the people stirred and rose to their feet, wandering the shallows. These were the shores of the dead, and horror soon stifled his curiosity. This place was evil, and he feared this gray beach was the doorstep to far greater suffering.

The surf surged, and he watched a man tumble through the whitecaps. The waves pummeled the poor man's pathetic form, and it made Dario angry and sad and afraid, all at once. *What did we do to deserve this?* Now, he was the one asking the question. And the only answer was the one he'd given to the refugees who'd asked him. *Nothing.*

Where are the Gales?

I don't know.

Ashen scoured the beach in a staggered line—a dozen slender silhouettes—hunting the shoals like fishermen with spears and nets. They caught the poor man by the arms and dragged him, but then an arrow shrieked across the beach, striking one of the shadowmen. The arrow came from the boat Dario had tried to wade to. One of the ghosts was standing, holding a pale purple bow. There were several small boats now, floating just off-shore at regular intervals. Another shrieking arrow passed overhead, glowing pale purple like the bow and the ghost holding it. Up and down the shallows, arrows flew, protecting those who'd washed ashore.

Rocks jutted up from the shallows like burned cakes covered in syrup—black and glossy. Dario paused atop the sloping safe-haven, gasping for breath. At last, some place dry. Others were resting here, tending their wounds. Blood stained the rocks, and it didn't seem like anyone had made it this far without getting cut by the sharp shells and bones littering the shallows. Bandages were passed around, since not everyone had washed ashore with grave goods. Some didn't even have clothes or a lantern. Those people gathered close, coughing, choking, and shivering. Water dripped from their bare bodies, tapping the ground next to their wrinkled toes. Meanwhile, Dario's small lantern sizzled and bubbled. The sparkling black fuel inside was already half empty.

Help is near.

What help? Where? He squinted inland, toward a gloomy wall of cliffs. Water and cloud spouted from geysers in the shallows, blocking much of his view. He sat down, and something on his back clattered against the rocks. *Nightfly*, he remembered when he saw the long wings of a flier curled in their resting position. Closing his eyes, he thought of his first flight with Madi. Her dark hair, tucked beneath her bandana. Her smile. Her voice. Her perfect eyes. Her perfect body. The tools hanging from her pockets. The way she walked. The way she touched him.

I have to get back, he thought, over and over. *I have to help her.*

Pale clouds drifted overhead, veiling the heights of this world. Was it Sky? Earth? Stars? The firmament of this world looked like porous rock, gloomy and full of holes, like a sponge. Dario squinted, trying to gauge the distance. It was far—very, very far. Even distant mountains struggled to reach the top of this world. But he saw ledges lining the cliffs and pillars of rock, meaning there was a way up. If he could at least reach one of those high crags, he could rest and continue upward. He emptied sand and shells from Nightfly's gloves and put them on.

Shadowmen were very close now. They moved methodically, stirring the shallows with their long, slender legs. Nets dangled from their hands, and their dark blades held no glint at all. People scampered from the rocks, injured, limping, dragging themselves like a bunch of seals fleeing back into the water. Then, the Ashen began to run. Water churned. Screams signaled their advance. All across the rocks and dunes, people fled inland—away from the surging waves, away from the shadowmen. There was nowhere to run but inland. Down the dunes, the dead charged further into the underworld, with desperate and fearful shouts, like a doomed army.

A chorus of panic filled the air—waves crashed, geysers spat water and mist, bodies tumbled in the surf. Never in his life—in all evacuations and retreats he'd documented—had Dario witnessed such chaos. Except, this wasn't a retreat. These were the first steps into an underworld.

We don't even know what we're running into.

Sand scattered as at least a hundred people fled inland, but Dario refused to go that way. Madi and Aerial were above, so he took to the sky. Nightfly chimed, and a black haze trailed its wings. Dario's lantern tugged at his neck, clicking wildly. Toxic air filled his lungs and clawed at his eyes. Plumes of white and gray cloud swept over the cliffside, but what color were the clouds? He couldn't tell.

Gulls circled the air, silent except for the flapping of their wings. He'd expected the birds to flee, but instead, the flock swarmed him, nipping at his clothes and throwing him off balance. The black birds made no sound, but when a gust of gloomy cloud brushed his face, he heard a dark cackle—the contorted call of a thousand sick birds. The icy sound gripped Dario's skin, making him think of the White Whisperer, the Black Knight, and the Gray Ghost. If the underworld was real, were they real, too? The sound grew, a chorus of screeches, and the birds attacked, pecking Dario's flesh, tearing his clothes, and throwing him off-balance. He tumbled back into the frigid water amid a splash of blood and feathers.

He emerged screaming. A long bone had pierced his side, and blood gushed out. There was a deathly magic in this water, clawing at the life in his veins, and he scrambled to his feet to escape the sensation. Chaos swirled around him, reminding him of battle—bodies floated in the water, bouncing lifelessly against the rocks. People ran toward the cliffs, shouting in fear. Shadowmen silently snatched them up and dragged them down the beach. There was nowhere to run but toward the cliffs, which were full of large caves. Dario eyed the dark holes ahead, fearing those jaws led deeper into the belly of death.

"Help!" someone shouted.

"Help us!" another pleaded.

Help is near, the ghosts' message had said. *But where?*

Dario didn't see it. Desperation turned his stride frantic. *I have to get back.* Ripples and rocks shook his balance, and he felt more frail than ever before. When he was on Lamptree, he was still a Celestial. Now, what was he? A corpse, separated from his wife and daughter.

He had no constellation. No battle cloak. No Galecraft. No heart. Just memories.

"Help," Dario whimpered with everyone else. If he didn't cry out, if someone didn't save him, he would never see his family again. Blood poured from his side, and his fingers turned red as he tried to stem the bleeding. *I HAVE TO GET BACK!* He tumbled again into the frigid shallows, releasing a bubbly cry for HELP!

Then, as he looked up, trying to keep his mouth above water, a burst of color erupted near the base of the cliff. Gale pierced the gloomy scene, and hope surged inside of him. People were running from the cliffs—dozens of them. Humans! Not shadowmen. They emerged from cliff-side caves, pulling small sleds atop the water.

"Here!" people screamed and waved. "We're here!"

One by one, the sleds diverted toward the calls. But so did the shadowmen. Geysers spewed water into the air. The torrent sparkled in the daylight, and then came crashing down, splattering atop Dario. He gasped as the water sucked at his wound.

Another geyser launched a torrent of water into the air, knocking a woman and child off balance. Together, they fought the torrent, screaming as the receding waters carried them back toward the sea. Dario reached out to them, but they slipped from his grasp.

From the caves, a young girl rushed to their rescue, pulling along a sled. She was barely a woman yet—still just a child. *These are our saviors? Children?* She moved without a word and glanced at him for just a moment. Her eyes were as teal as a winter storm, and Dario swore he saw the air frost amid her gaze. This was no normal child, he realized, seeing an icy mist shimmer across her thick battle cloak. She was a Celestial! The girl smiled and turned, puffing measured breaths as she raced toward the woman and child. Water splashed over her cloak, but the garb seemed to shed the waves completely, allowing her to move, weightless, through the surf.

Trust the Stranger in these strange lands.

Sleds rushed back and forth from the caves, nearly all of them pulled by young Celestials. Their cool teal eyes flickered like stars in a blizzard. One of them rushed to Dario, silent like the rest. Wet brown hair clung to the boy's cheeks. Like the others, he wore a teal-gray cloak, the color of a cold storm, which crackled with a frost as the boy helped Dario settle onto the sled. Shrewd eyes peered from his soaked hood, eyes which seemed older than the rest of him. Dario thanked him, and the boy replied with a silent nod.

The boy breathed heavily as he battled the shallows, shielding his head as geysers doused him. The water was frigid, but the cold hardly seemed to bother the boy. He slowed once or twice, redirecting course, but no matter what obstacles appeared—corpses, shadowmen, or rocks—the boy pulled for the caves, with Dario in tow.

What company is this? And how do they get their tasks without any constellations?

Dario didn't understand. This was the underworld, yet death was as real, horrific, and as rife as the world above. If death above led here, where did death here lead? Was there a world below this one? Did this cycle of suffering ever end? Dario shivered on his sled, feeling utterly betrayed—betrayed by his parents, betrayed by the Gales, betrayed by whatever beings created this world and put him in it, only to suffer like this.

By now, the cliffs were very close. Black birds circled the heights, where bodies littered the ledges. These corpses were contorted, making it obvious that these poor souls died trying to scale the cliffside. If they died while trying to climb out of the underworld, where were they now?

Water pooled where the beach met the cliffs. Dario's young rescuer trudged through, dragging his sled up a smooth rock and into one of the caves. Two women rushed over and tended Dario while he remained on the sled. They poured orange brews on his wounds, which stung and slowed the bleeding. They wrapped a large blanket around his shoulders and poured out a bit of red brew, which sizzled and warmed the blanket.

Meanwhile, the boy rested on a small rock and stared at the surf, panting. This was the last place Dario had expected to see another Celestial. "Thank you," he said.

The boy turned suddenly, as if startled. His eyes were so wintry blue, and as water dripped from his hair onto his eyelashes, they turned to snow. Dario smiled as the flakes formed, finding the magic very foreign and very beautiful. And yet, the boy's gaze was quite warm, comforting in a way Dario couldn't exactly describe. Whoever this boy was, his heart was too large for his small body.

Wiping his nose, the boy rose and gathered a new sled. Without a word, he hopped back into the shallows. A teal sash was bound to the boy's weapon—a glaive—bearing markings that Dario recognized. It was the same sash the sick woman in the caravan had given him. The same sash he'd given to Illio! Dario lunged for it, nearly falling from his sled. "Where did you get that?"

The boy frowned and guarded it by tilting his body away.

"Please, it belonged to my best friend," Dario said, hope surging in his tone. Illio was dead. That meant he was here, too! "His name was Illio Lire. Please!" he begged, reaching out desperately now. He needed Illio, more than ever. "You must have seen him."

The boy's posture shattered Dario's hope. A finger protruded from his soaked sleeve as he pointed toward the battered bodies that'd fallen. There, on a sharp formation of rocks, Dario saw a form he recognized. Illio's body dangled from a sharp ledge, caught by his legs. His chest was bare, and he wore a pair of makeshift pants. He'd fallen onto his back, and so his hollow gaze remained upward, toward a narrow ledge, where his grip had failed him. His hair and beard swayed in the wind, and what should have been a reunion was just another cruel passing.

"That's him," he whispered, watching a gull land on Illio's body. Anger and confusion churned his words into a frustrated slur. "I can't believe I'm doing this again—looking at him like this. I don't understand. This is the land of the dead. Where is he now?"

The faded gull pecked at Illio, and Dario took his anger out on the boy's silence. "SAY SOMETHING!"

"Leave him alone!" one of the women said, shielding the boy from Dario. "Exile can't speak. None of the Celestials in Company Snow can. They would have tried to save your friend if they were here, but they can't be everywhere at once. We were only able to rescue a few from the shallows that day. I'm sorry."

"We're already dead . . ." Dario muttered, tasting blood on his lips. He'd expected loneliness and suffering in the underworld, but he'd never thought it could get worse. "Where did he go?"

"There are more worlds below this one," said the woman on Dario's right.

"Many more," added the one on his left. ". . . We think."

The sled rocked back and forth as they carried him. Dario, meanwhile, stared at Illio for as long as he could, haunted by his hanging form. He wanted to walk to him and say something, if only to pretend to hear his voice again. Wind howled outside the grotto, cackling with Gloom. Dario's body grew cold, his stomach soured with nausea, and his head became very light. He'd always had someone to help him: Illio and Madi. Down here, without them, he didn't know what he would do.

The women paused, and Dario felt a tug at his shirt. Exile was there, hand outstretched, offering back Illio's sash. Dario snatched it and squeezed the sash tightly in his hand. The women frowned, but he missed Illio too much to care. *Trust the Stranger?* he thought, turning away from the boy's bright blue eyes. What did the Stranger do for Illio? Nothing.

Squeezing the sash sapped him of all his strength. His vision blurred, and the whole passage seemed to sway. A narrow boardwalk rumbled as people hurried back and forth, carrying sleds, bodies, and supplies. Cave openings littered the rock, howling with wind and splashing with saltwater. Cries echoed from the shallows, and sledders returned, some with shivering bodies on their sleds, some without. Blood seeped through Dario's clothes, and when he moved his hands, he felt warm blood filling his sled. The women quickly cut away the cloth, revealing a gaping wound.

One of them cursed and applied pressure. "This wound is deep. It's reopened. He needs blood!" she said, dousing Dario's flesh with brew. He cried out, writhing as his skin sizzled and stung. They carried him quickly now, pounding across the boardwalk. "He needs blood now!"

CHAPTER 14: DARIO

A ray of daylight pierced a dark cavern. Like a pale and passionless eye, it gazed upon a derelict cloudcrawler, lodged atop a high rock in the middle of a grotto. Long black vines clutched the hull, their surfaces turning green wherever they neared a lantern of Gale. The vessel teetered and creaked above a circular chasm. Every so often, the darkness gurgled and spouted mist, stirring the stale air. The scent of bile and blood wafted across Dario's body, along with the sound of buzzing flies.

A lone surgeon shuffled through a sea of cots and hammocks, checking on each writhing body. Dario watched her exhaustion set in, wondering if she'd reach him soon, hoping she had the skill to save him. Bit by bit, her black hair unraveled from her braid, and more and more blood stained her apron. When she reached Dario, she dabbed his face with a cloth, sopping up beads of cold sweat.

"What color does your blood brew?" she asked, applying pressure to Dario's side. His skin stung and tightened.

"I don't know what that means," he whispered. He clenched his fingers into a fist, forming a ball of pale-yellow flesh like an old onion.

His clothes were miserably wet and itchy with sand. The surgeon used a knife to cut portions of the red-stained cloth away. Her blade was cold, and the air stung the exposed wound. "Everyone's blood brews differently," she explained. "Do you know what yours does?"

"No," Dario answered. His shallow breaths came quickly, forcing what little blood remained through his pale body.

Illio's form still haunted him—the sand dribbling from his beard, the wind searing his skin. How many underworlds were there? He eyed the dark geyser in the grotto. Its slimy walls shimmered, and it belched black cloud, leading Dario to wonder—what kind of horrible world did that pit lead to?

The surgeon worked at a nearby brewing table, sorting through empty vials. Glass capsules clanked at different pitches, sizzling and bubbling as she added contents. Several large vats hissed, steamed, and dripped a shiny substance. The sounds reminded Dario of Adacus Lire, the company brewmaster. Gale brews were concocted by condensing and then combining different colored clouds. The effect of each brew could be altered through further distillation and combination. The possibilities were limitless, but it took people with great patience—people like Adacus—to sort the useful combinations from the harmful.

The surgeon lifted a brew to inspect it, clicking her tongue when she saw bubbles floating inside the vial. Dario was no brewmaster, but everyone knew bubbles meant a weak potion. Liquid fizzed, water boiled from a vat, and something warm splashed onto Dario's wound, stinging it. He felt a prick, and then the surgeon stirred a bloodied needle into her concoction. Dario's blood swirled and sizzled, turning the liquid inside the vial dark yellow.

"Your blood brews gold," she said with a sigh.

"Is that bad?" Dario asked.

"No, just rare," she answered, glancing around the cavern. Her eyes were red with exhaustion. She searched for a place to wipe her hands, but every stitch of her apron was stained in blood. "I need to find someone with your kind of blood before I can help you."

The sides of Dario's jaw soured with discomfort. He tried to sit up, but his stinging spine yanked him back toward his pillow. The fabric was wet with sweat and reeking of fresh blood and old wine—in fact, the whole cavern did. It reminded Dario of the pirate lairs south of Greenpond, without any of the treasure. The ocean surf echoed from a far passage. From there, a boardwalk curled around the side of the cavern, avoiding the dark geyser, which hissed and growled.

Refugees, survivors, the dead—Dario didn't know what to call them—they were everywhere, writhing, wandering, waiting in utterly hopeless positions. He guessed there were a hundred other people resting inside this wrecked cloudcrawler, with only a handful of attendants to look after them. Shadows coiled around the wreck, and a pair of Celestials, with wintry eyes, patrolled the vessel. Without a word, they held a cup of daylight brew close to Dario's skin, searching for hints of faded flesh.

Dario knew he wasn't fading. His heart burned too much with a mission: *I have to get back.* All he had to do was keep breathing. Breathing was easy, but he figured it'd be easier with more blood in his body.

"Cavern Four, can you hear us? This is Cavern Six."

An unnerving voice crackled and warbled. Dario shuddered with barely the strength to search for the sound. The voice echoed across the rotting cloudcrawler. Sometimes it sounded distant. Sometimes, it sounded close. Sometimes, it faded beneath the sound of rushing wind. But whenever Dario did hear the voice clearly, it mingled with the sound of a ghostly wail.

"This is Cavern Four. We hear you, Cavern Six."

". . . Cavern Four, don't send any pilgrims out yet . . . Cavern Five . . . silent . . . white sleighs in passage . . . . . . All Caverns be warned . . ."

Dario contorted his body as he searched for the source of the voice. The bones in his spine popped and pinched, seizing his legs beneath his blanket. He tracked the voice across the deck to a large device he'd never seen before. It was the size of a beer keg—bronze, sleek, and curled—like two shells fastened together.

"Teal clouds continue to rise in Cavern Ten. They need more warm clothing . . ."

A brown blindfold covered the woman's eyes, and a belt of tools crossed her chest. Curly hair drooped toward one shoulder as she tilted her head and gently turned the crank. The voices came and went as she adjusted it.

"Ledge-walker coming with supplies . . . Cavern Nine . . . White sleighs moving north. Wait for signal before sending pilgrims."

All across the old cloudcrawler, people listened to the device, sitting with their heads cocked toward the crackling voices. The contraption spun in mesmerizing fashion. As the woman turned the crank, it pulled thin strands of cloud from the surrounding air. Lanterns colored the faint strips of mist, revealing them to be purple. The cloud cycled through the contraption in waves.

Dario craned his neck, intrigued. Did this mean the voice was in those clouds? If so, it meant people could pass messages in this world without flying bottles. The voice sounded a million miles away, fraught with echoes and crackles, but still, it gave him hope. It meant there were others out there—organized and communicating—and by the sound of it, they were trying to escape, too!

". . . Four pilgrims reached World's End yesterday. Another party will depart Bold Sanctum after . . . . . . Wish them luck and life . . ."

The surgeon stood nearby, running her finger down the page of a book. "We need gold blood," she told the woman spinning the device. "Or he's not going to make it."

Dario focused on keeping his breaths calm. A chilled sweat pooled on his neck and trickled down his chest, filling his stomach with a familiar sensation. He'd felt it not so long ago—the sickening fear of death. At this point, he didn't care if they siphoned blood from a shadowman. He'd do anything to keep from falling away from his family.

"Gold? Are you sure?" Dario heard the blindfolded woman ask.

She spoke with a slight stammer. "You should test it again. Could be sand in the vial."

"I tested it twice. It brewed gold," the surgeon said, turning the page.

The blindfolded woman touched her fingertips together, counting. "Gold blood. Rare. Extremely. Extremely rare."

"Yes, Girli, but I'm certain there was someone who came through here who had it. Can you remember who?"

Girli continued counting her fingers. "Forty fraction deaths per hour. Waves every three and two fraction minutes. Average, two and five fraction survivors per wave. Purple blood, one in four. Red blood, one in six. Pink blood, one in eight. Brown blood—"

The surgeon snapped her book shut and pinched her brow. "Stop, Girli, please! You know the numbers, but can you remember the man's name? It was a very long time ago. His blood brewed gold, too. Who was he? He may still be on the Trail."

"Stranger on the ledge."

"Who?"

"The stranger on the ledge," Girli repeated. Her voice was monotone and matter-of-fact. "That's what they call him. He's one of Captain Imani's ledge-walkers. Never gave his name. He washed ashore three years, six months, and fourteen days ago. It was a green atmosphere. You said he had gold blood. I said you needed to wash the vial and retest. You said I needed to keep my thoughts behind my blindfold. I said—"

"Yes, I remember now," said the surgeon. "Pass it through the horn. Ask the Sky Doe to send that ledge-walker here. I need his blood."

Girli retrieved a tool from her belt and removed the bronze crank. She inserted the crank into a different hole and began to turn it. Now, cloud funneled out of the device instead of into it. The strand glowed purple—like the ghosts and boats floating along the shores of the afterlife. Dario squinted, sand dribbling from his forehead. After a moment of silence, he shivered with wonderment. A voice answered, as if it'd heard the whole conversation! Girli adjusted the crank again, and wisps of cloud siphoned through the device, sparkling. With them, came a ghostly response:

"Cavern Sixteen, we know who you're talking about. He came . . . days ago . . . supplies . . . lives on ledge . . . Might be difficult, but we'll try to send him your way."

The surgeon returned to Dario's bedside. "Someone is coming who can help you," she said, exchanging his bloody bandage for a clean one.

Dario nodded, letting his head slide further down his pillow toward his belongings, which were stacked on the ground next to him—Nightfly, his book, and Illio's sash, folded atop it. *My book!* He'd thought it'd faded in the world above. It was Galecraft after all. *Someone must have buried it with me,* he decided, gratefully imagining Madi tucking it against his chest.

He lifted it, and its weight shocked him. In the world above, it'd only ever weighed upon his mind. Here, it wasn't Galecraft any more. It was just a book, it seemed, and Dario would have to get used to how heavy it was. The binding remained firmly clasped, although much of its wax coating was chipped and weathered. Hopefully, it'd been enough to protect the pages from the sea.

Dario exhaled, relieved to see ink surviving on each page. Words were chipped and smeared, and some of the faces had faded somewhat. He squeezed the book against his chest. The grotto dimmed, and he already felt forgotten. He was responsible for these stories. Would they survive this place? Would *he* survive this place?

Dario writhed beneath his sweat-stained sheets. His muscles grew stiff, twitching. Brittle bones ached beneath his skin, feeling hollow—not his own. This condition had haunted him his whole life, but now that Constellation Lire was gone, he worried it might overpower him.

"I'm not a Celestial anymore, am I?" he asked the surgeon.

She shook her head.

"So, I can fade?"

"Only if fear suffocates your hope."

"It won't," he said, steeling his eyes.

She smiled and brushed a hand through Dario's hair. His scalp tingled. He wasn't used to having hair. "I can tell."

Attendants looked after him through the night, but soon, feverish dreams confused him. Dark figures stood over him, looming silently. They reached through his skin, removing his bones one by one, stacking them like a charred skeleton—covered in shadow. Sweat blurred his vision, and he tried to dream of Madi, but every time he thought of her, a colorless hand ripped through his mind, shredding the memory.

He woke with a shout. The surgeon stood over him, tying a string around his arm. "It's alright," she said with a comforting smile. "You were dreaming. Hold still."

She placed a small red shard in his left hand, its warmth buzzing like Galecraft. The longer he held the rock, the more it pricked his palm. "Don't let go," she said while placing Dario's other hand in a large basin of water.

"Give me your hand," she said to a man standing nearby. Her voice was notably less compassionate.

The man's muscular forearm passed across Dario's chest. He wore a "bit of luck" on his wrist—smooth bits of colored glass. In the world above, colonists sometimes gave a "bit of luck" to a Celestial before they departed for a task. Most Celestials carried one or two bits. The leather band on this man's wrist held dozens. The colored glass glistened as the surgeon placed the man's hand into the basin next to Dario's.

First, she cut carefully into Dario's hand. Oddly, no blood came out. But when she cut into the man's wrist, blood spilled freely into the bowl. A crimson line weaved through the water, winding from the stranger's wrist into Dario's exposed vein. His hand tingled. Then his arm. Soon, his whole body buzzed like someone had just wrapped a warm blanket around his heart and offered his soul a drink. Dario closed his eyes and sighed as life rushed back into his veins.

"That's all for now," the surgeon said.

The stranger removed his hand, and the water in the basin sank some. His stool scraped the wood floor as he stood. Blond hair, bleached by dayclouds and saltwater, covered much of his face. He bandaged his hand, then lowered his sleeve, hiding the wound. Candlelight danced across his face, which was weathered by wind. A messy beard covered his chin, but his gaze was as grim as a shadowman's visage—and unmistakably familiar.

"Vetricus?" Dario muttered, recognizing him.

The man's eyes cooled, withdrawing into the darkness of his hood. Every hair on Dario's body stood on end, and an unexplainable excitement rushed over him. Maybe it was the influx of blood. Or maybe it was the thought that he'd had something to do with bringing down the most powerful Celestial in the sky.

Vetricus' expression darkened, and his hands disappeared into the folds of his cloak. "How do you know my name?" he asked.

"I saw you before I died," Dario answered. If Vetricus was here, it meant Company Minoan killed him. But something was wrong. The surgeon had said he came through here a long time ago. She must have been mistaken. This WAS the Celestial from Lamptree. Dario's chest went taut with fear. How long had he been unconscious in the Sea of the Afterlife? How long ago had he died?

Vetricus leaned closer—earnestly, cautiously. He spoke in a very, very low voice—acutely annunciated. "You saw Vetricus Perth?" The whisper was filled with energy and fear, and he looked left and right before speaking again. "You're certain?"

"Yes," Dario said, recollections of Lamptree abuzz in the forefront of his mind. "You wanted my map book, remember?"

Vetricus turned away. Then he turned back as if to say something. Then he turned away again. He wrung his hands and stared vehemently toward the floor, as though trying to burn away whatever thoughts were forming. The surgeon, meanwhile, cleaned her tools and vials, but kept her head tilted toward the conversation.

"Lamptree exploded," Dario told him. "You must have died in the explosion."

Vetricus stared at the basin of water—at his reflection in the blood-stained liquid. He strangled the stool he'd been sitting on, shaking as if fighting the urge to hurl it across the deck. He squeezed so tightly that blood seeped through the bandage on his hand. Candlelight glimmered in his eyes, which looked furiously ablaze.

"I'm afraid I couldn't have," he said, his voice softening. "Because that wasn't me."

"But—I saw you."

"You didn't see me."

"But you said you're Vetric—"

The man pressed his palm to Dario's mouth, muffling the name. His skin was callous and cracked, smelling of climbing chalk. "That is my name," he whispered. "It is *not* the name of the man you saw above, though he uses it. And I assure you, he's not dead."

"Who is he?"

"My twin brother," Vetricus replied softly. He stroked his beard, smearing the hairs with chalk from his fingers. "Did he speak to you?"

"He wanted the maps," Dario replied.

Vetricus leaned close, shielding the conversation from those nearby.

His weight made Dario's cot sag. "What maps?" he asked, panic seeping into his tone.

Chills covered Dario's body. It was obvious now, this was not the same man he'd seen on Lamptree. The Celestial on Lamptree had looked down at Dario with the confidence of a god. This man clung to Dario's cot with desperation in his brown eyes.

"Maps to cities of escape," Dario said, finding no reason to lie. "If you can decipher them."

"Did you give it to him?" Vetricus asked, barely audibly.

Dario shook his head. "It was destroyed."

Vetricus relaxed, and Dario's cot creaked as he rose. "Good," he whispered. He massaged his bandaged vein and glanced around the room. People were beginning to stare. He stroked the back of his neck, adjusting his deep hood.

He started to walk away, but the surgeon caught him by the sleeve. "He'll need more blood," she said.

"More of mine?" Vetricus asked, holding his wrist.

"Yes, yours."

A voice crackled from Girli's bronze device, and Vetricus cocked an ear toward it. *". . . attacked by a faded lion . . . Herds crossing the Riddled Road. Pilgrims beware. Horses. Gazelle. Many vermin. Faded predators prowl among them."*

After the word *horses*, Vetricus stepped toward the galley, and the fiery stove glowing there. Survivors slurped bowls of soup while listening to the crackling voice. The ghost's voice became muffled, as though he were speaking through wind and rain. Everyone stopped what they were doing, anxious, until the voice became clear again. The device's body was cracked and chipped. Even now, a faint *crack* crawled across it, and bronze flakes floated to the floor.

Dario's hair stood on end. Was he really hearing a ghost? Had the people here really learned to communicate with them? This was only the second time he'd come near a ghost. The first time was when Company Lire was tasked with burning down and rebuilding a haunted bridge. He would never forget the whispers in the air, the words scrawled across the bridge—strange sayings and pleadings for help. Whoever haunted that bridge was very lost and confused, dangerously so, as they'd killed six refugees, but Dario still pitied the poor being afterward.

"What happens when a ghost's haunt decays?" he asked the surgeon.

"Their anchor to this world weakens, and they're swept away."

Dario studied the device, noting its rigid texture. The top was wider than the base, like a horned seashell. "What do you mean, swept away? How can the waves get to him here?"

The surgeon lowered her voice as Girli looked over, concerned. "Because he isn't *here*. He's on a boat, alone on the Sea of the Afterlife, fighting tides and torrents to keep us informed. He's merely anchored to our horn." Her voice wavered, hinting of distaste. "We shouldn't be talking about this now. Not here," she said, turning to Vetricus.

"You need to eat and rest," she told him. "Speak to the steward for rations. You'll have to sleep here on deck, since there isn't room anywhere else. We're not equipped to help this many people washing ashore. Something is going on up there. Something bad."

"I shouldn't stay here." Vetricus turned away, his voice muffled by the cusp of his hood. He eyed the rows of cots, and those writhing atop them. His posture wavered amid their groans, as though he couldn't decide whether to help them or run from them. "I'll sleep out on the ledge."

Dario eyed his book, wishing he had the strength to unlock its pages. He had to learn more about this man. He had to learn more about this place. People above didn't know enough about the underworld, and they needed to. Someone needed to tell them what happened after death, and how badly people here needed help. Someone needed to prove that the Gales knew about this suffering, and yet they did nothing. Prayers echoed elsewhere in the grotto, but Dario didn't pray. He plotted.

CHAPTER 15: MADI

Bright yellow clouds flowed along the easternmost end of Trade Gap valley, bathing these gentler hills in a mellow light. Beneath the buttery atmosphere, vineyards lined the slopes, speckling them in red, green, and purple. Dozens of refugee wagons churned along a beaten path, bordered by a stone fence and a cherry orchard. As far as Madi could see, these were the last fruitful lands before the Trade Gap emptied into a barren plain, stained in gray.

Bandico rested the horses and suggested that everyone stretch their legs. They dismounted and meandered the hillside. This borderland between the Carnation highlands and the Carmine desert was a battlefield, a beautiful but sobering contrast between Gale and Gloom. Two atmospheres clashed—one colorful, the other cold, distant, and discomforting. It strained at the emptiness in Madi's heart, whispering to her that all good things would one day fade.

Bereket stood watch in his ballista nest. The turret creaked as he scanned the honeyed horizon. Madi's whole body ached. Her soul gasped at how lonely a life could suddenly feel. It'd been four days since she'd buried Dario, and her emotions fluxed between sorrow and numbness. All the while, life fluttered by.

Panima sat silently with Aerial in the grass, while Corlan and Wodan sulked along the stone fence. Only Bandico seemed in high spirits. With a burst of excitement, he hopped down from the driver's box, muttering something to himself—or to Raven. Madi followed him into the orchard, where the knock of a woodpecker echoed. Rows of curled branches rained white leaves onto a soft bed of grass. Farmers patrolled the nearby vineyards, carrying lanterns as they harvested. Wherever they walked, healthy color spread to fruits and leaves. But outside of their lantern's reach, crops slowly faded.

"What do you see?" she asked him.

Bandico stepped over a log, shielding his face with his hand. Daylight streamed through the leafy white canopy, meeting the wide brim of his black hat. "Bees," he answered. He grit his teeth and gazed up at the branches, eyes sizzling. "I saw them swarming somewhere up there, but I keep losing them in the light. Can you see them?"

Branches creaked. The woodpecker knocked. White leaves chattered in the breeze, shaking beneath a sky full of burning constellations. Every sound filled Madi with a sense of emptiness—one sound in particular: the call of the Lamptree bird. It'd been following her for days, and now, it wailed somewhere in the hollow.

"I can't. I'm sorry," she said, rubbing the chill from her arms.

Bandico let out a thoughtful hum while tapping his fingertips together. His hands emerged from his oversized sleeves as he stretched an arm into the air. Healthy mists weaved through the trees like tiny specks of dust, glittering with every color imaginable. With subtle *snaps* and *sparks*, the haze followed Bandico's fingers, forming an elegant hive as large as a pumpkin—grayish-gold and full of combs, crevices, and crannies. When he'd finished, he tipped a small vial toward the empty hive, letting out a few drops of a citrus smelling liquid—lemon, like the pines of Lamptree Forest.

"We don't have to find them. Their scouts will find us," he said, tapping his Galecraft. "Bees swarm when they're looking for a new home, and I've got one for them. All I ask for in return is a small, sweet tax."

Sadness welled within Madi's chest, stoked by his choice of words. A home was all she'd ever wanted—*but Celestials don't have a home. We go where our starlight drags us.*

She eyed the beehive's flaky texture. "I didn't think Shades could use Galecraft," she said.

"As long as our glyphs outshine our curses, we can."

Branches swayed overhead, revealing pockets of empty sky. High above the golden dayclouds, the firmament was an oily black, glittering with hundreds of constellations. Every shape and pattern told a story. Madi didn't know how to read them, but she couldn't deny their beauty. Her gaze passed from constellation to constellation, wondering what kind of people each company was made of based on the form. Was it elegant? Was it harsh? Was it bright, or desperately dim—like Company Lire's had been.

"Dario loved looking at the sky," she told Bandico. "He said it was like reading a book—or a regal tapestry, always shimmering, always moving, visible for all people to admire or condemn. He used to say that it wasn't fair that the Gales could issue whatever task they wanted, while their own stories and motives remain hidden."

"He's right," Bandico mumbled without as much as a blink skyward.

"You would have liked him," Madi said, smiling. "I think you two have a lot in common."

"He enjoyed murder, too?"

"You don't enjoy it."

Bandico sighed, as if to rid his tone of sarcasm once and for all. Madi sensed more emotion in this one short breath than in all he'd ever said or done. "The sky says I do, but who can judge a motive?" He tipped his hat, as though to risk a glance at the stars, but then he spat into the mud next to his boot. "Everything I've done, Madi, I've done for my brother. Everything that's happened to me was to prevent something worse from happening to him. But I don't think anyone gazing at my glyph from their bed at night will ever see that."

As he spoke, Madi watched Constellation Perth. Marred with shimmering scars, like a shattered window, it was the only cursed constellation bright enough to see.

"Sembetra never said what company you were with," Madi said.

"Then she respected my wishes."

Madi held her breath for a moment, then exhaled. "You're not in Company Perth, are you?"

"Would it matter?"

"Yes. They pillaged my home. They've pillaged many people's homes." A tear slipped down Madi's cheek, the screams still fresh in her mind. "Please—I just—I need to know."

Bandico's hat hid all but his indecipherable grin. Then, he raised his chin slightly, letting Madi see his eyes, and the gentle white glow coming from them. "No. I'm not a Perth. I'm a Witterwen," he answered. "After me and Bear were stranded in the Long Dark, we had no choice but to work for one of the night syndicates. They put him in the mines, but they trained me to be a Little Light."

"What's that?"

"We were guides. Our eyes are blessed by the Green Grinner."

Blessed? The blood dripping from his pupils might say otherwise. Unsettled, Madi turned away until he'd wiped his cheek. She scanned the branches, finally spotting a bee. "How old were you?"

"I don't know. Eleven. Twelve maybe. The glass cartels use young Celestials to safeguard travelers through the Long Dark. More trustworthy, you know? It's a con, like all the Grinner's tasks. Candlelight Colony is a festering hive of parasitical people. Raven says that I fit right in. The oracles make a fortune, while kids like me completed tasks to keep their glyphs from falling."

"Is Raven following you now?"

"Step for step since we were kids."

Wind rustled through the wood, and Madi listened carefully for Raven's footsteps. For a moment, she thought she heard the faint *crunch* of leaves, but then Bandico's timing beads clattered, and he drank a brew. After that, there was nothing—nothing but the wail of the Lamptree bird. Madi searched the grove. The bird's call echoed through long branches and drifting white leaves, but the harder she looked for it, the more the sound swirled inside her mind.

"I think someone is following me," she admitted. "Like Raven follows you."

What did Madi know about ghosts? She'd never dwelled on the topic long. Dario had talked about it on occasion, but she'd always changed the subject. The afterlife was a realm of rumors. Many of them frightened her, because if they were true, it meant death didn't free someone from magic.

As far as she knew, only Celestials could become ghosts. It happened when their glyphlight was stolen from their corpse and . . . corrupted. Madi didn't know what that part meant. Dario had heard rumors that some companies used ghosts like spies—slipping between the world of the living and the dead, gathering information and confusing reality. Based on what Madi had seen Raven do in the Roots district, it was probably true. Raven had extinguished torches, shattered windows, and opened doors without a trace. It hadn't frightened her much in the moment, but now, the idea of a third soul—here, in this grove—it terrified her.

"You think you're haunted?" Bandico asked.

"I don't know," Madi whispered as the air grew cold. "It used to just be a feeling, but now it's more real—sometimes a sound, sometimes a figure. I've had dreams the past few nights. I wake up on Lamptree, all alone, but there's someone else there. I can feel it. One day, a flying bottle came for me. It was in my hand, but Corlan couldn't see it."

Bandico glanced toward a swaying branch, as though Raven were sitting up there, giving her opinion. He nodded a few times before turning back to Madi. "Raven says that there are no ghosts in the sea around her."

"She can see them?" Madi asked.

"Usually," Bandico answered. "Sometimes they hide, but they can't hide their boat or anchor."

"Wait, what now? A boat?"

"Yeah, a boat. You know, little wooden things that float."

Madi huffed. Sometimes it was impossible to tell if the Shade was being serious or not. "Ghosts travel in boats?"

Bandico nodded. "On the Sea of the Afterlife."

"Stop. Are you serious or is there a punchline coming?"

Bandico pinched his nose, groaning. "I wish."

"Please," Madi said, stepping closer. She tried to catch Bandico's eyes, but he dipped his hat low. "Something is happening to me. I've never felt a magic like this before."

Bees explored Bandico's baited hive. As he watched them, he asked, "Do you know how Celestials become ghosts?"

"Not exactly."

More bees buzzed toward the hive, and Bandico sat down at the base of the tree. "It happens when a Celestial's glyphlight is brewed with cloud and poured over their bones. I've seen dens in the Long Dark, where the Grinner's oracles bury these Celestials. When people die, they fall into the Sea of the Afterlife, which carries them to the shores of the underworld. They're asleep until they wash ashore. But when a Celestial's corpse is doused in brewed glyphlight, they wake up when they fall into the water. They're buried with very specific grave goods—a small boat, oars, rope, timepieces, and an anchor. The Sea of the Afterlife flows toward death, but ghosts can survive by finding haunts, and anchoring to them. Most of the time, they choose objects. Sometimes, they choose people."

Madi grimaced. The answer had become too far-fetched, too quickly. Anchoring to people? With a boat? In an invisible ocean?

"You think I'm lying?" Bandico asked. "I told you, I'm what anchors Raven to this world. Her boat, it's right there. I can see it, bobbing up and down," he said, pointing. "If not for me, the Sea of the Afterlife would carry her into the underworld. She can see a bit of our world around me, like an island, and she can slip between hers and ours. It used to be a major inconvenience, but now, I've learned how useful it can be for someone of my profession."

"You've seen all this?"

"Are you not listening?" Bandico asked, his gentle voice growing grim. "If I hadn't seen it, I never would have believed it. Without my medicine, Raven will manifest. When that happens, you will be able to see her, and my life will speed into her veins more quickly. When that happens, I can see bits of her world. Yes, I've seen it. It began as a nightmare. Now, it follows me everywhere."

Bees buzzed around Bandico's hive, inspecting every entrance. But instead of excitement, Bandico's voice wavered with fear.

"I've seen black waters. Waves swelling like mountains. Dark skies, full of falling stars."

"Falling stars?" Madi interrupted. "I've seen them, too! Above Lamptree! In my dream!"

Bandico cocked his head, narrowing his eyes until the white shimmer faded from his scarred pupils. He tapped his chin and glanced toward the swaying branch again. A cold air drifted there, and Madi saw black water dripping from the bark, which was quickly beginning to rot. Raven really was there—and the branch was dying.

"You saw stars falling across the sky, above a black sea?" Bandico asked.

"Yes."

Bandico looked back toward the swaying branch. Icicles dangled from it now, dripping dark water amid the daylight. "What do you think, Raven?" He was quiet for a time, inspecting Madi. "Yeah. Odd indeed."

"What'd she say?"

"Why aren't you dying?" he asked, rising. He peeked at his hive, where a mass of bees gathered now. "Ghosts cause their haunts to decay. Anything Raven touches dies." Just then, the swaying branch cracked. It fell to the ground, shattering the ice that'd formed. "See?" Bandico said, pointing. "One day, that will be me."

"I told you. I don't know what's happening to me."

"Your company reached the top of a city of escape. Why are you still here?"

"Because my company left me behind."

Madi squeezed bitterly against her daughter's empty pouch. Her lips quivered, stinging with sorrow. The words had just slipped out, and she couldn't believe she'd said them. She'd never told anyone what had happened at the city's summit, not even Dario.

Bandico crossed his arms, contemplative, as he watched the swarm of bees move into his baited hive. "Left behind? Why?"

"My company fell apart," Madi answered. "Magic tore us apart."

No clear memories of the climb came to mind. She'd buried them too deep and stacked a new life atop them. Instead, she thought of making toys—hammering, chiseling, stitching, painting—that's when memories of her past sometimes leaked through. Every toy she made bore traces of her past. Every chiseled face was once one of her friends. Their painted grins and glass eyes reminded her of what all Celestials really were—puppets.

"We were tasked against each other," she revealed. "Like a game, to see who could reach the top. It began with a task from the Blue Lady, to clear Ashen from the lower levels of the city and secure sacred sites. When we'd finished, we resisted the temptation to climb. It wasn't our time to escape, and so, like loyal Celestials, we sealed the gates and departed." Madi raised her eyes, catching a constellation shimmer through the leaves. "But then the sky quaked, and more tasks came—from the Yellow Watcher, the Green Grinner, and the Purple Prince. They sent us back into the city, higher and higher. The rewards became greater and greater. But the tasks became more and more tangled, and my company more divided."

"Isn't that always how it is?" Bandico asked. "The Gales only cooperate when the Gloom forces them to. Some might say the shade is what really holds this world together."

Madi watched the farmers cure their crops on the hillside. Gale spilled from their lanterns into the vibrant vineyards. "No, colonists are. We—I mean—*they* are the instrument of magic. The brushes for the paint. My company was ambitious and we thought the answer was to try and please all the Gales."

"Bad idea," Bandico muttered.

"I know. That's why I became a toymaker."

She carved through wood so that her mind didn't dwell on the flesh she'd carved through. She blew away sawdust so that her mind didn't dwell on the blood she'd sprayed into the air. She painted brave smiles on her toys to forget the pale expressions of her dead friends.

"We all wanted our constellation to shine bright for the world to see," she admitted without adding any emotion to her words. Gritting her teeth, she kept the memories trapped deep inside her chest—buried with the name, Nariah Maya. "Every task teased our imaginations with escape and the rewards that would follow. We vied for the Gales' favor. They vied for our obedience, and it drove us apart. It drove us *mad*."

Madi remembered a time in her workshop when she'd ripped one of her toy creations in half. Sometimes fits of frustration, guilt, and anger broke through her act as Lamptree's toy-maker.

"I was on a task with the last person I trusted. My best friend. Her name was Cry Maya." Tears slipped from Madi's eyes as she thought of Cry's face—a face she'd refused to draw on any of her toys. "Cry thought I was going to betray her, so she betrayed me first. On a bridge, about three-quarters of the way to the summit, she pushed me from the city."

Bandico eyed Madi's flier. "You couldn't fly back?" he asked.

Madi wiped her eyes, fighting hard to keep Cry's face out of her head. She imagined herself in her workshop after one of her fits, surrounded by splintered wood, shattered glass, and broken toys. She'd clean it up and start all over. She'd lose herself in work through the night, clinging to the promise of morning. Entertaining Lamptree's children had proved a better medicine, and far more addictive, than any of the brews or bottles she'd tried to bury her past in before.

"No, I couldn't fly," she replied. "Clouds rise quickly at those heights. Miasmas are everywhere. I could only fall and pray. So, I prayed to the Pilgrim, and I lived."

"You didn't even see the summit?" he asked. His tone turned impatient, and he began to pace. In each hand, he tapped his thumb to his fingertips. "Are you sure there's even a way out up there, or is this just another dead end?"

Madi frowned. She was looking for comfort, but all he was looking for was an escape.

"Look, I'm sorry about whatever happened to you," he said, coughing. "But I can't afford any more dead ends. I'm running out of time. I need to escape. It's the only way I get rid of Raven."

"As you wish," Madi answered, regretting that she'd told him anything. "I'll mark down what I can remember on your map, but you're going alone. I'll find a home for Corlan. Panima and Wodan are old enough to make their own decisions about what they want to do."

"The oracles won't lift your daughter's curse."

"I heard you the first time."

"Still don't trust me?" Bandico asked.

By now, the swarm of bees had moved into his new hive. He took a bit of cork from his pocket and plugged the entrance. One bee lingered outside, but Bandico left it behind.

"I don't know," Madi whimpered, watching the bee buzz aimlessly around the tree. It weaved back and forth, and she pitied its panicked patterns. That was exactly how she felt without her company. That was exactly how she felt now, without Lamptree, without Dario. Alone in an empty world, without any sense of direction. "How can I? I hardly know you."

"Well, I know you," Bandico replied. "You'll do anything to keep climbing. It was the first thing I saw in your eyes. It's a good thing."

"You don't know a thing about me."

"I forged your identity, Madi. And we're more alike than you think," Bandico said, his hive bobbing at his hip. "Your greatest fear is to be alone again, like you were when you were sobbing in Sembetra's arms. Admit it, after what's happened to you, you feel like a ghost, clinging to your daughter to live. She's the only thing keeping you tied to this world now, and you'll kill anyone to keep her alive."

Madi's eyes widened, and she drew back, but something inside her whispered that he was exactly right. Nariah Maya whispered, deep from within Madi's chest—*You'd do anything to keep me locked down here.*

Bandico swaggered from the orchard, carrying his hive over his shoulder. He'd made his point. *Maybe we are similar,* Madi thought, watching him greet his brother. *Running from magic. Trying to save ourselves while saving someone we love. Afraid we can't do both.*

A stone tower overlooked the hillside, and from it came a shrill *clang*. Immediately, workers fled the fields, and the caravan of refugees compressed, like sheep squeezing through a gate. A shadowman crept atop the hillside. Its dark form moved from rock to rock, tracking the caravan like a wolf. Madi pointed it out to Bandico, who cupped the brim of his hat before looking.

"Alright tree urchins, back to the wagon," he said. "I'll be riding through the night, so try to get some sleep if you can."

Wind rustled through the vines. Shadows stretched across the orchards as daylight dipped behind the hills. Nearby wagons sped their pace to keep up with the dayclouds. Nobody wanted to ride through the night, but Bandico seemed to eagerly await the coming darkness. He climbed confidently into his driver's box, the pale glow of his eyes growing. Madi wished she shared his confidence. But nightfall worried her, the shadowman in the hills worried her, the future worried her, as did the past. Dario, Lamptree, Aerial's curse—anxiety came from every direction, chewing at her stomach. She hadn't eaten, she'd barely slept . . .

A flock of crows burst up from the vineyard with harsh caws, interrupting her thoughts. Panima and Aerial were nearby, but Corlan and Wodan were nowhere in sight. Bereket called out for them, turning his ballista toward the fleeing crows. Something was coming—black boots in the vineyard. Mist leapt toward Bandico's fingers. Wisps of cloud crackled as he crafted an elegant black bow and an arrow. Arm outstretched, body rigid, weapon poised— he scanned the vineyard, where leaves rustled loudly in the dying daylight.

"Corlan, come," Bereket said as the boy emerged with a cluster of grapes in his hand.

In the daylight, his hair was a radiant gold, but now that darkness approached, it dulled to a more dusty brown. As he ran, he smiled.

And Madi found it miserably unfair. How could he smile after all that'd happened?

"Where's Wodan?"

Corlan pointed to the black pair of boots. "He's coming."

It wasn't a shadowman after all—just Wodan. Soot stained his uniform, and his black hair fell over his eyes as he trudged back to the wagon. He didn't even notice the brothers' weapons aimed at him. He was too busy looking through his pockets. After finding a few of them empty, he panicked, scouring the rest of his body until he found his small piece of crissle rock. He stared callously at the bit of unrefined lantern fuel before climbing back into the wagon.

Panima sat in the grass, holding Aerial. She twirled a dandelion between her fingers. Aerial opened her mouth and leaned forward, repeatedly trying to eat the flower, but Panima pulled it away at the last moment, touching her nose to Aerial's each time. Aerial giggled, but the Lamptree girl remained expressionless. When Bandico called her, she smothered the flower between two fingers and silently climbed into the wagon with Aerial.

Madi was the last to climb back onto the wagon. She peeked toward the plain, where the Carmine Keep jutted up from a mesa, its jagged towers glinting in the Gloom. A long sigh of uncertainty pushed through her lips. Obey the oracles, or run to a city of escape? The choice was like deciding which cliff to leap off of. But Bandico had a point. The chances of the Red Rider lifting Aerial's curse seemed slim, but still, it felt unwise to ignore that chance. What would Dario have said? Surely, he'd want to run, but would he risk Aerial's life?

No. One step in the wrong direction, and her curse would burn forever. Madi had four days to make this decision, but instead, she'd spent four days wishing she could turn back time. What a magic that would be, and what a terrible price it would cost.

The rear hatch to Bandico's wagon clapped shut, and Madi stumbled inside the dim cabin as though she was climbing into her own coffin. Old instincts warned her that traveling with the brothers beyond Carmine was a mistake. They were Shades, feared far and wide for violence, desperation, and unpredictability. All it would take was a wave of Bandico's hand, and he could cull this Galecrafted wagon, killing everyone inside.

Yet, in the two most dire moments of Madi's life, Bandico had appeared, seemingly out of thin air—like a ghost—to help her. Coincidence or not, his presence was beginning to have a comforting effect.

"I think its kinda cozy in here," Corlan said.

Panima rolled her eyes, revolted. "Cozy is NOT the word. There's what? One pillow?"

Corlan shrugged. "Bandico doesn't seem like a pillowy kind of person. He's got treasure boxes, though. That's cool!" The latch clicked open, but then Corlan's face soured. "Empty."

"He emptied it to give Aerial a place to sleep," Panima said while lowering Aerial carefully into the box, alongside the sole pillow.

"Was there money inside? I bet it was full of glass!" Corlan peeked into the box, curling his nose. "Whew. Doesn't smell like money."

"Brews," Wodan grunted from his bunk.

The wagon lurched forward. Warding brews chimed from the horses' harnesses, reminding everyone of Bandico's ghost. The kids spoke very little after that, and their eyes glinted in the dark as they searched the creaking cabin for a sixth figure. Madi did too. She perched beside the porthole window in an alcove opposite the bunks, expecting to see Raven's reflection in the glass. This alcove was just about the only place she could tolerate inside of this wooden box. She didn't understand how the others could sleep with all of this shaking and bumping.

Starlight beamed through the window, illuminating the floor of the cabin, where Corlan slept flat on his back, hands tucked behind his head. His body bobbled with the rumble of the wagon. Madi squirmed, unable to fathom his posture. After a time, he opened his eyes and lifted the toy she'd made into the pale light. A small crack split the side of the soldier's head.

"I could fix him, if you'd like," she whispered.

"No, I like it. Makes him look tough." Corlan brushed his finger along the split wood and then peeked at Madi. "Panima said you made it, and all the other toys at the festival, even the flying ones. All by yourself?"

"All by myself."

"I bet it took all day long."

"Yes, all day."

"Every day?"

"Every day," Madi whispered, remembering her cluttered workshop, filled with formations of soldiers, lines upon lines of them.

"Why?"

Madi gazed at the toy in Corlan's hand, and the brave expression painted on its face. "It makes me happy," she answered. "And keeps my mind occupied."

"You sound like the officers," the boy replied. "They use that word a lot with the crew, except they don't make toys, just ammunition. They stay occupied a lot, but I don't think it makes them very happy."

Officers? Crew? Madi studied the boy and his motley assortment of clothes. She was beginning to wonder if he hadn't stolen one piece of clothing from ten different houses. His eyes grew heavy, and starlight danced peacefully across his face. She guessed he was eight or nine years old, too young to work the docks.

"You spent time on a cloudcrawler?" she asked.

"My whole life. This is the first wagon I've stowed away on. Bandico caught me pretty quick."

"I had a feeling you weren't from Lamptree."

"Can I still keep my soldier?" Corlan asked, winking an eye open.

"I don't know," Madi said, smiling. "I'm sure I wrote 'For Lamptree children ONLY' on there somewhere."

Corlan chuckled. "I'm one of the stowaways," he revealed. "We're like a company, except we're not Celestials, just ordinary kids. A bunch of us hide on cloudcrawlers. We go all over. The governors call us a gang of miscreants, so that's something, I guess. Lamptree was the fifth colony I've been to." He yawned and let his chin slide onto his shoulder. "Do you always have parties like that?"

"Once a year."

"Well, it was definitely my favorite place to visit so far."

Mine, too, Madi thought as she watched the boy drift to sleep. No wonder he did so well in this rickety wagon. This was just another cabin to him. Another journey. Another unknown destination. His calm made her aching heart jealous.

Aerial slept lightly inside Bandico's treasure chest, wheezing and whimpering. Madi watched her for a time before resting her head against the porthole. Torchlight flickered outside, illuminating a wagon full of refugees. In the driver's box, a young girl slept on a woman's lap, covered in a red blanket. Madi yawned, tempted to sleep by the steady clop of hooves, the gentle chime of Bandico's warding vials, and the distant whir of starlight. Wagon wheels churned, reminding her of the windmill on her balcony. She imagined herself there, in a perfect twilight, and her eyelids started to grow very heavy.

Madi gasped, shaking her head and tugging her hair. She dared not sleep, else she might wake up in one of her haunting dreams on

Lamptree. She climbed up the ladder into the pleasant night breeze. Insects sang from the hillside. Wagons rattled nearby, bathed in torchlight, but Bandico drove in utter darkness.

"Can't sleep?" he asked, his body shrouded by the night.

"Afraid I'll dream," she replied.

"I know that feeling," he replied. "Here, catch."

Madi reached out, feeling her way across the dark deck. Something squishy struck her in the chest, surprising her. It dropped to the deck with a *slosh*.

"Sorry," Bandico said, chuckling.

"He forgets we can't see like him," his brother said, pouring out a cup of daylight brew. It sizzled and sparked, illuminating the deck. Bandico groaned, leaning away.

Madi found a leather flask at her feet. "What's this?"

"Brew, but not the magic kind," Bandico answered. "Mead, from my old hives."

The wagon shifted as Bereket slid closer to his brother, making room for Madi in the driver's box. Madi uncorked the flask and sat down. The bench was softer than it looked, and warm from Bereket's weight. She sniffed the brew, catching a subtle sweet sting in her nose. With a gentle squeeze, she drank. Warm liquid rolled onto her tongue. She preferred drier drinks, but Bandico's was wildly sweet. The brothers laughed together as she spat up, coughing.

"Too much honey," Madi said, grimacing.

"No such thing," Bandico said. "Not all my batches hit so hard, but this one warms you faster than a den-friend."

Bereket let out a deep chuckle and drank from his own large flask. Madi took a second sip. The liquid burned down her throat, crashing onto the entanglement of emotions burrowed inside her body. Bandico was right about one thing: it felt good, like a warm waterfall. She blinked slowly, letting her head rock back. Starlight darted through gaps in the clouds.

The brothers chatted quietly, and Madi let her body rock to the rhythm of the rumbling wagon. Sip after sip, her nerves slowly settled. Sip after sip, her mind muddled. She yawned, and a hot breath rolled across her lips. This was a mistake, she realized, corking the flask. She was tired. Her dreams were waiting, and now she lacked the will to stay awake.

CHAPTER 16: MADI

Madi woke up in her bed on Lamptree, surrounded by warm blankets and pillows. Overhead, a staircase coiled around a small library platform toward an attic door. Books lay open on the floor, their pages rustling in a gentle breeze. A coral vine clung to the stair, boasting clusters of brilliant pink flowers. Some of the petals drifted through the darkness, landing on her blankets. As soon as she saw them, Madi jolted upright, cursing. She'd let her guard down, and now she was back inside her cottage, dreaming again.

Arched windows lined the wall next to her bed. In the past, she'd enjoyed waking up in the morning as dayclouds beamed through the glass, filling her entire home with light. But now, the dark sky outside was full of falling stars. They rained from one horizon to the other, filling the air with a sense of dread. Her conversation with Bandico immediately came to mind. When Raven haunted him, he saw falling stars too. *So who is haunting me?* The cabin appeared empty, but Madi knew she wasn't alone.

Stepping over a small stack of books, she studied her home. The mess was exactly as she'd left it. Clothes covered the floor, muffling her steps. There'd been no time to clean while tending to Dario. The kitchen was completely dark, but a gentle glow came from the far side of her living quarters, where the fireplace crackled with light. She crept toward it, screeching when a dark body came into view. She latched onto its neck, lowering her hip and throwing it as hard as she could. With a hollow *thud*, it toppled to the ground, completely rigid.

Sewing needles and fabric fell to the floor, and Madi's face soured. She'd just tackled her tailoring mannequin.

Aerial's crib was empty. Dario's cot on the balcony was also empty. This was once the most comforting place she knew, but now, its emptiness unnerved her. She added a log to the fire and stoked more light into the dim room. Embers spewed into the air, illuminating her shrine to the Pink Pilgrim. The large wooden statue was carved from the wall, and it depicted a hooded pilgrim sitting on a throne. A long travel staff was in the statue's right hand, a wooden bottle was in its left, and a silver bowl was at its feet. Every few days, Madi lit incense inside the bowl when she prayed.

Something dripped in the kitchen, a slow, steady tap. Floorboards creaked as Madi descended a short staircase to investigate. The darkness frightened her. This was her home, and yet she felt like she'd wandered into someone else's house. If not for the familiar scent of wood polish, and the dark silhouette of dirty dishes stacked in the sink, she might have convinced herself otherwise. The Lamptree bird wailed outside, and Madi opened the front door to look for it. Falling stars hissed overhead, and something fluttered between the branches.

"Who are you?" she called out. "What do you want?"

She eyed the falling stars, remembering what Bandico had told her about the Sea of the Afterlife. The horizon was completely dark, swelling with the rise and fall of giant waves.

"I don't know what you're trying to tell me!" she shouted. Her voice echoed across the empty Mossroad. "Please, where are you?"

Glass shattered inside Madi's cottage. She quickly crossed the kitchen, back into her living quarters. There, in the light of the fire, a bottle had broken.

"More bottles . . ." she mumbled. ". . . How unhelpful."

She stooped to the ground, where bits of broken glass glimmered. Where had this bottle come from? It was almost as if it'd fallen from the statue's hand, but that was impossible since the shrine was carved from wood . . .

Shadows stretched across the floor, and when Madi looked up at her shrine, she screamed. Wood had become flesh. The statue was now a woman, and she was moving! Madi fell back, scattering the shattered glass. A ragged breath filled the room, like an old woman's. The Pilgrim coughed and clutched her chest. With a weary groan, she leaned forward in her shrine, nearly collapsing onto the floor.

Madi scrambled to her feet, balancing the woman. She was shocked to feel flesh and bone beneath the Pilgrim's knitted poncho. The Pilgrim's breath tickled Madi's ear. It sounded exhausted, but it felt powerful, like she'd been holding her breath for eons. White hair, streaked in silver and blonde, spilled from the Pilgrim's hood, which fell to her shoulders, revealing a face far more beautiful than Madi had imagined. Judging by the coughs and groans, she'd imagined some sort of hag, but this woman was neither old nor young. She seemed—apart from time. Youth polished her skin, but age creased her expressions. A wreath of pink and white petals adorned her hair, and beneath them, a pair of cunning eyes glared powerfully.

Firelight flickered on her face. Was she angry? Sad? Or in pain? Madi spotted hints of each. Tiny beads adorned the woman's white cloak—a pale knitted poncho. The Pilgrim was always depicted as wearing such. Madi was too afraid to speak, and the Pilgrim seemed too exhausted to open her mouth. So, in the warmth of the crackling fire, they were silent for some time.

"Why do you all insist on hearing with your ears?" the Pilgrim whispered at last. Her voice was like a morning breeze—peaceful, soft, and apace. "Why don't you trust the heartbeat we've given you?"

The voice cut through Madi's skin, causing her to shiver. Broken glass crackled as she backed away and bowed, not knowing how to respond. Was this really happening? Was this the Pink Pilgrim? In *her* home? After a thousand unanswered prayers, now her revered god was here—sitting across from her messy bedroom.

The Pilgrim clutched her stomach. All of Lamptree seemed to creak as she sat up in her throne, grimacing. "What don't you understand about my messages, Madi?" she asked gently.

Madi's mouth hung open, and she couldn't manage more than a croaked syllable here and there. The only thing keeping her from collapsing from fear was a subtle hint of doubt. The Pink Pilgrim harnessed winds and shaped worlds. She ruled from her throne above, writing tasks in starlight. This couldn't possibly be her. This was Bandico's mead, turning her dream sideways.

"You see, Madi, this is why we speak through bottles and dreams." The breadth of the Pilgrim's voice softened as she smiled. Suddenly, she seemed so familiar, so safe, so kind. "When we speak face to face, you all say it is too much, or you say nothing at all."

When Madi heard the Pilgrim say her name, she relaxed somewhat. "I-I'm sorry," she replied, focusing her breaths. Excitement made her smile, but then reverence made her afraid. She lowered her gaze from the Pilgrim's pained posture. "It's really you," she said, looking up again. "I can't believe it. You're real! Well, I-I always knew you were real, but I never thought you'd . . . you know . . . bother . . . with me . . . . . . Should I stop talking?"

The Pilgrim chuckled and hummed. "You speak like you pray."

"I ramble."

"Only when you're afraid."

Madi risked a longer look. Pain crippled the Pilgrim's proud posture, but there was still so much power in her gaze. Why did she seem so familiar? Madi had never seen this woman before in her life, but being close to her now warmed her heart, as though seeing family.

"It's really you . . ."

"You've seen me many times, Madi."

"When?"

"Every day, but not in this form." The Pilgrim coughed. "I find no joy inhabiting a body which travels the world. My delight comes from inhabiting a place where people travel to. You already fell in love with my true form," she said, glancing toward the window, toward the branches. "Which is why my favor rests upon you."

Chills scoured Madi's arms. A god's true form could be anything, even a— "Lamptree?" she asked as leaves drifted through the open window. They skittered across the floor toward the Pilgrim's brown boots. "You're Lamptree?"

The Pilgrim nodded weakly, her hair caught by the breeze.

Madi teetered, unsure of how to react. She sat on the hearth and bowed her head in her hands. The fire warmed her back, and soon she was sweating. Part of it made sense. Lamptree was unlike anywhere else Madi had ever known. But the Gales ruled from above, writing tasks in starlight, and Lamptree was destroyed.

"I'm afraid I don't understand," she admitted.

"I know," the Pilgrim replied. "And you want answers."

"I just want to know what I should do."

The Pilgrim wheezed, and Lamptree's branches creaked. "I'm afraid I could tell you all you wish to know, but you would still be unsure of what to do. I have the power to obtain any answer I desire. Yet, even now, I wonder what is right. I wonder if we will win this war, or if the people we created will escape in time."

Shadows grew on the walls, and Madi shrank away from the Gale's words. The fire provided no warmth, and all of Lamptree seemed to teeter and sway. Windows clapped open as the room tilted. Glass slid across the floor, and dishes crashed in the kitchen. Madi spread out her arms, balancing herself, and the Pilgrim gripped her throne with an ached cry. The sound of a roaring wave echoed outside.

"Where are we right now?" Madi asked as the room righted. "A dream? Inside my head, right?"

The Pilgrim's words came slowly, painfully. "Your body is asleep on Bandico's wagon. Your mind has manifested in the Sea of the Afterlife, with me," the Pilgrim replied. "I thought you would understand when Bandico explained this place to you."

Understand? Understand what? Madi peeked at the Pilgrim. The woman's chin dipped toward her chest, exhausted, but her eyes remained fixed on Madi. "What are you saying?" Madi asked timidly. "You're my ghost?" It seemed blasphemous to even suggest it.

Firelight flickered against the Pilgrim's flawless skin. White hair curled around her face, glowing in the light of the fire like a grim mist streaked by daylight.

"Yes, but only since the colony's most recent destruction."

"Most recent destruction? Lamptree has been destroyed before?"

"Yes. As a ghost, I have manifested myself through many people."

"But if you're a ghost, that would mean—"

The Pilgrim blinked her eyes, lifting her gaze as Madi paused. "It means I am dead," she admitted. She lifted her poncho, revealing a large hole beneath her heart. There was no blood dripping from the fatal wound. Instead, a steady current of pink mist floated from her body, disappearing as it rose. "And my soul is bleeding. The clouds you see, rising from the earth, rise from the lowest of our worlds, where Lamptree first fell."

Madi stared at the wound. Her heart tilted like a sinking ship, capsizing her confidence in—everything. She had a million questions, but now she feared the answers.

"Are you certain you want to know more?" the Pilgrim asked, no doubt sensing Madi's hesitance. "Revelation will not make your path any easier. Answers may ease one concern, but add two more."

Madi wrung her hands together. Her thoughts bit like ice despite the fire at her back. "I-I'm not sure," she stuttered. The Pilgrim's wound disturbed her. What did it mean for Aerial? What did it mean for Dario? What did it mean for the world? "I just want to know what to do."

"I already told you," the Pilgrim said. "Go with Bandico. But apparently you find bottles unhelpful."

"You want me to go to the city of escape?" Madi asked, walking toward her daughter's empty crib. She moaned and clasped her hands in front of her face, distraught. "But if I don't reach the Carmine Keep, Aerial's curse will kill her."

"Not if we are quick," the Pilgrim said, massaging her wound. "You may choose that other path, but I will have no choice but to depart from you and haunt another. I have tasks to tend to before my time ends. The oracles may lift your daughter's curse, but without me, you will not survive."

"You're keeping me alive? But Bandico said ghosts leech life."

"My dear Madi, you do not have enough life to give me," the Pilgrim said, chuckling. "I am not the ghost of a mortal. My spirit bleeds into the worlds, so it is, in fact, the worlds that leech from me." Madi clasped her hands together as she paced, hugging herself and touching Aerial's empty pouch. Normally, she'd cradle her daughter right now, but Aerial's warmth was gone. All warmth was gone. "So, these really are the last days?" she asked.

The question seemed to pain the Pilgrim even further. She moaned and gripped her chest, crying out. Lamptree quaked. The fireplace flickered, illuminating pictures on Madi's wall—but not the pictures she remembered hanging. These were pictures of the past. Seas surged. Mountains rose and crumbled. Lightning cut through the sky—the Purple Prince's Spear.

"They are *our* last days, but not yours, if our plan succeeds. We should have listened to him! The youngest of us. Our poor little brother. The one you call the Brown Hood. He warned us of a foreign magic, roiling on the fringes of our creation. We could have prevented all this."

"The Gloom?" Madi asked, eyeing another portrait. The Brown Hood stood behind a legion of his fabled mud golems, firing a bow toward a mountain in the sea.

Lamptree shuddered as the Pilgrim opened her eyes. "No," she replied. "The Gloom was not supposed to be our enemy. Those invaders were cruel gods—creators like us, with their own worlds, their own people. In those days, a foreign dawn pierced the borders of our creation. Mountains bridged the shores of our world with the shores of those wicked beings. Waters rose. Waves crashed. My sister's sea surged against the sea of some other goddess. Storms brewed in two opposing skies. Cataclysm!"

Firelight painted the room in a fiery glow. Meanwhile, Madi studied the pictures on the wall—the Teal Stranger walked amid a blizzard. Searing flames billowed from the Red Rider's shield, and his crimson lance jutted into the heart of a mountain like a strand of blood. Madi couldn't imagine all of the Gales' power in one place. She'd seen what a legion of Celestials could do with Galecraft—uproot the foundations of a world.

"In the lowest of our realms, we fought to protect the worlds we'd created," the Pilgrim said, staring into the fire, which *snapped* and *popped*, devouring the log Madi had added. "Thousands of our Celestials died. The enemy was relentless—and their own heroes fought against us." The Pilgrim dipped her head, and a tear fell into her lap. "We needed help. Our world, our people, all of our creation depended on us. I can still remember fearing for every newborn who breathed my air, for the children who whispered my name to the wind. If we'd lost that war, our enemy would have smothered them all with a smile."

"And?" Madi asked, wondering how the Gloom fit into all this. This contradicted every history book she'd read. It was treason to suggest that the Gales weren't in complete control. "You lost?"

"No," the Pilgrim whispered. "We schemed, and we won."

The Pilgrim stared toward the fire, uttering a verse from an old song that Madi recognized. Bandico sang it quietly on deck, almost every day:

> *"To whom do the Nine Gales pray?*
> *Together, they combined to birth the Black Knight.*
> *Divided, they died to summon the Gray Ghost.*
> *Absent, their last breaths spoke the first White Whisper.*
> *When the Nine needed help, they prayed to the shade."*

The Pilgrim's shadow danced in the light of the fire. "Victory, but at a terrible cost. We created the Gloom and the Three Shades—the dark side of our very being. They won us the battle. They ravaged our enemy's worlds, which was to be their reward, but then they returned unsatisfied, with hordes of shadow. They wanted more—the worship of our people. It was an impossible request. The Gloom taints the very air our people breathe, and we'd had an agreement. My older sister, the Arbiter, tried to reason with them, but they killed her. My eldest brother rode after them into that foreign land, his red shield burning hotter than I'd ever seen. That was over a thousand years ago, and I haven't seen him since. That was the day this war began. The Ashen attacked, overwhelming my sisters and brothers. Overwhelming our armies. Overwhelming me. I crumbled. My limbs cracked. Black and white fire consumed me, and the last thing I saw was our eldest sister, the Yellow Watcher, shining as a cloudcrawler. Mirrors glinted with light as she carved the pillars of that world in two to protect the worlds above."

The fire hissed, and the pictures on the wall shifted, depicting battles and figures too fierce for Madi to believe. This talk was treason, but the Pilgrim spoke with conviction and clarity while oracles always gave vague answers. Tears welled in the goddess' eyes, and she truly appeared to have witnessed these events. "Why haven't I heard this story before?" Madi asked.

"Because they're buried with the dead. News falls through the worlds faster than it rises," the Pilgrim answered. "Remember, this world has enjoyed peace for hundreds of years without reason to fear the Gloom or its shadowmen. But now, the tide has finally risen. The Ashen climb the roots of this world, and if they defeat the remaining Celestials, they will climb into the next. That is what the fools on our thrones fear. That is why they've deceived our oracles."

Shooting stars soared slowly through the air, and Madi immediately thought of Dario. He was right! He'd been all along. "You mean someone else has been writing our tasks all this time?" she asked, shuddering. "Who?"

The Pilgrim's glare burned, hotter than the fire. Sadness flickered in her eyes, alongside betrayal. "They were mortals, once haunted as you are. Now, they are pretenders. They used the knowledge we revealed to find our thrones and seize the power that our nine realms provide. They know the truth about the Gloom, and they think they're safe from it."

"So, the oracles don't know they're being lied to?"

"No, it seems they do not. They've forgotten how to read the true depths of the sky."

What about Sembetra? Did she? A headache throbbed inside Madi's skull. The Pilgrim was right. These answers were more of a burden than a relief. The whole world was dangling above a dark jaw. Was there any way to survive this? The Pilgrim had just admitted she didn't even know. Madi hung her head, paralyzed by hopelessness. This was the end of the world. Not even this dream felt safe. The only way she could think of to survive was to find an escape—out of time and trouble—but even if she did, it would be an eternity spent trying to repair a broken heart that would never heal. Dario was gone.

Her mind turned to the caravan of refugees. They were fleeing to colonies when they needed to be making for cities of escape. Why weren't the oracles saying anything? "Dario was right," she whispered. "The Gales—I mean, the people ruling on your throne—they don't want us to escape. Why?"

"You may call them Gales," the Pilgrim said sadly. "So long as they sit in our seats and wield our power and command our Celestials, that is what they are. They are very powerful now, and they will grow more so as they uncover our magics. What they lack is a love for the worlds WE created. They care only to protect their newfound power, and they'll sacrifice our creation to keep it."

Madi's skin tingled as the Pilgrim spoke. So that was why the oracles and their inspectors were so obsessed with searching for magic. The Gales above wanted more power. She paused at the window, eyeing Dario's cot. The sheets were mangled from hours of his writhing. Her heart ached—and it'd been aching—for so many days now that it felt like a shriveled grape, squeezed between two gears, over and over. "Where is Dario?" she asked, sapped of all strength.

The Pilgrim opened her palm in the light of the fire. Bits of her flesh drifted away, like dust. If the Gales themselves could die and wither away, what hope was there for anyone?

"In the world beneath yours," the Pilgrim replied. "Bandico was not lying, and for Dario's sake, you were fortunate to have listened to him."

Madi collapsed onto the window, weeping. What fortune was there in this? Dario was wandering the underworld alone. He deserved rest, not suffering. She'd watched him slowly die, and now she'd feel his absence for the rest of her life, knowing he was down there somewhere.

"He doesn't deserve this. Was there any way you could have saved him? You should have saved him instead of me," she whimpered, tears smudging the glass. "I want to wake up. Let me wake up now, please!"

"You don't think I share your pain?" the Pilgrim asked. Tears streamed down her face too. Strands of her hair clung to her cheeks, and her voice wavered like a tree in a storm. "Your sorrow is but a wisp of mine, daughter! Do you know, Madi Amriel, toymaker, what it's like to create from the void? To birth a people and then fail them? Do you know what it's like to love a world and wonder if you're powerful enough to protect it? Do you know what it's like to hold a million souls in your hand, and fear you're not strong enough to hold onto them? To fear you're not the most powerful being in the void? To learn that there are distant gods who would snatch you all from us for the joy of it."

Madi dropped to her knees. Maybe she didn't know what it was like to create a world, but she knew what it was like to create life. She knew the feeling of holding a child in her hands, wondering how she would ever keep her safe. Now, the task seemed impossible. *If gods struggle to protect their own children, how can I?*

The Pilgrim cradled Madi's head on her lap, where Madi felt utterly depleted. She heard no heartbeat in the Pilgrim's chest—only something like a strong wind. "I favor you so much, Madi, because your love for family is like mine, and you yearn to find a place for them to be safe." She curled her fingers through Madi's hair, whispering like a mother.

Madi regretted asking these questions. The answers had cast such a shadow on her heart. "Is there any hope?" she asked.

Lamptree swayed. The room creaked. Dark water sprayed against the windows, where the shutters clapped in a gust of wind.

"There is a place. We will lead you there, but everyone must climb before it's too late! Everyone must know. They must be told. Follow our bleeding souls to the place we've prepared, an escape we've created—into the void, and a new world we've created."

"Follow the rising clouds?"

"Yes."

"So, there's a chance for Dario?" Chills covered Madi's body, and she lifted her head. A smile crossed her face as she imagined him flying through the air toward her. "There's a chance I will see him again?"

The Pilgrim's eyes were closed and her voice weakened as she repeated, "Yes . . . yes," over and over. She wheezed, gripping Madi's hand. "But there is also the chance that you may not. The journey will be difficult for those far below. So many people stand in their way, and so few obey."

"I'll listen," Madi said, squeezing the Gale's frigid hands and bringing her lips to them. "Please, I'll do anything you say to bring my family back together again."

"Then go," the Gale whispered and wheezed. "Return to the city where I found you, and tell people to climb."

Madi gasped as she woke to a bitter breeze. Her head rested on the side of Bandico's green driver's bench, where she'd been drooling. Bereket had placed a furry blanket over her, which buzzed with his noticeably pungent Galecraft. As she stretched the stiffness from her body, her feet kicked her empty flask of mead. She groaned, holding the sides of her throbbing head.

Clouds of daylight threaded the horizon, where clouds meandered upward, toward the stars. It was so obvious now! The currents of mist were a trail. They each lingered for a while in this world, but then they wandered upward, making Madi shrink in her seat. She'd promised the Pilgrim she'd listen, but now the thought of jumping into a divine plan made her shake.

Beneath a silvery atmosphere, a gloomy plain surrounding Bandico's wagon, which he'd pulled to the side of a large crossroads. Long caravans of refugees rattled along the road, turning toward the Carmine Keep, which was now clearly visible. Birds circled its stone towers, where large lanterns of Gale dangled above a moat of molten lava. The Red Rider himself was rumored to have once resided in that citadel, and after her dream, Madi believed it.

Bereket and the Lamptree kids sat on a grassy mound not far from the wagon. He beat on a drum and hummed. Meanwhile, Bandico remained on deck tending his new hives. Bees circled his black hat, and his face was veiled by a net.

"Make a decision?" he asked.

Madi watched the refugees flee toward the Carmine Keep, then she scanned the constellations peeking out from behind its gold parapets. Her world had flipped upside down. She felt trapped, like a grain of sand in a clock, caught between the rising tide and the stars above. The Gales—whom she'd once feared—were dead and drifting with her. She'd made her decision, but it was just as the Pilgrim had said: answers had eased one concern, but created many more in its place.

"I have," Madi said. "I'll go with you, but I'll have to speak with the children. They should go to Carmine."

"I already spoke to them. They cling to you like honey," Bandico said quietly. "I used to know what that was like. They said they're staying with you, wherever you go. So, where will it be?"

"West and then north," Madi said, pointing to the road beyond Carmine. "I'll write down everything I can remember about where we found the city."

Bandico grinned and signaled for everyone to mount up. While hundreds of refugees turned toward the safety of the keep, his wagon rumbled alone into the wild. The stars watched them, and as Madi cradled her daughter close, she felt their gaze turn hot.

CHAPTER 17: DARIO

ar is a riddle. To end it, someone has to solve it. The longer the riddle takes, the more people suffer. Why are the shadowmen fighting the Gales? Why do they snatch colonists from their homes? Where do they take them? Why don't the Gales want their own people to escape?

Dario put down his pen, sensing his spine was about to seize. It'd become predictable while lying on this rickety cot—usually just as he was getting comfortable. He grit his teeth so as not to groan. His back tensed, contorting every muscle. Something was inside of him, tugging his spine in directions he didn't want to go.

WHAT IS HAPPENING TO ME?

When the seizing finally stopped, Dario sat there panting, watching a bead of sweat slide down his nose onto the page. He scribbled the question into his book, below the others. Anger stewed inside him, and the longer he sat in this stinking cave, the more violent his spasms became. How long had it been now? Days. Maybe weeks. It was all beginning to blur, and his impatience burned.

Red cloud steamed from the grotto's geyser, curling around the decrepit cloudcrawler, heating it like an oven. Slime caked every surface, slick from the constant movement of cloud. Water dripped from the vines overhead and pattered into a puddle near Dario's bed. The torturous sound was like the drip of time itself, tapping his brain.

I have to get back.

Every day, a ledge-walker came and led healthy pilgrims

away—along the Underworld Trail. That was the name for the network of hideouts connecting each world with the one above it. Dario still had trouble believing that such an organization existed, but whenever he asked the crew of Cavern Sixteen about it, they assured him that Captain Imani was real—that's all they would ever say about the Trail or its leader. The surgeon, Krisha Mesa, and Girli, the haunted horn operator, were both volunteers. They helped smuggle people upward, but so far, Dario had been deemed too dangerous to move. To pass time, he spent much of each day writing, recording the stories of these forgotten people—the dead.

> *Ten volunteers went out today with sleds, to help Company Snow gather people from the shore. Only seven returned. They bring wounded from the beach each day, but in these conditions, only a few survive. Without clean beds and proper brews, there's only so much Krisha can do. We have little food. Disease runs rampant, and those who fade are quietly killed and thrown into the pit below.*
>
> *The healthy huddle around Girli's haunted horn, waiting for a ledge-walker to come and guide them along the Trail. I wonder how many of them survived to the next safehouse, or how many now lay dashed upon the rocks—like Illio.*
>
> *This place is godless. The Gales have abandoned this world and these people. We climb alone.*
>
> *~Dario Lire 15.14.2f*

Krisha held a cup of daylight close to Dario's body, checking for hints of faded flesh. There was barely any brew left inside the glass. The yellow liquid bubbled, releasing a sugary scent into the air. As the brew evaporated, Dario's bed went dim.

"I'm not fading," he told the surgeon. "I'm ready to get out there."

"I know, Dario, but I can't allow it. Not yet," she said. "I'm sorry. Your condition would be too great a risk for your ledge-walker and other pilgrims."

Dario sat up, feeling around for Nightfly. The flier clattered as he dragged it closer. "I'll make my own way then."

"Please don't," Krisha said earnestly. "The ledges are too dangerous, and you don't know the way."

"The way is up. Straight up, until I see starlight."

"The Ashen watch the heights. They control the underworld passages." Krisha wiped her hands on her apron and sat on the cot across from Dario. "Listen to me. It's too dangerous. I know this is the last thing you want to hear, but you have to be patient, or you're going to find yourself a world further away from your family."

Dario dropped Nightfly, letting it rattle to the floor like a pile of bones. "It's like you *want* me to fade."

"No, Dario, I don't."

"Then why do you snuff out every shred of hope I have?"

"I tell you the truth, because I'm confident you *won't* fade," Krisha admitted. "I don't want you to trap yourself down here, like I've trapped myself . . . and my best friend."

"Girli?" Dario asked, glancing toward the haunted horn. A ghost sang now, his voice echoing crudely throughout the old cloudcrawler. Survivors sat near its base, listening, while Girli turned the crank, filtering cloud through the horn. "You're both trapped?"

"She is, because of me, and I won't climb until I solve it."

Dario opened his book. "Do you mind if I write this down?"

"It's fine, I suppose. Here, I'll pour out more light."

Krisha refilled her cup with water and emptied a drop of daylight brew into it. The water sizzled and evaporated, surrounding Dario's bed in a healthy glow, easing his strained eyes. He touched his pen to the page, and she continued.

"I was a Celestial in the world above, with Company Mesa. Girli was an inventor. I fell during the siege of Reeftown, and she blew herself up while testing a prototype of the haunted horn. Don't worry. She's given me permission to joke about it. She says she'd blow herself up again for science. Her reason: because she'd never have learned that her horn needed a ghost to work if she hadn't. Anyway, we died on the exact same day, hundreds of miles apart, but we washed ashore together six years ago, and we've stayed together ever since."

Dario had no idea the haunted horn was Girli's invention. If only companies in the world above knew about this technology. They wouldn't have to use flying bottles. Tears glistened in the surgeon's eyes as she watched her friend fidget with her fingers and sway in her chair. Every day, Girli wore a different colored blindfold. Today, it was purple. She sat with a peculiar tilt to her head, twitching and grimacing every-so-often, reminding Dario of his own spasms.

"I was in your position," Krisha continued. "I had friends, a company, a life I HAD to get back to, and now she's paying the price. There's something wrong with the bones in her head. I don't know if it's because of the way she died or some other reason, but pressure builds up inside her skull the higher she climbs. I didn't know it at the time. She warned me she wasn't feeling well, but I wanted to climb faster. I was selfish and impatient, and now she's blind because I made us keep going."

"She'll die if she climbs too high?" Dario asked, watching Girli squirm in her seat. She counted her fingers, muttering numbers and statistics to those around her.

The surgeon wiped her eyes. "Yes. She's trying to invent something to protect herself for the next time we try to escape, and I'm trying to figure out a way to heal her, but so far, nothing has worked."

"So, you think my spine will break if I fly up there?"

"I don't know, but I've never seen blood or bone behave like yours. I've been comparing your blood to Vetricus' after each transfusion, and while they both brew gold, there's something different about yours.

If I can learn why, I could help Girli, and maybe even other people."

Dario closed his eyes, uncertain if he was ready for more bad news. "Just my luck—confused bones *and* confused blood."

"It's no different than Vetricus' at first glance, but after a few hours, your blood fades to white while his remains gold."

A hot sweat gripped Dario's body—nervous and tingling. "White? Like Ashen blood?"

"Yes," Krisha answered, lowering her voice. "Identical to my eye."

"What's that mean?"

"I don't know, but if you're willing, I'd like to study you further."

"I'd like to leave," Dario replied. The last thing he wanted was to stay in this cave while Madi and Aerial climbed further away from him. "I need to climb."

"And the Underworld Trail will help you, but it's going to take time. I have a proposition," Krisha said while moving to Dario's bed-side. She knelt on the dirty deck. Roaches scattered as daylight brew dripped onto the boards. Her voice became desperate, and she clung to Dario's dirty bed sheets, begging. "Join us. Volunteer as an agent for the Underworld Trail. We need people like you. There are thousands, hundreds of thousands, maybe millions of people, trapped in the worlds below. The worlds are a ladder, and without Captain Imani's network, most people couldn't climb. You have that tender fire in you. It's why you talk to people in the beds beside you, writing their stories in your book. It's why you draw pictures of Exile and Company Snow in the surf. It's why I know I can tell you the truth without worrying that you'll fade. Your compassion for people burns. You want justice, you pity the weak, and you don't give up. The Trail desperately needs people like you. The *Gales* need you. They have a story too, and people need to hear it, but they need to hear it from someone like you, else they'll lose all hope."

"The Gales?" Dario riffled through the pages of his book, tilting it so the surgeon could see the faces on each page—hundreds of desperate and distraught refugees. "I watched parents bury their children. I told families they'd make it through this war together, knowing it was a lie. I listened to orphans cry their hearts out to the Gales, and do you know what the Gales did?"

Krisha shifted uncomfortably. "Dario—"

"NOTHING! They did nothing. *I* was supposed to be the answer to their prayers—me, a Celestial—but in my heart of hearts I knew we'd all been betrayed." Dario closed his book and gripped the binding tight, drawing a deep breath. "Don't worry. I'll tell people what the Gales have done, in excruciating detail."

"Dario, we're on the same side."

"It doesn't sound like we are."

"Dario, the Gales are dead," Krisha said bluntly. Daylight brew glistened against her bloodstained apron. "They died a long time ago, in a world far below this one, and they *are* helping us. You've been reading their story backward."

Dario felt his face fall numb. It'd become paralyzed somewhere between perturbed and perplexed. His mouth hung open, and his pen sank toward his bed sheet, staining it in a puddle of ink. He tried moving his lips, but little more came out than tiny gasps of disbelief. A million questions squirmed through his brain all at once. Did the oracles know? If the Gales were dead, who was controlling the companies? Who had he spent his entire life grumbling against?

"Do you know where the clouds come from?" Krisha asked.

"Deep underground, from evaporating crissle rock," Dario replied, reciting what Illio had told him. Crissle was compacted cloud—Gale squeezed into a small space over thousands of years. People refined it to fuel lanterns. Dario was no geologist, neither was Illio, but it sounded logical enough.

"That's not true. Why would the Gales' clouds rise from

subterranean crissle, if the Gales themselves resided in the world above," she said, pointing across the grotto, to a pillar of green, brown, and gold clouds rising from the geyser. The chord of currents slithered above the crippled cloudcrawler, blanketing the hideout with a thick jungle atmosphere. "Do you know how much crissle it would take to form a cloud that large? It'd take a vein larger than any ocean we know of. It's impossible. These clouds bleed from something far more powerful—the Gales themselves, where they laid down their lives to reveal the Trail—the trail we follow." The surgeon leaned close, whispering. "Time is running out for everyone, Dario, not just you or your family. If we don't all escape before it's too late, none of us will."

Dario opened his book. His pen hovered above the page, but he was too shocked to write, too skeptical. He'd never heard anything like this before, not from anyone he'd ever interviewed. He grew cold beneath his bed sheets, and he needed a moment to collect himself, but Krisha kept talking, and he was too curious to stop her.

"When the clouds stop flowing, anyone who hasn't escaped the Gloom never will," she said. "Nine Gales. Nine colored currents. It's no coincidence. The clouds are their blood, Dario, and so long as their souls bleed, we have a chance to help people escape."

Dario remained silent, still too stunned to decide if he believed it all or not. The implications were worse than dire. The Gales created these worlds. If they were dead, what chance did anyone have against the Ashen?

"The truth is disturbing," Krisha said. "And we don't tell most people right away. Not all at once at least, but I know the truth won't make your hope fade like it would others."

The truth? To say such a thing was treason—at least in the world above it was. Illio would have been outraged. He would have sat here and debated Krisha until her ears bled. He'd said a thousand times:

the Gales were good, and they could never die.

Dario's spine seized, making him lose grip of his book. It tumbled to the deck's slick surface, stained in blood, sweat, and saltwater. Had all this been for nothing? He stared at his pen—his weapon against the Gales—and he felt purpose bleeding from his heart.

"So, whose tasks are the Celestials following?" he asked.

Krisha picked his book up from a puddle. She softened her tone, no doubt trying to calm him. "We're not sure exactly, but we believe that they are the Gales' heirs—once human, like us, but then granted great power. Very little information comes from the worlds above, and our ghosts risk their souls to bring us what little we know. Everything they've learned coincides with the conclusions in your book. The Gales' heirs use the celestial companies for one thing—power."

As Krisha spoke, volunteers carried survivors into the cavern. Water dripped from the sleds, saltwater and blood, sloshing beneath soggy boots. Moans and gasps echoed, and Krisha rose, barking commands, drowning out the sound of the distant surf. Dario sat silently for a long time. He watched the wounded arrive on sleds. He watched cloud seep from the geyser and slowly rise through holes in the rocks above. He listened to the ghost inside Girli's invention relay reports from other caverns—weather, tides, and Ashen activity. Slowly, the Underworld Trail took shape in his mind, and he imagined all of Lamptree's lifts with their intricate gears to help them rise. He narrowed his eyes and smiled somewhat, beginning to wonder if it really was true.

But that night, he doubted again. A lifetime beneath the constellations and a thousand conversations with Illio made him uncertain. The Gales were above. The oracles were their eyes. How could such a revelation be unheard of in the world above? The Gales were dead? Imposters ruled from their realms? Dario shook his head, smearing his pillow with sweat. If the gods who'd created this world couldn't prevent their own destruction, how could they help Dario and his family escape theirs?

Darkness settled over him, a loneliness in the night. The deck was dim—except for the galley, where the oven glowed deep red. Smoke slithered from it, shimmering as an attendant patrolled the deck, cupping a crude candle. Supplies were running low, otherwise she'd be using brew. A formation of lights moved across the far side of the grotto, catching Dario's eye. Shadows stretched in the darkness, stirred by the shifting light, and something else—flakes of snow.

They fell softly upon Dario's bed, melting onto his skin. Overhead, a teal cloud curled around the hideout's severed top decks. The snow drifted toward the line of torchlight, and Dario felt the urge to follow. He limped through the wounded, watching their silent silhouettes writhe in the dark. They all looked like shadowmen, and soon, some of them would be.

Snow blustered over the bulwark, which Dario gripped tightly as he explored. His bones seemed eager to move as well, but not toward the lights. They tugged him downward, toward the gaping abyss. Clutching the hull, he peered toward the edge of the grotto, where water pooled at the entrance to a subterranean river. There, Exile sat atop a large wooden raft, tying his glaive to the deck. The primitive vessel had a flat base and two fenced decks, like crude scaffolds—colorfully decorated and connected by nets and pulleys. Grape and tomato vines dangled from one deck toward the other, where a small staircase led to an enclosed chamber. Mist veiled a small wooden catapult, which gave off a faint sound Dario recognized—the hum of Galecraft. Company Snow didn't use wagons. They used rafts!

He tread carefully as he neared. This part of the collapsed cloud-crawler was slick with moisture, and the damaged hull tilted toward the geyser below. The deck creaked, and Exile looked up, blinking his wintry eyes. He untied a rope from the tiller, and soon, the raft's large water-wheel began to spin, carrying the vessel toward a dozen others near the mouth of a flooded cave.

"You're leaving?" Dario asked, fear pinching his heart.

Exile nodded, clutching his raft's long wooden tiller. He brushed a strand of wavy brown hair from his eyes and studied the rocks ahead.

"For a task?" Dario asked, feeling a sudden closeness to his rescuer. So, this was what it felt like to rely on Celestials for protection. No wonder colonists always prayed for more companies. The thought of Company Snow not being in the cavern or in the surf outside was more than discomforting.

Exile nodded again. His face was so youthful, but the squint in his eyes and the weary smirk on his face told Dario that this was far from the first task this boy had obeyed.

"How do you get tasks down here?"

Exile pointed to his telescope. Tied crudely to the bulwark, the long scope was angled downward. Waves rolled into the shallows, where corpses and starlight mingled. The violent surf churned the waters, and Dario saw nothing of note. But when the water calmed, he saw a glimmer, a reflection of a sky he thought he recognized.

Company Snow floated slowly into the dark channel, one young Celestial to a raft, their eyes shimmering like ice. A current of teal cloud flowed overhead, and snow danced across the decks. "Exile!" Dario called, feeling a bond he should have felt earlier. This boy was a Celestial. A brother. *He saved my life, and I've the sinking feeling this is the only chance I'll ever have to thank him.*

"I never should have taken this from you!" he said, reaching into his pocket and retrieving Illio's sash. "Keep it safe for me, please."

Exile took it and tied the sash to his glaive, which he held high for Dario to see—a promise, to keep the tiny memory of Illio safe. Dario shivered. Past memories flowed through his mind, losing his company, losing Madi, losing Illio. As Company Snow floated into the subterranean passage, he feared this pattern would only continue. Stalactites dangled above their rafts, and then darkness devoured them. The last thing Dario saw was Illio's sash waving atop Exile's glaive.

A teary voice came from behind. "I wish they wouldn't go."

"Girli?" Dario turned, finding her on the steps to the deck above. She sat with a crumbled device in her hands—bits of bronze. Her haunted horn was completely decayed, completely silent. There was no purple glimmer, because the ghost inside was gone. "Girli, I'm sorry."

"I am sorry as well," she replied. "I'll build another. But every time a new ghost volunteers to haunt my horns, I feel sad. Am I the one sending them into the world below?"

"No, they volunteered," Dario said, sitting beside her. "Just like you volunteered. We're all in this together, right? Like a bunch of gears, spinning side by side."

Girli wiped her nose on her sleeve. Tools jingled from her shirt, reminding him of Madi. "I appreciate the relatable analogy."

Dario watched the last of Company Snow's rafts disappear. "Do you know where they're going?"

"You are not an agent of the Trail, therefore I may not disclose any details of their task."

Dario chuckled. She spoke so awkwardly. At first he'd found it slightly strange and rude. But now he knew her story. She'd climbed too fast with Krisha, and now her skull was squeezing her brain just like Dario's spine squeezed his nerves. The similarity sparked a kinship.

"Any chance you'd tell a nosy archivist?" he asked.

Girli tugged a blanket around her shoulders, and flakes of snow settled atop it. "Zero, unless you were to reconsider Krisha's offer."

"I want to, but it's still too much to believe all at once."

"You don't believe?" she asked, turning toward him. A white bandage sheathed her eyes, but her brow creased softly, desperately. "What about Company Snow? They're proof? Surely you investigated their past."

"We never got around to an interview," Dario replied, tapping his book's binding. "It'd have been a good one though. I meant to ask Exile how his company managed to descend an underworld passage."

"Descend?" Girli said, smiling cryptically. "Typical archivist, asking questions backwards. Company Snow did not descend. They climbed. From a world far, far below. Because *that's* where it all started," she whispered. "Exile has never seen the world above this one. But do you know what he *has* seen? Gods dying to preserve their people. He saw where the Trail began, and he's followed it here, rescuing people along the way. Rescuing you."

Dario's skin tingled, and he smiled toward the teal clouds above. They billowed up from below, through holes in the earth, and snow drifted from them. Then he laughed. Something in him clicked, like the cogs of Krisha's story had finally aligned.

"I had no idea," he mumbled.

"You didn't ask," Girli said, feeling for Dario's book. When she found it, she flipped it over on his lap. "You have it backwards, Mr. Archivist. We're not falling. We're climbing. Talk to Left-Foot, the ledge-walker. She traveled with Company Snow. She can tell you their story."

"I will," Dario said eagerly.

He believed her. This was the evidence he'd needed. Not all Celestials came from the world above, which meant there had to be a power below. The thought flipped Dario's perspective of his world upside down. Purpose surged back into his heart. He twirled his pen between his fingers and touched it to the page:

> *War is a riddle, but I've been asking all the wrong questions. Who are the Gales really? How did they die? If their blood is creating a trail, then where are they leading us? I fear more for my family than I did a day ago. I fear more for Illio, and the fate of Company Lire. But now, for the first time in a very long time, there's something I can actually do to help them. I found a group of people like me, who want to help others climb. I've never written so quickly, nor so fervently in my life. I'M NOT ALONE ANYMORE.*
> *~Dario Lire 15.14.2f*

CHAPTER 18: DARIO

That evening, Dario volunteered to join the Underworld Trail. Krisha and Girli were overjoyed.

The surgeon nearly dropped a vial of orange brew she'd been condensing, and the horn operator smiled for an entire half-second. Their reaction encouraged Dario, until he thought of what Madi's reaction might have been. The decision would delay his climb, but what choice did he have? He couldn't afford to part ways with the Trail. Even if he was strong enough to fly back to his family, they'd need the Trail's help too.

If only Madi knew the truth.

Krisha studied Dario's condition for three days—three full, fruitless days—squeezing bone and inducing spasms without deducing even a hint of its cause. Afterward, she arranged for Vetricus to guide him along the ledges to the Trail's headquarters, hidden in a cloud-crawler called the Sky Doe. Dario emerged into a wailing wind, which whipped his face, waking him up to where he really was. He'd been stuck underground for a month now, listening to Girli's haunted horn warn of the world outside. Now, he stepped into it for himself—into the crushing sensation of being a world below Madi.

Vetricus waited on the ledge, a narrow slice of land bordered by a sheer cliff on one side and a sheer drop on the other. His lantern dangled over his shoulder by a string, and in the time he'd been waiting, color had spread to a small area around him—grass as gold as wheat and an old brown fence.

Far below, cloud spouted from the geysers on the coast, plumes of gray, black, and white. Dario guessed what color the currents were, based on shape and movement. Dashes of white cut quickly ahead of the others—those were probably pinks. Thick billows of gray smoke lingered above the shallows, spitting wet ash atop sledders in the surf—dark blues, most likely. Madi had made it look so easy. As the geysers spouted cloud, Krisha's warning shot to the forefront of Dario's mind.

When the clouds stop flowing, anyone who hasn't escaped the Gloom never will.

Vetricus hopped from the fence, snatching his travel kit from the grass. Two coils of rope hung from his belt, and his sword jingled against a harness. His windswept hair highlighted an undeniable energy—the air of a once mythic hero, Dario thought. But unlike his twin, he moved with a humility. Dario couldn't say exactly what it was. Maybe it was just the wind, or perhaps the weight of death, but he walked with a burden.

"Am I the only volunteer?" Dario asked, seeing no one else.

"Just you," Vetricus said. "Thinking of going back?"

"No," he answered. Purpose pulsed deep within him, quickly pushing out the reply.

"Right then, let's trim our lamps. Gloom this thick will evaporate our fuel fast."

Vetricus' lantern clicked and hissed as color spread from it. He turned a small knob, dimming the lantern's colorful glow. Dario throttled his own Galefuel. The knob squeaked, and the color around him waned. Gloom closed in, baring shadows like teeth. Dario had a hundred questions he wanted to ask, but Vetricus raised his hood and walked swiftly into the colorless world. Wind swept across the cliffs. Waves battered the beach below, where faded walruses gathered. Lanterns fizzed and clicked. Dario draped his lantern over the front of his left shoulder, close to his face, so that the air entering his lungs would cure first.

The ledge, which was wide and grassy at first, narrowed until Dario couldn't find any safe place for his feet. The sheer cliff to his right met the sheer drop to his left, forming a jagged collection of crags. Ropes and ladders had been driven into the rock, and Vetricus instructed Dario on where to step.

Dario pressed his back against the cliff, hesitating. With each dizzy breath, he felt his spine tugging him from the ledge, as though his own body was fighting against him. *What's wrong with me?* he thought, his sweaty hands clutching the ropes. Pebbles crackled downward, dragging Dario's gaze toward the shallows. Whitecaps danced around sharp rocks as bodies bobbed in the water.

He inched along awkwardly. If only he hadn't wedged his travel pack between Nightfly's folded arms. Every time the weight shifted, he lost his balance. He reached for the next rope, but as he stretched, a sharp pain shot through his neck. His spine seized, throwing him the other way, into the open air.

Hands quick to his gloves, Dario activated Nightfly, spreading his arms and stabilizing himself. He glided back toward the ledge and perched next to Vetricus, clutching the cliff like a bat. Together, they watched the travel kit tumble down the drop. Vetricus cursed as it splashed into the water.

"Was there something important in that pack?" Dario asked.

"Yes. Very. All the extra biscuits I stole from the galley."

"Oh . . . Sorry."

"You will be when you taste the slop they give out where we're going."

Vetricus uncoiled a length of rope from his shoulder. He attached his harness to a hook and then swung across a small gap. Dario flew next to him with ease. He'd forgotten how good this felt. In the air,

Nightfly's glistening spine had control, not Dario's bones. *This is much better*, he thought, smiling. He pulled through the air, passing Vetricus, who did not seem so pleased.

"Careful," he warned. "Flying is dangerous down here. It's a good way to get—"

A huge shadow careened down the cliff, startling them both. Vetricus swung to the next ledge, narrowly avoiding a giant creature with faded flesh and long, angled wings. It had a beak the size of a canoe, with teeth like spears. Nightfly pinged as the creature snapped its jaws. Bone and metal collided. Dario panicked. His lantern crackled and he couldn't tell what color the closest clouds were. They must have been pink, blue, or green, because they were slippery and fast.

"In here!" Vetricus shouted, waving his sword.

Dario followed the glint to a narrow opening in the rock. As he flew toward it, a shadow engulfed him. The Gloom hissed, and sharp claws closed in around him. With a strong pull, he tumbled into the rocky passage, cutting his arms and the side of his head. Claws scraped the cliffside, but Vetricus sliced his sword across the creature's leg, drawing white blood. It retreated, as silently as it'd ambushed. The last thing Dario saw was a long bulbous tail. He sat gasping on the ground. His bones throbbed from the tumble. He removed his gloves, and Nightfly curled up against his back.

The ledge-walker helped him stand. "You alright?" he asked.

"Yeah, what was that?"

"A faded pterosaur," Vetricus said, wiping his sword clean and sheathing it.

"A faded what?"

"Pterosaur. You know, flying dinosaurs. I hope there are still healthy dinosaurs in the world above."

"Some, but not flying ones," Dario answered as he brushed himself off. "We've got big slow ones that eat leaves."

"Oh, brontosaurs." Vetricus nodded. "Here we've got big fast ones that eat people. Sometimes, they just rip your arms off so the shadowmen can drag you easier."

Dario knew it was just a joke, but he couldn't grace it with a response. He'd been thinking about Company Lire, imagining their fate. He hoped they weren't all as gruesome as Illio's.

"Sorry." Vetricus sighed. "Galicus always said I had poor comedic timing."

"Your brother?" Memories of Lamptree flashed vividly—Vetricus' twin.

"Mhm. He was always the actor, not me. When we were young, he went to a school for dancers while I went to school for duelists." Vetricus raked a hand through his hair, staining his brow with chalk. "When you saw him on Lamptree's stage, did he say anything about his companions?"

"No, I've told you everything I know."

Vetricus let out a frustrated huff. "You said Galicus came into the hall alone, but did you see any other Perths on Lamptree?"

"I'm not sure. I might have seen your company in the swamp near the base of the tree."

"What were they doing?"

Dario hesitated, answering only when the ledge-walker pressed him further. "Pillaging."

Vetricus cursed, slicing his sword through the end of a gnarled root. "I know, but why? They would never do that. Can't they tell he's not me?" he groaned, looking upward.

"Was your brother always a part of Company Perth?"

"He was *never* a part of it. I fell alone. I didn't even know I had a brother."

"Wait, then how do you remember him?" Dario asked.

"That's a long story," Vetricus replied reluctantly.

Dario waited, imagining what kind of magic could return lost memories. His earliest memory was falling with his crutch, twirling through the air as a child, feeling the numbness of betrayal. But what had happened before that? Dario's glyph had provided hints—his parents had thrown him from the Purple Prince's realm—but that's all he knew.

Eventually, Vetricus elaborated. "More than just lost souls wash up on these shores," he revealed as he walked along the passage. "Lost memories can too, but those shoals carry a steep price."

His voice faded around a corner, and Dario scrambled to follow. "Can you show me where?"

"No. You'll need a ghost to ferry you into those waters." Vetricus stopped and turned, his face stern with a warning. "Keep your mind in the present for now, friend. I spent years searching for my memories of the celestial world. I found some, and now I wish I never had. They don't heal past wounds. They make them worse."

Dario dropped his chin. Under different circumstances, this news would be life-changing. His lost memories were out there—memories of his parents and a childhood in the celestial realm. But recovering those memories paled in comparison to recovering his family. Vetricus was right: such life-altering magic would have a life-altering cost. What had Vetricus paid? Even now, he saw something burdening the ledge-walker. For someone who'd found lost memories, his expressions were still filled with so much doubt and uncertainty.

"So, your brother came from the celestial world?" Dario asked. "Did he fall? Or did he climb down?"

"I don't know." Vetricus pressed both hands against the passage wall, touching his forehead to the rock. "He came to steal my glyph and my company. I don't know how it's possible, but he is my twin, so . . . maybe there's a magic connecting him to my glyph . . . I don't know. If he climbed down a city of escape, it must have been destroyed. Otherwise, he wouldn't be searching for another way back up."

"That's why you were glad my map was destroyed."

"Yes. I don't know why Galicus wants my name and company, but he must have known I'd refuse, else he would have at least tried to reason with me, right? He didn't even speak to me. I was so stunned to see a reflection of myself, I didn't react. Then I was dead." Vetricus shook his head. "But how has he convinced my company that he's me?"

The ledge-walker sped his pace, and Dario flew close above him. The passage emptied onto another ledge, further from the coast, overlooking the vastness of the underworld. If not for the giant stalactites far above, he would have forgotten this place was underground. The sky was vast, and ledges lined every cliff wall, winding upward like a maze of staircases. Waterfalls cascaded atop them, emptying into the shallows. Geysers spouted mist, cloud, and water high into the air with a loud, hissing *sploosh!* Rays of daylight shot across the immense land, darting through lonely trees, and casting long shadows across pale peaks.

Dario's lantern clicked and fizzled. Such a small lantern could not color such a vast place. The ledge weaved atop two deep ravines like a crooked spine, and gloomy trees grew up from the earth at every angle. Vetricus trimmed his lamp again, and Dario did likewise. The lanterns calmed and quieted, coloring just a tiny area around them.

Clouds billowed from geysers and journeyed upward, through holes in the rock. Dario untrimmed his lantern for a moment, just to see what color the clouds were. The nearest current was bright orange. Every tree, no matter where it grew, reached toward it, seeking to feed from its nutrients. High above, the clouds squeezed into carved channels like they were veins. Dario's skin chilled, and he sensed a strange fondness for the clouds. Here he was, in a different world than Madi. Yet, one day, she might gaze upon this very same current.

"Krisha told me something in the cavern," he said, watching the currents billow. "She said the clouds are the Gales' blood. When they stop flowing upward, we won't be able to escape anymore."

Vetricus clambered around a large rock, and stones dribbled into the abyss. Daylight beamed against his blond hair, which looked pale now, almost gray, on account of his trimmed lantern. He glanced at the clouds, dipping his hands into a bag of climbing chalk.

"Is it true?" Dario asked him.

"It can't be," Vetricus answered, still squinting skyward. He attached his harness to a hook and began to climb, speaking between grunts. "I served the sky my whole life. I bled for it. I watched newborn Celestials fall from the stars, bodies limp and unconscious. Every few years, they rain down like meteorites, infused with magic, but stripped of memory. If the Gales are dead, who sends the celestial reinforcements down? Who binds them to their glyph? Who sent me? Who sent you?"

Dario remembered falling as a Celestial. The sound of that child's voice—his voice—it scarred him still. Weeping, wailing as his parents stood over him, watching. The thought made his heartbeat slow and shallow, like a dull blade, rubbing his rib cage.

"I serve living gods," Vetricus said. "They sent me to fight in this war. They wrote to me in starlight, and my company bled to complete their tasks. Captain Imani and her rebels would have me believe that was a lie? They would undo everything my company, and hundreds of others, have bled for."

"Rebels? Krisha said they were smugglers."

"Sure, we smuggle people up through the worlds. That's why I joined—to right my brother's wrongs. But you'll see when we get there, Dario. The Sky Doe isn't a crippled cloudcrawler. It's a warship, built for one task: to breach the celestial realms and take control of the Gales' thrones, one by one."

"A coup?" Dario asked, smiling. The thought energized him. As a Celestial, he'd fantasized about becoming powerful enough to march into the world above—to present the Gales' crimes to its people and look his parents in the eyes.

"And Imani wants you to lead her army?" he asked as Vetricus slid his harness along the rope and clipped it into another hook. "Will you?"

"Absolutely not. It would destabilize the war, and my brother has gone and done enough of that. The Gales and their companies are the only reason we haven't already lost. If there really are old Gales bleeding to death in worlds far below, what can they do? Like I said, I serve *living* gods."

Dario disagreed. As he flew beneath gargantuan currents—those long, winding veins of cloud, Krisha's revelation became more and more clear. If the Gales were dead, it would explain so many things, such as why his prayers went unanswered. Deep down, he'd always *wanted* the Gales to be good, but the fact that the gods ignored him made him feel like there was either: something wrong with them, or something wrong with him.

"So, you don't think the Underworld Trail leads somewhere safe?" he asked Vetricus. "What about the clouds? What about Company Snow?"

"What about them?"

"They're one of the old companies! Their existence proves that the dying Gales are not a myth. Look here," Dario said, opening his book to the most recent page.

Vetricus resisted. "That is a *very* large book, and I am a very slow reader."

"Just this page. Read."

. . . One of the ledge-walkers told me that the Stranger herself cre-ated Company Snow a millennium ago. She said it happened before the Gales died. Our gods desperately needed soldiers, so the Teal Stranger descended as a blizzard upon a ravaged village. Snow covered the corpses of those killed, most of whom were children. When the storm ended, the dead rose up from the snow and have fought for the Stranger ever since, as silent as the winter storm they were reborn in.

I wish I'd had time to ask Exile about this. He's ageless, frozen in time. Madi would be ecstatic. She's always dreamed of magic like this, of places out of time and trouble . . .

"Okay, I know who told you this," Vetricus said without finishing the page. "Rule number one in the underworld: don't believe any story Left Foot tells you."

"She said she knew who *you* were," Dario revealed as the ledge-walker turned away. "She said there will never be another Celestial like you. People called you arrogant and accused you of only ever thinking about your company, but she said you cared for the lowliest—even a young refugee like her."

Vetricus' shoulders sank, and his proud posture turned humble. "Like I said, don't believe anything she says."

"She seems reliable."

Vetricus snorted.

Dario closed his book and chained it to his belt. "It's obvious. You wouldn't have volunteered if you didn't care. You wouldn't obsess over stopping your brother if you didn't."

Vetricus spun, snatching Dario by the collar. "I want my *NAME* back! My *COMPANY!* That's all, Dario. I don't care about the stories in your book. I've seen the same suffering you've seen. I've read the same sky and pondered the puzzle of tasks it presents. What of it? The

Gales are our gods. They dwell above. They are not the enemy—the Ashen are."

Vetricus crouched behind a rock, pointing. Far below the ledge, a formation of shadowmen weaved along a lower ledge. Black wagons coiled downward, carrying—something. Dario couldn't make out what it was.

"I've never been able to please all the Gales," Vetricus admitted while the caravan quietly descended the distant cliff. "Their wills have confused me to this day, but no matter who rules the stars, my enemy is the Ashen. Maybe I'll read your book one day," he whispered. "But I'm loyal to the sky."

He sounded so much like Illio, and he wasn't wrong. The Ashen were a threat, but were they the only threat? Dario didn't think so. The weight of the book on his belt, and the truths within, was growing heavier and heavier. "Where are the Ashen going?" Dario asked as the dark silhouettes marched the distant path.

"To the deep worlds," Vetricus replied, inching his way along the ledge. "We should move."

They crept in silence for a time. Dario's spine kept him to a crawl, but finally, Vetricus said it was safe enough for him to fly again. It was a long, silent journey after that. The ledge-walker seemed to have lost his interest in conversation. He remained silent until he'd reached a lamppost and wooden pier jutting from the ledge. There'd been other lamps along the path, but this one was lit with a pale glowing orb. The ledge-walker grasped his hood and looked left and right. After studying the surroundings, he pulled a rope attached to the lamp post. It was tied to a bell, but there was no clapper inside. The bell shook, silently stirring a blanket of white fog. Mist veiled much of the chasm, lingering like a white lake.

Dario cleared his throat. "Do you mind if I ask a question about Galicus?" he asked, his mouth parched from the journey.

Vetricus rubbed his wrist where Krisha had exposed his vein. He tilted his head toward his lantern and took a long breath. "Depends on the question," he replied.

"Do you think he could be working for the Trail?"

Wind rolled across Vetricus' cloak, but he stood motionless, arms crossed—more like an idea than a man, but a very different kind of idea than his brother. "I don't know, but Captain Imani assured me that he isn't." Vetricus' voice wavered, and for a moment, it sounded as though he simply missed his brother. "I've no idea what he's doing. He gave me no hints. Nothing. Just a blade in the back. But I saw something in his face that day, something that wasn't an act—a rage that not even his twin brother could stand in the way of. He's on a warpath, Dario, and he's going to get my company killed. I know it, and I have to climb before it happens. That's my family."

Dario closed his eyes. His lips tensed with sadness. That word, "family," vibrated through every brittle bone in his body. He longed to hold Madi and Aerial again. His hands would feel empty until he did. "I guess we don't have to agree about the Gales," he said. "We both want the same either way. Besides, Illio would have sided with you anyway."

Vetricus grinned. "Course he would've."

By now, the ferry was very close. The vessel creaked, and its oars moved all on their own. There was no one on board. A rope slithered across the deck, curling around a mooring post as it reached the lamp post pier.

Dario's mouth hung agape. "It's haunted?"

"Don't be rude, say hello," Vetricus said, pushing him aboard.

"Hello," Dario said, scanning the empty vessel.

Frigid air nipped his exposed arms, and ice crackled as lines and netting moved all on their own. Wisps of purple cloud curled over the bulwark and weaved through barrels and broken boards toward

Dario's boots. He didn't move. Neither did Vetricus. And yet, through the purple haze, he thought he heard someone's boots bumping across the deck.

"Is this safe?" he whispered.

Vetricus stepped aboard. "Don't insult our ghost—I mean *host*. This is his haunt. Sit down. I'm certain this cloudcrawler is completely skyworthy. Look, it has . . . at least three working oars. You only need two, right?" He leaned against the hull, and the wood crumbled out from beneath him, revealing a vast chasm below.

"Sixteen oars is standard," Dario said, recalling a joke Madi had told him. He never understood why it was funny. "Eight on a light ship. Four on a bad day."

Vetricus crossed his arms and propped his feet up. "Well, you're in the underworld now. Three oars is as good as a day as you're going to get."

The deck creaked and crackled so badly, Dario was certain the tiny cloudcrawler was about to crumble to pieces. Invisible footsteps crossed the deck once more, and a rope slithered from its cleat. Vetricus chuckled and chatted with the ghost, asking mundane questions, receiving no answer. This was the most Dario had ever heard the ledge-walker talk or laugh. Maybe this was how he disguised his own nerves?

Dario was about to sit down when wood peeled from the long bench he was stooped over. There were several benches on deck, carved with hundreds of names. Was that a list of all the people this ghost had ferried? Dario cocked his head, noting the name *Stranger on the Ledge* was carved more than once. The rest of the hull was in great disrepair. Bolts undone. Hinges broken. This ghost ship was decaying, just like Girli's horn. The peeling bulwark made Dario sad, but it also ignited a sense of purpose, deep inside him.

We're all in this fight, Krisha had said. *If we don't escape together, we won't escape at all.*

Meanwhile, Vetricus walked to a wooden post in the middle of the ferry. There was a lantern on it. Glass chimed and a gear clicked as he inserted a fueling vial into the nearly empty lantern. Brew bubbled as it funneled into the contraption, and the colors on deck became more vibrant. "Payment for passage," he explained. "And he'll need your name, otherwise we don't cross."

"Dario L—"

"Not your real name. Codename."

"Oh . . . I picked Nightfly."

"Don't tell me. Tell him," Vetricus said, pointing as if he knew where the ghost was standing.

The vessel's tiller moved all by itself, steering the ferry between large rocks, bathed in fog.

"Nightfly," Dario said, stepping toward the tiller. The wooden stick swung toward him. He backed away, saying his code-name a little louder. "I'm Nightfly." But then the tiller swung away again.

Vetricus chuckled.

"You enjoy embarrassing me?" Dario whispered.

"Anything to make this crossing go faster."

Dario smiled. "So, you *do* get nervous."

Vetricus didn't answer. He turned away in his hood, toward the sound of invisible footsteps. Dario tracked the sound, seeing a puddle splash. Afterward, there was an eerie *scratch*, and the name *Nightfly* appeared on one of the long wooden benches.

The haunted ferry skimmed across the clouds, drifting from one current to another. An empty barrel rolled across the deck as the vessel tilted upward. Then Dario saw it. There, on a wide ledge, was the most colossal cloudcrawler he'd ever seen, larger than any celestial battleship—nearly the size of one of Lamptree's giant branches. It wasn't even finished yet! Construction teams carried supplies while mechanical lifts raised them atop a maze of scaffolds. Wooden beams curled across its open hull like a rib cage, and inside, Dario saw hundreds of people working. He counted six decks, seven if he included a smaller one near the top.

The Sky Doe loomed atop the ledge like a beached whale. Its uppermost cabins were complete, glowing with torchlight, watching like burning eyes as its body took shape. The ship was terrifying to behold—proof that this war was far larger than Dario had ever imagined. *This crawler is being built to withstand the power of gods.* Excitement surged through him. This was the rebellion he'd imagined being a part of since he was young!

The ferry's tiller creaked as the vessel passed below a stone arch and glided toward a pier with a lone lamp post, much like the one they'd departed. Other ledge-walkers guided volunteers from all directions, and Vetricus was quick to don his hood.

"This is as far as I go," he said, stepping onto the pier. He unfastened his harness and slung it over his shoulder, extending a chalky hand. "Good luck, Dario."

They shook, but then Dario hesitated in the shadow of the mammoth creation. "You're not coming with me?"

"I think it's best I don't go in there."

"How do I find the captain?"

Vetricus glanced upward, toward the captain's cabin. Light glowed from two curved windows, which overlooked the skeletal construction like two amber eyes. A silhouette paced behind the glass, pausing as they stared.

"No one sees the captain," he answered.

The vessel groaned as builders bent its bulwark into place. Torchlight peered out from behind the wooden beams, like a heart peering from an unfinished rib cage. Long shadows crept across the pier, and Dario drew back, chilled.

"Why not?" he asked.

"Because she's a ghost," Vetricus said, turning toward a rising ledge. "The Sky Doe is Captain Imani's haunt. The Trail won't make its move until she's strong enough."

"How long will that be?"

A wooden beam passed overhead, suspended from a crane. Dario flew over it, while Vetricus ducked and said, "No idea. Could be years."

"Years?" Dario's excitement deflated. "I don't have years." When he'd volunteered, he'd imagined weeks, maybe months. Not years.

"Get in line," Vetricus replied. "Some of the people I've guided through here have been waiting a lifetime to escape, and you've only just arrived."

Dario stumbled. His spine tugged his head downward, but he fought it, gritting his teeth as he gazed upward. A colorful blend of clouds sifted through holes in the rocks above. Madi was up there, somewhere, and every bit of Dario's being rebelled at the thought of years passing between them. Soon, his body shook, and his spine pulled him into a painful hunch, so he just sat there, gasping toward a bare bit of rock.

"You alright?" Vetricus asked. He leaned close, placing his palm on Dario's sweaty shoulder. The wetness washed the chalk from his hand, revealing fingers covered with scars. These cliffs had mutilated his hands.

"You've tried to escape on your own. How many times?" Dario asked him.

"Too many."

"Are you going to try again?"

"Yes."

Dario straightened his spine, fighting to hide his condition. "Let me go with you."

"I think about it, but I'm not trying again until I find my old horse. He's the only one fast enough to fly the Heights."

"Your horse? Babble, right?" Dario asked. "He's down here, too?"

"He fell with me. I assume it didn't sit well with him what Galicus did to me."

There wasn't a picture of Vetricus Perth in the world above without his flying horse. Madi had one in her library, with the schematics of Babble's saddle, though she'd admitted such a device was beyond her skill to create. Its eight bony arms were twice as long as Nightfly's, with twice as many joints. It'd sell for a fortune, she'd said—enough to fly to a city of escape and back ten times.

"I'll help you find him," Dario said.

"I've been searching for years," Vetricus said, rising. "But you're welcome to try. Find Captain Imani's First Mate, Dugan. He does all the talking. Request assignment to my safehouse. It's hidden not far from here, in a region called the Shelves."

He ascended a scaffold, where a dozen other ledge-walkers sorted through ropes, hooks, and ladders. They eyed Vetricus as he passed, some of them even standing at attention, like soldiers. He was the leader this motley army needed, and it frustrated Dario that Vetricus ignored them all, shrinking into the folds of his cloak. Winged dragoons watched Vetricus from a wooden tower. They carried crossbows, like Madi, and their fliers' glistened as they gathered and looked. Did they know who Vetricus was? Dario was beginning to think so. It seemed everyone in the cavern recognized that this was Vetricus Perth—everyone except Vetricus.

CHAPTER 19: MADI

Every day, the borders of Aerial's glyph paled. After two weeks, the edges of her light flickered faster and became more rigid. After a month of travel, the shape of her star folded in on itself, withering like a flower. The curse had taken root, and now it was spreading. Madi twisted a dial, focusing the lens of Bandico's telescope toward the center of her daughter's glyph. With each cold *click*, the patterns became clearer. Five strands of light formed a simple web of shapes, like a newborn flake of snow. More strands would form as Aerial grew, but for now, there were only five—and an ugly black scar sliced across them.

"Madi, we need to get moving," Bandico said while tending his hives. The net hanging over his hat muffled his restless tone. As the weeks dragged on, his patience had grown increasingly thin. Sometimes, he gave her only a few minutes to gaze, but she understood why. Enemy constellations loomed on the horizon. Celestials were on their trail.

"Just one more moment."

A bee crawled across Madi's fingers, tickling her skin with a faint *buzz*, but she tolerated it so as not to disturb her calibrations. The bronze instrument squealed as she focused more closely on her daughter's curse. The scar was a sixth strand, growing from the others, weaving around them like a weed. Shades of gray shimmered deep within its dark borders, forming strange patterns, strange shadows. Madi cursed, wishing she knew how to interpret it.

The top hatch creaked open, slamming against the deck. "She's shivering again, Madi," Panima called. Aerial's cries echoed through the open hatch—not cries of hunger or attention, but of pain. "I don't know what to do."

"I'm coming!" she said, quickly lowering the bronze scope.

Bandico culled his beekeepers mask and rushed to the driver's box. "Before you go, Madi, give us a heading." He punched his brother, who was asleep with his feet propped up on the storage chest. It gave a hollow rumble as Bereket shifted his weight. "Bear, wake up! Where's the map?"

Bereket yawned, growling as he rubbed his eyes. Madi had barely slept during the last month, but the poor brothers had slept even less. They took turns driving the wagon—Bereket during the day, Bandico at night. Beads rattled from Bereket's braids as he stooped and picked up the map.

By now, ink markings covered the crumpled piece of paper. They were Madi's attempts to make sense of where she was. She knew the city of escape was on the coast somewhere, far to the northwest of Carmine. But so far, she'd yet to even find the coast.

"How hard is it to find an ocean?" Bandico grunted, snatching the map. "We need landmarks, and that's our best one. Where is it?"

"We might be traveling too far west still," Madi said while peeking at the page. Wind nipped at the corners of the pathetic parchment. "I don't know. We should hit the coast if we turn north."

Bandico tossed the reins into the air. "I'd love to, Madi! Which way's north? You said there'd be mountains. I see grass."

These barrens were gray and completely faded to Gloom. Guttural groans echoed in the air—lofty whirs and distant dark clicks. Madi had hoped the sounds were just shifting starlight, distorted by the Gloom, but now she knew: this was the voice of the White Whisperer.

The sounds made her want to cry. She shivered as they trickled across the plain like a cruel hag's laugh. The gray atmosphere echoed like a bloated belly, and the longer the wagon rolled through it, the thicker the sensation became.

"Everything looks different on the ground," Madi admitted. "My company flew to the city. Landmarks were easier to see."

A pale tornado churned on the horizon, picking up gloomy earth and spitting it across the plain. More tornadoes formed. Judging by the speed and hue of the currents, Madi guessed they were pinks, browns, and blues. The storm looked fierce, and Bandico picked up the pace. He obviously couldn't read clouds. There was no outrunning a storm like that, not in a wagon at least.

Dust scampered across the deck, blown by the impending mud-storm. It brewed across the barren plain, obstructing Madi's view. Her empty stomach gurgled. It pinched doubly hard—from lack of food and from an overabundance of stress. The Pilgrim had been silent since they'd left Carmine a month ago. Madi had prayed for direction. Why didn't she get an answer?

"We're not talking about finding some rock or tree, we're talking about finding an ocean!" Bandico said with a slew of sarcastic curses. "An ocean. Yeah? And mountains. And a big tall city that towers into the sky. Right? Where is it?"

Madi rolled her eyes as he paced in front of her, like a caged animal desperate for an escape. Then, she soured her tone to match his. "Are you talking to me or Raven right now?"

"I'm talking to you," he answered, tugging her flying bandana, which pulled her gaze upward and mussed up her hair in one annoying motion.

She slapped his hand away.

"Let's all just calm down," Bereket suggested. "There's no reason to panic until the mead runs out." The bench creaked as he reached for his flask. He uncorked it and held it to his lips. A drop dribbled onto his lip, but then it was dry. He cursed loudly.

The hatch opened and Panima called again, "Madi, I don't know what to do!"

"Coming."

"I still need a heading, Madi."

"Just go that way!" she shouted, flailing her arm.

Bandico folded the brim of his hat over his eyes. "Excellent! That way! C'mon, Ascender. Turn, boy. She wants to drive into a mud-storm. Maybe a tornado will pick us up and throw us into the ocean we can't find."

Bandico jerked the reins. The wagon jostled, and Madi felt its weight fall out beneath her. She shuddered, clutching Bereket as the wagon dipped to the right.

"I got you," he said, gripping her tight. His deep and gentle voice was just what she needed after Bandico's constant sarcasm. Bereket peered over the bulwark. "You're alright. It was just a slope. We're not falling."

The brothers' lanterns clicked rapidly as they struggled to color the atmosphere surrounding the wagon. Brown clouds lingered low to the ground, and Madi tasted dust on her lips. She raised her scarf over her mouth just as the wind picked up. Pink clouds weaved overhead, mixing with blues. Tall grass trembled in the wind, and soon, rain fell alongside the dust, forming large globs of mud. They pelted the wagon, making muffled *thuds*.

Madi closed the hatch and descended, her boots slippery on the ladder. It was times like this she felt that her dream of the Pink Pilgrim was just a figment of her imagination. A god had chosen her as a haunt? Really? Then why did she feel more vulnerable than ever, like the hollow earth beneath her. Frustration forced out a groan. Bandico was like an annoying little brother, but she wasn't angry with him. He'd walked the Long Dark. If he'd been to a city of escape, he could have found his way back blindfolded. No, she was angry with herself for not remembering the way, and she was confused by the Pilgrim for not making the path more clear.

Inside the cabin, Panima and Corlan stood over Aerial's treasure chest bed, while Wodan watched from his bunk, twirling his crissle rock. If only there was a way to refine that rock out here—a rock that size could be smelted to fill at least five lanterns. Still, Madi doubted Wodan would ever part with it. She'd learned from Bereket that Wodan's father had mined it, just moments before shadowmen breached the Roots.

Aerial stopped crying as Madi cradled her, but the shivering continued. Beads of sweat slid down her daughter's nose, and her eyes appeared so desperate and confused.

"Is it the curse?" Panima asked.

Corlan waved his toy in front of Aerial, but she seemed in too much pain to notice. She coughed and squirmed and spat up a mixture of milk and bile.

"Why did they do this to her?" Panima whimpered, beginning to cry.

"She's a Celestial," Madi replied.

"Is there a cure?" Wodan asked from his bunk.

"Obedience," Madi replied, curling into her alcove by the porthole.

"But Bear and Bee," Corlan said. "They're cursed. But they do what they want."

Madi raised an eyebrow, peeking toward the cabin wall, and the ghostly etchings carved into the hull—into Bandico's brain. "Bee?" she asked.

"He said it's what the kids used to call him, in the Long Dark."

"Bear says he's killed people," Wodan said from his bed. "And Bandico *looks* like he's killed people."

Panima held a finger to his lips. "Quiet, he can hear."

"I've already told him. He laughed."

"I'm confused," Corlan said, staring at his toy soldier. "People say Shades are bad, but we're traveling with Shades, and the good guys are chasing us."

"Not all Shades are bad," Madi explained, thinking of her dream with the Pilgrim. "Like Bee and Bear . . . and Aerial."

"But why are Celestials chasing us?"

"Because the sky tells them to," Panima answered, and Madi nodded.

"Is Company Perth chasing us, too?" Corlan asked softly.

The cabin grew quiet. Madi touched her head to the window, peeking skyward. Constellation Perth loomed on the horizon, like a jaw, devouring the other constellations. They certainly appeared to be following, but their constellation was so vast, it was visible far beyond the Trade Gap—far into the wild, where only Ashen, Shades, and the lost wandered.

Bandico's cabin was cramped now, littered with scavenged supplies. He'd even added some hooks for hanging canvases for privacy. Panima returned to her bunk and pulled the white sheet closed. Corlan curled up on his bedroll, surrounded by odds and ends he'd scavenged from abandoned homesteads and old caravans—some rusty weapons, seeds, pots, some toys. Meanwhile, Madi opened the porthole, hoping to rid the cabin of its stuffiness. Some days, she didn't know what was worse, five stinking bodies in a cramped coffin, or the smell of the Gloom.

Thunder croaked overhead, muffled by mud. A thick glob of wet dirt spat into the cabin, and Madi quickly closed the window. The Lamptree kids slept soundly now, exhausted by a month of hard travel, but this wasn't always the case. They often slept poorly on account of Bandico's ghost. Panima complained about a lifeless chill in the air. Corlan said he'd heard boots bumping the floorboards. And Wodan said he'd seen a woman's reflection in the porthole once.

Outside, the warding vials chimed again, like chains tied to a gate. Galecraft was an extension of the mind, and Madi imagined Raven outside trying to force her way in. Timing beads clicked on the wall. They were tied to a sand clock, much like the one Bandico wore on his belt. Wagon wheels churned. Madi yawned, tempted to sleep by the steady clop of hooves, the chime of brewed potions, and the echo of starlight. She might have succumbed to sleep, if not for another, more sinister noise, slithering through the cabin.

The whisper was soft, impossibly faint at first, but rising. Starlight shimmered through the porthole, glistening against the cabin wall, revealing faint markings clawed onto its surface. Madi brushed her hands against the Galecrafted wall, feeling the fractured texture of the markings. There were words, but also drawings. In one of them, a line of children held hands while following a boy in a big hat. Shivers crawled up her arms. Were these etches depicting the Long Dark? Were these memories? Or nightmares? It was like Raven had dug her nails into Bandico's brain, reminding him of his past, but Madi didn't know what any of it meant.

The whispers grew louder, and soon Madi heard children singing, not just one voice, but many:

> *Please, Little Light, don't leave me here.*
> *They say you know the way back home.*
> *My mom's a queen. My father's rich. My brother knows a governor.*
> *I'm lost in the dark and I don't know the way.*
> *Stay, Little Light, please stay.*
> *They say you know the way back home.*

She searched her alcove for more etches of the Long Dark, but all she found were names scrawled into the wood. Raven's name was there, alongside Bereket's, and many others. Outside, the warding brews sputtered and the last bit of orange brew evaporated from the vials. The lullaby grew louder, and other sounds joined them—shrill cries, the clatter of gates, the rumble of footsteps. The Long Dark came to life—like a nightmare. Outside the porthole, Madi saw it slowly taking shape. Black gates. Crooked mansions. Children in rags. A vast darkness.

On deck, Madi heard Bandico cough and vomit and pop open a brew. Vials jingled, and she heard the brothers' muffled voices. Bandico coughed violently. The sand clock on the wall flipped, the timing beads reset, and soon, the nightmare outside the porthole disappeared. He must have drank one of his deafening brews, because all the whispers in the walls ceased. It was suddenly very silent, until the top hatch opened and Bereket's big boots scraped down the ladder.

The whole cabin creaked as the giant man climbed into the cramped cabin. He carried a cup of daylight brew. A warm glow stained his dark beard and braids. His eyes, gentle and cool, glanced at the walls. Surely, he knew the meaning behind the cruel carvings scratched into the wood, but he'd never said a thing about them—revealing where his loyalties lie. His hands shook, spilling some brew from the cup. Daylight splattered onto the floor and quickly faded.

"Is everything alright?" Madi asked him.

"Yeah, I just don't like cramped spaces, remember?"

Bereket stooped over Corlan. He checked the skin around the boy's eyes and ran his fingers through his hair. Of all the children, Corlan's skin appeared the healthiest, and now Madi knew why. He hadn't lost anything.

"I've been checking on them twice a day," Bereket whispered, moving to Panima.

She sat up quietly and held out her arms with a yawn. Bereket let the brew illuminate her skin, tanned brown from days lounging beneath orange clouds high on Lamptree's limbs.

Wodan was next, and he tried pushing Bereket away, but his hand had little effect on the Shade. "I'm old enough to check my own skin," Wodan said.

"There's a rule underground," Bereket grunted. "We always check each other's skin. Toxic clouds caught in the rock can kill as quickly as a cave-in. In the dark, faded flesh looks a lot like soot and mud."

"Wait." Wodan turned, furrowing his brow. "You worked a mine? How long?"

Bereket eyed his own shadow on the wall, his hands trembling. The cup of daylight shook, and his shadow danced. "Too long."

"What, a year? Two years?"

"Nine."

"NINE?"

Clearly shocked by the number, a hint of respect replaced the defiance on Wodan's face. He lowered the collar of his shirt, revealing a puddle of shadow, wriggling beneath the young man's skin. He was still fading.

"How you feel today?" Bereket asked, inspecting the flesh.

"Better," Wodan replied.

"Hearing voices in the Gloom?"

"Sometimes, but only when I'm on deck. Down here in the cabin, it's better. Reminds me of a tunnel."

Bereket's big friendly eyes peeked warily from behind his braids. "Me, too," he whispered while raking his beard. Madi saw his hand shaking, leading her to believe that nine years working a mine was too long for anyone.

Wodan lifted his chunk of crissle rock. It was pitch black, sparkling with tiny white dots. Light from the porthole passed across them, making them sparkle and shimmer with every color imaginable. "How much you think this would sell for in Half Light Colony?" Wodan asked. "You're from the Long Dark, so you've been there, right?"

"I have," Bereket replied, letting the rock settle in his giant palm. "Ooh, it's dense. Very dense. With this rock, I'd wager you could afford a cloudcrawler, a couple dozen wagons, and your own shop—or skip all that and just buy the governor's mansion."

He tossed the rock back to Wodan, who beamed. The appraisal had to be an exaggeration, but Bereket did whatever he could to keep the Lamptree kids happy. Sure enough, a faint ripple of Gale spread from Wodan. The shadow on his skin retreated, and his face shined for a moment.

Bereket sat down, and the bunk sagged. "You'll have enough glass to fill your kitchen with ale and your bedroom with women for the rest of your life."

"Why not fill it with toys?" Corlan asked.

"Don't worry, kid," Wodan said, matching Bereket's mannerisms. "I'll build a room just for you, with as many toys as can fit the shelves."

"Th-that's good," Bereket said, smiling weakly. He glanced at the cabin walls, quickly closing his eyes. His fists clenched and he brought them both to his chest. His voice darkened and his eyes peered out from behind his braids, like a child behind bars. Bracing himself against the cabin wall, he slowly moved toward the ladder. "Sorry, I-I'm having trouble breathing," he admitted. "I need to go topside."

The wagon lurched, and several of Bandico's treasure boxes toppled from their netting, blocking Bereket's path. He stumbled, and Madi curled into her alcove, worried the man might collapse on top of her. "I can't breathe," he said, reaching for the ladder. His thick braids lashed about his face, and his eyes swelled behind them. "I need to get out!" The shade's voice sharpened with panic. "Get me out!"

Madi helped him sit, and Bereket pressed his face to the closed window, breathing deeply. He groaned, letting his cheek slide down the glass. His eyes tilted toward the stars—muttering, whimpering.

"I got you," Madi said, squeezing his hand. "You're claustrophobic?"

"Yes . . ." the man said softly.

"I know what it's like, okay? My fear is just like yours. Breathe. The walls won't close in on you when I hold you, just like the earth doesn't open up when you hold me. Breathe, Bear."

His giant shoulders rose and fell. Slowly, his body calmed.

"Claustrophobic?" Wodan asked. "I thought you said you worked in a mine? You weren't just a lift-loader, were you?"

The beads in Bereket's braids clattered against the porthole as he shook his head. "No, I dug. The Green Grinner tasked me to dig in the mines, so I dug and I dug and I dug."

"For crissle?"

"For shadowmen," he replied. "We'd smoke them out of their lairs, but then we dug too far. A tunnel collapsed. We were trapped for days, six of us. We tried to dig our way out, but shadowmen are quick and quiet underground."

Madi's hands and feet began to tingle, and her own fears came to surface. Suddenly the wagon seemed to float and fall, and she gripped Bereket's coat.

His breath fogged the window until Madi opened it, and he gasped for air. Outside, Bandico's voice echoed from the top deck, but Madi couldn't make out any words. Most likely, he was arguing with Raven again.

"My brother wishes I'd never squeezed out from that hole," Bereket whispered, eyeing the walls. "I'm starting to wish it, too."

"Don't say that," Madi replied.

"Why not? He can't hear us," Bereket said as his brother shouted at Raven topside. "He's distracted. And it's true."

Bereket sighed toward the sound of his brother's voice, loud and upset, but still muffled. "It's my fault he's haunted. I escaped the collapsed mine, but he says I came out with two debilitating diseases: an intense claustrophobia and an irrational desire to help people."

"That's not an irrational desire."

"It is in the Long Dark, Madi. I was just a kid. I didn't know. I tried to help the other orphans, even when I didn't have the means. I rattled the nest and got caught by Elazela's thugs."

"I don't know who that is."

"An oracle. The Long Dark belongs to her. After I was caught, Bandico showed up to negotiate. Her terms were simple: she told Bee to bring her five young, unsuspecting Celestials, or I die. So, while I was sent back into the mines, my brother went out and led five young Celestials through the Long Dark back to Elazela, but then the number became ten."

"The number was twenty when Bandico met Raven. She was sent into the Dark to find us and bring us back to Company Witterwen. Or so she said. She was crafty, keeping away from the other children Bandico was guiding, and she was smart. Too smart. Somehow, Raven knew exactly what Bee was up to."

"What *was* he up to?" Panima asked.

Bereket eyed the Lamptree kids as they listened, wide-eyed, from their beds. He seemed worried this story might make them fade, and Madi was beginning to agree. "Maybe I should finish this story another time," he said.

"No, please, I can handle it!" Corlan begged.

"It's not you I'm worried about kid," Bereket muttered. "It's me. I don't want to think about it."

"We won't tell anyone," Panima said.

Bereket growled, cornered by curious faces. "My brother is a rescuer. He'd have rescued all of them if he could have . . . That's all you need to know."

"That's not fair!" Panima argued. "We chose to come with you, Bear. We deserve to know. What did he do?"

Bereket eyed the scratches on the walls—the line of children following the boy in the big black hat. "He . . . he obeyed Elazela. He brought young Celestials to her . . . and she killed them. She turned them into ghosts."

Madi could practically see the kids' hearts beating through their chests. They leaned toward Bereket, soaking in every word, mouths agape. Corlan and Panima's lips were trembling, but they each tried to hide—Panima curled a strand of hair over her mouth while Corlan bit his nails.

"Bandico and Raven agreed on a plan to free me, but the plan was a trap. Bandico barely got me out alive. But on our way out, we found Raven—the real Raven. Her body hung in a cage, flesh rotting beneath her crimson coat. She'd been dead for months, and all along, my brother had been plotting with a ghost. That was when we learned who Raven really was—one of the first children he'd ever lured to Elazela. That was the first time Raven tried to get revenge on my brother, and it wouldn't be the last, all because of me."

"But Bee said she wouldn't hurt us," Corlan said.

Bereket ran his fingers through his braids, glancing upward as Bandico continued shouting on deck. "She won't, but I'm still not convinced that she won't hurt him. We don't even know if she was part of our old company. Now, I know he's made a deal with her, but I don't know what it is. They're working together, but I'm afraid she's still going to kill him in the end. My brother isn't a bad person. He would have saved every last one of those children if he could have." Bereket glanced toward the Lamptree kids and their faces, aghast. He pointed to the haunted carvings, etched into the cabin wall. "If I'd died underground, none of that ever would have happened."

"He's not going to turn us into ghosts, is he?" Corlan asked.

"No, kid. I swear. We're going to get you out of here. I SWEAR. My brother rescued you in the forest, right?"

The children nodded, and their shoulders relaxed. The reminder comforted them. It comforted Madi too.

"He's a rescuer. I promise. He'll get you out," he said, clutching his muscular chest. "He'll get us all out."

Bereket opened his mouth to continue, but the wagon violently lurched to a stop. The children rolled to the floor and their belongings clattered against the wall. "Bear! Madi! Get up here!"

Bereket cursed and quickly climbed through the hatch, followed by Madi. Topside, Bandico stood atop his driver's box, hands on his sides, staring into a pitch black night. Where had the horizon gone? The constellations shimmered above, but there was no more reflection on the grass. Bandico scanned the surroundings slowly.

"What do you see?" Madi asked him.

"A hole," Bandico replied. "A big hole."

Bereket squinted. He grabbed the bulwark and began to dismount. "Where?"

"Stop!" Bandico shouted, grabbing his brother's arm. The word *stop* echoed, over and over, in front of the wagon. "Give me your cup," he said in a much lower voice.

Bandico took the daylight brew and poured it from the side of the wagon. Instead of splashing in a field of grass as Madi thought it would, the glowing liquid fell and fell and fell, disappearing before it'd struck anything at all.

Bereket cursed again as he lit the deck's forward torches. Madi reeled back, clutching the bulwark as a vast underworld passage was revealed. The horses nickered nervously in their harnesses, mere steps from a sheer drop.

The pit creaked and groaned, reeking like a foul breath. Dirt dribbled into the abyss, and Madi heard rocks collapsing far below. She leaned against Bereket, who placed one of his big arms around her.

"Let's back away slowly, yeah?" he asked.

Bandico clicked his tongue, and the horses turned sharply, curling around the edge of the abyss. Wind rose from the hole, catching Madi's hair. She closed her eyes, but the feeling of falling stole her breath away. Her hands wandered to her pockets, where she kept her flying gloves.

"I thought you could see in the dark? How'd we come this close to falling?" Madi asked Bandico.

"I *can* see. The horses can't," he answered. "I was distracted. I'm sorry."

The underworld passage was even larger than Madi had imagined, bordered by a crooked scaffold. Even in the light of the flare, she couldn't see the bottom. An old battlefield surrounded the pit. Colonial wagons, arrows, corpses—scattered all over. A banner, filled with holes, *clapped* feebly atop a cart. Black bugs skittered across the body of a man, whose hair and flesh were stained gray by the Gloom. His body hung from a toppled wagon, littered with arrows and scorch marks.

"Celestial," Bandico said, pointing to a girl. She lay near the man, rotting.

"How can you tell?" Madi asked.

"Their wounds. See the colonists?" he asked, pointing. "Just one fatal cut. Now look at the Celestial. Lots of little cuts, leading to one fatal wound. She was overwhelmed, and the shadowmen chopped through her cloak until she dropped."

The longer Madi stared into the abyss, the more she thought she heard a voice. The call was long and drawn out, something between a groan and a wail. It was difficult to tell if it was someone calling out a name or just the wind rising up the scaffold. Madi stood rigid, too afraid to step closer, too curious to step back.

"Where are the kids?" Bereket asked, realizing he'd left the hatch open.

Bandico closed his eyes, looking through his Galecraft, into the cabin's interior. "Still here. They're all looking out the porthole."

The ground shook, and the pit belched cloud, white with Gloom. Madi dropped her torch, and as it fell, it illuminated movement on the scaffold below. Shadowmen looked up at her. There were two. Three. Creeping upward. Pausing behind wooden posts. Peeking. Scurrying like rats.

"Wait. I remember this place," she said, eyeing another broken banner, clapping wearily in the wind. "I remember this! We've gone too far west."

"You're sure?" Bandico asked.

Madi's skin tingled when she saw another Celestial, contorted on the ground, surrounded by faded corpses. "Yes. I remember these banners. I saw this company marching toward this place three years ago! I saw them!"

Bereket shuffled toward his brother. "We've gone too far."

"I heard her," Bandico said. He peered upward, and his eyes glowed in the night. Instead of signaling the horses, he fidgeted with the reins, letting out a quiet curse.

"You're afraid to double back?" Bereket asked. "You think they're still on our trail?"

"I know they are."

"Who?" Madi asked.

Constellations crept across the horizon, closer now.

"People who really don't want us to climb that city," Bandico replied, taking a seat. "Let's go."

"You mean the Gales?"

"I mean anyone with skin in the game. It's a fight for favor, Madi. Pieces are moving. The trick is learning who's pushing them before it's too late. Throw anything we don't need over, Bear! We move fast!"

The wagon rumbled quickly, back the way they'd come. Madi sat next to Bandico, pondering his analogy. She'd sworn allegiance to the Pilgrim in a dream. Since then, she'd been motivated to find the city. But she had to admit, she still felt like a piece on a board. There were so many players: the Gales, the Gloom, the rulers in the world above, gods in the world below, the oracles. So many fingers, spinning webs all around. Who was pushing her? The Pilgrim? Could she be trusted? Madi hoped so. She was Lamptree, or so she said.

Bandico raced back into the storm. Something otherworldly pushed him. Starlight seared overhead, but he kept his eyes fixed to the dark horizon. Rain mixed with sand, pelting the wagon in mud, but he rode on, pushing Ascender and Two Ton to their limit. Lanterns crackled, with barely enough time to cure the air enough to breath. Madi coughed, so did Bandico, but he kept going, racing into the night.

Whose side was he on? She still didn't know, but there was something comforting about his desperation, something familiar. Lightning flashed as he cracked the reins. He was running too, searching for the same place Madi was—a perfect place, out of time, out of trouble, where all your fears and mistakes could be forgotten.

CHAPTER 20: MADI

Madi unfastened her harness and hung Flicker next to the porthole window. Starlight shimmered against its collapsed spine, which clung to the wall like a crab. Without lubricating brews, the arms were getting stiff. She'd been wearing it too often and flying too little. She stretched, yawned, and massaged her shoulders. Flicker's straps had dug deep into her muscles. Meanwhile, Bandico rode hard into a syrupy atmosphere.

Blue and brown clouds mixed, churning rain and dirt into balls of mud, which splattered against the wagon and drooled across Madi's window. Tornadoes ripped across the horizon, and one of them was very close now. The gloomy cyclones swallowed currents of cloud, scattering them toward the sickly horizon. Madi climbed inside her alcove, unfurled her bedroll, and adjusted Aerial's treasure chest. As the storm raged, she warmed beneath her blankets, listening to the beat of mud balls.

Aerial was awake in her bed, staring at Corlan's toy soldier. She slept poorly these days, and Corlan had been kind enough to tie his toy to the top of the treasure chest. Madi rolled to the edge of her alcove and peered down at her daughter who breathed rapidly through her nose, wheezing, grunting, fighting just to breathe.

Madi brushed her hand across the lid of the chest. Inside, Aerial's bright brown eyes sparkled like treasure. *She's the only thing keeping you tied to this world now.* Bandico was right. *And you'll do anything to keep her alive.* He was right about everything. Madi hid beneath her blankets, trying to escape Bandico's voice. But she couldn't. She was in *his* head, after all. Chills crawled up and down her skin, prickling her even as she hid beneath her pillow—even as she fell asleep.

Your greatest fear isn't the ground giving way. Your greatest fear is being alone again. A piece of paper doesn't change who you are. I don't think Madi Amriel can save Aerial, but I think Nariah Maya could. Your daughter isn't safe until you realize that.

A warm wind, smelling of crisp leaves, invaded Madi's sleep, carrying her into a vivid dream. She sat up quickly, striking her head on the base of a giant telescope. *Donk!* The sound echoed in a large circular chamber, sparkling with starlight. Madi held her head, groaning as she looked around, quickly realizing that the Pilgrim had pulled her into another dream. Incense burned from braziers. Pink smoke curled around white-budded vines and large wooden columns. She rose, rubbing the newly formed bump on her head. The room smelled like Lamptree—fragrant furniture and polished floors, all carved from the tree. But this was not a part of Lamptree she'd ever been before.

A giant contraption clicked and rattled throughout the room—an enormous telescope. Not a straight scope, like the one most people used, but a crooked, reflecting scope, with at least six mirrors. Dozens of lenses glinted in the dim dome, and she couldn't even count the number of dials and cranks attached to the device. She did, however, recognize some of the cogs. She'd crafted them for an anonymous buyer. Was this the oracles' observatory on Lamptree?

A wooden balcony confirmed her suspicion. It curled around the dome, overlooking a green leafy sea—Lamptree's canopy. Only a few other towers rose this high, flickering in candlelight—the Bottle

Catcher, the Kestrel Keep, and the mansions atop the Kingfisher Branch. The clocks in this room had been doused in daylight brew, and so the sand glowed faintly as it flowed. There were no candles here, no fires, no cups of daylight—nothing to dilute the stars.

When Madi gazed through the telescope, she saw Aerial's glyph. Her heart ached at the sight of the sickly strands. The amount of detail these lenses revealed was astonishing! Specks of light danced like snow, and the longer she watched them, the more she was certain they told a story. She squinted, determined to make sense of the movements, but the telescope suddenly re-calibrated. Gears churned, and Madi gripped the device, wishing it would stay.

"Lady Pilgrim, wait, please—"

Leaves crackled across the floor, and Madi sensed the Pilgrim's whisper. *"Keep watching."*

Cogs rumbled. The scope tilted toward the far end of the horizon, where the falling stars originated. The lenses followed a new trail of light, like a string, from Aerial's glyph to another, much larger star. Light danced here, too, but the motions told a far different story—a battle between love and desperation, between sacrifice and uncertainty, between survival and fear. Madi recognized it immediately. It was as though the scope had focused onto the center of her heart.

"This is my glyph?"

"Yes."

She pressed her forehead closer to the apparatus, careful not to touch any of the dials. Some of the patterns were familiar, common for all Celestials—symbols revealing movement, energy, and actions. Light bled from the patterns and faded, like drops of melting ice. Madi clutched her chest, feeling that same unsettling thaw leak down her heart. Her glyph was dying, but something else was growing—strange patterns with sparkling light, spreading like the roots of a tree.

"Is that your magic?" she asked.

The sweet scent of pine swept across Madi's nose as a warm breeze wandered into the dome. *"Yes,"* the Pilgrim replied. *"I am the wind which breathes life into all lungs. So long as my spirit rises through sea and sky, your glyph will not fall."*

"Do you . . ." Madi hesitated. It seemed irreverent to ask, but she was too curious. "Do you know how much longer your clouds will rise?"

The Sea of the Afterlife swelled, up and down, carrying Lamptree with it, creaking and groaning. Madi was afraid to think it, but the sensation made her god seem very . . . small.

"No," the Pilgrim replied softly. *"I've watched so many of you grow old. I've listened to your last prayers. I've felt your dying lungs try to pull just a few more breaths in. But I never truly understood how frightening death was for you—until now."*

The whole observatory *whirred* and *clattered* as the scope recalibrated. Madi looked again. The Pilgrim's patterns rose from the bottom of her glyph, she noticed, but other patterns formed near the top, pushing and pulling. Meanwhile, the middle of the glyph stretched thin. It was the perfect image of Madi's heart—squeezed beyond what she could bear. Her glyph was unlike any she'd ever seen before, and its foreignness frightened her. She imagined herself as a toy, lying on a workshop table while someone stuffed her with cogs and gears.

The room grew cold, and she released the telescope, cradling herself with a shudder. "Is that your magic, too?" she asked.

"No. This is what I wanted to show you tonight. To warn you: someone else is altering your glyph."

"Who?"

"Someone in the world above. Someone powerful."

Madi peered back into the device, hesitant, like she was peering into a nightmare. Tendrils crept across her starlight, like fingers—no, like hooks. She thought of her puppets, and the way she fastened strings to their shoulders.

"What kind of curse is it?" she asked, feeling the prick of magic on her skin. Something was changing inside her, causing her to shudder, and she didn't know what it was.

"It isn't a curse. It's a blessing." Madi sensed the Pilgrim hesitate. Incense circled the room, wary and slow, as though the god was pacing in thought. *"Centuries ago, we appointed sceptons to rule over cities of escape. Imagine a governor, but instead of governing a colony, they governed a large part of the world. In our name, they could curse. They could bless. They wrote tasks. They commanded companies. They controlled the horizon's gate. The pattern on your glyph is the mark of a scepton. Only someone seated on a Gale's throne could learn such magic and the means of writing it."*

Madi knew what a scepton was. She'd found letters planning an assassination during her first ascent of the city. Her palms tingled as she recalled how precarious a position of power it was. City sceptons stood on a coveted pinnacle, and their reigns were often short. The letters Madi had found proved it.

"What does this mean?" she asked. "Is someone up there trying to help me?"

"Someone certainly wants it to appear that way, but I fear a trap," the Pilgrim replied. Elsewhere in the observatory, gears squealed and telescopes tilted as though the goddess was squinting her eyes, desperate for information. *"But we must be wary. Very few oracles serve me in this age, and I know of no allies above. Such a blessing would surely . . . complicate . . . things for us. Do not accept this task. If they curse you, so be it. I will keep your glyph bright. Whatever you do, DO NOT accept the scepton's mark."*

Dario was right all along. He said the world above was full of schemers. Madi walked to the balcony, gazing up at the falling stars, wishing he was here, wishing she and Dario had been born in another time, when none of this was happening. "What do we do?" she asked.

Wind rustled across Lamptree's canopy, stirring the leaves.

"We hurry!"

Clouds of daylight crested the horizon, shooting light through the porthole onto Madi's face. She rubbed her head as she woke. The bump from her dream was gone, but the pain lingered. Boots rumbled above deck. The Lamptree kids were up from their bunks, and Aerial's chest was empty. How long had she been asleep?

At least the storm had ended. Now, a pleasant sound echoed outside, and she followed it, opening the hatch. Daylight crept across the gloomy plain, meandering like golden rivers. Orange clouds dipped below them, passing close to the wagon, soothing Madi's skin. All across the plain, sickly stalks of grass poked through thick globs of mud, eagerly reaching toward the honeyed atmosphere for nutrients. Meanwhile, the wagon's wheels squished at a slower pace than before.

Bandico and Bereket sat on the mid-deck, surrounded by the Lamptree kids—Panima sat cross-legged, holding Aerial. Corlan perched atop the bulwark, angling his wooden sword in the daylight, and Wodan took a turn in the driver's box. He'd been asking for weeks to drive, and it seemed Bandico had finally given him the chance.

The brothers seemed in high spirits, though Madi hadn't the slightest idea why. She scanned the horizon, where distant clouds curtained a mountain range. So they'd found the northern mountains. Finally, progress! The brothers sang together, alternating questions and answers. Bereket beat a drum, while Bandico did most of the singing. He sang more articulately than he spoke—as clear as a dawn after a very long night.

"Brother, what's the most important thing?
Swords? They can't cut the looming shadow.
Fame? It won't last the rising of the Tide.
Can you see the skylights falling?
Today the clouds are black, but honey is gold.
Sister, what's the most important thing?

Beauty? My face will soon be dark as dust.
Wisdom? If we were wise, we'd be living somewhere else.
Can you see the skylights falling?
Today the trees are white, but honey is gold.
Mother, father, what's the most important thing?

Baby. Brother. Sister. Son. Daughter. Anyone.
What's the most important thing?
Can you see the skylights falling?
Today our homes are gray, but honey is gold."

The children clapped when it was over. Bandico bowed, and Bereket tripped him. The kids laughed, and a bit of Gale rippled from the wagon. The scent of smoked meat rose from the deck stove, marking Bereket's first successful hunt in weeks. He carved bits of meat from a sizzling carcass and tossed lumps toward the kids' mouths for them to catch.

"This wasn't a free meal and performance. Expect it to be added to your bills," Bandico announced.

"But I'm just a kid!" Corlan said while chewing.

Bandico ran his hand through the boy's shining blond hair. "In my experience, kids pay the most."

Panima took a seat next to Madi on the rear-deck and stretched her body toward the orange clouds. "I miss the Sapling Gardens," she said, shielding Aerial's eyes from the dayclouds. "You ever been there?"

Madi nodded. She could still picture the bare bit of branch, leaning from Lamptree at the perfect angle. During amber atmospheres like this, it was one of the most popular places to lounge and watch clouds rise into the sky. She'd meant to bring Dario there . . .

Panima rolled up her sleeves. "My friends and I used to go there after school and just talk until the dayclouds disappeared," she said. "If I'd known the world was going to end, I wouldn't have said some of the things I did. I feel silly, being so upset about not getting the part I wanted in a dance." She closed her eyes and let her head rock back. "Things like that feel so pointless now."

Madi gripped Panima's hand, thinking of all the chores and errands she'd left behind. So many worries and cares—gone. "For now, but when we escape, all those silly things will matter to us again. Think about how easy auditioning for a dance will feel after everything you've been through!"

The young dancer smiled, pursing her lips.

"It's true!" Madi insisted.

"Is that why you became a weird toymaker?"

"Weird wasn't my intention, but yes."

"The older kids thought you were weird."

"I suppose they would," Madi admitted, closing her eyes. "But now, after what's happened, I'm certain they would give anything to see me and all the other weird people from Lamptree, again."

"Yeah . . ." Panima stared into Aerial's face, smiling bitterly. Afterwards, she exhaled and smiled more cheerfully, as though a heavy weight had fallen from her shoulders. "I think you're right."

As they spoke, a flock of birds flew in from the Gloom and landed on the bulwark near the lantern. They were large seabirds—albatross, Madi thought. Bandico crafted his bow, and the birds retreated some, but refused to leave the lantern. There were seven birds in all. They stood close together, eyeing the travelers and occasionally pecking toward the lantern.

"Don't hurt them. Please," Panima begged. "They need Gale."

"We need food," Bandico said, taking aim.

"We just ate!"

"What'd you plan on during the climb?"

She stopped and turned. "Climb?" she asked as everyone stared at her, smiling. Madi's body tensed. *What climb?* Her face flushed, and a hot wave of angst burned her from the inside out. Had they found the city of escape? She flashed a smile, but her panicked nerves wouldn't allow it to linger. Her heart and mind weren't ready to find it. In some ways, this journey—and this wagon—had become a tiny rest in time, where she could slowly recover from Dario's loss, alongside people she'd grown quite fond of.

Panima punched Bandico in the side, muttering something.

"Ouch. I thought you all had a plan. Nobody was saying anything."

"We did have a plan!" Panima replied. "Corlan was supposed to start it."

"I forgot what I was supposed to say."

Panima groaned. "We rehearsed it ten times!"

"You mouthed the words to me ten times," Corlan replied. "Why didn't you mouth the words to me this time?"

"Because this was the performance!"

Corlan puppeted his toy soldier like a ventriloquist, lifting its arms into a shrug. She took a swing at him too, but he ducked, peeking his toy out from the hiding place, shaking it as though it were shivering with fear.

"Amateurs, all of you!" Panima huffed. "Just tell her, Corlan."

The boy leapt out from Bandico's hives, eyes gleaming, hair shimmering in the daylight. "We found it!" He cried out, spreading his arms and running past Bandico and Bereket. He clambered up the bulwark again and pointed to a distant mountain peak.

"Madi, we found it!" Panima announced, matching his excitement.

She gripped Madi's sleeve and placed a small telescope in her hand. "Bee spotted it last night."

"There!" Corlan shouted.

"A little to your left," Bandico said.

"*There!*" Corlan repeated, pointing again, emphatically.

Madi looked through the scope, tracking his hand toward a formation of rock. Those mountains, she remembered them! The northern peak spewed red cloud and lava, which glowed bright gray in the Gloom. The middle peak was flat and barren. The southern peak spilled ice and water, which met the lava in the valleys below, spewing great froths of steam.

Gray trees with large and unruly branches swayed in the lowlands, while the mountainside bit into the sky like teeth. Billows of cloud crawled up the mountain, thinning as they split. Daylight streamed through the gaps, alongside something else, something unsettling. A shape rose through the sky, tall and dark, but it wasn't cloud or part of the mountain. As quick as Madi saw it, the clouds hid it again.

Pangs of excitement, and then of trepidation, toppled inside her stomach as she waited for a second glimpse. Beyond the mountains, a towering structure peeked at her momentarily. Something was there, a long, winding object, a hundred times taller than it was wide, ancient and otherworldly: a city of escape.

Everyone on deck cheered—but Madi couldn't. That was where Nariah Maya died, and the search for Madi Amriel began. Her stomach twisted. The city was real, despite all the memories she'd buried. It was still there, as though it'd been waiting all this time for her to return. Was there any possible way it could lead to safety? A month ago, Madi thought certainly not. Now, with her new little family and the Pilgrim in her pocket, there seemed a shred of possibility—if they could just get there fast enough.

Wheels churned through mud as Wodan struggled to find a dry

path. The albatross remained on the rear deck beside the lantern. Gale hissed gently from the glass, washing Gloom from the birds' feathers, turning their chests a healthy white, and their wings a beautiful brown.

"The moment I sense one bird driblet fall on my deck, I'm shooting," Bandico announced. "And you're cleaning the mess."

Corlan's face soured. "I wouldn't want to eat one of those ugly things. Hey! Maybe one will lay an egg. We could eat that."

"So, you're telling me, you won't eat an ugly bird, but you'd eat something that comes out its—"

A horn echoed, long and clear from the horizon. Bandico paused. His grin faded. Eyes narrow, he scanned the plain, standing up straight, like an alerted watchdog. He tipped his hat upward, squinting into the light. His eyes hissed the longer he looked.

"Out its what?" Corlan asked, still smiling.

"Shh!"

Bandico moved to his brother's side, scowling. "You hear it?"

"Yeah," Bereket muttered.

"Was it ours?"

"No."

Madi listened. Earth groaned in the Gloom, stars chimed, lanterns fizzed and clicked. Then she heard it again. This time, she was certain. Celestial war horns.

"Stop the cart," Bandico told Wodan. He hopped into his driver's box, seizing the reins from the boy. "Bear, craft your wagon."

The albatross scampered from the wagon. Their wings beat the air, and their shrill squawks put Madi on edge.

"What is it? What's going on?" Panima asked. She clutched Aerial close and searched the horizon.

The brothers moved quickly, pushing past the Lamptree kids without answering. The wagon came to a stop, shaking as Bereket jumped down and opened his palm toward the grass. Mist rose, and the hiss of Galecraft drew the attention of all three Lamptree kids. Wisps of cloud *popped,* and a large wagon took shape. A shadow overtook Bandico's smaller wagon, and earth sank beneath the weight of a rugged hull—round like a pumpkin and gray like stone. Iron spikes chattered as the wheels took shape. The bulwark was like a wall, and a large catapult capped the rear deck. Madi's heart sank—this was a war wagon.

Bandico kicked open a storage chest. Empty vials clanked as he retrieved the last two vials of protective brews, glowing brown near the bottom of the pile. He climbed onto the horses' harness, slathering the brew onto their hides. A barrel tumbled across the deck, rattling like a drum, stirring Madi's adrenaline. She looked toward the horizon again. The sky quaked. Starlight hummed. And soon, she heard drums and a company chant on the wind.

"Get below," she told Panima. She quickly doused the deck stove and cleared the driver's box. "Stow any loose gear."

Panima watched Bereket hitch Two Ton to his wagon. Then, she looked at the wagons and lances on the horizon. "Will they hurt us?"

"Not you," Madi promised, pressing her hands to Panima's cheeks. "If anything happens, tell them the truth. You're a colonist from Lamptree. Just do what they say. They won't hurt you."

The girl's lips began to quiver. "What about you?"

Madi didn't know what to say. She'd known Panima for little over a month, and now she felt like she was saying goodbye to Vishi all over again.

"I don't know," she whispered.

"Madi, take the reins. I'll ride with Bear!" Bandico shouted, clapping his horse's side. Ascender snorted, clearly exhausted. He scratched the animal's nose. "I know you're tired boy, just one more sprint. We're almost there. Think of the big green field you'll get when we escape."

"Bee, we'll need a driver if we're both lobbing rocks," Bereket called, climbing into his stronghold of a wagon. His cabin looked like a cave, and his driver's box was guarded by a barbed cage. If he was the bear, that was surely his den.

"I can do it," Wodan said. His face was pale with fear, but he nodded convincingly enough.

Bereket hesitated, then beckoned him. Large round stones lined his deck, which he hoisted over his shoulder and loaded into the catapult. Hatches clapped and chains rattled as the two brothers mounted their war wagon and helped Wodan into the driver's box.

Bandico's big hat bent in the wind. "Get going, Madi!" he said, waving. "Make for the forest's edge. Head straight for the city, through that saddle there. We'll keep them at bay."

The wagon lurched forward, tugging Madi's nerves to a gallop. She fixed her eyes to the nearest woodline, where gray trees swayed in a noxious atmosphere. Above them, the city of escape peeked over the mountainside for a moment before the clouds concealed it again. Questions raced through her mind, pounding her brain to the rhythm of Ascender's hooves. What company was this? What was their task? What was the Pilgrim's plan? Had she foreseen this, or was this just another complication she hadn't predicted?

"What should I do?" Corlan asked, unsheathing his wooden sword.

"Get below," Madi told him.

"But I can work a ballista. I've seen crews do it."

"No, you get below and keep my daughter safe. Can you do that?"

Corlan sheathed his toy sword and gave a sour nod. As he descended, Madi took a few deep breaths. They shivered out from her shaking lungs. One month crammed in a coffin with the Lamptree kids, and suddenly she had three younger siblings to look out for.

CRACK!

An explosion rocked the sky, and Madi spun in her seat, expecting to see Bear's wagon toppled and Wodan writhing on the ground.

Instead, a puff of smoke drifted high in the sky. *Please, Pilgrim! Help us!* She silently mouthed the prayer, wondering if the Pilgrim could even hear her outside of her dreams. *Please, don't let anything happen to them,* she prayed, watching the brothers scramble across the deck. Bandico stood with one arm outstretched, firing his bow across an incredible distance. Bereket cranked the catapult, his beard and braids caught firmly in the wind's grasp. They were her older brothers, and the further their wagon fell behind, the more she worried she'd lose them too.

A second rock whistled through the air, greased with brew. It shattered, scattering fragments of rock across the plain. This time, the brothers replied with a rock of their own. The catapult clapped. A stone hissed toward the celestial wagons, exploding and crackling. This rhythm continued, booming back and forth.

Black birds circled the air, watching the two wagons flee the company of Celestials. Ascender's black mane thrashed as Madi pushed the pace. Wheels screeched, spitting mud and dust. She kept the lead while Bereket's wagon trailed, trading shots with the Celestials. Gale smeared the gloomy landscape as the chase went on, painting a desperate line of color toward the gray forest's edge. All the while, rocks and bolts soared across the plain, cracking like thunder.

Madi wiped the sweat from her eyes, but still, the plain seemed to stretch out in front of her. The open ground made her hands tingle. She fixed her eyes to the trees, but the wagon rumbled violently across uneven terrain. Tiny holes filled the earth here, swallowing the mud. The ground gurgled, bubbled, and slurped. With every bump, she imagined the wagon sliding into one of the holes and falling into the world below. Through every dark crevice, she thought she saw a shadowman rising.

Watch the trees. Just watch the trees. See, they're not falling.

She desperately tried to focus, but after another wobble and rumble, the wagon seemed to slip. Was it just her fear? Or was the ground really sinking? Her entire body tingled as the force of gravity pulled her downward. She screamed and yanked on the reins. Ascender turned sharply, the wagon buckled, and Madi tumbled from the driver's box into the mud.

Her fingers and wrists sank deep into the soil, which latched onto her clothes. Mud spattered her face, and each panicked breath filled her nose with the foul scent of faded earth. The Gloom gurgled. The ground bubbled, and fear drowned her senses. Her head became so heavy, she couldn't keep it out of the mud. Paralyzed, she imagined fingers beneath the surface of the earth, pulling her downward. She couldn't move, and she couldn't breathe. All the while, the Gloom groaned, like a gray stomach about to open up and devour her.

Bereket's war wagon rumbled by, and a pair of boots squished into the mud beside Madi's head. A firm grip curled around her body, turning her toward the sky. "Hey. Hey, you're okay, Madi. I got you. We're not falling."

When Madi opened her eyes, Bereket greeted her with a weary smile. "Hello," he said cheerfully. He knelt beside her, panting, but his voice remained calm and comforting.

"You're not falling," he said while cleaning mud from Madi's hands with his cloak. "You're okay."

Madi couldn't stop shaking, even as she clung to him. His cloak buzzed between her fingers, and it was the only warm thing she felt. Every other part of her—every one of her senses—told her she was dangling above an abyss. She searched the pockets of her coat, panicking when she couldn't find her flying gloves.

"Left your flier in the wagon, eh?" he said. "Sounds like something I'd do."

"Don't let go," Madi muttered, clawing for a better grip of his cloak.

"I won't," he said, glancing toward the celestial wagons. Madi's vision blurred, and she couldn't tell how many there were, but they were close now—close enough to see riders and banners. Close enough to hear the wheels churn through mud.

"Don't let go!"

Bereket wrapped his arms around her and rose. Carrying her, he trudged through the mud. His voice was unnaturally calm.

"You know, I've been thinking. I used to sit on the floor next to my mother's bed while she slept. She was too sick to move, so I sat with my back against the door so nothing could get in. I was nine years old—probably only a hundred pounds. I tried so hard to act brave, but really, I was there because I needed her more than she needed me."

Mud squished beneath his boots. Rocks exploded in the sky, scattering shards across the plain. Madi flinched, but Bereket's eyes wandered pensively.

"One day, Bandico suggested we play cards to determine who goes out to scavenge. I lost. The one day I'm not there, with my back against the door, something bad happened."

Bereket grit his teeth and straightened his spine. Sweat trickled down his nose and dripped from his braids. His footing stumbled through the mud, but the slosh of his boots was soon drowned out by the rumble of hooves. Stones shattered in the sky amid flashes of smoke.

"Everything changed after she died. Everything got worse . . . and I just wish . . . I just wish I'd been there that day, with my back against the door for her. I doubt I would've been able to do anything. I doubt—I mean, I was a scrawny kid. Shadowmen would've—would've snatched us both. But at least . . . at least I would have been there, you know? Maybe if I'd died that day, things would be better for my brother. He's a good person, Madi."

"You are, too," Madi said, holding Bereket tight. "You both know my fears. And you both know exactly how to make me feel safe. You're the brothers I've always needed."

Bereket's breathing slowed. His knees buckled in the mud, and his arms trembled. He shook his head, panting. "No, we're not," he admitted sadly. Sharp bits of rock sliced across his shoulders, and his mask flashed—an ugly and monstrous thing. "We're not."

Glass crackled beneath Bereket's feet as he reached Bandico's toppled wagon. Ascender had ripped free of his harness, and the wagon had pitched deep into the mud. Bereket groaned as he opened the rear hatch and helped Madi inside. Pins and needles pricked her legs, preventing her from standing. She grabbed the edge of his cloak as he turned to leave.

"Get back in here."

Bereket gently brushed Madi's hand away. "Can't do that. There's a door here that needs guarding, and I won't be making the same mistake twice."

He turned toward the oncoming celestial wagons, and when he did, Madi saw the mangled backside of his battle cloak. Arrows and shards of Galecraft stuck from his armor, which was frayed and smoldering. Madi gasped, covering her mouth. He'd walked all that way, bearing the brunt of the bombardment. The rear hatch boomed shut, and she felt the full weight of Bereket's body sit against it.

CHAPTER 21: MADI

Madi crouched low, pressing next to Panima and Corlan as they looked through the window of Bandico's toppled wagon. Lances glistened, and riders circled. Hoofbeats pounded, kicking up globs of mud. She'd never imagined facing the sharp end of a celestial spear. She turned, gripping Panima's wrist. "Hold Aerial tight. Don't move until I say."

A volley of spears and arrows crackled against the wagon, but then Bereket emerged, swinging his club, scattering the riders. He lowered his shoulder into one of the horses, sending it tumbling. Madi moved to the opposite window, her breaths shallow. Where was Bandico? His brother needed help!

She found him freeing Ascender from his harness. He hopped into the saddle, but instead of riding to Bereket's aid, he turned toward the city of escape. Corlan and Panima huddled close, fogging the glass with panicked breaths. Their whimpers echoed in the quiet cabin.

"Bandico! Come back!" Bereket's voice boomed as he hurled a second rider from his mount. "*Pleeeaaase!*" The man's voice cracked, the younger brother inside him, crying out. "I swore to them! I swore!"

But Bandico kept riding.

Panima covered her mouth, tears spilling onto her fingers. "He's leaving?"

"No," Corlan whimpered. "Bear said he'd lead us all out. He'll come back. He has a plan."

Madi shook her head as the sour sting of betrayal sank into her jaw. Bereket had made that promise, not Bandico. Bereket defended his brother during the story of Bandico's betrayal in the Long Dark. And Madi had forgiven him, because she never imagined he'd do the same thing to her.

Bodies rumbled outside, battering the side of the wagon. Panima shrieked as Bereket wrestled a Celestial, pushing him away from the wagon with his giant club. He roared for his brother, but by now Bandico brought Ascender to a gallop. In front of him, the city of escape loomed, slicing through the clouds toward the glistening constellations. The Lamptree kids clapped the window with their palms, pleading with him to come back.

As their hands beat against the glass, the sound resonated and rebounded, as though a hundred hands joined them—a hundred other young voices, crying out in the Long Dark.

"Don't leave us! Little Light, don't leave us here!"

A deep vibration heated the cabin walls. Sweat stung Madi's eyes, and she pulled her hands away. A rush of whispers swept across the walls, sending a shiver through her spine. The sand clock ran empty. No flip. No reset. Bandico was out of deafening brews, and Raven's voice coiled through the chaos, sharp as a blade.

"Bandico. GO BACK!"

The voice was cold, and frost crackled across the porthole. Through it, Madi saw Raven in her long red coat following after Bandico, pleading with him.

"That vial is empty, Bee. I know you can hear me."

"I tried, Raven. I really did this time."

Bandico's voice broke, raw. The wagon shuddered, its walls shifting like mist, revealing jagged carvings—memories clawed into the wood. A younger Bandico, a younger Bereket. Children walking hand in hand. Children crying out in the darkness. Madi winced as Raven's voice sliced through them.

"Turn around, or I won't give you a choice!" she shouted. *"I'm not going to leave them!"*

"Why do you care?"

"I've been on this journey, too," she answered. *"Just because they can't see or hear me doesn't mean I haven't grown fond of them."*

"Go on then. Pick up your anchor and stay," Bandico replied. *"See how long you last without me."*

His timing beads continued clicking on the wall, rattling back and forth, reminding him to drink another brew. Madi eyed his empty brew chests. If Raven manifested, what would happen to Bandico? What would happen to his wagon?

"Your brother is back there!" Raven's tone shifted from emotional to practical. *"If he dies, everything you've done—everything you've become—would be for nothing."*

Madi's stomach twisted. Bandico wasn't turning around, and Bereket still needed help. She snatched Flicker from its hook and threw its harness over her shoulders, turning sharply toward the children. "Keep Aerial below deck unless I signal to you."

Panima hesitated, clutching the baby tight.

Madi ensured her crossbow was tightly secured in its sheath. She listened for the *click* and then grasped Panima's chin, looking her in the eyes. "I mean it. Watch for my signal. I don't want you in this cabin if Bandico loses consciousness . . . or worse."

Raven haunted the shade hard now, and her voice turned dark. *"If Bereket dies, he'll find out what you did."*

Bandico's grip on the reins faltered. He sagged in his saddle as though he was dragging his wagon behind him. *"If he dies, it won't matter. I'll never see him again,"* he muttered. *"This is his decision. Father said it would happen. It KEEPS happening, and I—"* He sighed loudly. Madi heard it slither through the wall. *"I keep making the same mistake."*

"TURN AROUND, BANDICO!"

"I can't."

The sound of wind swirled as Raven wailed. *"I'm staying!"*

"We can't!"

"You're out of brews, Bandico." Raven's voice slithered now. *"You can't stop me from taking shape. You can't stop me from helping them."*

"Don't!" Bandico's tone conceded. *"You'll trap us both!"*

Madi shuddered. This was only the beginning of a haunt? How much worse could they get? She'd never seen someone get haunted before, but Dario had heard stories. Ghosts could frighten their haunts to the point of unconsciousness. They could take control of their minds, and some said—their bodies.

"You know what the dead will do to me!" Bandico shouted. *"If we die here, I'll never escape the underworld. The city is right there, I can make the climb."*

"No. If you let our friends die here, I'll never let you."

Bandico and Raven shouted simultaneously. The cabin shook. The shade's voice waned, as though being swallowed by a raging wind and sea. Meanwhile, the ghost's voice grew. There was a brief hush, then a surge of energy—a weightless wind carrying an excruciating wail. Panima and Corlan ducked their heads as the sound gushed through the cabin. Black water dripped down the porthole windows, and Madi saw something she recognized from her dreams—the dark Sea of the Afterlife. The porthole shimmered with frost and magic, and the sight stole her breath away, freezing her in place! It was like peering through Bandico's eyes.

A black ocean surrounded the wagon. Dark waters surged, splashing over Bandico and throwing him from his saddle. He tried to run, but the waters of the Afterlife surrounded him, and there was nowhere he could turn but back to the wagon. Falling stars glided overhead, illuminating his frightened face. His big hat folded sadly over his brow, dripping with dark water.

Black water began to fill the wagon, frigid against Madi's ankles. The treasure chests shook and the walls peeled to a mist. This was it! Raven was haunting Bandico hard now, filling his mind. Madi made for the ladder, tugging Panima and Corlan.

"Out! Get out!" she warned them.

Corlan pushed the hatch open, and all the sounds that had been swirling within the cabin burst upward into the plain. Madi grit her teeth as she climbed, surrounded by the deafening noises. When she stepped on deck, she no longer saw the Sea of the Afterlife. Everything was as it was, except now, Bandico had stopped fleeing. He was trapped by an ocean no one else here could see. He jerked Ascender's reins, pulling back toward the wagon as though a giant wave chased him.

Celestials circled the wagon, and old instincts brought Madi's hands to her chest, where she opened her palms and prepared to craft her battle coat. She hesitated. Could she even craft it anymore? She hadn't in over three years. She searched the far corner of her mind, for a magic she'd left untouched. It was still there, like dusty armor, left in an attic. The last person who'd worn this armor was named Nariah Maya.

She swept her hands across her body, collecting bits of nearby mist and cloud as they rose from the earth. Like the silky layers of a cocoon, magic entangled her, curling through her clothes in a protective armor. The smell of mist and matter mingled, reminding her of war—and the mangled emotions that'd followed.

"Get off the wagon!" she shouted to the Lamptree kids. "It's going to cull!" Panima obeyed, with Aerial in her arms, but Corlan slid across the deck, tucking into a hiding place. Madi reached for him, but a lance grazed her leg, knocking her from the deck.

Bereket fought nearby, shielding Wodan. Bits of his battle cloak drifted in the air, shredded during the skirmish, but no blood had yet been drawn. Madi wiggled her fingers into her flying gloves, bringing

Flicker to life. Before she could pull into the air, a Celestial rounded Bandico's wagon, thrusting a lance toward her. The strike might have landed, but a cold and crackling *PING* stopped it. A figure, dressed in a crimson coat, rushed to Madi's side, sword outstretched. She deflected the lance and startled the celestial's horse with a withering wail.

Madi watched in awe as Raven Witterwen manifested. She took shape on the battlefield—as though her body had ripped free from Bandico's—and she was vibrant and full of color. She wasn't the naive orphan Madi had imagined, but a grown woman with a compassionate face. Dark brown hair skipped from one shoulder to the other, sliding across her soggy collar. Her crimson coat was slick with water and full of stitches, meaning she'd probably tailored it many times, adding to its length. Madi had always thought ghosts were caught out of time, but she was wrong. Raven had aged as much as Bandico—and she'd been all alone, adrift on that terrible dark sea for all these years. Filled with compassion, Madi moved to help Raven, noticing one bit of cloth on the ghost's coat that she hadn't mended—a knife-sized hole, just above her heart. Black water oozed from the wound, leaking from her coat as she met the blade of a second Celestial.

"Ghost! They have a ghost!" a Celestial shouted. "Warding vials, NOW! Douse the wagons! There she is! Throw deaf brews if you have them!"

Vials crashed, brews spilled, and Celestials flung all manner of magic toward Raven. Arrows—dipped in colorful deafening brews —came from all directions, whistling toward Bandico's ghost. She shrieked and ran, passing straight through Bandico's wagon, emerging on the other side. A celestial rider caught up to her quickly, hurling a spear into her back. The weapon passed through Raven like she was a mist, and she continued fighting. But Bandico stumbled to the ground, arching his spine in pain.

He gasped, and bits of his battle coat frayed from his back. When Raven was cut through the arm, a bloody wisp of cloud slithered from Bandico's sleeve. Sweat smeared his desperate expression, and Madi had never seen him so focused. He faced death, and Madi hardly recognized him. Gritting his teeth, he fired a slew of arrows, forcing the Celestials to maneuver.

Now, with his hatchets, he struggled. Celestials pecked at him, cutting away at his cloak. Raven suffered another blow, but he took the pain—groaning again. His eyes flickered beneath the brim of his hat as Celestials swarmed him. One of his hatchets fell to the ground, and he swung wildly and wearily with the other. Madi shouted to him, assuring him she was coming to help, but he didn't seem to hear. His form sagged, weary beneath his curses, weary beneath his ghost.

An arrow struck his battle coat. Then another. Madi fought her way toward him, the sick taste of irony running across her tongue. Just days ago, he was acting the part of the immature brother, frightening the Lamptree kids with stories. "The only way through a celestial's cloak is to tear it to pieces," he'd said. "Slicing with swords and hacking with axes is faster than trying to jab through with spears or arrows. Give me three shots and I can outsmart any Celestial. Two shots to the neck, and they get nervous. Trust me. Every time, they sweep their hand like this across their body, moving mist from the side of their cloak to reinforce the front. Do you know what they call an archer's third arrow?" he'd asked Corlan. The boy had shaken his head, and Bandico had answered confidently. "The killing arrow."

Two arrows stuck from Bandico's cloak, and he looked more than nervous. He swept a hand forward, stealing mist from the back of his cloak to reinforce the front. Beams of daylight burned his eyes, and he didn't see the Celestial flanking him, nor the lance poised at his spine. Madi moved to intercept, but her boots slid in the mud, and two Celestials held her at bay, spears *pinging* against Flicker's arms. All she could do was shout, but as soon as the warning left her lips, she knew it'd come too late.

CLAP!

A ballista bolt hissed from Bandico's wagon. The arrowhead glinted through the amber atmosphere, straight into the charging rider, catching him by surprise. A chunk of his cloak shredded into the air, curling around his bewildered face and spattering his cheeks in blood. The bolt spat out from the Celestial's back, dripping red. His lance fell to the ground, and he slumped over his horse for a moment before dropping into the mud. Glyphlight echoed above, shaking like a chandelier about to crash. Such a hush followed that Madi could hear the croak of the celestial's final breaths.

The kill came as a shock to all, and everyone searched for the source of the ambush. Atop Bandico's wagon, a head of bright blond hair peeked out from the ballista nest. *Corlan!* Madi's stomach turned hollow as celestial bows released a barrage toward the wagon.

"Covering fire! There's one in the turret!"

Corlan spun the ballista, trying for a second shot. His voice lacked the depth of manhood, but it was filled to the brim with bravery.

"Don't shoot!" Madi shouted, waving her arms. Flicker copied the motion, hurling her off balance. "He's not a Shade!" Flicker's arms clattered against a wall of swords and spears. Blades pricked her cloak, driving into her brain as though she was walking through one of Lamptree's thickets.

Arrows splintered against the ballista nest. Corlan dashed for cover, but a spear struck him in the back, throwing him from the deck. The spearhead pushed out from his chest, and Madi knew in that moment that the young stowaway was dead. He fell face down in the mud, motionless.

"Hold fire! It's just a kid!" a Celestial shouted, but it was too late.

Bubbles crept up from the mud where Corlan had fallen, and by the time one of the Celestials had turned him onto his back, his face was already pale white.

Panima shrieked. Bereket roared. Raven wailed. Her crimson coat curled around her body as she tried to break through to the boy. Lances and brews forced her back, and her form began to fade. Warding vials crashed around her—orange mist, washing over her like waves. A moment later, she disappeared with another wail. Bandico, meanwhile, slumped against Bear's wagon with two arrows in his chest. He slid slowly downward, smearing blood against the hull, but he was alive. He sat at the wheel of his brother's wagon, still breathing—but only because of Corlan.

Blood flowed from the boy's back, which firmly held the spear upright. All the places to stow away, and he'd picked Bandico's wagon. Tears streamed down Madi's face, blurring the Celestials surrounding her, but they didn't press the attack. Instead, they all looked at the young colonist and the Celestial he'd killed. Why would a colonist help a Shade? The Celestials were angry and confused, and yet, they clearly sensed something special about Corlan, just as Madi had during the course of this journey. In a battle between Celestials and Shades, the bravest voice to be heard was that of a young stowaway.

The atmosphere quaked, interrupting the reverence. High above the dayclouds, a giant constellation burned against a black sky. It groaned like a waking giant. Louder and louder, it thundered and boomed. The sound rippled like a drum against the horizon, and all at once, the Celestials looked skyward. Several small telescopes clicked open, rattling nervously.

"Vetricus Perth," one of them whispered. "He's here."

"Give him the field. Withdraw."

On the horizon, a lone rider approached. His cloak was gray and mangled like a vulture, for no Gale favored him anymore. Vetricus sauntered onto the plain, untouchable. Madi scowled as the air seemed to ache with the sound of Lamptree's victims. He paused atop a mound and looked upward—toward Constellation Perth. The giant web of glyphs let out a sound like a low horn—like the howl of a wolf—and a few moments later, the rest of Company Perth arrived, emerging from all directions toward the call of their pack's leader. Madi shuddered.

They've been searching for us.

"Withdraw!" The Celestial Commander's voice was urgent now. "Stay to our task. Withdraw."

"And the boy? He's dead. What do we do?"

"The Arbiter sees all. She knows we acted in self-defense."

"What about the body? Do we bury it? He's not fit for the underworld."

"He died defending a Shade. Let them bury him."

Madi's hands sank into the mud as she crawled toward Corlan. Horses squealed in the plain, and the beating of hooves turned violent. The Celestials were in full retreat, and they culled their wagons to flee faster. Madi pressed her hand to Corlan's neck and brushed his blond bloodstained hair from his forehead. There was maybe a glimmer of life in his eyes for a moment, but then no more. Squeezing the boy to her chest, she moaned.

"Madi," Panima whispered, her voice muffled beneath mud and tears. "Madi," she repeated.

Corlan's blood pooled on Madi's lap. It spilled onto her battle cloak—onto her mind. She sensed his warmth seeping into the creases of her brain, filling her spirit with a nauseating aroma. Was he falling into the underworld right now? How, when she was clinging to his body? She didn't want to believe it. She'd rather that magic were a lie, and there was no underworld at all. Then at least she'd know that Dario and Corlan were at peace.

"Madi?"

"WHAT!"

Panima recoiled. She was covered in so much mud, Madi could barely see Aerial in her arms. "She's not breathing."

Madi's tone melted, and her second reply slipped out more softly than the first. "*What?*"

"I can't feel Aerial breathing."

Madi seized her daughter, wiping the muck from her face. She felt for a breath. Nothing. Aerial's expression was limp, and her eyelids sagged over her beautiful brown pupils. Until this moment, she thought she'd felt the worst pain a person could feel, but she was wrong.

"Oh no. No, no, no . . ."

She pressed her hand to Aerial's chest. Beneath her tiny ribs, there was no heartbeat—just a subtle tremor, like all of her bones were about to break. Sweat seeped from Madi's skin as she burned with guilt, anger, and denial. There was a way out of this, somehow!

"What do I do . . . what do I do?" she asked, looking around.

But there was no one here to help. Panima covered her mouth, shivering. Bereket was slumped in the mud behind her, his cloak smoldering.

"Bandico!" Madi whimpered. "Bandico, help!"

He had medicine. He could do something. He'd saved Madi twice, and now she needed him to save her daughter. She'd forgive him for everything if he somehow could. But Bandico was unconscious now, too, and his wagon frayed to a mist. Madi sank hopelessly into the mud, praying. *Pilgrim, please. Use your power to save her. Let my glyph fall instead.*

Aerial's glyph flickered, and Madi felt her heart beginning to crack—the final cog in her body was about to break. The oracles' curse had grown like a gaping wound, pushing Aerial's light toward the earth. Constellations droned, buzzing like swarms of angry bees as their shapes shifted. Madi squeezed her daughter, looking around for a place to run—somewhere to hide from all this magic.

PILGRIM, PLEASE!

A horse neared, spitting mud. The rider dismounted and neared, pausing when Madi looked up. Mist curled around the wild gray cloak of Vetricus Perth. Blond hair dangled from his brow—glistening with sweat, like daggers. And he wore a stone cold grin, shielding any sign of emotion. What more fitting a face to see at the end of the world than his? He loomed like a vulture—eyes distant. Posture wary. Lips neutral.

Madi couldn't move. Her brain shook, and most of her thoughts evaporated—all except one: if she could go back in time, what day would she travel back to? When did everything go wrong? She chose the day Company Maya reached the city of escape. She'd turn her company around and never go back. She should have done the same thing this time, too . . .

Vetricus came closer.

"DON'T!" Madi shouted.

Vetricus cocked his head, and the daylight seemed to get lost in his dirty blond hair. "Don't . . . save her?" he asked in a tone, carefully crafted. Before today, she might have had the will to interpret it.

"You can't."

"Yes, I can."

Sure, he could graft her glyph into Constellation Perth, but that was a worse fate even than death. Give her daughter to the company who'd destroyed Lamptree, who'd pillaged countless colonies and murdered Celestials to keep their glyphs glowing? They were a doomed company, on one of their disgraced commander's doomed tasks.

Glyphs groaned in the sky, and Aerial's body grew heavy in her arms. Fear and loneliness crept over her, and the thought of seeing her daughter's eyes open again tempted her to treat with Vetricus. "Why would you help us?" she asked, cradling her daughter's frail frame.

"Because I can afford to," Vetricus replied, kneeling. "She's a Shade, and I'm sure you've heard, some call me their king."

Madi sank deeper into the mud. Vetricus was the Gray Lion. According to dances, he'd sold his soul to the Black Knight, and now that Madi had spoken with the Pilgrim, she believed the rumors.

"You're not anyone's king . . ." she mumbled.

Aerial's head slid down Madi's hand, and there was little warmth left in her body. Lose her to the underworld? Or lose her to Company Perth? Either way, this was the end of Madi Amriel. She could feel it in her chest—every spring and gear that'd kept her going for the last three years was broken. Her thoughts turned callous, and suddenly she found herself unable to ponder it any longer—*unwilling* to ponder it.

She turned her face away from Vetricus, but she left her arms open. A moment later, Aerial's weight passed from her hands to his. As she sighed, she felt Madi Amriel breathe her last. A cold and careless breath came next—blown from the loneliest corridors of her body.

Madi peeked at Vetricus, who closed his eyes and covered Aerial's face with his hand. She'd never learned the magic of grafting, so she'd no idea how it worked. Judging by Vetricus' expression, it was painful. In the sky above, Aerial's glyph flickered and stretched. Then, it suddenly flashed with light.

Aerial woke with a shriek. Her eyes glowed, full of life, and when she looked at Vetricus, it was as though she recognized him. After this magic, she would no longer be Aerial Amriel—but Aerial Perth. Her glyph rose upward, weaving into Constellation Perth like a vine crawling up a tree. As it settled into the bright formation of stars, Madi lost sight of it.

Vetricus rose and handed Aerial to a young woman in a bright blue cape. A needle-like sword hung from her belt.

"This is Lakayd. She'll tend to your daughter," he told Madi.

The Perth surgeon nodded. "I'll look after her," she affirmed. With a flick of her hand, she crafted some cloth and swaddled Aerial inside of it.

You'll tend to her? Madi thought, smirking sourly. Foul thoughts filled her mind, lonely and angry thoughts. *She was MINE to tend.*

The shade surgeon walked away, and Madi stared at Vetricus' boots as he rose. "We'll take you to the city," he said before leaving.

Madi nodded, despondent, and let her head dip toward her chest. Her daughter was alive, and yet she felt utterly defeated and alone. The sky had won. Aerial was now a prisoner of the celestial stage, like her mother. The hooks and strings were attached. The future she'd dreamed of was gone. The barred gates of Madi's heart unhinged, and Nariah Maya walked out.

"Madi?" Panima asked, sliding close.

Madi? Madi? The name echoed over and over, foreign to Madi's ears. Numbness dragged her gaze into the mud. There, she unclasped Aerial's pouch and let it fall to the ground.

She wouldn't be needing it anymore.

CHAPTER 22: DARIO

Wind howled along the ledges, ceaselessly whistling and wailing, whipping the rocks and washing their surface until they were smooth and submissive. Vetricus' small cabin shook, battered by each gust. He'd said this place was a bunkhouse for crissle miners once, and then stripped of its furnishings and repurposed as an Underworld Trail station. A sliver of morning light crept through narrow windows near the roof, where rafters creaked. Supplies lined the walls, and even after living here a month, Dario sometimes mistook the dark silhouette of boxes and barrels for a shadowman.

He slid from his hammock and stretched his legs toward an old oven, the amber remains of last night's fire. The slow crackle of heat comforted him amidst the relentless lashing of wind. He stoked the flame and poured his ration of beans into a tin cup, letting them warm beside Vetricus' simmering kettle. He then risked a journey onto the colder part of the floor, limping into the dark of the cabin, arms outstretched until he felt Nightfly's polished arms.

Without Nightfly, Dario was certain he couldn't survive down here. Keeping up with Vetricus wasn't easy, and every day, he was more grateful for Madi's gift. Every time he polished and cleaned it, he thought of her, wondering where she was. His bones grew more stubborn by the day, and the wind didn't seem to help at all. The ledge-walkers said there was dark magic in it. They'd warned him to stop flying out in the open, but Dario had to keep practicing. He had to escape with Vetricus, or he had to do it on his own—which meant he *had* to get faster.

He'd been rehearsing Madi's flying lessons for weeks, but each day, her voice became more difficult to remember—her gentle explanations, her loving warnings, her honest admission of her dream to fly with him. The constant whistle shredded his sense of time. It felt like years since Lamptree fell, but according to news from the haunted horns, it'd happened just shy of two months ago. Ghosts listed the names of those who'd been rescued by other caverns. Madi's was not among them.

I listen for my wife's name whenever Vetricus is out. He doesn't like hearing the names of the dead, especially when his company is involved. Our weather vane acts as a relay, picking up voices from haunted horns hidden across the underworld. We funnel the cloud with a differently shaped nozzle every few days, which acts as a primitive cipher, because the Ashen are also listening.

I don't know how the Trail survived before Girli's invention. Flying bottles are slow and easily intercepted, but haunted horns allow for near-instant communication. Ghosts slip in and out of our world, gathering and passing information through a current. Girli explained it like this: she said the worlds are stacked atop each other like a cake. Between each layer is a sea or a sky full of starlight. But the Sea of the Afterlife stretches vertically, sliding across all the worlds, connecting each sea and sky. In the cake analogy, she called it the syrup. I didn't like the thought of it—something thick and inescapable, seeping into every world, into every life.

Dario stretched closer to the fire, but the motion sent a sharp pain through the nerves in his arm, making him drop his book and breakfast. Beans splattered across the floor, and the cup clattered loudly. Vetricus rolled out of his hammock and tumbled to the ground with a shout. He ripped his sword from its scabbard, chest heaving. Even after he'd realized it was nothing, he remained on the floor, panting. His jaw hung open, while sweat slid from his hair, dripping from his eyelashes and clinging to his messy blond beard. The ledge-walker rarely slept more than an hour or two, and he often woke Dario with cries in the night.

He sheathed his sword and joined Dario near the fire, setting his kettle atop the flame until it bubbled. A small lantern hung from the rafters. Vetricus checked its fuel and set it closer to the gloom-stained water. The lantern *clicked* and *crackled.* Slowly, the liquid cured, becoming drinkable. Meanwhile, Vetricus sat and stared. Dario stooped and cleaned up his spilled breakfast. He struggled to stand until Vetricus silently helped him. He'd been quiet like this for days, and Dario didn't know why.

After equipping Nightfly, he flew up onto the rafters, to a little nook he'd made for himself where he could read and write in the light of the window. Today was another gray day. Only a hint of color stained the ledge, left over from Dario and Vetricus' last walk. They'd escorted six people to Tickman's Station, but by now, much of what their lanterns had colored had faded back to Gloom. It was probably for the best, since Ashen were always on the hunt for the Underworld Trail's hidden safehouses.

In the shallows far below, a dark surf battered the cliffside. A lone sledder waded through the water toward a body that'd just washed ashore. Wind howled, and whitecaps churned, but the sledder battled through them. Dario wondered where Exile and Company Snow were now. He thought of Krisha and Girli, in Cavern Sixteen, hoping they were safe. He thought of all the ledge-walkers, ghosts, and volunteers—all the cogs that kept the Underworld Trail churning. It fueled his sense of purpose and belonging, far more so than being a Celestial ever had.

"I thought we could search for Babble out by the Norian Spit again," he said, breaking the silence.

Vetricus sipped his hot morning drink, scowling afterward. "Why'd you move out here with me, Dario? Why waste your time? Why haven't you flown back to your family yet?"

Dario peered through the window. High above, long stalactites pierced a colorless sky. Ashen telescopes glinted from the underworld's highest cliffs, where they watched from wooden towers with nets to catch those attempting to climb or fly. He'd thought of racing through the Ashen blockade for days now, but something made him hesitate. Maybe it was his fear of failure, or maybe it was something Illio once said. *If we leave, who's going to help all these people?*

"You need to get out of here," Vetricus muttered. A log collapsed in the oven, causing his shadow to flicker on the wall. "You stay down here too long, you risk falling further, or worse. I want you to find your family. I want you to see them again before this all ends."

"I will, but I have to wait my turn," Dario answered. "And I promised I'd help find Babble. I owe you."

The ledge-walker said nothing afterward—not as they ate, not as they dressed, and not as they walked outside into the howling wind. They went to work building Babble's stable, reinforcing its fence with nails. All the while, Vetricus brooded. Dario sensed his friend's frustration growing, just by the frantic pattern of his hammer.

"What's wrong?" Dario asked him.

"I never should have read your book!" he said, bludgeoning a hopelessly bent nail into the fence.

Dario smiled. "Wait, you started it?"

"I finished it."

"When? I never even saw you reading."

"Every day. When you were out flying."

"Did my commentary make sense?" Dario asked, excited to hear his opinion. "Was each story cohesive to the theme? I want to keep my words brief since the interviews are more poignant. Is the book's purpose clear?"

"Sure, I guess."

"You didn't like it?" Dario asked, confused by his friend's lack of enthusiasm.

"No, because if it's true, I'm as guilty as the Gales," Vetricus admitted. "I built Company Perth. I obsessed over my tasks, growing my glyph, making our constellation shine as bright as it could be. I waged war on behalf of the world above, and you're saying I fought for the enemy?"

Dario didn't know how to answer. Vetricus spoke with the same zeal as Illio. *How do I tell him he was deceived?* Vetricus hammered slower and slower, weaker and weaker. With every strike, Gloom spread to the fence, painting it black.

"Celestial warriors are a noble bloodline," he said. "We came from starry streets, sacrificing a life of peace to protect people without any chance of winning their war."

"Their war?"

"With the Ashen. They're the enemy, and you completely ignore them. I could count on one hand the number of times you blame the Ashen for any amount of suffering. But on every page, you blame the Gales, and that means you blame Celestials. You blame me."

Vetricus' emotion caught Dario off guard. It was like arguing with Illio all over again, but this time, Dario knew the truth, and it gave him the upper hand. "They aren't the real Gales," he said.

Vetricus shook his head, uncomforted. "You're not listening to me. They're the Gales *I served*. By your logic, I deserve to be here. By your logic, my brother is the hero."

"That's not what those stories say."

Vetricus sighed and tapped the hammer against his palm. "Maybe not, but it's how they make me feel."

"It's alright," Dario said, disappointed but not surprised. "Illio didn't believe me either, and we got along just fine. He stood right next to me for many of those interviews, and he reached the same conclusion as you: the Ashen are the only enemy in this war."

"I didn't say I didn't believe you," Vetricus said, dropping his hammer and looking upward. Pain and guilt smeared his face. A weakness Dario had never seen the man reveal before. "I said I didn't *want* to."

After a brief silence, he rolled up his sleeve, revealing a grim shadow pooling there. It was darkest near the bone, where it seemed to latch. The shadow shimmered like water and seemed to rise like a flood, filling the body instead of crawling across it. Dario's face grew hot, and his scalp itched uncontrollably. It was like seeing a gaping wound, only this was a wound in the mind. A sharp sickness sliced through his stomach. Vetricus was too strong to fade, just like Illio was too strong to die.

"It started not long after I began reading, and I can't get it to stop," Vetricus admitted, rubbing the collar of his shirt. He'd been wearing long sleeves and thick clothing for weeks now, even indoors, and now Dario knew why. "I tried to fight it, but every time I turned a page, I started to believe you. I remember tasks that made no sense to me, but I completed them anyway. All I was thinking about was glory and gain. Constellation Perth had to grow. We had to survive. We had to keep shining, and we did."

As he spoke, Vetricus eyed Dario's book, tracking it as it dangled from its chain.

"I thought I was a prince, but I was just a pawn. Every page, I got angrier and angrier. I thought about what I'd do to the people who'd used loyal companies like that. How would I react? What would I do? What kind of person would I become? And guess who I thought of."

"Your brother," Dario whispered, feeling a sudden chill. A gloomy wind swept through the stable, knocking over tools, slicing through the fence, whispering the name *Galicus*.

Vetricus nodded. "Now, I don't know who I am. Up there, Vetricus Perth is called the Gray Lion . . . the Shade Prince. But that person isn't me. It's Galicus. Me, I'm no one. My past is meaningless. My future is his. I can't sleep. I'm not hungry. I have this constant head-ache—a black blur inside my brain making me . . . tired . . . telling me to close my eyes and forget."

"Spasms?" Dario asked.

"Not yet," Vetricus replied, inspecting his hand.

Dario rubbed his knuckles together, unsure of what to say. He always got nervous while talking to someone who was fading, so Illio always used to do the talking. Yes, you could help a fading person through encouragement, but one wrong word, and you might make their condition worse. That'd happened to Illio once, and the man faded in front of them. Dario would never forget it. The Gloom snatched life from the man's eyes—like the spirit inside him had just withered away to sand.

"People are dying up there, Dario, and the last face they see is mine."

"And the first face I saw clearly in this world was *yours*, when your blood was pumping into my veins. You see? Galicus is pillaging the world above. Not you. You're leading pilgrims across these ledges. Maybe if you'd told them your real name, you'd feel less guilt."

"They wouldn't understand."

"Then take your name back. Climb. Stop your brother. Someone needs to."

"Why stop him?" Vetricus asked.

"Because I don't want *him* taking control of a Gale's throne." Dario straightened his spine. "I'm one of the few people who can honestly say I've met both of you. Your brother could have saved me, but he didn't. You did, without question."

"I asked Krisha a lot of questions actually. You were unconscious."

"My point is, a name is just a name. People are going to remember you for what you do, and they're going to remember Galicus for what he does."

"That's easy for someone without a twin to say," Vetricus said with some humor. His expression grew more lighthearted, until it crashed with a dismal sigh. "My brother grafted someone today," he revealed. "This is the first Celestial he's grafted since stealing my company—they're the first Perth I know nothing about."

He climbed up the rocky roof of the stable to the cleft where he kept his telescope—a sad looking device aimed downward toward the surf instead of toward the sky. His lantern clicked quickly, spreading faint shades of color and curing the toxic air. The bronze scope squealed in the wind as he angled it toward trails of starlight in the shallows.

Dario clung to the fence, his hair and clothing whipped by the wind. From this height, he could clearly see how the shallows reflected the sky in the world above. The water was as dark as night, rippling with constellations.

"How does the starlight get down here?" Dario asked.

"You see the horizon?" Vetricus asked, pointing beyond the shallows, where waves rolled in from a black abyss. "Supposedly, the Sea of the Afterlife stretches upward, not outward. It bends and connects to the world above."

"So, we could sail across it, er, up it?"

Vetricus shook his head. "People try. They don't get far. That sea flows one way, and it carries two things: corpses and starlight. Only ghosts can navigate it, so long as they have a haunt."

Waves crashed onto the shallows, causing the water to ripple, and Dario's skin to tingle. If that was a reflection of the sky above, it meant Vetricus had been stuck down here for three years, looking through this telescope while Galicus turned Company Perth into Shades. One month had felt like a lifetime for Dario. He couldn't imagine what years would feel like.

"He's up to something," Vetricus said, adjusting the scope as it sagged. "I'm trying to make sense of it. Why graft a Celestial now? I'm worried it means he's making progress."

"May I look?" Dario asked.

Vetricus recalibrated the dials and stepped aside. Dario took a deep breath and placed his head to the cold scope, grasping the device firmly. His vision focused on a small glyph on the bitter-most edge of Constellation Perth. Light surged toward it, as though it were being sucked toward the center of the constellation. The glyph was similar in shape to Aerial's, but far too large to be hers. Most of its features were hidden by a black scar, which burned bright with a curse. Simple shapes shimmered and swayed, like a flake of snow, struggling to hold its shape. This Celestial was very young, and in very poor condition. A refugee, judging by the patterns, but that was every Celestial's story at that age.

"Whoever it is, your brother sacrificed a fortune to graft them in."

Vetricus peered through the scope once more. "That's what I don't understand. He's been meticulous so far, pillaging for his trove, storing power. He grafted that child for a reason, but I can't imagine what it could be."

"You think he's found a city of escape?"

"I think he's close, and if he climbs, he dooms everyone in my company, including that poor kid."

CHAPTER 23: DARIO

Dario always returned to the ledge before dark, but today, he'd cut it very close. Dayclouds disappeared into the upper passages, leaving only a few pale pockets of light for him to follow home. *"What color are the nearest currents?"* He heard Madi's voice every time he flew. *"Look at their shape, Dario. Look at the way they move. If you trim your lantern just right, you can test a cloud before you slip."*

His heart ached. He missed her so much. Each day was agony. Was she safe? Did she have a plan? Every night, he fell asleep thinking of her. What company was she with? What secret had convinced her to hide her identity from him? He tried to dwell on their first flight together—one of his favorite memories—but the relentless wind scattered those delicate thoughts. Shades of black and white mottled a maze of cliffs and ridges, where long shadows crept out from the rocks. The surf looked colder in the evening, foaming and frothing far beneath the Shelves' Safehouse.

The wooden bunkhouse peeked from the rocks like a snail, hiding within its shell. Vetricus had no doubt already set out fresh traps, doused all the lights, and locked the doors. Wind whistled through Babble's empty stable, lifting a loose canvas. Something lunged from beneath it—something dark and hairy. Dario pushed back with his gloved hand. Nightfly mimicked the motion, striking the ambusher with a wet *clomp*. He squinted at the toppled shape, realizing that it was just a bale of hay.

Dario quickly knocked on the safehouse door using the most recent entry code. The darkness made him jittery. Down here, he wasn't a Celestial anymore. Down here, the Sea of the Afterlife swayed on the horizon, spilling fallen starlight into the shallows, forming a rippling reflection of a sky somewhere far above. The only other sources of light were pale fires and telescopes glinting on the Heights, where shadowmen searched for signs of the Underworld Trail.

The wooden peephole slid open, and Vetricus peeked into the night. His gold hair glowed within the dimly lit interior, and he brushed it to the side as he opened the door. "You alright? What happened?" he asked before Dario had even crossed the threshold.

"I was attacked."

Vetricus' hand went immediately to the hilt of his sword. "What?" he asked, stepping outside.

"By your haystack."

Dario thought his friend might grin at the joke, but he didn't. Vetricus cocked his head sourly and itched his beard. He closed the door and barred it. Dario had been intent on lifting the ledge-walker's mood, but nothing seemed to stop the spread of shadow on his skin. A small fire crackled in the oven on the far side of the room, and a red glow burned across the floor, warming Dario's chilled fingers and toes. Vetricus stirred the coals, and a flare of light revealed his frown.

"I told you to stop searching for Babble," he said. "He's dead and gone from this world. The longer you spend out there, the greater the chance you give away our location."

On the wall, a small warning flag was in the alert position. It was red, with a number painted in its center. As Vetricus tucked it back into its box, Dario realized he must have tripped the trap during his landing.

"Sorry, but I still believe we can find him."

Vetricus slumped over his desk, caliper in hand. A candle burned next to him, melting into a pile of wax on the edge of the parchment. Shadow snaked across the top of his hand, burrowing into the knuckle of one of his fingers, which began to twitch.

"It doesn't matter if we find him," he mumbled. "I don't even know who I fight for anymore."

"The Trail," Dario answered.

"I don't trust them," Vetricus replied. "I can't. Not after reading your book. There are too many similarities between the Gales tasks for me up there, and the Trail's tasks for me down here."

Dario frowned. He hadn't sensed any such similarities. "You're helping people escape."

"They're preparing for a war, Dario. You've seen the Sky Doe. You've seen them try to recruit me to fight."

"To help people escape," Dario answered.

As he hung Nightfly on the wall, his spine tugged hard. His bones felt frozen—locked into place by the wind. He worried his condition was getting worse, and the only time he could move freely was when he wore his flier. Once he'd thawed, he took off his outer garments and hung them by the lantern. The capsule clicked and colored some bits of faded fabric.

"Maybe. Maybe not." Vetricus looked up, dully. "I wager if you'd interviewed more Celestials in your book, they might have justified their actions same as you. My point is, the Gales I thought I was serving are dead, and dead gods cannot win a war against living ones."

"They're not trying to win. They're trying to help us escape before it's too late."

Vetricus grinned, and his sad smile soured the air. "I'll believe it when I see it." He turned back to his map, clearly cutting off the conversation. "A message came through for us today—orders to guide a volunteer to the Low House."

"Not to Tickman's?" Dario asked. The Low House was one of the ground level safehouses. It was hidden inside of a flooded clock tower, not far from where Dario first washed ashore. He remembered seeing its large clock face glowing just above the surf, like a giant round star, making it an easy landmark. Sometimes he practiced flying near it, and it always gave him the chills. That abandoned clock tower supposedly led to an underworld passage.

"No," Vetricus replied. "This volunteer is bound for the deeper worlds. Left Foot is guiding her here, then we'll take her to the Low House."

"She's traveling downward?" Dario asked. "Why wouldn't she be climbing?"

"The Trail needs more volunteers down there than they do up here." Vetricus' calipers clicked as he measured a route. He leaned close to his dying candle as he studied his map and scratched some notes on the parchment. "Before you do anything else, I need you to put together three travel kits. I'll need my longest ropes for this. Also, add the two-four clips to my harness. I don't want to use the four-fours on a downward route."

"Right," Dario said, realizing how many duties he'd left unfinished today.

He hobbled about the old bunkhouse while Vetricus plotted a route. Floorboards creaked. The fire crackled. Wind whistled against the windows, but Dario felt quite warm. At night, with Vetricus here, this small hideout was the only place he considered safe. After putting the travel kits together, he prepared a bunk for the volunteer, wondering all the while why anyone would willingly venture deeper into the underworlds. Maybe they were looking for someone? *I would certainly go if Madi or Aerial were down there somewhere.*

As he worked, a faint voice crackled from a copper cone on the wall. The cone was attached to a pipe which led to the weather vane on the roof. Girli designed the contraption herself and every safehouse had one. They looked like ordinary weather vanes, with spoon-like appendages that spun, but really, they collected the voices in the clouds—the voices that came from the haunted horns scattered about the underworld. The weather vanes made a terribly loud squealing noise, therefore most safehouses had to be very careful when they used theirs. But out here on the ledges, the squealing was muffled beneath the constant wind.

Vetricus listened to the haunted horns before every walk, slowly turning a small wheel to track the various voices. Cloud seeped through the copper pipe, hissing as it transformed into an audible voice.

"*. . . attempts to clear Weeman Passage of debris have failed. Ledge-walkers beware. Cari's Steps are not safe for travel either. A storm destroyed all the ladders. A ledge-walker is on route to repair. Hold fast for my next words . . .*"

As Vetricus twisted the small knob, the voices crackled and changed. Dario recognized many of them now—the voices of the underworld—ghosts bound to haunted horns, hidden in the safest of places. Some sang. Some entertained with instruments. Others relayed important information—over and over, all day long. Comfort and communication, they were the Underworld Trail's most important tools.

"*. . . with a message for the Stranger on the Ledge:*"

Vetricus cocked his head as his code name crackled from the copper cone.

"*Per your request, information concerning the horse, Babble, has been relayed. No Caverns have a record of the animal washing ashore, though we've received one report of a flying horse beyond Cavern One. Your message has been relayed.*"

"Message? What message?" Vetricus asked, rising. "How do they know Babble's name?" he asked, turning. His chest heaved, and his eyes burned, irate, in the oven's crimson glow.

Dario pinched his lower lip. This was going about as well as he'd expected. "It was me," he admitted. "I wrote a letter to Krisha and Girli about our search for Babble."

Vetricus pushed his chair aside. It raked the floor and fell.

Dario stood where he was, confident despite his deep hunch. "You asked for my help. We're hurling a hook into a sea when we need a net."

"Dario, they said Babble's name along with my code name." His eyes swelled, afraid beneath his windswept hair. "Anyone listening to that voice will put together who I am."

"People already know who you are," Dario replied.

"Not everyone," he muttered. "When did you put out that message?"

"About a week ago."

Vetricus touched his forehead, cursing quietly. The copper cone continued relaying messages, and the ledge-walker's tone grew leery. "You should not have done that. That name will only get us into trouble."

"Your name is all we have to find Babble." Dario limped to the nearest bunk and sat down. Vetricus' posture worried him—his hollow gaze, his empty expression. "You're fading because you don't want to hear it anymore, but if you want Babble to find you, we need to shout it out."

"It's not MY name anymore," he groaned, kicking his chair, cracking its spine. "My life belongs to someone else. Chances are Babble has flown back to my brother already, thinking it was me."

"Nope. You're wrong. Babble fell with you, right? He saw what happened. He's looking for YOU, Vetricus, not your brother. Have you ever considered that? What if Babble can't find you because you're hiding? I can't escape without you, so I'm going to shout your name as loud as I can—until Babble hears it, until your brother hears it, until your heart hears it."

"Don't be so dramatic," Vetricus said, turning his back. "I'm not another story for your book. Keep me and your fancy handwriting out of it."

"Too late."

Vetricus glared at his ledge walking equipment—his ropes, hooks, and harness. He tossed a bag of climbing chalk onto the bunk, and a puff of white powder spewed into the air.

"Look, I don't know what sort of hopeful things you've written about me lately, Dario, but I promise my heart would agree. I'm a selfish, arrogant person who thinks he can do anything. Believe me, I want to redeem myself, but your book taught me that the price of my redemption is just too much. I-I don't think I truly want my name back anymore. It weighs too much. I can't save enough people. I can't delve deep enough. I can't win this war. I can't do what I know would make me feel better."

Dario groaned, frustrated by his friend's skewed interpretation. He could hear the shadow inside his voice, and he feared he was running out of time. "You can start by stopping your brother and saving your company. We'll worry about the rest of that after."

"What if we're wrong about him? What if Galicus is on a holier mission than I ever was?"

"I don't think so," Dario admitted. "He's working with the Ashen. I saw it."

"I need to get back," Vetricus groaned. He leaned against his desk, letting his eyes glaze over his map. "But I'm too tired, Dario. It's hard for me to keep going out there. You know how in your book you say you feel all those stories clinging to you. You feel responsible for them, and the weight makes your book too heavy to carry. That's how I feel about helping people climb. I can't do what people expect me to. I can't save enough of them."

Dario's chest tensed at the reminder. His book sway at his hip, and recently it'd felt like a useless burden, like a pack full of rocks. Everyone down here already knew the truth about the Gales, and everyone in the world was out of reach. "I can be very selfish at times too," Dario shook his head, ashamed. "I actually believed I was going to climb into the Gales' realms and change the world by publishing these stories. Now, I'd toss them into the sea if it meant finding Madi and Aerial again."

He shrugged, unsure if this was just another selfish response.

"Down here, my book has lost much of its purpose. Sure, I'll keep writing, but now I'm down here with many of the people I wrote about. What motivates me now is that I can actually do something to help them. I think when you find Babble, you'll feel that way too."

Vetricus sat in silence for a time, staring at the safehouse door. Dario found himself doing the same, and he wondered if his friend was as worried about the future as he was. They both flinched as a loud knock shook the door.

"See, Babble might be here already," Dario muttered, trying to salvage the mood.

Vetricus' sour expression remained skeptical. "Unless you taught my horse how to knock on doors, that's not him. Move," he said, pushing past. "It's our volunteer."

The door rumbled again. This time, Dario made out a hasty entry code. Vetricus opened the peephole, gripping his sword with his other hand. "We've no more room, I'm sorry," he said, using an identification challenge.

Wind swirled outside, spitting wisps of gloom through the peephole. "There's always room for the weary," came the correct response.

"Who sent you?" Vetricus asked, using the second part of the challenge.

"The children," a woman replied.

The answer gave Dario the chills, not because it was correct, but because he recognized the voice. His heart swelled, pushing against his ribs with terrifying force. Vetricus opened the door, and the volunteer hurried inside. Her hood was torn on one side, revealing a large tattoo on her neck. The ink speckled her skin in precise patterns—Constellation Lire, at its zenith.

"Eljay Lire?" Dario asked, limping toward her.

Eljay lowered her hood and looked with two astonished eyes. "Dario? DARIO!" She clasped his cheeks with cold fingers, smiling widely. Then she hugged him. "You're alive!"

"Define alive."

Eljay laughed joyfully and gently hugged him. She'd remembered not to tug on his spine. Not even death could rob Eljay Lire of her empathy.

A second woman stepped inside—the ledge-walker code-named Left Foot. She'd come through here several times recently, escorting important volunteers. She wore a black hood, hiding all but a scar on her chin. Her harness jingled as she helped Vetricus bar the door. The wind howled and seemed to push against them.

"You're late," Vetricus said. "Tide's ebbing."

"We know," Left Foot replied. She cursed the darkness and then shook Vetricus' hand. "I'll bunk here until you return. Good luck out there."

Vetricus nodded toward the row of bunks, where Dario had just laid out fresh linens. They sparkled white beneath the safehouse's narrow windows. Left Foot tossed her gear atop one of the beds. Dried mud dribbled from her belongings. She clapped her hands against her cloak and reached out toward the fire. Her clothes smelled like the shallows—a mixture of salt and sadness.

"I wouldn't rest here more than an hour," she told Eljay. "Time isn't on your side."

"What do you mean?" Eljay asked, releasing Dario. Concern swelled in her eyes, but they remained as perceptive as ever.

Vetricus tapped his map with his caliper. "The underworld passage beneath the Low House is only open during low tide, and I just heard the time tables on the horn. The tide is coming in."

"Can't we just wait until the next low tide?" Dario asked as he guided Eljay to the bunk nearest the stove. "Here, take this bed. It wobbles the least," he told her.

She eyed the pillow, but remained standing with her gear in her hands. "It doesn't sound like I have time to stay," she said. She yawned, and her silent breath made Dario uneasy. He'd watched Eljay die. He remembered her groan as shadowmen tore her to pieces. Now, she stood here, wearing one of the Trail's travel coats. As much as he pitied her weary posture, it also frightened him. The reunion reminded him that Madi and Aerial were a world away.

"Did any other Lires make it?" he asked her.

Eljay sat down, clutching her empty travel kit against her chest like a deflated heart. "I don't know. I washed ashore alone. I might have heard Koka's name on the horn, but I'm not sure. If it was her, she reached the Riddle Rock safehouse two weeks ago. What about you?"

Dario's throat knotted as an image of Illio's body formed, fresh in his mind—his wet and weathered flesh, the sand spattering his wounds. "I washed ashore the same beach as Illio. He didn't make it."

Left Foot offered Eljay a cup of hot water, which she sipped slowly. Her eyes watered some as she stared into the fire. She was very fond of Illio. All the Lires were. A song crackled from the copper pipe on the wall, barely intelligible amid all the hissing of cloud. The weather vane needed to be adjusted, so Dario rose and turned the wheel. The motion stung his spine, but soon, the instrument became clear. A happy song battled the thick air of sadness that'd settled over the room.

"The children from Cavern Seven love this song," Eljay said. "I wouldn't be here if not for them. They scavenge the northern shores for supplies. When they saw me lying there, they brought me in before the shadowmen found me. I thought I'd somehow survived the battle in the marsh, until one of the orphans told me she recognized me from the world above. It was quite the surprise."

"I'm not surprised. You've helped so many," Dario said. He smiled proudly at his old friend, but she seemed too tired to notice.

"That's not what I mean," she whispered. "I meant this place. The underworld. It's real. World atop of world, stacked like dead bodies." Eljay folded her hands over her nose and mouth, pinching her eyes as tears formed. "I've heard that ghosts ferry children to less dangerous shores if they can, but many of them still don't make it." She released a nervous breath while looking Dario straight in the eyes, whispering, "They die in the shallows, Dario—infants like your daughter. I've heard they can fall very, very far before they're rescued. There are orphanages in the worlds below, deep in the gloom. That's why I volunteered. Everyone talks about climbing, but nobody mentions who we're leaving behind."

Dario thought of Illio again, briefly, but then fears about Madi pushed everything else away. He imagined her running from shadowmen with Aerial in her arms. "I don't want to leave anyone behind, but I have a family to get back to," he said.

"I know," Eljay said. "I'm sorry. That isn't how I meant it. But you know how I am.

Dario nodded. If there was a lost child, Eljay wouldn't rest until they were safe.

"You're ready then?" Vetricus asked.

Eljay's eyes drifted toward the bunks and the pillows neatly laid upon them. She blinked slowly as a peaceful song echoed from the weather vane. As far as Dario knew, this might be the last time she ever listened to a haunted horn or had the chance to rest. She'd volunteered to descend deeper into the grave, and no one in the room seemed confident she'd ever walk out.

"I'm ready," she answered quietly.

Dario set a fresh travel kit on her back, and she seemed to sag beneath the weight. Afterward, he began putting on Nightfly. "That's *yours?*" she asked as he eased into his harness. She gently touched one of the curled up arms. "It's beautiful."

"Madi gave it to me," he answered. He aligned the flier's spine with his own, just like Madi taught him. He stood up straight, aided by Nightfly. "It's where I got my code name."

Eljay let out a slow, appreciative whistle. "You're Nightfly? The children talk about you. They say you're fast."

"I need to be faster," Dario replied.

Eljay raised her hood, covering her light brown hair. A few loose strands dangled in front of her two exhausted eyes, which suddenly flared with a fiery confidence. "You're going to fly back sooner than you think, Dario. I believe it."

"I hope so, and I hope to see you again."

"I hope so, too," she replied, embracing him.

"Save your goodbyes for when we reach the Low House," Vetricus said, stepping between them. "We've got a ways to go."

Vetricus unbarred the door, which squealed open, spilling black fog into the room. Darkness veiled the ledge outside, and they all hesitated. Wind howled into the bunkhouse, scattering the stove's coals and hurling the room into utter black. Dario stepped back, bumping into Eljay. Nightfly's arms rattled against her travel pack.

Sparks scattered as Vetricus struck a piece of flint against one of his steel climbing hooks. With a warm *fizz*, a torch ignited in his hand. The bunkhouse flickered in orange and black, illuminating Left Foot's worried expression.

"The shallows are dim tonight," she warned. "Be careful."

Wind tore her hood back, revealing the extent of her scars. The sullied pink flesh crossed her lips and then split like the roots of a tree, reaching into her hairline. Something had tried to snatch her from behind, and something in her tone warned Dario that it'd happened during a night walk.

"Good luck," she said, retreating into the bunkhouse. The door clicked shut, and Left Foot was quick to bar the entrance.

Outside, hints of the rocky ledge shimmered in shades of gray. Shadowmen always hunted in the dark, wearing it like a cloak. Dario's skin grew cold, and for once he agreed with his bones: he didn't want to move.

Vetricus jingled as he walked, and his hooks glinted in torchlight. He dipped his hands in climbing chalk, whispering, "Let's go." The night seemed to swallow his voice. Wind howled, surf smashed the rocks, and somewhere far in the distance, voices wailed.

Eljay followed, turning back toward Dario when he didn't move. "What are you waiting for?"

"Confidence," he replied. "You've walked at night before?" he asked Vetricus.

"Once, yeah. I broke six bones," he said, peering toward the ledge. His face was less than certain. Once he'd measured out a deep breath, he stepped into the dark.

As silently as shadowmen, they walked. For hours, Vetricus led the way across lips and ledges and ladders. Eljay looked too exhausted. Every time stones crackled, Dario thought she'd fallen. She needed to rest, but it was too late to go back and too dangerous to stop. Plumes of colorless cloud billowed silently in the night—filling Dario with dread. How much life did the old Gales have left to bleed? How much longer would their clouds rise? Every magic had a cost, and this one seemed frighteningly expensive.

Vetricus and Eljay wore torches on their harnesses and kept their lanterns trimmed low. The idea was to keep the torchlight nearly colorless. That way, Ashen spotters would mistake them for other Shadowmen. Vetricus had promised that it'd worked a dozen times, but he'd already admitted that he'd only walked at night once—so somebody's math was off.

Wind swirled, churning the clouds. Dario had no choice but to fly slow, carefully testing each current as it came. Sometimes, Vetricus and Eljay outpaced him on foot. Darkness curled around him like two hands, and Dario felt trapped—like a bug inside a fist. To cheer himself up, he thought of Aerial and all the lightning bugs she'd squished during the Lamptree festival.

The surf roared, churning the Sea of the Afterlife. The shallows swayed, a glistening blanket covered with constellations. Waves crashed. Starlight shifted. Down here, the sky didn't quake—the sea did—and large waves followed.

A shrill cry made Dario shudder—the shrieks of those washing ashore, disoriented in the utter black. Every night, the shores of the underworld echoed with such sounds, keeping Dario awake. He peered downward as a voice pleaded for help. The shallows glowed with starlight, revealing several shadowmen moving toward the sound. After a panicked and gargled shout, the voice was silent.

Eljay gripped Vetricus' hand as she stepped onto a ladder. Sharp rocks had reduced her boots to mere tatters. She bled now, and the wind eagerly licked up each drop. She crossed the gap slowly, and voices rose from the abyss—many now, shouting for help, splashing through the dark. Dario closed his eyes, unwilling to peer downward.

But this only made the haunting sound ring louder in his ears. Petrified cries. Hopeless wails. They shouted names into the night, names of people who were a world away now.

"Keep moving," Vetricus said, after clearing his throat. He'd hidden it for hours, but sounds of the underworld were weighing heavily upon him.

The fuel inside his lantern clicked, faster and faster. The sound meant the lantern was struggling to cure the air. Sometimes, it meant shadowmen were near. Dario eased back with his gloves, spread his arms, and widened his fingers. This caused Nightfly's wings to latch more strongly to the nearest mists. Something wasn't right. Eljay's lantern painted the ledge in a pale white glow and while there should have been three shadows, Dario saw four.

Vetricus lifted his lantern upward, cursing as it let out a rapid sequence of quick *clicks*. On the rocks above, a shadowman crouched in wait. Startled by the faceless figure, Dario swept his arms backward, pulling himself away from the ledge. The Ashen hurled a net toward Vetricus, who swung across a gap, narrowly avoiding it. His travel pack raked the cliffside, letting out loud scrapes and rattles.

The shadowman's net caught the edge of the ladder, knocking Eljay off-balance. She jumped onto a steep slope and slid downward, calling out to Vetricus for help. The ledge-walker descended quickly, looping a rope through his harness and rappelling. Hooks and travel kits scraped the flat rock, which was full of large holes. Something stepped out from them, something long and slender and dark with shadow. Dario retreated further out over the water, where the air was prickly with an unknown presence.

He squinted, but Eljay's torch moved too erratically now, with scarcely enough light to illuminate every shadow. They all seemed to shift in the darkness, and soon the cliffside swayed with movement, filling Dario with fear. Spiders, he realized, dozens of them. They were as large as barrels, covered in hair, and gray with shadow. They skittered and skipped across the rocks, coming from all directions, completely silent.

Dario pulled toward his friends, spreading his fingers outward, telling Nightfly's wings to grip the mist. Eljay's torch tumbled toward the shallows, and the last thing Dario saw was Vetricus trying to free her from the arms of a slender shadowman. Rocks crumbled. Lanterns clicked. Dario hovered blindly—helplessly—until a rope snapped. Eljay shrieked, Vetricus shouted, and then the ledge was silent.

All that remained was the reflection of a hundred glossy eyes, watching Dario from the rocks. Forming a fist in both hands, he dove downward, toward the churning waters and the sound of nightmare. The spray of surf stung his face, and even the tiniest breaths tore at his lungs. Large waves rolled in from the horizon, glittering with fallen starlight. His eyes swelled, blurring what little he could see—dark shapes in the shallows.

"Vetricus! Eljay!" he called, flying low. He found a figure standing knee deep in the water. "Vetricus?"

The figure reached upward, silently wrapping around Dario's neck with two wet arms—wet and scratchy, like soggy leaves. Without Nightfly to stabilize his spine, he'd have drowned then and there, but with a flick of his wrists, he broke free before the shadowman could pull him into the water.

"Vetricus!" Dario screamed between coughs. His skin burned, and suddenly, his bones felt very hot, like they were about to sear through his flesh.

"Here!" he finally replied.

There was a loud *scratch*, and then a *hiss*, like the lighting of a match. A bottle of daylight brew fizzed in Vetricus' hand as he raised it, revealing his position. Waves threw him off balance, and his travel pack floated in the water next to him—half submerged. Wet hair smeared his forehead, slicing between two fearful eyes.

Figures followed the light of his brew, approaching from all directions. But they weren't shadowmen. They were the dead. Waves rolled across the shallows, and people waded through them toward Vetricus, crying out. They swarmed the ledge-walker and his light, clinging to him. A large wave rolled over them all, and they pulled him under. Vetricus emerged with a roar, and they clung to him, gargling and gasping.

A harsh wind muffled their cries, slathering the night air with the sound of suffering. Dario's mouth dropped agape. The taste of salt made him sick, reminding him of his first day on these shores. Mist swirled atop the water, stirred by wind and surf. People splashed and squirmed, fighting the current. A few wore lanterns around their necks, those fortunate enough to have been buried. Most, however, were naked, or in rags. Their skin shimmered and slipped against one another as they vied for position next to Vetricus.

A shivering child clung to his arm. Two men fought for grip of his cloak. Another held fast to his travel pack, locking the ledge-walker in place. Dario circled the scene, unsure of what to do. If he flew too close, they'd pull him under too. Vetricus moaned, looking up at Dario.

I'm too tired, the silent gaze said. *It weighs too much: my name, the price of redemption.*

For a moment, Dario feared Vetricus was about to surrender himself to the waves and currents. *Stop!* He wanted to shout. Vetricus Perth was the man who'd saved him. His blood was in his veins. His friendship was all that kept him going some days. This was when he should have rushed to the ledge-walker's rescue, ripping him free and saving him. *Just like he saved me.* But Dario couldn't. His fingers froze with fear, and the wind bullied him. Guilt tugged his head into a sag, and when he saw the book on his belt, he clenched his jaw, breathing deep, trying desperately to conjure enough bravery to be like the people he'd written about:

Totep, the ferryman. Avita, the schoolteacher. Elduko, the ranger.

They were brave, but now they were all likely dead, trapped in this underworld. Every time Dario tried to pull toward Vetricus, that thought made him hesitate. *I have to get back. I have to get out of this nightmare.*

Vetricus strained to keep looking at Dario. Fighting to stay above water, the muscles in his neck bulged. His body tensed, but his expression remained humble and understanding, which made Dario want to weep.

He knows what I'm thinking.

Vetricus thrashed as another wave rolled over him. Water spilled from his mouth onto his beard, making his voice haunted and unrecognizable. "Go!" he shouted, choking down water. "Go!"

The word haunted Dario. It emptied his heart of all warmth, just like when Illio died. He imagined that day, when Illio would have shouted the same thing. *Go, Dario! Get back to them!*

The urge to flee coursed through Dario's muscles, but unlike that day in the swamp, Dario couldn't flee. The weight of his book anchored him in place. How dare he carry a book full of heroes if he couldn't muster the courage to be like them? The answer frightened him: because I love my family so much, and I'm beginning to believe I'll never see them again.

A wave billowed over the shallows, carrying swollen corpses. The surge carried Vetricus and those with him toward the cliffside, where white torches stained the surf. Ashen hunted the beach there, and one of them already grasped Eljay by the hair. As Vetricus washed ashore, they were quick to grab him and the other survivors. Dario looked upward, toward the world above, tempted to fly, anchored by his book. Trapped between love and guilt. It tore his heart in two, but then, something large flew overhead.

The wind and waves seemed to subside, and the sound of a gallop echoed softly in the sand. Without a word, the shadowmen fled, releasing those they'd captured. When Dario looked up, a black horse emerged atop the dunes. Its saddle was empty, but as it reared, eight spindly arms stretched out from a mechanical saddle. A rider appeared briefly atop the horse, wreathed in red smoke and raising a crimson lance. Two fiery eyes peered out from a ghostly black hood, and Dario felt the sharpest chills he'd ever felt in all his life. All his fears subsided. Only guilt remained—a sharp guilt, as the Red Rider's two bold eyes surveyed the scene.

Once the Ashen had fled, the rider disappeared, but the horse, Babble, remained.

CHAPTER 24: MADI

Numb. Sapped. Dried of all tears. Madi's spirit was drowning, and she needed just a moment to breathe. She dug her nails into the bulwark of a Perth wagon, begging the Purple Prince to pause time for her. But the Prince was dead, and time kept flowing, turning each day more gray.

Company Perth raced toward the city of escape, smearing Gale across the coast with their lanterns. Celestial cloudcrawlers pursued the trail, pounding the beach with catapults. The bombardment had followed them for two days—through the gloomy forest, across the mountain saddle, and onto the northern shores. Even now, rocks whistled overhead, exploding against the dunes and scattering sand into the air. The Perths traveled in a loose formation, hunched in their saddles, lances resting on their shoulders. Rays of light pierced the clouds, drifting like spotlights. Like a pack of weary wolves, the Shades prowled toward the city apace, confident despite their fatigued forms.

The gloomy seaside smelled more like sweat than salt. Waves lapped the shore, white and languid in a lazy breeze. Madi rode atop the surgeon's wagon, which was black and red like a poisonous widow's lair. Spools of fabric peeked from barrels, poked by sharp needles. White cobwebs clung to the windows, and spiders crawled across the hull. Apparently, this Shade kept spiders for silk, like Bandico kept bees. Madi hated spiders—she hated everything about this wagon—but she tolerated it to be closer to her daughter. For two days, the surgeon had tended to Aerial, Bandico, and Bereket. They slept in silk hammocks, suspended from the ceiling, and every time Madi gazed upon her unconscious daughter, she felt the steady buzz of magic lift from her body.

Panima tugged at Madi's sleeve, but Madi resisted the pull. Her world was crumbling. Why turn her ear to another problem she couldn't solve?

"Madi, please talk to Wodan," she begged. "Something's wrong with him. He won't stop staring at his rock. He won't let me check his skin either. I'm scared he's fading again."

"I'm scared he is too," Madi replied. "But I've nothing to say that will comfort him. If my body wasn't born from starlight, I'd be fading too."

A shadow covered Madi's heart, dousing every thought in a dreary haze. She touched her chest and felt nothing—no motivation, no hope. All the pieces of her heart had fallen silent. All the gears had stopped grinding. Dario was dead. Nothing remained of Lamptree but a ghost. Aerial was a Perth now, bound to the company who destroyed her life.

Panima sniffed and started to speak, but then a dark shadow engulfed the wagon. The city of escape rose upward like a vine, climbing unpredictably through the sky, a thousand times higher than Lamptree. Its cruel visage filled the air with dread—a cold concoction of desolation and decay. Company Perth's wagons traveled well within the city's chilling shadow now. Old roads converged from the seaside toward the mound of structures, which were stacked, one atop the other, and glued by gatehouses, bridges, and roads. Clouds clung to the city's carcass, and debris tumbled through them—large chunks of stone—thundering against the ground as they landed. Bones littered the fields here, but Madi doubted they'd been killed in battle. Judging by their contorted positions, these people had fallen—without a flier to save them.

Skeletons marred the earth at all angles, contorted as though they were bowed in prayer. Even as lanterns colored the lush coastal plain, it was a sad sight. The surgeon's wagon creaked, and Madi peered upward, nervous. The city groaned. Even Vetricus seemed wary of the sound, and had since slowed his pace.

A chilling cry pierced the silence. Bereket bellowed from his bed, groaning as the surgeon used magic needles to stitch his giant body back together. Madi's stomach was still nauseous from watching the woman stand over Aerial, elegantly weaving mist and matter into her skin. Fleshcraft was illegal. The use of Galecraft on organic matter was grisly, nearly always ending in some sort of explosion. Dario had written about cases of such magic being used for torture. Madi had warned the surgeon not to touch her daughter, but the woman—Vetricus had called her Lakayd—insisted that Fleshcraft was the only way to curb curses during grafting.

"What of the pain?" Madi had asked.

"She's a Perth now," Lakayd answered while working. "We tolerate extraordinary amounts of pain."

"And what if you die? What if you lose focus? This is Galecraft. If it culls inside my daughter's skin, it will explode."

"I don't lose focus. My family's wounds are my life. And if I'm somehow slain, half of this company will explode."

Lakayd smiled confidently, but then caution crept into her expression until concern had carved it to pieces.

"We've had no choice," she'd added while looking at the column of Shades riding nearby. "And I'm well protected."

Lances resting on their shoulders, cloaks thick with mist, Company Perth marched with an invincible air. Wodan watched them from the surgeon's top deck. Spiders skittered away from his presence, and he brushed silk from his clothes. He clutched his piece of crissle rock, which glittered in comparison to the dull texture of his skin.

"They're afraid," he mumbled, glancing at the caravan. "I hope they're all killed."

Madi looked at the boy, surprised by the venom in his voice. His eyes darkened behind an unquenchable anger.

"Please, don't say that. If they die, Aerial dies," Madi told him. "They won't hurt you, Wodan. You can climb with them to safety or you can surrender yourself to the Celestials, but you must be completely honest with them about everything. Not a single lie."

The azure atmosphere grew quiet, and the bombardment finally ceased. The celestial cloudcrawlers had to stay atop thick currents, forcing them further west while the Perth caravan stayed course. Wisps of blue cloud wandered overhead, and soon, rain pattered the road leading to the city. Company Perth navigated a long line of colonial wagons which were stopped in front of the gate. They'd been abandoned here a long time, and dust floated from each carriage as they rotted in the Gloom.

"He's one of them," Wodan whimpered, heartbroken.

"What? Who?"

Wodan nodded to Bandico's wagon. The Shade slouched in his driver's seat. Perths rode through the fog nearby, and on occasion, he spoke to them. Their silhouettes were as sinister as shadowmen, but Bandico didn't seem at all disturbed. Were all Shades allies? Madi didn't think so, in fact, she'd heard that shade companies rivaled each other like packs of wolves. They roamed the Gloom like lions, preying on the weak, vying for territory and for glory. Only the strongest survived. And right now, Company Perth was the strongest. So why would they help two lost Witterwens?

"Look, he's talking to them again," Wodan whispered as Bandico dipped his chin and muttered something to a passing Perth. "He's one of them."

"They're not," Madi assured him. "I asked Bandico to his face."

Wodan snorted. "Then he lied . . . to your face."

So Wodan believed Bereket was a Perth. That would explain why he was fading again. Madi breathed easy for the first time in days. "Wodan, listen to me. There's not a chance in the world that Bear is a Perth. He'd make the worst Shade," she said, unable to imagine him pillaging Lamptree's branches.

"No, it all makes sense now," Wodan continued. "They snuck in through the mines. That's why Bear acted so strange when I told him about it."

"What? Who?" Panima asked, joining them.

"My dad," he whispered. "That day . . . before it all started, we heard a lift rising in the mines. It was supposed to have been broken and barricaded, but someone opened it. Someone strong. Someone who knows how those kinds of lifts operate."

Wodan's voice was grim and matter-of-fact, but Panima tried to comfort him. "You think Bear broke into Lamptree?"

Wodan gripped the bulwark, as though he might leap from the wagon. He pressed his hands hard against the hull, cursing. Veins bulged from his neck where the Gloom was spreading again.

Madi restrained him gently, unsure of what to say. He really believed this? She tried to put the pieces together: Bandico had been inside Lamptree days before its fall. Was he lying about his task? Where was Bereket? He couldn't possibly be a Perth. He was as large as a grizzly, but as gentle as a cub. She tried, but no—no, the pieces didn't fit. Sembetra hired Bandico years ago, and she never would have hired a Shade.

Below deck, Bereket cried out again—his voice pained and ragged. Not long after, Lakayd climbed topside, wiping blood from her hands onto an elegant cape of blue silk. She squinted through the rain at the city of escape, grinning when she saw it. The wagons slowed, and a stone gatehouse came into view. Columns bordered a large wooden door, gray with Gloom. The colossal city eclipsed swathes of daylight, and Madi felt the crushing weight of magic all around her.

"Your daughter is getting stronger already," Lakayd said. "I gave her some brews to help her sleep, but the power of our constellation will do the rest. No curse can reach her now."

Madi stared at the ground, pondering something Bandico had said. *Admit it, after what's happened to you, you feel like a ghost, clinging to your daughter to live.* It was true, now more than ever. The only reason Madi tolerated the surgeon and her wagon was to stay with Aerial. The only thing she feared was losing her daughter. But now she feared something else. What if Wodan was right?

No, he can't be.

"What about the Bee and Bear?" Panima asked.

"How kind of you to ask," the Shade replied. "Bandico is alive, but it's costing him much of his power to heal. I don't know how much longer he can outlast his ghost. Bereket will be fine. I've brought him back from far worse. Did he tell you about the time I sewed his arm back on after he'd wrestled with a faded lion?"

Madi narrowed her eyes, feeling a sickening pressure build up inside her head. She tried to breathe normally to hide her shock, but soon she felt herself gasping. She needed time to stop. She needed it to stop right now, so she could just *think* for a moment. Too many emotions had numbed her senses, and she either found herself weeping uncontrollably or standing stone still, like she was now. Home. Friends. Daughter. Brothers. Soon she wouldn't have anything.

"Oh, I suppose he wouldn't have," Lakayd said, clearing her throat. "He's awake now, actually, and he asked for you, Wodan."

The young man leaned on the bulwark, watching the forest. There, a faded buck stood alert, staring back. "Bereket Perth?" Wodan asked. "That's his real name?"

Lakayd nodded. "We're not what you think."

Her answer severed something inside Wodan, his final strand of hope. Madi watched it snap in his eyes, which quickly grew dull.

"Yes, you are," he mumbled, turning away. "And you're all going to die up there."

The young miner eyed his rock, and with a dark glare, he hurled it into the plain. As the wagons stopped in front of the city wall, he jumped from the deck and walked toward a bare tree not far from the road. Panima rushed after him, but he ignored her, sitting beneath the tree.

"Don't leave us," she wept. "Bear wants to talk to you. Let him explain."

Wodan pushed her away and yanked his hat over his eyes. It was too late for him. His father was dead, and no apology, no explanation, would ever change that. He would never forgive the Perth brothers. But would Madi?

She stood frozen, watching Wodan retreat further into his grief. The weight of betrayal pressed against her chest, making Lamptree's desolation hurt more than usual. Could she look Bandico and Bereket in the eye and offer them forgiveness? They'd become her brothers, and so she'd wait for their answer, but the longer she watched Vetricus, the more she felt Wodan's hatred creeping into her own heart.

For a long time, Vetricus stood in front of the city gate with his sword resting on his shoulder. Without a word, his Shades watched patiently, as though their commander would whisper some secret phrase. Hooves clopped the stone street as the horses shifted, restless. Rain pattered Vetricus' hood, splashing onto his cloak while he stood in the shadow of the groaning city.

Finally, the gate creaked open. Shadowmen pushed the giant doors, eight to a side. Panima reeled back, clutching Madi's sleeve. Horses raised their heads and snorted as their riders gripped their weapons. Lakayd drew her needle-like sword, and other Shades angled bows and lances.

"Lower your weapons. Trim your lanterns," Vetricus said, gesturing for his company to follow. "We've been granted safe passage."

Panima quickly ran to Wodan. "Wake up, we're leaving."

Wodan's arms and legs were crossed as he reclined, almost peacefully, beneath the tree. He was probably so exhausted, he'd fallen asleep. "Wodan?" Madi called when he didn't rise.

Wodan's hat covered his face, and when Panima removed it, there was nothing beneath but a face full of shadow. Gloom consumed the young man's flesh, and his faded corpse rose, faceless and naked in shadow. In the dim daylight, there stood a shadowman. Without a word, he snatched Panima's sleeve. The girl reeled back, slipping in a puddle. Vetricus and his Shades turned toward the commotion, but before they could react, Madi unclasped her crossbow and put a bolt through the corpse's chest, pinning it to the tree.

Wodan hadn't warmed to her the way the younger kids had, but as his faded body went limp, her bottom lip began to tremble. He'd fought the shadow for months, and Bereket's comfort had nearly cured him. Bereket Perth. It still sounded wrong. Couldn't Wodan have held on a little longer? At least long enough to hear the brothers' explanation. Surely, they had an explanation. Maybe they had no choice, captive to Vetricus or to a curse?

Either way, Madi had to take the shot. She had to, not just to kill a shadowman, but to silence a whisper inside her head:

They know how you survived, Nariah Maya. They know what Lamptree is. The Gales will destroy it. Destroy you. DO NOT GO BACK! Please. I studied your glyph. Saw your death.
~Your friend Sembetra

Every part of Sembetra's prophecy had come true—everything except her own death. The gate of the city was open now. Vetricus guided his black horse inside, and as Madi followed, she doubted she could cheat death a second time. A formation of Ashen guarded the avenue, with shields and spears as shadowy as their skin. Rain fell softly onto their faded flesh, glistening like beads at first, but then filling with a dark mist. The formation parted, allowing Company Perth onto a wide street. Footsteps shuffled as the shadowmen backed away from the wagon, avoiding the Gale coming from the lanterns. They stared silently, tracking Madi with featureless faces.

Like Wodan, these Ashen were people once, now stripped of everything that'd made them unique. From human to shadowman—from colorful skin and personalities to empty shells, controlled by an invisible hand. This was the most docile Madi had ever seen them, and in many ways, it was more eerie than when they crept through the darkness.

Hundreds of shadowmen watched Company Perth enter the first district, some from the street, some from rooftops—completely silent atop the creaking structures. Had they made this city their home? Madi had never seen an Ashen eat or drink or sleep or play. They only hunted. More likely, this force was a garrison. But why weren't they stopping Company Perth?

She eyed the stars, bathed behind a watery atmosphere. Rain slid down the rooftops, splashing the roof of her wagon as it passed beneath. The abandoned city groaned and crumbled. Meanwhile, stars glistened and chimed. What did the patterns mean? That was always the question Dario was asking. What were the enthroned Gales scheming? Finally, Madi began to understand his frustration. She felt it burning in her gut, wrenching her shriveled heart. Finally, she understood his book, his distrust, his desire to disrupt whatever it was the world above was doing.

Colossal buildings formed the core of the city, which sprouted from a labyrinth of smaller homes. Mist crept through every alley, and it all seemed to congeal in the Gloom—a rising mass of structures, like stone giants clambering atop one another, reaching for an escape. Vetricus paused at a second gatehouse. An Ashen guardian stood in front of it. Madi shuddered when she saw the giant shadowman, who was even taller than Bereket, with a club twice as thick. The guardian turned and lifted a bar from the gate, which rumbled open.

What kind of magic had Vetricus stumbled upon to pass through this way? The Ashen opened the gates voluntarily, which meant the Gloom wanted Company Perth to climb. Whose side were they on? *Whose side am I on?* Madi wondered. The Pilgrim seemed more powerless than ever, trapped in the Sea of the Afterlife with nothing but an ancient plan to save her people.

Once through the second gate, she felt the road rise. Here, streets coiled around an old, flooded reservoir, spilling from the bowels of the city like black blood. An enormous statue lay face down in the water, broken. Perth lanterns colored the statue's face, cheeks, and parts of its hair gold, but the rest remained deathly white. It wasn't until a bridge carried the company into the third district of the city, that Madi felt like she was truly escaping. What would happen to Aerial in the world above? Would she be free of Company Perth? Madi doubted it could be that simple. Her only option was to stay as close to her as possible, and hope for a way to free her.

In this third district, a junction reminded Madi of the inner workings of a toy. A giant wheel, a hundred times larger than any carnival wheel, spun ever so slowly, carrying platforms to the districts above. Mist spilled from a second wheel high above the first, connecting multiple districts like gears. The system of lifts and bridges reminded her so much of Lamptree.

A lone Ashen guardian stood watch over the road here. Two faded animals—tigers, Madi thought—crouched by its side. A dozen Celestials lay at their feet. A hint of fallen glyphlight sparkled atop their skin, which had yet to rot or turn gray. But soon it would. Cobwebs stained their flesh. How long ago had they died? Had they all fought the guardian at once? Or had these warriors each fought alone, seeking fame or escape?

Dayclouds drifted into the distance, leaving the city in darkness. Gulls perched atop seaside towers. The birds themselves seemed silent, and yet, the nearby Gloom gave off an eerie echo, like the sto-len screech of a thousand seabirds. Madi clasped her arms together, wondering if it was her imagination or the White Whisperer's voice riding the wind.

In this district, the city's architecture changed once again, as though an entirely different people had constructed it. Unlike the stacked stone of the first two districts or the clock-like bronze of the third district, the fourth district meandered outward, over the sea, with sweeping bridges and tall towers.

To pass time, Madi challenged Panima to a game: find a window that wasn't circular. Stone towers, smooth like glass, vaulted high above the sea, each with its own pointed roof and parapets. Every single one of them had one, large round window, glistening in the night. Panima fell asleep soon after the game began, but Madi kept studying the architecture—wondering why each tower had only one window, imagining each lone circle as an eye peering from its abandoned home.

White clouds rose from the sea, weaving through the towers and turning teal once they'd reached the Perths' lanterns. Ice crackled be-neath the wagons, and soon, rain turned to snow. Many of the Perths replaced their wagon wheels with skis, and the company slid upward, through an eerie silence.

This was a much calmer journey through the city than when Madi flew with Company Maya. If not for the nervous knot coiling inside her stomach, she might've called it peaceful. Company Perth didn't have to fight shadowmen. They didn't have to avoid traps or fight guardians. They didn't even have to navigate the maze of roads. Even now, a shadowman gestured to Vetricus, pointing out where to go.

For hours, Company Perth coiled upward, weaving back and forth through the rising streets. Some districts were as small as one of Lamptree's branches. Others sprawled like the bridges of Greenpond, with twisting avenues and alleys. Scenes of panic told a troubling tale—skeletons stranded outside locked gates. Jars left at wells. Furniture stacked against doors. Wagons surrounded by mounds of decaying Ashen corpses.

The road narrowed, and mist curled around a sign which read: *Epitaph Passage.* Here, murals covered the walls—some sketched by children, others by skilled artists. Madi untrimmed her lantern, letting Gale spill onto the artwork. These scenes depicted an epic struggle—a journey upward, from underworlds far below to this city. Hope flickered inside Madi's dark heart as she thought of Dario. Could he really climb back? If people could escape the underworld, then where were they all? Why were there only rumors?

The caravan slowed, and even Vetricus eyed the walls, tilting his vial of daylight toward one of the scenes. Panima woke, wiping her eyes with a yawn. Snow glided across the road. Lanterns fizzled and squeaked. Gale splashed outward, and the murals glistened with color. Panima clutched a blanket to her chest, pointing.

"Is that what the underworld looks like?" she asked, yawning again.

One particular mural crawled up the wall of the entire district, portraying people climbing up through cracks in the earth. Their silhouetted forms were desperate, and shadowmen climbed after them. Colorful clouds weaved throughout the entire mural, forming a trail and chilling Madi's skin.

"I don't know," she answered.

Suddenly, the caravan stopped. Perths cursed and muttered to one another, eyeing Madi. Vetricus paced atop a crumbled stair, sword perched on his shoulder, cloak fluttering. Several of his Shades stood on the steps beneath him, gazing through telescopes. It was quiet at first, but then a commotion echoed, and Madi felt the shades' attention turn toward her.

Madi scrambled toward the steps, pausing when it ended abruptly. Clouds lapped at the crumbled stone, and a lofty wind lifted the edges of Vetricus' coat. Madi tracked his gaze upward, to where the district ended. A giant gap loomed above. For a mile at least, there was nothing but open sky. Far above the gap, there was more of the city. Buildings and streets dangled from the sky like a black icicle, but it was far, far above. Debris dribbled from it, and Madi dropped to her knees. Someone had severed this city.

It was a dead end.

Vetricus, however, didn't seem surprised. He stood atop the severed stair. A lofty wind bounced off of his confident posture, and through his dirty blond hair, two deliberate eyes peered at Madi. Constellations blazed above him, sparkling with symbols and patterns. *The scepton's blessing,* Madi remembered, feeling a chill. Constellation Perth echoed in the sky. Starlight smeared quickly, like the enthroned Gales' pens were scratching the sky just above their heads.

"You knew the city was severed?" she asked him.

"I suspected it."

"Then why come this way?"

"Because I have a scepton," Vetricus answered from atop the stair. "And if the scepton wants her daughter's company to survive, she'll do exactly as I say."

CHAPTER 25: DARIO

Dario's lantern hissed, clicking frantically as it colored a wide beach. Red and blue clouds spouted from nearby geysers, spattering the shallows in a hot rain. Each drop sizzled as it struck the cold water. Steam curled around Dario's body, which shivered, tingled, and chilled. Forces were on the move, and after what he'd just seen, he felt like he was finally a part of something—a fight for truth, justice, and survival. Babble's saddle was empty now, but a moment ago, a Gale had appeared briefly upon it—the Red Rider!

Dario quickly documented the scene in his book. Exposed bone pushed against wounds in Babble's flesh, but no blood poured out—only a dim red mist, which seemed to keep the wounds sealed. A powerful presence filled the air, which smelled acrid and ancient. Even the survivors who'd washed ashore were hesitant to approach. Instead, they gathered around Eljay Lire. She lit another torch and dug through her travel kit, fishing out dry clothing and supplies for as many as she could.

Dario counted six survivors, huddled in the night, hiding behind a crude driftwood barricade. Four of them carried grave goods and wore small vials of lantern fuel around their necks. The other two were naked and speckled in sand. They coughed and gasped as Eljay tended them first, wrapping blankets around them. To ease their breathing, she untrimmed her lantern, letting out swathes of Gale. The glass capsule hummed, and an atmosphere of color spread across the beach. Meanwhile, shadowmen gathered atop the dunes, watching.

Rain trickled down Vetricus' hair as he stared into his horse's eyes and caressed his black mane. Their foreheads touched, and Vetricus glanced toward the empty saddle. "Dario, did you see anything . . . strange . . . a moment ago?"

"Yes," Dario answered while writing. "I saw someone riding Babble, and then they disappeared."

Vetricus' jaw tensed. He'd no doubt hoped for a different answer, but Dario couldn't lie. He knew what he saw—a rider, wreathed in red smoke. Vetricus cleared his throat. His hands shook, and he'd yet to touch the saddle. First, he scooped up some sand and tossed it. The specks scampered across the saddle, unhindered. Next, he took a long piece of driftwood and prodded the air with it. The saddle appeared empty, but Dario was certain he'd seen a Rider.

"I'm afraid to mount up," Vetricus admitted, his face harsh with hesitance.

The air tingled with magic, making him nervous. There'd be a price to pay for sitting in that saddle again. But what? Vetricus wrung his hands in anguish. He'd been searching for Babble for years, only to find him bound to an ancient power.

"I would be, too," Dario replied.

"What do we do now?" Vetricus whispered.

Rain pattered Babble's bold posture, his eyes alert in the night. The animal flicked his ears and seemed to understand the question. He lowered his head, then his hoof, etching something into the sand:

RIDE

Dario drew back, now fully convinced that the horse was haunted. A thick and powerful air surrounded the animal, making him afraid. He'd hated the Red Rider. He'd quietly cursed the oracle on Lamptree—but this was not that same god. This was a different being. But who? Dario's hair stood on edge as he imagined what kind of god this was. Bold. Brave. Brazen. Bloody. If the rumors were true, this was the Gale who'd charged into a foreign world long ago to avenge his fallen siblings. But could he be trusted? Did they have a choice? Dario didn't know. The thought of a dying and desperate god made him think of cruel and crooked contracts.

But there was something honest about the Rider's arrival—something timely—something comforting about his guise as Vetricus' old horse. Maybe the Red Rider was here to help, and he needed Vetricus Perth to do it, not some stranger on the ledge.

"I say you ride," Dario whispered.

Vetricus eyed the shadowmen, creeping across the dunes, then he watched Eljay tend the survivors. Hot rain trickled down his conflicted expression. Finally, he closed his eyes and settled into the saddle. He gripped the reins, and Babble shifted softly in the sand. After a long breath, he whispered, "Fine. One last climb."

Babble leapt from the dune, and eight spindly arms shot out from the saddle. Vetricus drew his sword, which seemed to glow red in the night, and the Ashen withdrew. Babble galloped silently through the air, carving a crimson mist through the Gloom. Dario didn't know how the saddle worked, but it made him think of Madi. It made him hope she would see it one day.

Meanwhile, Eljay placed her travel coat around a small girl's shoulders. "We need to get out of the water," she said, guiding the shivering girl. "Where's the closest safehouse?"

"I don't know," Dario replied, squinting into the darkness. The only landmark was the Low House on the far side of the bay, where Dario had washed ashore. The face of the giant clock tower glowed like a pale star, still miles away.

Shadowmen fired arrows from the dunes, pecking the driftwood barricade. Babble swept downward, and two swords seemed to strike from Vetricus' hand—his silver blade and another, concealed in a crimson smoke. Two shadowmen dropped dead. The others withdrew while Babble soared upward. Telescopes glinted from the Heights, where Ashen outposts turned their scopes toward the commotion. Soon, faded spotlights beamed from dark towers, bathing the flying horse in a pale glow.

Babble streaked across the sky, and Vetricus hurled his hand forward. Dario thought he might have thrown a rock, but then the sky flashed red, and a crimson lance shot out from Vetricus' hand, striking the wooden tower and burning it like a matchbox. Flames lit the sky, outlining Babble's winged silhouette. Vetricus stood high in his saddle. He raised a victorious fist and bellowed like a child. His hair sparkled like a king, and the joy in his posture reminded Dario of his first flight with Madi. *That day on Lamptree, she made me believe in myself again.* And as Vetricus howled, Dario wondered if the Stranger on the Ledge finally believed in himself again.

He circled a second tower, weaving between arrows, nets, and spotlights. Soon, a second watchtower erupted into flames, illuminating the coastline. Waves rolled onto the shallows, carrying the cries of the recent dead with them. Ghosts ferried them, and their tiny boats shimmered on the horizon, reminding Dario of the frightful day he'd woken up on these shores. Eljay splashed into the surf, toward those washing ashore.

"Don't leave the shallows," Dario told her, fearing she'd be swept away. "Stay here. I'll go!"

"How will you bring them back?"

"With this," Dario said, tying one of Vetricus' climbing ropes to his harness. He tugged the line to prove it was tight. Then, with an assuring smile, he took to the air.

The pitch black horizon ripped his smile away. The night was so thick, he could barely see the rope dangling beneath him. It skimmed over the surface of the water, splashing and snaking in the wind. If not for the web of constellations glowing in the shallows, he'd have seen nothing at all.

Rain pattered Nightfly's ten glistening arms as they mimicked the rhythmic pull of his arms and fingers. Wind howled, and clouds swirled. The nearest currents were rose red, laced with strands of blue. Blues made flying wet, slippery, and slow, but Dario had found that if he touched all of his fingers together and stroked like he was swimming, he could cut through blue atmospheres more quickly.

"Take the rope!" he shouted to a man stumbling in waist deep waters.

Raindrops rippled atop the waves, and it was difficult to tell survivors apart from shadowmen, but this man had been calling out. The surf swelled, and darkness devoured Dario's sense of direction. "The rope! The rope there! Hurry!" he shouted.

Once he felt the man's weight on the rope, he pulled for the shore. Red atmospheres, unlike blues, were easy to cling to while moving fast, but slippery while moving slowly. The added weight made this more difficult. Dario struggled to stay near the surface of the water. If he flew too high, the exhausted man would surely lose grip of the rope. Too low, and he might drown.

Dario squinted in search of the shoreline. Vetricus and Babble galloped across a dune near the driftwood barricade, which was now aglow with a campfire. Dario misjudged his landing on account of the extra weight and plowed headfirst into the sand, scattering sharp shells. Vetricus grinned and stroked Babble's side.

"All that practice landing on narrow ledges and you crash on a flat beach."

He looked like a different man, beaming with confidence—like his brother on Lamptree. Meanwhile, Babble's eyes burned red, cooling to brown as Dario cleaned himself. He spat sand from his mouth and wiped seaweed from his hair. It wasn't how he'd hoped to land in front of the Red Rider, but at least his friend's humor was back.

"You have to make a decision," Vetricus said, turning to Eljay. "Are we holding our ground here, or do we make a run for the Low House. The tide is ebbing, and we can't do both."

Eljay stooped over the newest survivor and helped him stand. "We can't leave," she answered while watching a distant wave swell in the pitch-black night. A young child shrieked as the wave crashed, and Eljay immediately ran toward the sound. "We'll wait till the next tide!"

Vetricus circled the barricade, fending off two shadowmen as they reached for a survivor. An arrow whistled from the dark, smacking Babble's side. The horse squealed. Red mist flowed, but then the wound closed. So that's how Babble had survived the underworld on his own all this time—the Rider had kept him alive.

"I don't know how long I can hold them," Vetricus warned, re-gaining control of the reins.

"We can't run," Dario said. "These people are too exhausted."

Vetricus circled the camp once more, eyeing the dazed souls within. Dripping wet, lacerations on their legs and feet, faded flesh begin-ning to surface—they were in no condition to move. To survive, they needed the Trail.

"Hold fast, all of you," Vetricus told them, gazing upward, where flames licked the dark sky.

"We need help," Dario whispered.

"Help will come."

"Who?" Dario asked, thinking of the dragoons on the Sky Doe. There were hundreds, but all he'd ever seen them do was hide. "Cap-tain Imani never risks revealing her troops."

"She will this time."

Dario watched one of the survivors wrap a splint around her leg.

He feared only a few would ever make it off of this beach. "They won't know where to find us."

Vetricus spurred Babble into the air, amid a plume of red mist. "Then I'll have to shout my name a little louder."

All through the night, a crimson lance guarded the driftwood barricade. All through the night, Eljay added to the fortifications and tended the wounded. All through the night, Dario pulled the suffering to shore. Blood trickled down his back where his rope had cut into his skin. His lantern fuel ran low, and the capsule clicked as it smeared color across the sky. His arms ached. His lungs burned. But he couldn't stop. No. Since dying, this was the most alive he'd ever felt. As the dead floated in from the Sea of the Afterlife, he imagined each story in his book. Those were people he'd wished he could have done more to help. Now, he was a cog in the Underworld Trail, and he had to help.

As he flew back and forth, thoughts paced his mind—ideas he wanted to write down. *Our survival is a book, and we are the pages that hold it together. We survive by holding fast to one another, and we reach the end of this climb by stacking our stories one atop the other, chapter by chapter.*

Dayclouds flashed. At last, bright currents spouted from geysers, filling the cavernous sky with pale rays of light. But where was the help? Vetricus had been circling high in the air, swooping downward like a falcon. But now, he faced a large formation of Ashen, creeping close to the barricade. Eljay was just a speck on the beach, rushing from one side of the barricade to the other. Children followed her, helping her, just as they had in the world above.

Dario groaned as he plucked another person from the surf. He worried his tendons might snap before he finished this trip. A wave swelled, and he pulled upward to avoid it. Dayclouds slipped between the red and blue atmospheres, like grease through gears. He tugged hard with his right arm to avoid slipping, but then he felt the weight on his rope go slack. The survivor had slipped.

Wind howled. Rain and surf clashed—cold seawater and hot rainwater. His muscles ached and his eyes strained to stay focused. As he searched for the survivor, he panicked and tasted the same fear he'd felt on the day he'd washed ashore—the day he'd begged for help. The survivor came up gasping, but before Dario could reach him, someone else grabbed the man. Dario cursed, fearing it was a shadowman, but then he saw a teal sash—Illio's sash.

Exile lifted the survivor from the water and placed him on a long sled. Wintry eyes peered from behind his wet brown curls. Illio's sash fluttered from the shaft of his glaive.

"Exile!" Dario called.

The boy smiled and pointed to a formation of small colorful craft floating across the shallows. There were at least a dozen, each unique and decorated, and now, dressed for war. Company Snow was back! Rocks hissed through the air, followed by volleys of arrows.

The Gloom roiled, as if miffed by the silent Celestials. Colorless clouds churned, and from the far side of the bay came another fleet—but these ships were faded and moving fast, with black sails. Black nets dangled from their hulls and hundreds of shadowmen peered from the bulwark. Dario flew too close. He balled one fist and opened the other, pulling quickly to the side as rocks cracked and exploded. Shrapnel missed him narrowly, striking Nightfly with a worrisome *ping!* Shattered rock skittered across the surface of the water, where even more ghostly ferries had gathered. Shrieking arrows flew from them, but as the Ashen fleet arrived, the ghosts withdrew.

A horn blew, but not a bold or brave blast. It was a sickening sound, and Dario realized that it wasn't a horn at all, but the wind. Like a gasp of death, it announced the arrival of a second Ashen fleet—this one in the air. Three faded cloudcrawlers. Shadowmen wearing fliers, dozens of them, and even more faded creatures—bats and bugs and something far larger—a faded pterosaur, far larger than the one that'd nearly swallowed him whole.

Exile rushed ashore, pulling his sled. Meanwhile, his company turned to face the oncoming tide of shadowmen. Dario counted twelve small rafts—not nearly enough. Images of Company Lire's final march formed in his mind, and he didn't want Company Snow to fight. He didn't want their companionship to end like his company's had.

A tense hush muted the shallows. Dario's lantern clicked and fizzled, and color fled the sky as shadows massed in the Gloom. He looked skyward, toward the giant stalactites dangling above. If there was ever a moment to chance an escape, this was it. Dario spread his fingers, poised for an upward pull, but something held him in place. His book dragged his gaze downward. Exile. Eljay. Vetricus. Illio. Their stories were still unfolding, and Dario worried that if he abandoned them now, they'd never reach a peaceful end.

Drums echoed in the Gloom, but then a brave drum answered. Again, it sounded—a trickle of beats, followed by a loud *BOOM*. Pale smoke smeared the horizon, glistening with daylight. He squinted toward a gap in the clouds, and his lips curled into a smile when he saw three large shapes—corsair-class cloudcrawlers, flying the flag of the Underworld Trail. Large white banners with black arrows and circles fluttered atop their battle towers, and crews of at least a hundred dragoons stood at the bulwark.

Dario thought of his notes for his book. *What started as a silent trek through the night grew into the largest battle the underworld had ever seen.* He merged with the flying formation and felt the brave drums vibrate against his bones. Dragoons prepared to take flight. Their fliers glistened, and the soldiers carried crossbows in the spines of their fliers—just like Madi. They faced the oncoming Ashen with stoic expressions. These weren't frightened survivors huddled in the safety of a cavern. These volunteers were eager to fight. For a long time, they'd been waiting to push into the Gloom. Dario had seen it since he'd arrived. Captain Imani's army had been waiting for a leader, and now it had one.

Babble soared atop a red cloud, and Vetricus' sword glinted in the daylight. At once, the dragoons let out a loud cry and leapt into the air. Dario flew with them, chills covering him head to toe. This was the Third Dragoon Regiment, from the Sky Doe. Dario recognized their brown and gold uniforms—motley, yet matching. Part of him wanted to perch on a rock and record this battle. Something big was happening here. Something that had never happened before, as far as he knew—the Trail was beginning to fight back.

Vetricus led the dragoons straight toward the faded pterosaur. Some dragoons stayed near him while others landed on the shallows, firing their bows in echelon. Shadowmen fell all across the beach— faded horses, faded creatures, white sleighs. The fighting withdrawal worked with great effect until a formation of flying Ashen flanked the dragoons, catching Dario by surprise.

The clash was like the crack of a whip. Fliers snapped. Wings broke. Bodies tumbled through the air, flailing, wrestling, locked in a deathly struggle until splashing into the water. Dragoons cried out as they fell. Shadowmen fell, too, but always silent. All Dario could think of was the day Madi gave Nightfly to him: *This one is built different*, she'd said. *It's bone-root, not flex-wood. You could stop a sword without a scratch.*

Nightfly clattered as a winged Ashen collided with him. Its shadowy flesh looked soft, like wet sand, but it was as solid as black ice. Dario wrestled with the shadowman as it fumbled for something—maybe a knife. Its shadowy hands came free from his gloves, and for a moment, it latched onto Dario with wet and itchy fingers. Its face was empty, cold, and silent.

The Gales made you? Dario recalled the rumors, his skin frigid. *You fought to protect this world once? What are you now?*

Their flier's entwined. The shadowman jabbed a dagger toward Dario's throat, but its flier snapped, and Dario sliced Nightfly's wings across the thing's body, freeing him just before he struck the water. The wave swallowed them both, separating them, and chewing Dario to pieces. Dark water churned, and Gloom filled his lungs, remind-ing him of his first miserable day in this world. Around and around he rolled, holding his breath until he'd washed ashore, not far from Eljay's barricade. Ears ringing, Dario looked at his hands. His gloves were torn, and Nightfly's wings curled back toward its spine. Sharp shells had sliced his fingers, and blood seeped into the water. It was like that first day all over again.

Dario trudged toward the barricade. Wind battered his body, and the waters rose to his waist—frigid water. At least the rain was warm. Each sizzling drop soothed his skin. Parched, he licked his lips and tasted blood. Something tugged at his waist. His rope, he thought it must be. But the rope was gone. He'd untied it a long time ago. There was no rope at all—only a thick red flow of blood pouring from his gut.

Dario opened his coat, cursing when he saw three gaping holes in his stomach. Suddenly, his senses sharpened, and he heard Eljay screaming. She leapt from the barricade, catching him as he began to lose balance.

"It stabbed me," Dario muttered as he fell into her arms. Whitewater passed between them, turning red as his blood spilled out—Vetricus' blood. "It stabbed me," he whimpered again, trying to push the wound closed. "When?"

"Hold on, Dario!" Eljay's voice faded in and out. "Look at me!"

Hot rain spattered Dario's face, and it was the only warmth he could feel. Or were those tears? A sharp, clawing cold gripped him, and then all his pain subsided. His spine stopped tugging, his teeth stopped chattering, and his wounds stopped burning. He recognized this sensation. It was the numb before the fall. *Please, no.* His eyes wandered skyward. Madi was up there, somewhere, but for the first time in his life, he truly wondered if he'd ever find her again.

As he stared, Vetricus and Babble soared over a current of cloud— victorious. Babble's wings blazed like a fire. Daylight glinted from his blade, and there was a great shout as the faded pterosaur fell. Eljay looked up at Vetricus, too, his blond hair shining like a crown, and she no doubt saw a hero, which he was. But Dario already missed the stranger on the ledge—his friend. His brother whose blood flowed through his veins.

"He'll find us," he told Eljay, fighting not to choke. "Don't worry. He'll find us."

Eljay stroked his head, sobbing. "Us?"

"Me and Illio. He'll find us . . . and we'll climb . . ."

Dario listened to his own voice fade. The sound of battle ceased. Babble flew overhead, but soon, his silhouette dipped behind the clouds, and all Dario could see were falling stars. They came toward him like a wave, and soon he felt himself falling again, slipping into another world. But this time, he wasn't afraid. This time, purpose fell with him—like a twirling crutch, or a book, chained to his waist.

CHAPTER 26: MADI

Madi opened her eyes to the flash of falling stars. From one end of the sky to the other, they flickered and faded like lightning, illuminating the corpses of the dead as they fell into the Sea of the Afterlife. Slumped and unconscious, the distant bodies disappeared with a splash.

She found herself on an unfamiliar balcony. The branch protruded from Lamptree like an arm, and it had five gnarled roots curling upward like fingers. Maybe it was just Madi's imagination, but if it was a wooden hand, she'd woken up in the center of its palm. Waves surged below. The surf splashed across the balcony, distasteful and cold, splattering Madi's face. Black water shimmered down Lamptree's bark, where torchlight glowed dimly within open windows—revealing the Pilgrim's waning soul.

This dream felt different than the others—colder and more vivid— though she couldn't say for certain why. Maybe it was because death felt closer than ever, and she felt very small in a world that was spiraling out of control.

Lamptree creaked and groaned as it was carried by massive swells of water. Much of its trunk was submerged. A falling star soared overhead, illuminating an object in the water. Madi clutched the edge of the balcony, squinting through the frigid surf. There was a small boat! It floated this way, battling black currents. Even now, unconscious bodies floated by, carried toward the underworld. The vessel came close, and Madi only saw one person—a woman, wearing a dark red coat.

Raven climbed onto Lamptree's catwalks. Boardwalks swayed beneath her weight, and a soggy lift rumbled, carrying the ghost upward. Her presence unnerved Madi, because it proved that this wasn't *just* a dream. This was a vision of a very real place—the Sea of the Afterlife. Ghosts lived here. Madi was just a visitor.

Still, excitement spurred Madi to greet her. She felt a warmth she couldn't describe. She'd never truly met Raven, but she'd spent many nights trying to put together what kind of person she was. *Brave and funny,* she'd decided. *Kind, persevering, and clever . . . very clever.* This was all proved true three days ago when Raven had prevented Bandico from fleeing.

Madi hurried inside, clutching her collar tight as another wave splashed across the branch. The balcony, it turned out, led to the governor's private box inside the Ringed Hall. The Pilgrim sat in Governor Kipp's throne, watching silently. Once again, Madi couldn't quite tell if the Gale was angry, exhausted, or just deep in thought. She blinked gently, but her eyes held such power.

"Someone's here," Madi whispered. "A friend."

The Pilgrim nodded knowingly, and the large doors of the Ringed Hall opened on their own. Leaves skittered inside, and Raven entered with them.

"Hello?" she called, tramping dark water across the stage. "Madi Amriel? It's Raven. I know you're here." She lowered her voice. "I think you're here." She lowered it again, to an innocent echo. "I *hope* you're here."

"I am," Madi said, revealing herself.

Raven squished across stage, throwing her arms into the air. "Yes! I knew it! I knew I'd find you here! Bandico said this shape in the water couldn't be Lamptree. But I said it was, and it is!" she said, covering her mouth with a gasp. "Lamptree, adrift in the Afterlife. This is . . . scary."

She studied the Ringed Hall with a keen and slightly suspicious slant to her head. She'd somehow predicted Madi would be here. Did that mean she suspected the Pilgrim was here too? Raven's dark hair glistened. A wet strand curled across her forehead, dripping water onto the stage.

"How did you get here?" Madi asked.

Raven smiled and pointed. "In my little boat."

She carried a rope and anchor over her shoulder. With a weary exhale, she let it drop. It landed on the stage with an unnatural *boom*. Magic filled this place, making Madi's skin crawl. Water dripped from Raven's hair and clothes, and yet, she'd entered with such contagious energy. Candles flickered on the tables behind her, where clean bowls and plates lined fresh tablecloths. The ghost extended her hand, and when Madi shook it, it was unexpectedly real—and warm.

"It's about time we met properly," Raven said.

Madi glanced upward, catching sight of a falling star. "Proper?" she asked as Lamptree swayed and groaned. "Forgive me if nothing feels proper in this world anymore. It's all falling apart."

"Tell me about it." Raven balanced a plate as it slid from a table toward the floor. More dishes tumbled, and she caught them until her arms were full. "No simple decisions. Only slippery ones. You can't afford to drop them, but you can't really grasp them well enough to make sense out of anything. Same goes for the friends we choose."

Madi couldn't have said it better herself. Recent events raced through her head, over and over, too quickly to examine, too painful to dwell on. Lamptree swayed all the while, and soon, she lost her balance. Raven dropped the dishes and caught her, reeling Madi into a firm hug. "We're going to climb out of this," she whispered.

Madi let her cheek settle on Raven's shoulder, ignoring the garment's foul smell. Her words were too sweet, and right now, Raven was the only stable thing in her life. The hug was a speck of dry ground while all other emotions careened in a flood of emotion.

"When all this started, I used to whisper you questions to help me get to sleep," Madi admitted.

"I used to answer them," Raven replied.

"Really?" Madi smiled at the thought. "I always made up your answers in my head. You gave good advice."

"I do try."

Raven's collar itched Madi's face. The jacket was slimy, cold, and frayed—the loneliest attire Madi had ever seen. A rotting aroma filled her nostrils, but she tolerated it. She needed this. She gripped Raven tight, prolonging the embrace, but then she noticed something: only one heart beat between the two of them. Raven's chest was still, and ice cold water drooled from the hole in her jacket, stinging Madi's skin as it dampened her shirt.

"Sorry," Raven said, pulling away. She adjusted her jacket and wrung the water from her hair onto the stage. "You shouldn't think too highly of me, Madi," she said softly. "I could have warned you about Company Perth's plan, but I didn't. I'm as much a coward as Bandico."

"No, you're not. We would have died in the plain if not for you."

Raven squirmed, figiting with one of the many patches holding her coat together. "You don't understand. I've haunted Bandico for years, reminding him of his past, refusing to forgive him. I'm a big part of the reason he's terrified of the underworld. I've burrowed deep into his mind and planted seeds of fear that will only keep growing. You need to know: I wanted Bandico to suffer. I *hated* him." Raven's voice softened as her chin dipped toward her coat's collar. "I hated him because I used to love him like all the kids in the dark loved him.

I looked up to him. I trusted him. I wanted to stay with him. And then . . . he betrayed us."

Raven took a long breath.

"I intentionally twisted the idea of death against him. It was easy, considering his past, but now, its turned on me. Every fearful question he asks himself, I begin to ponder. The disease I created has spread to me. I worry that I'm going to die even if our plan succeeds," she said miserably. "The only reason I have any life at all is because I steal it from him. What if I can't follow him out of this world when he escapes? I'll be left here without anything to anchor to, on a sea that flows only toward death. What if I'm already doomed? That's why I stopped hurting him. That's why we made a deal. Bandico Perth has been my anchor since we were kids, and now I'm terrified of losing him."

Madi scanned the Ringed Hall, recalling the day it'd filled with smoke. "So, he is a Perth."

"He is. Please, don't be angry with him."

"How can I not?"

"Nothing on Lamptree went to plan. They were supposed to pillage for the trove and steal Dario's map."

"And the Ashen?" Madi said, her tone blistering, heated by sharp pangs in her heart.

"That was Vetricus!" Raven replied. "The others didn't know. They never help shadowmen, and they never pillage more than they need to curb their curses—most of them at least. Bear refused to enter your colony. He stayed in the forest," Raven said, sounding more and more like Bandico. Even the intonation was the same. The words rolled off her tongue in a slow, deliberate fashion, quickening as if to emphasize some obvious truth. "Company Perth isn't your enemy. We need each other if we're going to survive this climb. We can't break apart now. It's only going to get more dangerous . . . for all of us."

Madi listened, desperate for a reason to forgive her friends. She was eager to deflect her rage to someone else—to Vetricus. It would certainly simplify the entanglement of emotion she was far too exhausted to sort through. "Vetricus?"

"Yes. He's . . . angry, Madi. Out of control."

"But Company Perth belongs to him," Madi replied, thinking of Aerial healing on her tiny silk hammock.

"It doesn't have to," Raven said, catching Madi's attention. Her tone shifted again, just like Bandico's when he made a bold suggestion, which made her wonder. Was Raven mimicking Bandico? Or was Bandico mimicking Raven? Or were they simply melding together—a desperate ghost and her haunt. "Not everyone in Company Perth agrees with his rebellion," Raven continued. "I could name a few who are still true Celestials at heart, starting with Lakayd. She made the grafting process as painless as she could for Aerial—at her own expense. The sky has declared you a scepton. That means power: enough to control Vetricus. And maybe . . . enough to remove him. Bandico is worried he's dragging us into something big. Something too big to escape."

"Where is Bandico now?" Madi asked.

"Pacing inside his cabin. If I haunt him, he'll be able to see this place. Should I?"

"He's had three days to speak to me," Madi said. "I don't think he cares what I think."

"He does, Madi. He just hides it. Wait here. I'll be right back."

Madi believed her. Memories of the journey tempted her to smile fondly—the safety of Bandico's cabin, the brothers' songs, honey mead, their affection toward Aerial. She had to know if they were ever her brothers, or if it was really all just an act.

Raven tugged on her anchor, holding it with both hands as she tracked it across the stage. Soon, she disappeared. A minute later, movement caught Madi's eye. At first, it was just a shadow in the dark, but then she saw a big hat and a long black coat. Bandico paced back and forth, tapping his fingertips together with each step. Stage props surrounded him, forming the interior of his wagon. The air grew thick and blurry—as though two dreams merged. Was he here? Or was he somewhere else? Madi couldn't tell. Props on the stage shifted into the shape of his wagon. A round mirror came to rest where his porthole window would have been.

"Get out, Raven," he said abruptly. "GET OUT OF MY HEAD!"

Bandico paused, breathing heavily. He stared at his reflection, watching sweat drip down his forehead. The white glimmer behind his eyes burned, and he punched the mirror, over and over. The sound made a meaty *thud*. All of the props around him shook, but the mirror didn't break. Instead, Bandico did. He cried out, holding the side of his head. Then, he collapsed onto the ground.

After opening his eyes, he stood up and sighed. When Madi heard the breath, she knew he was here. She stayed quiet as he studied the sea of props on the stage. Raven's anchor moved with him as he explored. He paused in front of a prop from the Toymaker's Dance—a wheel with children painted on it. He poked it, and the mechanical prop spun. The painted children followed a toymaker, hand in hand. A sad song seemed to rise from it, and Bandico took off his hat, running a hand through his short black hair. The prop stopped with a sudden *click*, but he kept standing there in the dark, no doubt thinking of the children he'd guided through the Long Dark—the children he'd betrayed.

When Madi whispered his name, he spun around, startled. He looked different without his hat—vulnerable and sad. He quickly put it back on, angling it downward.

"Are you in my dream, or am I in yours?" he asked.

"Mine, I think," Madi replied.

Bandico paced between the tables, peering into cups and lifting covers from plates. "Makes sense. If it was mine, there'd be food."

"Was I your company's plan all along?" Madi asked him, testing Raven's story.

"No, you were the backup," Bandico said without making eye contact. "I was supposed to steal from a mole inside one of the oracles' vaults, but Dario beat me to it. The plan tumbled out a garbage chute after that. Now, I've no idea what Vetricus is doing. When I told him about you, he was against the idea. Said he didn't want to rely on anyone outside the company. Now, you're our only hope. So, are you going to do it?"

"Do what?"

"Walk out there as a scepton and save my company."

Madi let out a sour exhale. ". . . my daughter's company."

"Isn't that convenient." Bandico smirked briefly. "Here's a rule I follow: magic is never free, and when it comes with a choice, it's a good sign you're already trapped."

"I'm aware of my situation," Madi said, walking toward the table. Her boots echoed in the empty hall as she stepped over the long wooden bench and sat down across from him. "I need you to tell me: what will Vetricus do if he climbs out of this world?"

"No idea. He doesn't tell me anything anymore."

"WHAT WILL HE DO?"

Bandico threw his arms into the air. "I don't know, Madi! What he says and what he doesn't aren't the same anymore. He *says* we're going to end the war. Is that really what will happen? No idea. I'm not sticking around to find out. Once we get to the top of this city, I'm gone. I'm dumping Raven and finding my own escape. There's no forgiveness for people like me in the worlds above. And in the worlds below, the dead don't forget. People like me and my father—we have to dig out of our own graves. We have to walk into our own horizons."

"We've all made mistakes," Madi said, searching the room for Raven.

Where was she? Madi itched her nose as magic tingled in the air. Had she manifested in the real world? Was she creeping through Bandico's cabin right now?

"You don't get it," Bandico said quietly. The wooden bench creaked as he sat down, staring at one of the golden plates on the table. "There are some things . . . that should just never be done."

"Bereket told me what you did in the Long Dark," Madi revealed. "You were in an impossible situation. People find forgiveness for those sorts of things."

Bandico dipped his hat further, and his hands retreated into his oversize sleeves. "Not that."

"What then?" Madi watched him fidget with his coat's cuffs. "It's obvious you're sorry."

Bandico shifted uncomfortably in his seat, tossing napkins onto the floor. "I'm only sorry it has to be this way. Our world is rotting, and only rotten people rise from the pile."

"It doesn't have to be that way."

"It does for me," he answered, looking upward. His eyes were wide open, innocent, spilling a pale white glow. The longer she looked into Bandico's eyes, the emptier it seemed his heart was. He groaned and wiped his cheek, tugging on the brim of his hat until all but his lips were concealed. "The night our father abandoned us, he warned me, *'If you want to climb to safety, you have to climb alone.'* He said, *'One day, you're going to have to leave your brother behind,'* but I never listened. I loved my brother too much."

Bandico's shoulders tensed. He rocked his head back, eyes closed, fists clenched, breath trembling.

"If only I'd listened, then it never would have happened . . ." he said, his voice breaking down, softer and softer.

Madi waited, watching more emotion seep from the man in that moment than during their entire journey. He gripped the tablecloth, trying to hold it back, but she saw it spill from his eyes—a tear, stinging and sizzling as it slipped free, stained in blood. Bandico's magical eyes flickered, and for a moment, she thought she saw the eyes of a child.

"I was thirteen. Bear was eleven," he said at last. "Our mom couldn't move from her bed. Her constellation wasn't healing her anymore. Shadowmen had been searching for us for days. We had to move, but no matter what I told Bereket, he wasn't going to leave her. He'd guard her door every night, but I couldn't get father's warnings out of my head. We had to climb. So, one day, when Bear was out scavenging, I let the shadowmen in, and then I hid. I heard them drag our mother away. I-I heard . . . I heard her call out for me." Bandico slammed his fists on the table. Dishes clattered, and a long *thud* echoed through the hall. "She knew I was there. She knew I'd done it."

A second tear slipped from his altered eyes, painfully it seemed, judging by his grimace. "No son . . ." Bandico's voice broke completely now, and he struggled to speak. "No son should ever do such a thing to their mother." His chest heaved, and Madi felt her own eyes turn warm. "She'd only ever loved us. She was the light our father never was . . . and I snuffed it out because I was scared we were going to die. That was the first time. I've lost count of how many I've killed since then, and no matter how many people I save along the way, I'll never find forgiveness or peace." He brushed his face with his sleeve and took a deep breath. "All I can do now is find a place where I can just forget."

Madi stood silently, stunned. She'd imagined a bloody past, but not this. How could she ever trust him again? How could Raven? And yet, the ghost seemed to. She'd asked for Madi's forgiveness on his behalf. What did she see in the Shade?

Bandico stood up slowly and fixed the place where he'd been sitting—plates and bowls back in place. He sniffed a few times before returning to his more usual mannerisms. By the time he was done, it was as though nothing had changed, except for two blood-stained tears on the tablecloth.

Now she knew, his whole character was a charade atop a frightened child. Since that day, and that horrible thing he did, he'd yet to grow out of that fear. Then, Raven came along and fed off of that fear, turning him into the Shade he was now.

Madi pressed her lips together forgivingly, realizing this was her first real glimpse at who Bandico Perth truly was—the Little Light, trying to right his wrongs. Was this the boy that Raven once knew? 'He'd always wanted to be the hero,' she'd said. Now, Madi knew why. He was trying to right a wrong, trying to fill a hole he'd never be able to—trying to be brave, trying to lead, trying to overcome a fear he'd never be able to outrun. It was sad and pitiful, but Madi wondered how long it would be before her own life sounded the same.

"Now I know who you really are," she said, grabbing his shoulder as he passed. He looked away from her, wincing. "You're like me," she said, tugging his chin. "You've done wrong. Real wrong. And you might never be forgiven by the people you wronged, but you've already been punished. You're my brother, and I'm glad you're my brother, especially now that you've told me who you really are. I'm excited to see more of the real you for once."

She hugged him, but he felt numb in her arms, hardly breathing. Gloom clung to his battle-cloak, a gray mixture of a fabric and smoke, weaved atop his long black coat. There was a warm heart under there somewhere. His tears proved it.

"Does Bereket know?" she asked quietly.

"No, and he can never know," he muttered. "I'm done protecting

him. I'm sorry, Madi. I told you who I am, but I'm not changing."
He looked her in the eyes, whispering. "There's nowhere for me to
go. I'd rather spend an eternity searching for a place to forget, than
settle somewhere I'll never be forgiven."

"A word of warning, Madi," he said as he pulled away from her. "If
you accept the scepton's throne, this city will become the epicenter of
the world. The war will come here, dragging refugees from all over.
You're going to want to help them all." He shook his head. "Don't
even try. Wolves will come. You protect yourself. You protect Aerial.
Find a way to climb as quick as you can. GET OUT. You're a good
person. If there really is a safe place at the end of the Underworld
Trail, I hope you reach it someday."

"What about you?" Madi asked.

Bandico wandered toward the edge of the circular stage where a
brown curtain veiled a tunnel. "I'll make my own horizon," he said.

What did he think people would do to him? How would such a
safe haven work? A world without an underworld? Did he really plan
on outrunning his past forever, doomed to walk the future alone? That
sounded like more of a punishment than a paradise.

Madi eyed the Pink Pilgrim in her throne, recalling her words. *You
will lead the lost to this city.* Then, she called after Bandico. "What if
I can help change that?"

"You can't."

"But I've already thought of a task for you," Madi called after him.

Bandico paused at the curtain.

Madi chuckled, tasting a brief hint of hope in his posture. "As
scepton, I'd ask you to guide people here, to the city of the
escape. Your glyph would become famous, a light for the lost."

"What kind of people?"

Madi glanced at the children painted on each stage prop. "I think
you know."

Bandico grinned. His body shimmered and began to disappear. The stage curtain fluttered, and as it swayed, he vanished.

"He's waking up," Raven said, reappearing. She hurried toward her anchor. "I have to go. Be careful, okay?" she whispered, hugging Madi. She coiled her rope and returned to her little boat, drifting away with the tide.

Madi expected to wake up, but the dream lingered. The Pilgrim glared from her throne, eyes cool and powerful in the dim chamber. "Scepton?" she asked.

"You don't approve?" Madi asked.

"No, but we may not have a choice," she answered. "Our enemy wants this, but it does grant us a window of opportunity. Once their mark on your glyph glows, the oracles and their army will have no choice but to obey you. We'll have to be careful about what we do next. We need time, and Vetricus' impatience worries me. His allegiance is unclear. He wants to climb the city quickly, but we control his pace."

"How?" Madi asked.

"The city is severed. I will plant myself on the severed stair and cross the gap, but in order for me to grow, I will need you to fill this city with people and with Gale."

"Plant yourself?" Madi looked around, arms tingling. "You mean Lamptree? How?"

"Through your Galecraft."

Madi smiled, filled with a sudden joy. It felt so foreign. "We're going to build Lamptree again?"

"Yes, and you will rule as scepton from this throne. You will call the lost and the desperate, the weak and those in search of refuge. And they will climb my streets to freedom."

Lamptree's stage was dark and dirty, and Madi imagined it clean and glowing again.

"But," the Pilgrim continued, "should you accept this magic from the world above, you will not be able to escape until they appoint you a successor. You will save your daughter today, but one day, she may escape without you. Do you understand?"

"Yes. I'll do whatever you think is best," Madi replied.

"Best?" The Pilgrim sat back in her throne, dried leaves drifting across her lap. "I wish I knew."

High atop the city of escape, Shades and Celestials fought over control of the severed stair. The sound of battle swirled beneath the constellations, which shimmered quickly now, recounting the battle for the world to see. Company Perth was surrounded, and it seemed their light would never last.

Madi stared at her glyph, alone in a vast web of stars. Her dream, which had been so hopeful, ended in crushing loneliness. She wept as she thought of Company Perth climbing to freedom with Aerial while she was bound to this city. The price of magic was once again too costly—but for her daughter, she would pay it.

Madi stretched out her hand and summoned Gale toward her palm, crafting something she hadn't seen since the last time she stood in this city. Her wagon was smaller than Bandico's, but more elegant, with two curved decks, like wings. She opened the cabin door and was struck with the scent of her past. After all these years, every detail lingered in her mind, down to the deck of crook cards she'd left on the floor.

Wood creaked as Madi stepped inside the cold heart of Nariah Maya. A crossbow leaned against her old cot, next to bags of brews, maps, and supplies for the climb. The smell made her want to cry. Beryl's hair lined the cushions. Beryl was a fruit bat, Madi's pet, and the inspiration for many of her flying toys. She'd died in this city too.

"You'll need a horse," Bereket said, startling her.

Madi hugged him, relieved he was alive. He limped with Two Ton to the front of the wagon and helped her with the harness. "Do you feel like a scepton yet?" he asked.

"No, I feel like a toy," she answered.

"But you're the toy-*maker*," Panima said, offering Aerial's empty pouch. Aerial squirmed in her other arm, bright eyed and full of energy.

There was something inside it, and Madi covered her mouth when she saw it: Corlan's toy soldier. The wooden grin was brave, and the marble eyes alert—just as Corlan had been. Sorrow squeezed at Madi's soul, but something held back the tears—purpose. One day, people were going to climb up from the underworld and flee into this city. One day, Dario and Corlan would climb these very streets.

"You put this in here?" Madi asked, smiling at the toy.

Panima shook her head, eyes glassy and sad. "No, Corlan must have."

Bereket peeked at the toy. "He knew he was going to die . . ." he muttered.

The toy's sturdy grin filled Madi with a sense of bravery, as though Corlan were right there with her. The Gales had a plan. *And I'm part of it*, she thought, her skin prickly with purpose. *Like a cog in a lift.*

"We're going to see Corlan again one day," she told them.

Panima placed Aerial into her pouch, and Madi buckled a little. Her daughter was noticeably stronger now, kicking her legs into Madi's stomach. Her eyes widened when she saw Corlan's toy, and her toothless mouth curled into a smile. With her daughter at her chest, Madi climbed into her wagon. Bereket and Panima waved as she set off toward the severed stair. Vine-covered towers loomed overhead, where the Lamptree bird called. Mist curled across the empty streets, and Madi wondered how she could ever fill them again. But she would. Lamptree would grow, and one day, Dario would see it.

A flash of light filled the sky, and Madi felt her heart glow ablaze. The light was blinding, like a dazzling dawn had sprung upon the city summit. A lone sky-quake muted all the others, but it was tender and lofty, like a bird flying above the chaos. The howl of battle came to a stop, and the two battle lines looked up, shielding their eyes. A glyph blazed above, unlike any they'd likely ever seen before.

Stars shivered and echoed. Battle lines separated, clearing a path for Madi's wagon. A hundred bewildered faces gazed up at her—Shades and Celestials—and the whole courtyard fell silent. The wagon's wheels churned atop broken stone and shattered vials. A miasma glimmered around the battlefield, bathing it in a dreamlike light, like a frozen flash of twilight.

Standing atop the severed stair, Vetricus bowed his head subtly. His Shades were gathered loyally around him, cloaks thick like vultures. Telescopes clicked. Lenses glinted. All across the battle line, eyes lifted toward the stars. Madi lifted a hand, gesturing peace, and the Celestials allowed her to pass.

Oracles emerged from their wagons—six of them, clad in red, blue, green, and purple. Madi dipped her chin slightly, and they bowed in return—reluctantly. They weren't pulling her strings anymore, which was why Madi smirked. But who was? The thought kept her from growing too comfortable.

"Nariah Maya," an oracle's voice rumbled from her hood amid a plume of blue smoke. "These are troubling times. Perhaps a scepton's star will provide some much needed clarity. We are prepared to offer whatever council you need as you embark on this most arduous task. But first we must demand that you hand over Company Perth. The sky clearly demands their fall."

"Does it?" Madi asked, her confidence growing. The oracles had just asked her permission, and it made her feel as light as a feather. She hadn't rehearsed anything to say, so she just tried to sound confident. "Is that why the sky has bestowed this blessing on my star? The only clear thing I saw during my ascent was suffering."

"Because of him," the oracle replied. Smoke hissed from her hood toward Vetricus. "Their actions prove we must take more drastic measures against the Shade companies."

"Their actions prove that this war has weakened the sky's grasp on their companies," Madi told them, settling into her role. She darkened her tone and added a fair bit of neutrality to her voice. She'd always hated this stage, but that didn't mean she didn't know how to act on it. "We need every sword we can craft in this war against the shadowmen, and I have a grip on this one. If Company Perth wants to escape, they'll obey *my* tasks."

The oracle protested, fuming. "This is unwise," she warned. "Heed my words, young scepton. Your authority is not absolute. You are still subject to the sky."

"Then let the world above settle the matter. You have your tasks. I have mine. Destroying Company Perth isn't one of them. My task now is to restore this city," Madi said, peering beyond the courtyard, toward the empty streets and gray buildings below. "And to fill it."

"That will take years," an oracle said. "This place is a ruin. Where will people stay until it's repaired? In shacks out in the plain for the Ashen to pluck at their pleasure?"

"No. I'll show you," Madi said, turning Two Ton toward the summit.

The oracles and many celestials followed Madi, watching her dismount at the severed stair. Small stones crackled beneath her boots and dribbled toward the district far below. Sweat trickled across her palms and her head began to swirl. Would this city crumble out from beneath her? She thought it might, and she wouldn't feel safe until Lamptree's roots coiled around this city's spine like a splint.

After a deep breath, she reached out. Mist gathered toward her palms. Lamptree was fresh in her mind, and she felt power rushing through her veins—the Pilgrim's power. Celestials gazed upward, whispering words of amazement as Madi crafted a branch overhead. Vetricus and the rest of Company Perth moved as roots coiled around the severed stair, forcing them back into the courtyard. Meanwhile, brown bark weaved upward, forming colossal branches. Starlight twinkled through sprouting leaves and vines.

Madi continued upward, adding details such as Lamptree's thorns and blossoms. Tears streamed down her face when she formed the Mossroad—glistening green, without a hint of being burned. Mist obeyed her every thought, rushing to wherever she pointed, fashioning treehouses and gatehouses and small houses and big houses.

Dawn came, full of blue clouds. For hours, Madi crafted in the rain. Sweat and tears mingled. Rain pattered Flicker's arms as she flew upward, crafting the tops of the tree. When she crafted the steps to her cottage, it was as though she'd reached her heart's very core. Joy churned inside Madi's chest, like gears grinding back to life. Aerial squirmed in her pouch, squawking toward every leaf and flower.

The blue showers moved on. Purple and green clouds rose, looming like a flat sea, covering much of the lower city in a perfect twilight. Bats and birds flew toward the branches, eager to breathe Gale from the celestials' lanterns. They camped on the Mossroad while Company Perth crafted their company tower somewhere deeper inside the city. The smell of food rose through the branches. Music echoed, and for a short moment, Madi felt as though she'd traveled back in time, to the start of the Lamptree Festival.

She gripped the door of her cottage, curious as to the condition of her home. She found it just as it was that day, before Dario had been taken—just as in her dreams. Books and clothes strewn about. Curtains drawn. Madi hadn't remembered any of this, but the Pilgrim had. *This isn't my Galecraft,* she realized. *It's hers.*

Madi walked through her kitchen toward the balcony door, glancing briefly at the Pilgrim's wooden shrine. Before opening the door to the balcony, she prayed that she'd find Dario asleep on his cot. Was that kind of magic possible for a dying god? Maybe it was. With a loud *squeal,* the door opened.

The cot was there, and even a crutch, but not Dario Lire.

EPILOGUE: MADI

I'm going to try to start keeping a book, like Dario did—like Dario does. It took eight days for me to finish crafting Lamptree, but only two days for it to begin fading. Gloom creeps across the city, and sometimes I feel like I'm in a world of my own. Lamptree isn't anywhere near tall enough to bridge the gap yet, and our lanterns are already running low. Several companies remain in the lower districts, scouring the streets for Ashen. Meanwhile, the Perths keep to their company tower—Fortingale—which they've hidden somewhere I haven't managed to find yet. According to Bear, it's deep within the ruins, where sagging stone and mist form caverns of debris.

A few days ago, I wrote my first task for Vetricus. The oracles gave me brewed inks, tuned with starlight, and they instructed me on which patterns to use. And yes, before you ask, I confirmed with Vetricus' astronomer, Seneca, that the patterns weren't curses. I wrote the task on the floor of the Ringed Hall, and as it seeped into the wood, starlight moved above us. The sky quakes regularly up here. Even now, it rumbles, reminding me that there really is another world up there—and another below.

Vetricus' first task was simple: Lamptree needs more colonists and lanterns to survive. In order for the city to rise, it needs to be filled. Since these branches are his only hope for escape, he has no choice. I'll admit, I was grinning when he departed with his Shades. This kind *of power tastes good—seeing Vetricus bitterly obey is a small victory for Lamptree. He emptied these streets, and he'll fill them again.*

Panima lives with me now, and I don't know what I'd do without her. Aerial has fully recovered—and some. Constellation Perth has filled her with energy and strength. She's barely six months old, and already, she's trying to walk! It frightens me sometimes. I've spent the last three years running, and now I'm dangling between two worlds, mummified by magic. Front and center on the stage I fought so hard to avoid. Is she still my daughter, or is she a Perth?

Bereket asked if he could remain in the city a while longer before going out on task. He doesn't trust anyone here. Sometimes, I catch him guarding my cottage through the night, with his back pressed against my front door. I don't need it, but he's my brother, and brothers overdo everything when they love you.

Bandico left earlier today, southward, to begin his task: guide children from the Long Dark. I can't see the countryside right now because of the clouds, but whenever I do see the horizon, I wonder when Bandico will reach his old home, and if his heart will ever find the same purpose I've found here atop this city. I hope he does.

I imagine the day he emerges from those dark borders. The wind will catch his hat, and his eyes will sparkle beneath it. He'll wait for a moment, squint into the light, and then beckon a line of children. They'll follow him out of the darkness, hand in hand, shielding their eyes. Bandico will mutter something to Raven, something about being happy for once, and then he'll lead the orphans here—to the City of Escape.

www.ingramcontent.com/pod-product-compliance
Lightning Source LLC
Chambersburg PA
CBHW020011120726
47903CB00004B/1243